MW00615451

DEAD DOWNWIND

DEAD
DOWNWIND

—— **A Historical Novel** ——

Ten harrowing days that changed aviation history

BILL RIDDLE

COMPASS ROSE PRESS

Publisher's Cataloging-in-Publication
(Provided by Quality Books, Inc.)

Riddle, Bill, 1946–
     Dead downwind : the ten harrowing days that changed
aviation history / Bill Riddle.
     p. cm.
     ISBN-13: 978-0-615-21694-2
     ISBN-10: 0-615-21694-3

     1. Rodgers, John, 1881–1926--Fiction. 2. United
States. Navy—Fiction. 3. Air pilots, Miliary—United
States—Fiction. 4. Aeronautics—United States—
Fiction. 5. Hawaii—Fiction. 6. Historical fiction.
I. Title.

PS3618.I385D43 2008   813'.6
                                QBI08-600182

Printed in China by Everbest Printing Co. Ltd

To the Bass River Beauties: Mildred, Judy, and Susie

Author's Note

This is a fictional treatment of the true story of the incredible series of events that led to the near demise of U.S. Navy aviation. It begins in 1924, three years before Charles Lindbergh flew the Atlantic. All of the major historical events recounted occurred when and as described. Headlines and news articles quoted are verbatim as published. Public quotes attributed to historic individuals are also accurate.

Many of the photographs in the book come from rare, archival sources. While the quality of some of the images is problematic, they are invaluable to a reader's sense of accurate historical context.

Modest creative liberties have been taken with lesser individuals and events. Personal conversations, love interests, and related characters are purely creations of the author's imagination.

—B.R.

dead downwind *adv., adj.* (often abbreviated as DDW): **1.** A sailing and aeronautical term, indicating a condition wherein the wind originates from directly behind a ship or airplane, "dead" meaning exact or precise. The origin of the term is commonly thought to refer to the location where the wind would most effectively carry the odor of a corpse.

Introduction

By the mid-1920s, America had arrived as a major player on the global stage, youthful, vibrant, and headstrong. The great experiment in democracy was emerging as an unmitigated success. Out of the shadows of the previous decade—the Spanish flu pandemic, brutal labor strikes, and the harsh realities of the First World War—the country was feeling its oats. Women had won the right to vote and now entered the workplace in droves. A strong sense of national pride prevailed, along with the conviction that America could do anything she put her mind to.

Running water and indoor plumbing were no longer just for the rich. Similarly, electric lights glowed brightly throughout the land, and the telephone was fast becoming commonplace. The first radio stations had just begun broadcasting, and news could now shoot across the country in hours rather than days. The immediacy of communication brought about a national coherence heretofore unimagined.

The country was experiencing an unprecedented economic boom, and unemployment was at an all-time low. A dime and a promise bought a dollar's worth of stock. As stocks grew in value, a dollar's profit easily turned into ten dollars more. The American dream of wealth and prosperity appeared well within the reach of the common man.

This decade was christened the Roaring Twenties with good reason. Hemlines rose right along with the stock market. With Prohibition in full swing, bootleg liquor business boomed. Speakeasies sprang up in cities, and vest-pocket flasks were *de rigueur*. People looked the other way with a wink and a nod to the so-called "blue laws." Not surprisingly, organized crime burgeoned in the wake of this casual attitude.

As a U.S. Territory, Hawaii prospered along with the rest of the country. Over the years, an assortment of nations had coveted the island archipelago primarily because of her unique geographic location. Hawaii's strategic significance as a shipping and military port of call would play a huge role in her destiny. By the twenties, the influx of American business capital and military expenditures contributed to a healthy financial portrait. The rapidly growing pineapple and sugarcane industries had replaced whaling as Hawaii's economic mainstay. Meanwhile, the recent advent of tourism would soon shape Hawaii's future as much as her military value.

During these times, the U.S. Navy found itself under fire, from within and from without. After the war, the navy had reduced its ranks, releasing or demoting scores of middle and junior officers. The vast majority of the remaining old-school senior brass staunchly believed in a battleship navy. As such, their vision was somewhat clouded when it came to new technologies. This myopia seriously threatened the fate of a modern, postwar navy, as did deep congressional funding cuts.

The officers that remained in navy service after the war were strictly monitored. All aspects of their lives came under intense scrutiny. During these repressive times, the military frowned even on interfaith marriages, while divorce or interracial marriage could kill a career.

Navy pilots endured especially stringent review. Pilots were expected to be superior physical specimens. Eyesight was of utmost concern. Corrected vision was not an option in the 1920s navy, and failure to pass an annual eye exam would ground a pilot forever.

As with many old-boy networks, personalities, connections, and private life counted for a great deal. Families with long and illustrious backgrounds often raised and educated sons to continue their legacy. John Rodgers, the protagonist of this story, was born into such a dynasty.

In 1793, his great-grandfather, the first John Rodgers, had enlisted in the U.S. Navy the very day it was founded. As a young officer he commanded the three-masted brig, *Constellation*, at the siege of Tripoli. Promoted to admiral in the War of 1812, he captured twenty-three ships.

Rodgers' first cousin was Commodore Oliver Hazard Perry, who also served during the War of 1812. Perry was the hero of the Battle of Lake Erie. It was he who spoke the immortal words, "We have met the enemy and they are ours."

Rodgers' son followed family tradition serving in the U.S. Navy during the Civil War, as a skipper of ironclads. He commanded the ironclad *Monitor* as well as her less famous sister ship, the USS *Weehawken*. In the *Weehawken*, this John Rodgers captured the Confederate ship, *Atlanta*, during the battle at Fort Sumter and was subsequently promoted to admiral. In the U.S. Navy of the 1920s, much would have been expected from the scion of such thoroughbred lineage.

Following the horrors of the First World War, many Americans argued for isolationism. They put their faith in the vastness of the Atlantic and Pacific oceans as the country's greatest protection from the threats of a still-unsettled Europe and the ominous rumblings in the Far East. Congress attempted to address this increasingly strident national groundswell through legislation designed to limit new warship construction.

Several trying years of negotiations between the United States, the British Empire, the Empire of Japan, the French Third Republic, and Italy produced the Washington Naval Treaty, finally ratified in 1923. Awash with good intentions, the primary goal of this compact was to prevent a repeat of the international naval race to build battleships that occurred prior to the start of the world war. America's fervent isolationists praised the treaty, but military realists were skeptical.

The U.S. Congress displayed considerable naïveté in their negotiations with the other signatories of the Washington Naval Treaty. As a condition of signing, Japan and Britain demanded significant shipbuilding concessions. They each claimed that their island nation status warranted the continued construction of warships. France signed the agreement, though subsequently circumvented all of the terms. Italy paid lip service to the treaty but totally ignored the terms of the agreement from the start.

While the Washington Naval Treaty was being negotiated, the Treaty of Versailles held Germany in a challenging situation. As both the instigator and the vanquished of the Great War, Germany was required to pay significant war reparations to the victors. Initially, the war-torn country met some of the demands, but ultimately failed to live up to most of the treaty's stringent terms. The edicts intended to constrict Germany's shipbuilding were soon circumvented. Before long, the German shipping industry was building hulls with double-plated armored skins under the guise of safety concerns for "commercial" vessels.

Eventually, the United States was the only major power observing what had been intended as a global cessation of warship construction. While England, Japan, France, Italy, and even Germany built new vessels, most of America's aging battleships were put into mothballs and barely kept afloat. Instead of building new ships, the navy was required to revamp older ones as new military needs were identified. For example, in order to experiment with a prototype for a ship capable of launching and landing wheeled aircraft, a massive old coal freighter was reconfigured into what became the nation's first aircraft carrier.

Because of the Washington Naval Treaty, America's postwar navy was left in an exceedingly vulnerable position. By the mid-1920s, the United States Navy had not laid a keel for a new battleship since 1919, just after the end of the war. In fact, the navy would not do so again for a full twenty years.

By 1924, almost every other major global player could claim air superiority over the United States. America, the birthplace of powered aviation, now ranked eighth in the world, right behind Poland. The disparity was growing larger as the decade approached its midpoint.

At this time, the army and the navy each had their own air divisions, and fought tenaciously to hold on to them. England had determined that a separate aeronautical military service branch was appropriate for their country, and an outspoken contingent here felt the United States should follow suit. America's top brass, however, believed this was the wrong decision. They felt that aerial support of ground troops and ships needed to be more closely coordinated. They strongly resisted the creation of a third entity that some were calling for, an independent Air

Force, an idea aggressively championed by Army General Billy Mitchell, much to the intense irritation of both the army and navy. No one had yet recognized the possibility of a compromise between the branches of the U.S. armed forces.

It was against this backdrop of military vulnerability and U.S. political infighting that the twentieth-century John Rodgers and his intrepid crew undertook the challenge of a lifetime. The outcome of their daring exploit would alter the course of aviation history.

Commodore John Rodgers: A founding father of the U.S. Navy. He served from the 1790s through 1838. His first assignment was as a young officer aboard the USS *Constitution* ("Old Ironsides"). He distinguished himself in innumerable battles and eventually rose to the position of Secretary of the Navy. He is the great-grandfather of Commodore John Rodgers, the principal character in this story.

As stated in the Author's Note, this reproduction may appear problematic, as may others to follow. They are, however, invaluable to a reader's sense of accurate historical context.

Commodore Oliver Hazard Perry: The brave victor of the Battle of Lake Erie in the War of 1812. He is best known for the quote, "We have met the enemy and they are ours." He was also John Rodgers' great uncle.

Admiral John Rodgers spent his entire life in the U.S. Navy, serving as a young midshipman aboard the frigate USS *Constellation,* as the skipper of the *Weehawken* (sister ship to the ironclad *Monitor*), and as the guiding force in the establishment of Annapolis as the U.S. Naval Academy. He was Commodore John Rodgers' grandfather.

The following lyric is from a song that was composed by patriotic balladeers in 1811. In the years leading up to the War of 1812, British ships were illegally removing American seamen from U.S. flag vessels, claiming they were British subjects and therefore subject to British navy impressment. Foremost of these was the forcible removal of several born and bred Americans from the U.S. vessel *Chesapeake*. These actions went unchecked until then-Commander John Rodgers (great-grandfather to our story's protagonist), at the helm of the frigate USS *President* off the eastern seaboard, encountered the sloop of war HMS *Little Belt*. Since the countries were not officially at war, the song retold the story of a brazen attempt by Rodgers to lure the cocky British into a gun battle to recover some of the kidnapped Americans. Thirteen men were killed and nineteen wounded aboard the *Little Belt* before she struck her colors, while only a ship's boy was slightly injured aboard the *President*.

"Captain, Commander, and Senior Officer of the American Navy" John Rodgers had restored some pride to our fledgling country and was declared a hero. The song "Rodgers and Victory" was sung throughout the States to the tune of Yankee Doodle Dandy.

You all remember well, I guess, The Chesapeake disaster,
When Britons dared to kill and press, To please their royal master.

That day did murder'd freemen fall, Their graves are cold and sandy;
Their funeral dirge was sung by all, Nor Yankee Doodle Dandy.

"Where are you from?" bold Rodgers cried, Which made the British wonder:
Then with a gun they quick replied, Which made a noise like thunder.

Like lightning we returned the joke, Our matches were so handy;
The Yankee bulldogs nobly spoke, The tune of Doodle Dandy.

Chapter 1

Friday—July 18, 1924

8:45 AM Hawaii Time

Commander John Rodgers was anxious. He wondered why he was being called before top navy brass on such short notice. Punctual by nature, John had arrived fifteen minutes early for this meeting. He was dressed in his best uniform, his hat tucked securely under his arm. One could almost have shaved with the creases in his slacks.

John entered the anteroom of the Pacific Fleet Commander's headquarters. As commander of the Ford Island Air Base, John's office was large, but this room was easily three times bigger than his. John checked in with the plainly dressed civilian woman at the utilitarian reception desk. She politely asked him to be seated, and offered him a cup of coffee. John declined. He'd already fortified himself with two cups at home, and navy coffee was notoriously strong. The last thing he needed this morning was the jitters.

After a short wait, the intercom on the woman's desk crackled, and she rose to escort Rodgers into an even more impressive office. A desk, two opposing chairs, and a leather sofa occupied the right side of the room, while a massive, highly polished, mahogany table with a dozen straight-backed chairs around it was to his left. Several stacks of papers were piled neatly on the glossy finish. The view from the windows was of Pearl Harbor's "Battleship Row," where millions of dollars of navy gray lay anchored.

John saluted his superior waiting for him behind the table. Rear Admiral William Moffett had arrived from D.C. without fanfare the night before. The admiral perfunctorily returned the salute, then came around the table to shake Rodgers' hand.

"John, it's good to see you again." The fifty-two-year-old Moffett wore his years well. He carried himself in the practiced manner of a superior, but without any trace of pretension. Nonetheless, Rodgers tensed in anticipation. Moffett may have been a sailor's sailor, but he was also Washington brass.

Firmly grasping the hand extended to him, Rodgers replied, "Admiral, the pleasure's mine."

In 1921, the U.S. Navy had formed its own aviation bureau, BURAERO, to counteract Army General Billy Mitchell's vociferous personal campaign for Congress to create an independent national air force. As Mitchell's headline-grabbing tirades gained popular support, the navy realized it needed a strong voice behind closed doors in Washington, as well as in the press, if it was going to hold on to any kind of naval-air division.

Admiral Moffett, a brilliant Annapolis graduate and war hero, had distinguished himself repeatedly as an innovator—a man who didn't hesitate to think outside the box. While commanding the battleship *Mississippi* in the Great War, he had been the first to launch scout planes from ships. The seaplanes, launched and retrieved by crane, had allowed the Admiral to extend his horizons and coordinate his fleet better than ever before. After the war, he had pushed the navy to experiment further with the launching of aircraft from naval vessels. Although not a pilot himself, he had foreseen great possibilities for further aircraft–warship coordination in future conflicts. Consequently, Moffett, considered the patriarch of navy aviation, had been the obvious choice to head BURAERO. As such, he was responsible for all naval aviation projects.

"John, I didn't come all the way from Washington for an inspection tour," said the admiral. "I came because naval aviation needs a kick in the pants."

John remained silent, listening carefully.

"That damned Billy Mitchell wants a single air corps to control all military flying—a separate branch of service he'd presumably be in charge of. Now, it's not that I don't agree with him about the future importance of airpower. He's right in that regard. It's just that his plan would effectively eliminate navy aviation."

Rodgers could hear Moffett's frustration build as he continued: "Mitchell has flat-out ignored our achievements with dirigibles, and seaplanes launched from navy warships. Now he's focusing on our success flying wheeled planes off the *Langley*. Hell, he wants to be in charge of all aircraft; even those being launched off our own damn carrier! If Mitchell had his way, the navy'd become wet nurse to *his* flyboys. It's bullshit, but nevertheless people are starting to listen to the self-promoting peacock. Plus, Mitchell's father is a senator, and with all that wealth and influence pushing his agenda, it could happen.

"Mitchell claims our aircraft are only good for short-range patrols. Well, it's my job to show them Billy Mitchell's wrong. The future of naval aviation must include aircraft of all types. We've got to prove that the navy knows what it's doing with our flying boats, and it's going to take something spectacular, something that will make a splash on the front pages and get people talking!" The admiral paused and looked John square in the eye. "That's where you come in."

"Sir?"

"Mitchell complains that all we can do with our so-called 'lumbering seaplanes' is to fly shoreline patrols, and according to him, that's a job better suited to ground-based craft. If we hope to keep our funding, we've got to convince our illustrious elected officials that navy seaplanes are capable of flying long-range missions. To that end, I've already earmarked two new planes that are being built at the navy yard in Philadelphia for a special project. They will be the next generation of our PN7 series—as you know, a well-established patrol craft. These planes aren't fast or revolutionary, but they are dependable workhorses, and we should be able to count on them for more than just puddle jumping.

"I've also allocated additional funds for the construction of a new, commercially designed seaplane. I know it's a shot in the dark, but it could help our cause. It's an untested prototype, but the designers are champing at the bit to prove its capability, and we're getting it at cost. So that'll give us three specially built planes designed for long-distance travel."

Here, Moffett paused, staring intently at the man in front of him.

"John, I need your help. What I . . . what *we* want to do, is fly these planes nonstop from San Diego to Hawaii. I'd like your opinion on the feasibility of such a mission."

John hesitated, momentarily taken aback.

Moffett turned and stepped behind the table. "I can sense your concern. Please speak freely. This is why I'm here."

"Sir, begging your pardon—the PN7s are great planes, but to my knowledge they can't even fly from San Diego to San Francisco nonstop, let alone across the Pacific. Nothing can. I mean you're talking twenty-five hundred miles!"

Admiral Moffett leaned over, spreading his meaty palms flat on the tabletop. "I know what I'm asking seems impossible. But that's the point. The navy needs to accomplish the impossible, something that will amaze the country." Sitting down slowly, Admiral Moffett continued, "I know I'm asking you to stick your neck out on this, but if the new planes were properly designed and outfitted, do you think it could be done?"

"Sir, what's the projected cruising speed of these new planes?"

"Seventy knots."

Thinking out loud, John mused, "If the planes could maintain seventy knots for the entire trip they would have to remain airborne for more than thirty hours. With the amount of fuel needed to stay aloft that long, I doubt they could get airborne. They just aren't powerful enough."

Moffett nodded, "I'm ahead of you, John. I'm having the planes outfitted with specially designed Packard V-12s. Each of those babies will produce well over 500 horses, so we're talking almost 1,100 horsepower per plane."

Still dubious, John replied, "Sir, the engines sound impressive. That's certainly a huge jump in horsepower, but the kind of physical challenges you are suggesting are downright monumental. We'll need extensive flight tests to see if flying the distance you're talking about with that kind of extra weight would be even remotely possible."

"OK John, fair enough. But let's assume for the moment that the planes *can* take off carrying the fuel they're going to need. What other considerations are there?"

"Well sir, to begin with, just finding these tiny Hawaiian Islands will be tricky. It's difficult enough to navigate over land in a bouncing plane. Plus, when we fly cross-country, there are geographical landmarks to guide us, or we follow railroad tracks, but there's nothing but ocean out there. It would be a lot easier to fly from Hawaii to the States; the Mainland would be hard to miss."

"Yes, John, but that's just the point. I need you and your men to pull off something that's really tough, not take the easy way."

"Yes, sir, point taken. But if the weather closed in and shut out good sextant sights, we could be in serious trouble."

"Agreed, but John, you're the best damn navigator in this man's navy. I'm confident in your abilities."

"Thank you, sir, but it would still be tough . . . ." John thought for a minute, then asked, "Would we still use five-man crews?"

"That's what the planes are designed for, and we need to make a case for their practicality. What else?"

"Radio communications. We'd be out of range for virtually the entire flight."

"True, but you would have the other two planes."

"Yes, sir. What's your time frame for the mission?"

Moffett responded, "Sometime next year. Maybe eight or nine months from now."

"That'd be good, sir. Late spring would probably give us the best weather conditions." John paused, mentally reviewing the challenge Moffett had set before him, then asked, "Admiral, are you locked in on San Diego as the starting point?"

"Why do you ask?"

"Well, sir, it's just that even though San Diego seems closer to Hawaii, it may not be the best solution. Hawaii is further south than anywhere in the States. But the California coastline curves eastward as it travels south. In fact San Diego is so far east that San Francisco is actually a couple hundred miles closer to Hawaii despite being so much further north."

"Interesting . . . well, let's look into that. Anything else you can think of?"

"Not at the moment, sir."

"Then I guess we're down to brass tacks. Can it be done?"

Rodgers hesitated, then made his decision. "Sir, honestly it'd be a stretch, but if we can solve the fuel, weight, and navigation problems, then yes, I think so."

"John, that's why I came to you. If anyone can pull this off, it's you. I know I'm asking a lot, but would you be willing to head up such a mission?"

Sensing the unique opportunity to prove himself, John quickly replied, "Yes sir, of course."

Moffett positively beamed. "Great! I have to work out the details, but you might want to start thinking about your crew and who you'd choose to skipper your second plane. I want you to be in overall command of the mission, but you need to know that I've been painted into a political corner about the third crew—the one for the new plane. I'll fill you in on that when it's settled. In the meantime, keep all this under your hat.

"I've got to head right back to the States. I've got a surprise up my sleeve for our dirigible skeptics. It involves your old pal Zachary Lansdowne. Anyway, I'll send you word once we're ready to move forward on this project. Thank you, John."

Once again, the admiral extended his hand. Recognizing that he was being dismissed, Rodgers shook Moffett's hand, thanked him for the opportunity, saluted, and then retired from the office. As he made his way down the long hall and out of the building, John considered the innumerable hurdles to be cleared in order for the project to succeed. He wondered if he had just opened a door to his own advancement or accepted an assignment that would blow his career out of the water. "My God, what have I gotten myself into?"

Commander John Rodgers

Rear Admiral William Moffett: Chief of BURAERO, the navy's fledgling aviation arm.

Chapter 2

Monday—July 28, 1924

5:55 AM Hawaii Time

Finishing his shower, Commander John Rodgers twisted the ceramic-and-brass faucets shut and carefully stepped over the side of the claw-footed tub. He toweled dry and reentered the bedroom quietly, hoping not to disturb his sleeping wife.

The summer sun shone brightly through the screened bedroom windows. As usual, the morning sky was a crystal-clear cerulean blue, punctuated by puffy cumulous clouds along the serrated mountaintops of the Koolau range. Gentle trade winds cooled the room.

Out in the yard, a pair of mourning doves huddled together on the fence, their plaintive cries mixing with the staccato chatter of dozens of mynah birds in the large banyan tree in the backyard. The full-throated song of a cardinal occasionally pierced this orchestral overture. John loved the daily tropical-morning symphony. He loved Hawaii.

He dressed quickly, as the sheer, white curtains hanging from the window next to his dresser danced gently along the bureau's surface. The reflection in the mirror confirmed that at forty-three, his broad shouldered, modestly muscled former swimmer's frame filled his well-fitted uniform quite nicely. He also noted it was time to trim his close-cropped regulation haircut, the style he'd sported during twenty-five years of navy life.

John began his standard morning ritual. On the dresser sat a hand-carved koa wood jewelry box that he had found in a small shop in Waikiki. John flipped open the lid and took out his Annapolis class ring, setting it absentmindedly on top of the thin curtain material resting lightly on the bureau. Then, out came his pilot's license. It read "Naval Aviator license number 2." John had been the U.S. Navy's first pilot personally trained by Wilbur and Orville Wright. Next, he removed one of his most prized possessions, his chronometer, and secured it to his left wrist. He pinned his navy name tag and insignia of rank to his uniform.

Continuing his ritual, John slid back the seemingly solid front cross-piece of the koa wood box, exposing a small recessed drawer. From the hidden drawer he lifted a pair of wire-rimmed glasses and stowed them in his jacket pocket. Commander Rodgers' eyesight was deteriorating, a fact he knew would abort his career as a navy pilot, should it ever come to light.

The soft breeze increased almost imperceptibly, causing the sheer curtain to billow outward like a miniature spinnaker. This delicate, curvilinear sail was anchored only by John's Annapolis class ring. For an instant, the gossamer curtain looked like a toy sailboat moored to the dresser. Then a slightly stronger gust overcame the weight of the ring, pushing it unceremoniously off the dresser. John winced as it banged loudly on the hardwood floor. He quickly bent to retrieve it, hoping the noise hadn't wakened his wife.

Ethel stirred briefly, murmuring in her sleep as John tiptoed from the bedroom. He proceeded quietly through the house, across the screened-in veranda, and out the front door. He crossed the well-tended lawn and picked up the morning paper. Out of the corner of his eye he spotted a solitary Pacific Golden Plover standing mute sentry on the front lawn. John smiled and greeted the spindly-legged avian traveler. "Well, hello stranger . . . . Welcome home. How was Alaska?"

John marveled at how each April, these birds fly more than 3,000 miles nonstop from Hawaii to Alaska, mate, and hatch their young. Then in late July, they wing their way back to Hawaii. Although capable of flying at speeds up to fifty-five miles per hour, they are not gliders. They must pump their rakish, swept-back wings nonstop for the entire voyage.

Neither are plovers waterfowl; they are unable to land on the water to rest. Yet somehow they always find their way back to these little dots of land in the middle of the Pacific—to the same patch of lawn, year after year, for twenty years or more. As a navigator, John was fascinated by this miraculous annual transpacific achievement.

Newspaper in hand, John retreated to the semi-privacy of the veranda. There, he donned his glasses and quickly scanned the entire paper. When finished, he hid them away again, gathered up the two glass quart bottles of milk from the milk box on the stoop, and headed back inside.

As he went about the business of preparing his standard breakfast— coffee and toast with homemade guava jam—he heard Ethel stirring in the bedroom. By the time he settled at the table with plate, mug, and newspaper, she shuffled into the kitchen. When she didn't acknowledge his "Good morning," he resigned himself to another silent meal. He slid the society section over to her place.

Ethel poured coffee into a mug, then added milk and sugar. Bending over the stove, she lit her first Lucky Strike of the day, before dropping onto the sturdy kitchen chair. She deliberately avoided John's eyes as she picked up the paper at her place.

Married nearly twenty years, John was well aware that Ethel had been unhappy for some time, but he wasn't sure what to do about it. He was also aware that his career could tank if they were to split up. As far as navy brass was concerned, divorce was a sign of instability, an unacceptable trait for a leader of men.

They sat drinking their coffee in silence. By now their relationship had deteriorated beyond fights and Ethel's angry recriminations. Once the country club queen of Maryland's high society, Ethel had imagined herself destined for a marriage that would maintain her elite social status, whether military or civilian.

John understood that the past three years on Ford Island had been especially hard on her. She desperately missed her friends and family, and had been plagued with serious bouts of homesickness. He had tried to make her see how remarkable it was for him to have been promoted to commander at a time when the navy was forcing the majority of officers to accept a reduction in rank, but she was not persuaded. As far as she was concerned, all his promotion had done was to land them on a remote island base, an island within an island, really, smack in the middle of the Pacific Ocean.

The tiny community of Ford Island offered no social life and little other diversion for a military wife. Grocery shopping offered a break in the tedium, but her daily trip to the Pearl Harbor Base exchange was more of an ordeal than an entertainment.

For this expedition, Ethel first had to dress up "properly," as befitted the wife of an officer—girdle and stockings, heels, makeup, the works. There were no cars on Ford Island. In fact, except for airplanes, bicycles were the only mechanical mode of transportation. Ethel certainly wasn't about to ride a bike, so she then had to walk several long blocks to the shuttle landing. There, she'd have to wait in the heat—or occasional shower—for the irregularly scheduled open-air personnel ferry. The quarter-mile trip across the harbor often meant wet seats and salt spray. When she reached the other side, she was forced to wait again to board a crowded bus to the store. The return trip was worse, as Ethel then had the groceries to struggle with. It was hardly what she had envisioned for herself at the outset of their marriage. Life on Ford Island was a far cry from the white gloves, tea-and-cotillion navy Ethel had signed on for.

That they had never been able to have children didn't help her frustration. The fact was that in this posting, while John was fully engaged carrying out his responsibilities, Ethel was left high and dry, with a lot of time to stew about it.

As it had become clear to her that they'd be stationed there for some time to come—John wouldn't be considered for further promotion for another couple of years—she'd grown increasingly bitter, rarely missing the opportunity to belittle him and his work. More and more, though, she seemed content to simply freeze John out.

Seeing that was going to be the case this morning, John rose, took his dishes to the sink, and rinsed them. "Well, I'm off." No answer. Ethel was occupied with the society page, or pretending to be. Sighing, he mumbled a quiet "Goodbye," left the kitchen, and headed off to work.

Before the porch screen door had closed, Ethel folded the paper and pulled another cigarette from the pack on the table. She lit the new one off the still-smoldering butt, and inhaled deeply. Checking the kitchen clock, she decided she had better get moving if she was going to make her appointment in downtown Honolulu by nine.

7:12 AM Hawaii Time

As the commanding officer of the Ford Island Air Base, John was five minutes by passenger launch from mainland O'ahu, but light years apart from its madness. Living and working on an island in the middle of a bustling major seaport like Pearl Harbor made for interesting contrasts. While some, like Ethel, may have felt life on the tiny island confining, if not downright claustrophobic, John found that the stretch of water between Ford Island and Honolulu allowed for a more easygoing pace; the spit-and-polish strictness of navy regulations seemed more relaxed than on other American bases.

The brisk ten-minute walk to John's office at the airfield followed a well-worn, unpaved path through knee-high grass on a field that was dotted with gnarled *kiawe* trees. This morning he briefly disturbed twenty or thirty miniscule red-beaked Java Rice Finches that rose and swarmed as one, only to drop a few feet away into the seed-bearing grass. He marveled at the tiny birds, so light that they barely bent the stalks.

As John walked, he reviewed his marital impasse. Certainly he was not the perfect husband, but he felt he had worked at their relationship. He was puzzled that his advancing naval career seemed to be the primary bone of contention with Ethel; but this was a strange contradiction. When they first met, Ethel had seemed to be attracted by his family's distinguished naval background, as well as enamored of his own status as a naval officer and pilot. She had even insisted that he wear his dress whites for their wedding.

As he crossed the hard-packed reddish-brown clay that served as the runway for the navy's wheeled aircraft, John's spit-shined shoes became coated with red dust. Fifty yards farther on, he walked beneath the shade of the century-old Chinese banyan tree fronting the sturdy concrete structure that served as headquarters for Naval Air Station

Ford Island. His office in sight, John knew it was time to clear his head and focus on the running of his command. His mind clicked into business mode as he climbed the three steps up to the covered porch, entered the building, and marched briskly down the short hallway. He stopped in front of a wood framed door with a smoked-glass window. The painted gold-leaf letters simply read, "Commander, NAS Ford Island."

John burst energetically into his office, catching one of his lieutenants by surprise.

"Morning, Byron!"

The junior officer had been slouched in a side chair and now jumped to attention. A quick "at ease" from his superior brought a sheepish grin to the lieutenant's face.

"John, you did it again—caught me with my sails aback!"

Lieutenant Byron J. Connell had served under John for two years. During that time, their initial mutual respect had evolved into a close friendship. Like Rodgers, Connell was a naval aviator, as well as a pilot. He was slender, weighing in at a wiry 148 pounds, and at just under 5'8", he was considerably shorter than John. At thirty-one, Byron was still a bachelor. His baby face, fair skin, blond hair, and blue eyes gave him a vulnerable quality women found attractive. Although perpetually juggling several ladies at a time, Byron's true love was flying. Nothing else mattered as much to him.

The oldest of four brothers from a relatively poor family, Byron Connell embodied Horatio Alger's American dream. His folks had instilled a strict work ethic in him and pushed him hard. His bright mind and conscientious work in high school had earned him a full scholarship at MIT, where he'd buckled down and made an exceptional record for himself.

Settling into the morning's work, John asked Byron for the day's master flight log, which the lieutenant quickly produced. John noted that all but two of the seaplanes were scheduled for aerial surveillance flights. Those two planes had been rolled up the ramp on dollies and were "on the hard," undergoing routine maintenance.

John saw that he and Byron were scheduled to fly recon together. He was pleased. Lately, one of the reasons he loved to fly was the sense of leaving his troubles on the ground.

"Is our plane ready?"

"Aye, sir," was Byron's quicksilver response. "Full and floating."

"OK. Give me a couple of minutes to review this stack in my in-basket. I'll meet you at the pier in twenty minutes."

Saluting smartly, Byron bounded from John's office. He was off to preflight the twin-engine seaplane.

John waited a moment after the younger man had left, then walked over and locked the office door. Removing the forbidden glasses from his pocket, he put them on, and began reviewing the latest in an unending cascade of paperwork. At least these were problems that were relatively easy to fix, unlike his situation at home.

Several minutes later, having waded through the pile, John stepped into the adjacent locker room. He stripped out of his uniform and donned his flight jump suit. He also grabbed his weathered leather jacket, cap, and goggles. To the uninitiated these outer clothes may have seemed out of place in an 86° tropical paradise, but they were necessary. It was amazing how cool it got at 2,000 feet in an open cockpit, flying into a sixty-knot wind.

Striding purposefully toward the piers that served as temporary homes for the aging aircraft, John watched as an F5N seaplane, identical to the model he and Byron would soon be flying, lifted off. Saluting the ground crews that swarmed about the bulkhead, he marched down the pier and approached his plane. The wood and fabric twin-engine biplane was painted a dull navy gray. Bobbing uneasily in the water she showed her age. The plane still wore wartime insignias on her slab-sided gray fuselage.

The two crewmen designated to care for the plane were buzzing around their charge like a pair of drones tending a queen. The taller of the two, Chief Mechanics Mate William H. "Wild Bill" Bowlin, had served on Ford Island longer than almost any other sailor currently stationed there. He'd been assigned to the base shortly after it was first commissioned and placed under John's command. From the start, Wild Bill had more than proven his worth. He was a masterful jack-of-all-trades and as such was a real asset to John. The chief mechanics mate could tear apart any engine and tweak it to run better than it had when new. He was almost as good with boats and radios. Bowlin was ruggedly handsome: 5'10" tall, 175 pounds, and built like an outfielder. A transplanted twenty-six-year-old native of Indiana, he loved everything about Hawaii. He did have an untamed streak, though, which accounted for his nickname. Wild Bill spent most of his time off-duty pursuing *wahine* and bootleg booze, and trying to steer clear of the Shore Patrol.

The other crewman hard at work on the seaplane was Otis G. Stantz, a.k.a. "Sparky." Most radiomen in the navy end up with the nickname "Sparky" and hate it, but anything other than Otis would have been OK with Stantz, so "Sparky" it was. Sparky Stantz was the same age as Wild Bill Bowlin and, coincidentally, also from Indiana. He'd been on base a little over a year. Sparky was smaller than Bill, with darker hair and skin. Standing 5'8" without an ounce of fat on his slim frame, he weighed in at 150 pounds soaking wet. Billeted together, the two noncommissioned officers had become inseparable over the last year. Although Sparky seemed to follow in Wild Bill's wake, he managed to hold his own when the two of them pushed the envelope too far. Their scrapes were notorious, but thankfully, from John's point of view, infrequent. Sparky's goal in life was to be the best damn radio operator on the planet. Most who knew him would attest that he was pretty close.

As John prepared to board the plane, Byron was already in the aft pilot's seat. Wild Bill and Sparky stood on either side of the lower wings, each waiting for his cue to start an engine. John climbed past Wild Bill up onto the port wing, and then into the front seat, automatically compensating for the rocking motion of the floating plane. He strapped in, then signaled over his shoulder with a thumbs-up. Looking to his left, Byron shouted "Ignition!" and Wild Bill started grinding on the long steel crank that jutted out of the port engine's nacelle. The spinning crank caused the portside four-cylinder gas engine to cough almost immediately to life. If anything, the harsh chopping sound of the wooden prop slicing through the air was even louder than the noise of the unmuffled 105-horsepower water-cooled power plant. The combination was deafening. Wild Bill removed the crank handle and stowed it onboard, then quickly clambered off the port wing, back onto the pier. Because the din made verbal communication impossible, Byron signaled Sparky to repeat the sequence for the starboard engine, and Sparky worked his crank with identical results. His job done, he too, descended safely to the pier.

Sparky cast off the stern line, and Wild Bill released the bridle that tethered the nose of the plane. The aircraft drifted inelegantly until it was twenty feet or so from the dock. Byron eased the throttles forward and the roar intensified. He used the foot pedals to work the tiny waterbound rudder, which simultaneously turned the less effective vertical tail-mounted one. They taxied the short distance to the western side of Ford Island—the less trafficked area designated as the seaplane "runway." Once lined up on the buoy, Byron checked both the bay and the air for traffic, then pushed the throttles to the stops.

The F5N moved sluggishly at first as she tried to muscle her way through the water. As graceful as she was when airborne, she left much to be desired as a boat. Then the plane slowly gathered speed, her churning props shooting dense spray behind her, momentarily creating a saltwater fog in her wake.

Waves of any size were virtually nonexistent in placid Pearl Harbor, and the calm surface actually made it more difficult for the plane to get up on the step. However the twin wings' massive amount of surface area prevailed. Once on the step, the ungainly seaplane continued to accelerate, then suddenly and deftly lifted off. The din decreased sharply as the seabird left the water, and the ugly duckling became a swan. Byron pointed the nose skyward and the fragile craft responded. They banked to the left, and completed a brief pass over the array of naval might assembled in Battleship Row. Banking back to the right they followed the harbor entrance toward the ocean. Once past Hospital Point, Byron eased the plane into a third, slower turn to port and began running parallel with the shoreline. To their left and forward, they had a view of Honolulu and then Waikiki. Diamond Head stood out in the distance, decked in its summer colors of light greens and tan. Below them on the right side of the plane were the teal and yellow-brown reefs separating the tiny Pacific outpost from the ever-deepening blues of the open sea beyond. There wasn't a whitecap on the surface—no trouble as far as the eye could see. John took a deep breath and relaxed. For the moment, he was content to let the majesty of the ocean to the right and the lush, green mountain valleys on their left refresh his soul.

11:55 AM Hawaii Time

Wearing a red pillbox hat pinned atop her dark hair, Ethel exited the Dillingham Transportation building in downtown Honolulu and chain-lit another Lucky Strike as she walked out to the curb. With her purse slung over her arm she opened the fringed crimson parasol to deflect the tropical sun, and tugged at her white gloves. She paused in front of the art-deco building at the bottom of Bishop Street and gazed longingly across the street at commercial Pier 10, where the *Mariposa* was busily docking. The passenger-freighter was being maneuvered by a stubby tug belching gray smoke. Ethel had read that the sister ship of the *Mariposa*, the *Lurline*, recently set a record on a transpacific crossing from Honolulu to Los Angeles. Ethel murmured longingly to herself, "Five days to the Mainland. . . ." and crossed Ala Moana Boulevard, carefully navigating the busy midday traffic.

Boat arrival days were happy occasions for most, but generally not for Ethel. Envious of those free to travel, she frowned at the cheerful faces crowding the rail onboard the ship. They were waving energetically to the many equally excited lei-carrying greeters below. A dozen or so bronze-skinned local youths lined the wharf, diving into the murky water between the ship and pier, competing for the coins flipped from above. Ethel briefly wondered why the authorities allowed this dangerous activity.

Ethel's take on the scene was further soured by her physical discomfort. She had dressed up for her appointment, and now couldn't wait to be out of her girdle and heels. She weighed her options, then turned and walked briskly to the queue for a taxi back to Pearl Harbor. To hell with the expense, she wasn't going to bother with public transportation today. If only John had shipped a car when they'd been transferred. Better yet, if he had been a flag officer, she would have had her own driver. Never mind. Soon, none of that would matter.

Ethel heard the Kawaiha`o Church bells chime twelve times. Her morning meeting had gone well. It wouldn't be long now.

4:33 PM Hawaii Time

After John and Byron had completed their air surveillance patrol, they headed for the tiny Ford Island Officer's Club, a casually comfortable, unsophisticated watering hole for officers and noncoms alike. Here, formalities were cheerfully overlooked.

They'd only just slid into a booth when Kiles Pope, a fellow pilot, joined them, crowding in next to Byron. Chief Petty Officer Kiles Pope had logged more hours in flying boats than anyone else in the navy, perhaps even the world. Pope was also a master mechanic. He loved the technical intricacies of airplanes and he was not happy unless elbow deep in engine oil. At thirty, he was a deeply religious, devoted family man—the happily married father of six. His lanky 5'11" frame carried 185 pounds. With a long nose and horsy features, he couldn't be considered handsome, but competitive by nature, he had lettered in three sports in high school, where his skill as a first baseman had earned him honorable mention All-State honors.

Above all else, Pope was a pilot of uncommon skill, probably the most natural pilot John had ever met. He seemed to be able to anticipate every nuance of the wind. To Kiles Pope, a plane was an extension of his being—something he wore rather than flew.

John liked both men. To him, Byron and Kiles epitomized the best of the navy.

Prohibition was in full swing so the men ordered Coca-Colas. With baseball season fast approaching the World Series, and college football right behind, the convivial conversation centered around sports.

Kiles, a die-hard Washington Senators fan, threw down the gauntlet. "Did you hear how Walter Johnson mowed down the Yanks yesterday? He's still the best."

Knowing Kiles's obsession, Byron needled him. "The best what? He's so far over the hill, he's on his way up the next."

Kiles shook his head sagely. "Just watch. You'll see. The Senators are unbeatable this year. What do you think, John?"

John chuckled, "Heck, I don't know about the junior circuit, but the Giants, now *there's* a team. John McGraw's got those guys humming. And Frankie Frisch is devastating from either side of the plate."

Byron chimed in, "Well, I'm not betting on either of them. Not while Babe Ruth still has his eye on the ball."

Kiles shifted gears. "Hey, speaking of eyes, did you guys hear about Dick Baldwin? Right after he finally got his promotion and his dream assignment at the Naval Air Field in Philadelphia, he flunked his eye exam. They busted him from flight duty. Damn, that would kill me! I wouldn't know what to do with myself."

Byron didn't miss a beat. "Kiles, you'd probably just get your wife pregnant again. It seems like that's all you do between flights anyway."

They all chuckled at this. It was a standing joke.

Byron continued, "That brings up the fact that flight physicals begin next week." Turning to John, he added, "At least that's not a concern for you, 'eagle-eyes.' Hell, you scare me when you read those tiny bottom lines on the chart. What does that make your eyesight, John, 20-5?"

"20-5! Isn't that like four times better than 20-20?" queried Kiles.

Thinking of the time he'd spent surreptitiously memorizing contraband copies of each year's eye test charts, John just shook his head in mock embarrassment, and deftly changed the subject.

"Hey Kiles, are you going to give us some competition in the races, or are you still sailing solo?" He was referring to the upcoming annual interservice regatta. John and Byron were the defending double-handed champions, having soundly defeated Kiles and his partner the year before.

Kiles shrugged. "Hell, you know no one can give you two a race in those scows. Anyway, I've promised Lilly that I'd spend that weekend with her and the kids. She really could use help with those hooligans. But just you wait 'til little Bobby gets old enough, and then we'll give you both a run for your money."

Byron chuckled. "Well, that may be, but we'll sure miss you hounding our stern this year. By the way, you should see the *bow* of our boat, one of these days. It's really pretty."

Kiles smacked Byron's shoulder, and the three friends clinked Coke bottles.

John Rodgers' pilot license. Considered a consummate navigator, Rodgers was also the first naval officer taught to fly by Orville and Wilbur Wright. His license indicated he was "Naval Aviator No. 2."

Honolulu circa 1924

First built in 1918, the F5N seaplane was the navy's most common patrol airplane in Hawaii. Like all navy heavier-than-air aircraft, she was a biplane. She had been constructed at the NAS Philadelphia, as were almost all navy aircraft. Her body was fabric and wood over a metal framework, while the wings and tail were similarly fashioned over hand-hewn ash ribs. These frames were covered with tautly stretched canvas. The fabric was painted with noxious "dope" paint, which served to seal the fabric and stiffen it. This provided the wings with the smoothly curved surfaces necessary for flight. The heavily doped canvas made them waterproof as well.

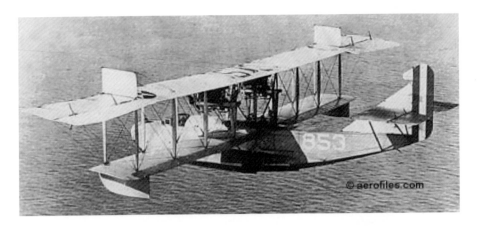

U.S. Navy F5N flying boat

At the plane's bow, the hull looked something like the prow of a powerboat. The shape then quickly changed to a flattened "V" as it ran back toward the stern. Partway back on the bottom, the seaplane's fuselage was engineered with a built-in "step"—basically a vertical notch upward about mid-ship on the hull's belly. Aft of the step, the rest of the hull became an almost flat horizontal surface rising and narrowing as it neared the tail.

A step was necessary for a water launch. As a seaplane gathered speed, she would eventually rise up on only the front section, or "step," The amount of the plane's surface in contact with the water reduced dramatically once the aircraft was "up on the step," which helped to further increase the speed of the craft. As the plane accelerated, it would begin to skip across the water. This skipping action, coupled with the increase in velocity, was similar to the process that allows a surfer to ride on top of a wave, rather than to plow through it. As the aircraft skimmed across the water, it would finally attain enough speed for the lift of the wings to overcome the tensile strength of the water, and the plane would rise into the air.

The F5L shown here in wartime camouflage paint. Dramatically underpowered, it was a slow and deliberate plane that took a considerable distance to get airborne.

A navy-gray painted version of the venerable F5L seaplane. Shown here in calm waters, it was floating unusually level. It would normally lean at an ungainly tilt on one wing float. Its twin engines were started via hand-cranks.

A closer look at the front half of the F5L seaplane. It is pictured above on a commonly used wheeled dolly. Note the carved wooden propellers, suspended radiators, and multiple guy wires crisscrossed between the wings.

Chapter 3

Friday—August 1, 1924

7:45 AM Eastern Time

Footsteps echoed crisply off the polished floor of a long office hallway in Washington, D.C. The civilian aide's pace was quick but not rushed. He stopped outside a dark brown wooden door, where a navy guard in immaculate dress whites stood at parade rest. The seaman curtly acknowledged the bespectacled aide, then turned and knocked twice on the solid door. When a brusque "Enter!" came from within, the guard opened the door and ushered the aide into Rear Admiral William Moffett's office.

"Good morning, sir. Welcome back." The aide quickly deposited several letters and the morning edition of *The Washington Post* in the admiral's in-box. Before Moffett could respond, the aide turned on his heel and left, closing the door silently behind him.

Back in his Washington office after the 5,000-mile trip, Moffett was catching up on the pile of paperwork that had been waiting for him. Even seated behind the impressive wooden desk, he was an imposing figure. A framed Medal of Honor hung on the wall behind him. A gold-fringed American flag and a matching Department of the Navy flag flanked the window. A writing set was strategically placed on the desk in front of him, the two pens angled like the gun turrets of a battleship. The hand-carved wooden nameplate read: "William A. Moffett, Chief, BURAERO."

Looking up from his correspondence, Admiral Moffett noticed that the newspaper had been folded open to an article on page three. A terse headline caught his eye: "AIR POWER." Groaning out loud, Moffett reached a large hand across the desk and grabbed the paper.

"That damned Billy Mitchell is at it again!"

Scanning the article quickly, he read that General Mitchell had charged that the navy was not using aircraft to their best advantage. Mitchell was quoted directly, speaking in his usual bombastic style: "While we have been proving the war-worthiness of planes by sinking battleships, the navy continues to pigeonhole their air power by using their heavy, slow seaplanes and dirigibles for shore patrols. A unified air force would use lighter and faster planes for that duty." The rest of the article just seemed to pour more fuel on the fire.

Moffett was torn. On the one hand, he concurred with Mitchell, but he found the way Mitchell massaged the facts intensely annoying. Yes, he had managed to sink a battleship by aerial attack, and to his credit, his flyboys had done it in twenty-one minutes—but there had been a considerable number of extenuating circumstances behind the story Mitchell touted to the public. The ship they sank certainly wasn't one of the huge dreadnoughts that commanded the high seas of the present day. His target, the *Ostfriesland*, had been an old, decrepit hulk, a German prewar tub that had been pre-holed and scheduled for scuttling. If left alone, it probably would have sunk of its own accord. At the time of Mitchell's attack, it had been securely anchored fore and aft in calm waters; the old ship had literally been a sitting duck. On top of that, Mitchell had his aviators use extremely large, heavy bombs—so heavy, in fact, that they would have been impractical in an actual battle. Plus, his airmen had flown in so low and so slow that a well-aimed pistol shot might well have downed any one of the sluggish Martin bombers. Nevertheless, *The New York Times* had turned the event into front-page news: "No fleet afloat is safe if it loses control of the air." Moffett was amazed that the press, and by extension the public, didn't seem to care that the ship hadn't made any effort to defend herself.

The week after he'd sunk the *Ostfriesland*, Mitchell further irked his superiors with mock air attacks on New York, Philadelphia, and Baltimore.

He even had a squadron circle Annapolis, an act specifically designed as an affront to the navy. These "attacks" were executed purely for their propaganda value, and in that regard they'd been highly successful. Headlines across the country began trumpeting Mitchell's clarion cry for an independent air force.

Mitchell had continued to feed the public disinformation by referring to hard-framed navy dirigibles as "bags of gas." He also did not correct reporters' questions regarding the explosive properties of these so-called gas bags, simply glossing over the fact that unlike other countries, the U.S. Navy dirigibles used inert, nonexplosive helium rather than highly combustible hydrogen.

Moffett had to admit, it was an easy flame to fan. Germany, Great Britain, and France, the leaders in the lighter-than-air craft industry, had no access to supplies of helium gas, and were forced to use hydrogen, whose explosive instability had been demonstrated in numerous dirigible disasters.

Moffett agreed with Mitchell on the need for more and better aircraft, as well as the prognostication that planes would be both important and effective as instruments of war in the future. Where they parted company was that Mitchell didn't think the navy should have its own, independent air wing, and Moffett was adamant that it should.

But Mitchell was not Moffett's only worry. At this moment, military aviation in America was in a precarious state. Funding was at an all-time low. Moffett was also concerned with recent reports that indicated a massive buildup of military aircraft in virtually all other countries that had participated in the Great War, and even some that hadn't. Japan was reported to have built more planes in the last twelve months than the United States had in total, and despite the terms of the Treaty of Versailles, the Germans were once again flexing their aviation might.

Admiral Moffett shook his head and tossed the newspaper into his out-box. It irritated him to see the press lapping up the half-truths Mitchell was spouting. It infuriated him that the army and the Department of War permitted the general's flagrant grandstanding. But Moffett had learned from Mitchell. Two could play this game. It was time to wake America up. He picked up the phone and asked for a long-distance operator.

General Billy Mitchell, photographed in France during the First World War

The World War I German battleship, *Ostfriesland*

The *Ostfriesland:* An anchored, derelict German battleship being sunk by General Billy Mitchell's planes after the First World War. This episode, although lionized by the press, would haunt Mitchell's career. A provocative self-promoter, Mitchell blatantly disregarded specific orders as to the size of bombs to drop and the altitude from which they were to be released. Although this picture is a poor reproduction, the moment that it captures—the actual bombing of the *Ostfriesland*—makes it worth including.

Chapter 4

Monday—August 4, 1924

8:00 AM Hawaii Time

John had summoned Lieutenant Byron Connell, Lieutenant Kiles Pope, Chief Mechanics Mate William "Wild Bill" Bowlin, and Chief Radioman Otis "Sparky" Stantz to his office for a meeting. As the four men filed into the austere space, Rodgers said, "At ease, gentlemen. Close the door, and be seated." He came from behind his desk and leaned against it as he addressed the men.

"Gentlemen, as you know, naval aviation is at a crucial juncture. There are people, some of them important people, who question the navy's need for aircraft—any aircraft. Many consider navy aircraft capable of nothing much more than shoreline patrol duty, and unfortunately, the public listens to them. Even some of our own brass are mired in the belief that the navy would be better off using aircraft funds elsewhere. However misguided they may be, those opinions carry weight. Therefore, if the navy is to continue to stay in the air we must do whatever we can to alter these perceptions.

"We've been offered a unique opportunity to make naval history. I've asked you here because each of you is the best at what you do. I want to extend to you the chance to volunteer for a very important project. It's a bold plan, and one that will necessitate some personal sacrifice."

Looking specifically at Kiles, John proceeded, "I don't want to sugar-coat this. The planning and development will mean long hours, and eventually will take you away from your families for several months. The ultimate mission *will* be hazardous." He let that sink in. "However, if you choose to join me as my crew, we will have a shot at ensuring the future viability of naval air power." John paused, then dropped the bomb. "Within nine months, the navy will fly three brand-new, specially prepared planes *nonstop* from California back here to Hawaii. We're to crew one of them."

Silence—then Byron spoke first. "Holy cow! That's incredible! This is Moffett's plan, isn't it? We all wondered why he was here." Looking at the excited faces around him, he continued, "I don't think there's any way you could stop us from joining you!" The other three laughed and nodded enthusiastically.

John was touched. "OK guys, I appreciate your support, but be sure. If anyone isn't one-hundred-percent committed, I'd like to know now. It won't reflect badly on you." No one spoke as John surveyed the room.

"Well . . . ?"

Byron answered for the group, "Sir, looks like we're all in."

"That's great." John continued, "I will be in overall command of the mission. There will be three planes and three five-man crews. We'll fly the point. I think all of you know Lieutenant Allen Snody—he's a good man. I spoke with him this morning and he'll be in command of the second plane. He's gathering his crew as we speak, so I'd appreciate it if you kept this news to yourselves until he's announced his choices.

"Both our plane and Snody's are already under construction at the navy factory in Philadelphia. They are the latest iteration of the PN7 patrol seaplanes you're all familiar with, except they'll have new Packard engines." Pausing for effect, John said, "Those engines will be rated at over 500 horsepower each."

At this, Wild Bill gave a low whistle.

John smiled. "That's right, those babies will be massive, and they'll need to be fed accordingly. The planes will be configured with extra-large fuel tanks, but we'll still need to carry reserve drums. We won't know the estimated range until we see how much extra gas we can get aloft, but remember our goal is Hawaii, so we're hoping for about twenty-five hundred miles. The planes are each to be designated PN9s—Patrol, Navy, ninth generation.

"As I indicated, there's a third plane. Admiral Moffett has redirected some funds and is having it built at a commercial factory in Seattle. This seaplane will be a new prototype. I know that it'll be a twin-engine craft, and a lumber company, Boeing, will be the manufacturer, but beyond that, I'm still in the dark. The crew for this plane will be under the command of Lieutenant Commander James Strong. I've heard of Strong, but haven't yet met him."

"I have," Byron muttered. "He's a prima donna."

John shot Byron a glance. He'd follow up on this later.

Kiles spoke up, "Sir, when are we talking about going?"

"Good question. We're planning the trip for late spring to take advantage of the strong trade winds at that time of year. The flight should take close to thirty hours. As you can imagine, flying nonstop, we're going to need all the help we can get. Those tailwinds could make all the difference."

"Sir, where are we leaving from?" asked Wild Bill.

"San Diego was the original plan, but I'm lobbying for San Francisco. It's a little closer to Hawaii than any other West Coast port. And we should be able to better use the east-northeast tailwinds that are downwind from there, rather than off our stern quarter as they would be out of San Diego.

"And speaking of San Diego, our planes will be shipped from the East Coast through the canal and up the West Coast. So we'll be heading to San Diego in either case, to pick up the planes. If San Francisco becomes the point of departure, we'll use the flight from San Diego as a long-distance shakedown. Strong will pick up his plane at the factory in Seattle and then meet us wherever.

"We won't be shipping out until spring, as the planes won't be ready until then, but training and planning will begin immediately. Questions?"

The room was silent, but the excitement was palpable. Rodgers concluded the meeting. "OK then. Dismissed."

Talking animatedly, the crew filed out, except for Byron, who held the door as the other three left. "John, do you have a minute?"

"Sure, what's up?"

Closing the door, Byron said, "Sir, this mission could be a real turning point. I mean, if we pull this off, we may never have to worry about any more rank-reduction sweeps from the brass in the future. This stunt could guarantee our job security."

Rodgers nodded. "I've considered that, and I sure hope you're right. But damn it all, Byron, just finding these tiny islands in the middle of the Pacific will be a major accomplishment. You know, when we're halfway between here and California, we'll be at the farthest point away from land that you can be on earth! Honestly, even if we *can* get the planes airborne with enough fuel, it's a hell of a stretch to fly those planes that far. And if we fail, well . . ."

Byron grinned. "We won't fail. We've got the best damn crew in the navy. Kiles has more time flying seaplanes than anyone, and you and I . . . hell, we can fly anything with wings. No one's better than Bill to keep those big engines humming, and Sparky knows every tube and wire inside a radio. He's also one of the best scroungers I've ever seen, especially when it comes to jury-rigging something in an emergency. And John, if anyone can find these islands, you can. You're one hell of a navigator."

John shrugged, touched by his lieutenant's faith. "Well, we'll see, won't we?" Then, feigning fierceness, he growled, "Now get the hell outta here, and let me do some work!"

After Byron had left, John closed the door, took out his glasses, and cleaned them with his handkerchief. Wrapping the wire rims around his ears, he picked up the top sheet in his in-box. Even with glasses, he found he now had to hold the page at arm's length to be able to read it.

Lieutenant Byron J. Connell
  John Rodgers' second-in-command on the mission, and his best friend.

Chapter 5

Wednesday—August 6, 1924

3:45 PM Hawaii Time

Wild Bill Bowlin and Sparky Stantz were in the hangar, perched on stools in front of a well-worn workbench. From the jumble of wires and metal on the bench, it was hard to tell whether they were in the process of reassembling or disassembling what had once been a radio. Their focus was not on the project at hand, however. These two sailors were in the midst of a high-stakes negotiation.

"Aw shucks, Sparky, come on! Did you get her phone number or not?"

"Steady on, Wild Bill, I told you, she lives with her calabash auntie, and they don't have a phone."

"Well, how the heck are you going to meet her again?"

"I walked her *home* from the beach—this means I know where she lives! They have a cottage in Waikiki. Don't worry, I'll work it out . . . . Damn, she's pretty."

"Yeah, you said that already. So when are you gonna introduce me?"

"I'm not crazy! I don't want you hornin' in on me. But . . ." Here Sparky paused for dramatic effect.

"But what . . . ?!"

"But she does have a sister."

Wild Bill jumped on that. "She does? Is she taller than Lei? You know our agreement . . ."

Sparky grinned. "D'you think I'd have told you about her if she wasn't? Yeah, she's younger than Lei by a year, but she's a little bit taller. Her name is Lani, and—you'll love this—they both dance hula at the Moana Hotel."

"All right! Now you're talkin'. How can I meet her—and when?"

A Cheshire cat smile spread across Sparky's face. "I've already set it up. We have to be there after the sunset show on Saturday evening."

Bill slapped Sparky's back and let out another enthusiastic "All *right!*" His mind was already racing forward to the weekend. "So Saturday night's all set! Hula dancers, huh?"

"Hey, loverboy—we got three days to go between now and then. What do you say we get this radio workin' so we can grab something to eat?"

Wild Bill grinned. "Okay, let's get back to work. Makes the time go faster, anyway."

Smiling to himself, Sparky turned back to the ailing radio. He was pleased to be in the driver's seat this time. Bill usually took the lead with women. But Bill was right; they did have a deal. Whenever there were two women up for grabs, their agreement was that Sparky got the shorter one. This plan had worked for them, up to now.

In fact, the approach had often played out to their advantage. Once, at a church mixer off-base, they had asked a couple of attractive young women to stand back-to-back in order to settle their bet over who was the taller of the two. Won over by boyish midwestern charm, the girls had giggled and complied. It had been the perfect icebreaker.

This time, however, things were a little different. It wasn't just a question of who wound up with whom for an evening; Sparky was really taken with Lei. He was thankful she was the shorter of the two.

As he tinkered with the radio, Wild Bill wondered aloud, "Do you think there'll be any problem getting off duty early enough on Saturday?"

"Nah, Commander Rodgers and Lieutenant Connell are racing in that interservice sailboat race this weekend. They'll be outta here early, and we'll be off duty in plenty of time to catch the Waikiki shuttle at four."

"Great!"

Sorting through the pieces on the workbench, Sparky asked, "Have you ever seen those two race that little boat? I watched 'em practice last week. They're somethin' else! They move like a precision drill team when they're tackin' that thing. Damn, can they make it fly! They hang out on those hiking boards so far that, I swear, their toes are the only things inside the boat."

"Well, whaddaya expect? Rodgers has seawater in his veins. His family tree reads like a *Who's Who* of U.S. Naval history."

Noting that Sparky seemed duly impressed, Wild Bill volunteered another tidbit. "Didja know Cal Rodgers was his cousin?"

"You mean Cal Rodgers, as in the first person to fly a plane across the country?"

"Same guy. Took forever. Somethin' like three months, 170 hops or so, but he did it."

"Jeez, I guess that's why the old man's so driven to succeed. Runs in his blood. He's pushed himself to be the best damn navigator in the navy—and he hates to lose at anything."

"Yep. I'll tell you, he's damn near unbeatable in that little sailboat of his."

Sparky just shook his head.

"Well, you can be sure of one thing; whatever job the navy gives him gets done right. That's why I love workin' for the guy!"

Commander John Rodgers was considered one of the best navigators in the navy. By the turn of the twentieth century, navigation was no longer a dark art, but it took a steady hand, a good chronometer, and mathematical skills not everyone could master. He is seen here taking a site with his sextant.

Aviation pioneer Calbraith Perry Rodgers, John Rodgers' first cousin. Seeing John fly inspired Cal Rodgers to get his own pilot's license. Just weeks after receiving his license, Cal Rodgers purchased this Wright Flyer Model B with the intention of capturing the 50,000 dollar prize awaiting the first person to fly cross-country in less than thirty days. In this 1911 picture, Cal Rodgers is airborne in his Wright Flyer, attempting the crossing. He would not win the prize, as the trip would take eighty-four days. Cal Rodgers would also break more bones than he could count, including both legs, his collarbone, an ankle, and several ribs.

Cal Rodgers' Wright Flyer was sponsored by the Armour Corporation to promote its soft drink, Vin Fiz. They paid Rodgers three dollars per mile for the effort.

Cal Rodgers' journey was a nationwide sensation. Pictured here is the white Vin Fiz boxcar that followed the epic journey, carrying multiple spare parts.

Shown here is one of the innumerable crash landings that Rodgers, with a mere forty-one days' experience flying, endured during the cross-country adventure. There is no official count of the number of crashes, but by the time Cal Rodgers reached California, the only parts that remained intact from the original aircraft were the rudder and the oil pan.

Calbraith Perry Rodgers was a big man. He stood 6'4" at a time when the average height was 5'7". Like his cousin John, he was related to a compendium of American heroes. He was the grandson of Admiral Matthew Perry, who opened Japan to the Western world, and he was grand-nephew of Commodore Oliver Hazard Perry, famous for the Battle of Lake Erie.

Although Calbraith Rodgers failed to reach California in his target of thirty days, he finally did land at Long Beach, where he was greeted by several thousand spectators. Almost three months after taking off from Sheepshead Bay, New York, Cal taxied the plane until its wheels were wet in the Pacific Ocean. He may not have won the prize money, but his accomplishment thrilled the country, and Cal was hailed as an aviation pioneer. Sadly, he died several months later, crashing into the shallows of the Pacific Ocean on a demonstration flight.

Chapter 6

Friday—August 8, 1924

5:45 AM Eastern Time

"Oh my god." The words, barely whispered, escaped from Navy Commander E. F. Robinson's mouth as he caught sight of the airborne behemoth streaking directly toward his ship. Out of habit, he reached for his binoculars, but there was no need for them; the dirigible was already too close. It had eluded earlier detection by approaching from the east, using the scattered cumulus clouds and the blinding early morning sun as cover.

Robinson had been right in step with the other Washington naysayers when it came to considering dirigibles as nothing more than vessels for airborne reconnaissance. Personally, Robinson viewed Rear Admiral Moffett's assertions about the use of dirigibles in full-on sea battles as downright laughable. This was the navy, and to Robinson, "navy" meant fast-attacking, well-armed warships, not toy balloons. He had privately scoffed at the war games that had been scheduled. Now, however, although his aerial attacker had been clearly described in Robinson's orders, nothing could have prepared him for the breathtaking size and speed of the silver torpedo bearing down on his ship.

Robinson was in charge of the USS *Patoka*, a ship whose keel had been laid just five years before, near the conclusion of the war. At 417 feet long, with a sixty-foot beam, she was the largest oil tender the U.S. Navy had in service—a fact Commander Robinson was proud of. Indeed, except for a few of the great battleships, she was bigger than almost any other ship in the navy.

Seven days ago, the *Patoka* had sailed alone from the Norfolk Navy Yard in Virginia, where she had undergone a radical transformation—much to Robinson's annoyance. Despite the relatively peaceful postwar climate, the entire refit had been performed under a veil of secrecy. The ship now included twin cranes capable of off-loading and retrieving seaplanes, an innovation which Admiral Moffett had introduced during the war, and one Robinson could understand. When launched from ships, seaplanes could easily scout great expanses of ocean, making them much more effective at enemy detection.

To this end, three small, identical single-engine seaplanes were presently secured to the *Patoka*'s deck. Fairly slow and deliberate, the lightweight fabric, wood, and wire biplanes were principally designed for reconnaissance missions, but had also been outfitted with light-caliber automatic weapons for air-to-air defense. However, the conversion of the *Patoka* into a primitive aircraft carrier was only one piece of her recent metamorphosis.

The more significant alteration by far, and the one that grated on Commander Robinson, was the tall, ungainly tower that had been constructed on the fantail of his ship. The pointed steel structure rose more than 125 feet into the air and bore a strong resemblance to the Eiffel Tower. Perched on her very stern, the peculiar spire towered over the ship and made her look downright unstable.

Robinson had disagreed with the concept from the outset, quietly cursing the abominable structure as yet another one of Moffett's wild ideas, but because of its top-secret status, he was unable to explain the purpose of the bizarre refit to anyone. Consequently, during the course of construction, Robinson had been forced to bite his tongue as his pride and joy became the target of considerable derision from his fellow officers.

However, the new tower was not uppermost in Commander Robinson's mind at the moment. His attention was concentrated on the imminent attack. To his intense surprise, he found he was going to have to call upon everything in the *Patoka*'s arsenal to meet the dirigible's challenge.

As the rising sun glinted off the speeding silver tube, Robinson ordered, "Battle stations! All ahead flank! Prepare for evasive maneuvers!" His command was repeated over the intercom, and the *Patoka*'s deafening Klaxon blared as 160 able-bodied men dashed to their positions.

The *Patoka* had been steaming along at more than eleven knots when the attacking aircraft had first been sighted. Now she was being chased down as if she were standing still. Robinson checked his instruments. According to the gauges, the *Patoka*'s engines were dangerously close to redlining, but even so, his ship was not accelerating fast enough. He desperately willed the massive vessel to gather speed.

Robinson knew instantly that there was no time to launch the airplanes. Even if there had been, what could they do? They would have been like flies trying to bring down a charging rhinoceros. The threat was approaching so rapidly that there was hardly time for his crew to get into battle gear and prep their weapons.

Although a support ship, the *Patoka* was not entirely without armament. Robinson watched as men on the foredeck quickly uncapped the twin five-inch cannons and spun them as far as the turret would turn to the starboard side. Not far enough. Additional teams manned the four forty-millimeter antiaircraft guns. These "ack-ack" guns fired shells that would burst at preset altitudes, creating a shrapnel zone designed to destroy attacking aircraft. There were four turrets: two located amidships, and two positioned further aft on either side. As he watched, Robinson was horrified to recognize how the dirigible effectively neutralized what he had considered to be formidable weapons. If the shells were set to explode as low as the zeppelin was already flying, they'd be like antipersonnel mines, killing all exposed sailors on his own ship's deck. And this was just one way the *Shenandoah* was about to humiliate the *Patoka*.

At the helm of the American built zeppelin ZR-1, a grin spread across the skipper's face. The sunrise approach had worked. Maneuvering under cover of night from miles away, he had positioned his airship directly behind and almost due east of its unsuspecting target. All night long, he'd operated the lighter-than-air craft in dark mode, maintaining position at an altitude of 2,000 feet. From this elevation, it had been easy to locate and stalk his prey. The *Patoka* had been operating with nominal running lights, but with her unusual stern tower lit up as it was, she might as well have been a Christmas tree.

With the newly risen sun and sparse clouds as cover, the gigantic craft dove at top speed for the stern of its quarry. The ZR-1's six individual 300-horsepower engines were at full throttle, frantically spinning the half-dozen propellers. Their combined might hurled the monstrous silver giant along at more than seventy-five miles per hour—an almost unimaginable pace. With the forward control pod suspended fifteen feet below the superstructure, and the engines located considerably aft, the noise level was surprisingly low. Although the swift ride was silky, it still took some adjustment on the part of the crew; airsickness was not unheard of, even for these experienced aviators.

When flying at altitude, the velocity of the 680-foot-long colossus was hardly noticeable to those onboard; but now, as it dived toward the *Patoka*, with the ocean surface rushing by, the speed of the craft was exhilarating. The massive ZR-1 was soon screaming less than two hundred feet from the surface of the North Atlantic. As the zeppelin devoured the distance to its victim, it seemed like something straight out of a Jules Verne novel.

Six duralumin doors swung open, exposing yet another surprise. Suspended within her bowels, the ZR-1 had six .30-caliber Lewis machine guns trained on the USS *Patoka*'s four semi-exposed antiaircraft gun crews. The zeppelin's machine guns were mechanically gimbaled, allowing them to change targets effortlessly. They were easy to aim, as they were primarily designed for air-to-air defense. Today, however, their purpose would be to cause mayhem among the crews manning the *Patoka*'s heavier and less maneuverable weapons.

The expert machine gun crews on the ZR-1 already knew that the *Patoka*'s larger, forward-mounted cannons would be of little threat because of their extremely limited range of motion. Those big guns couldn't face more than five degrees aft of amidships; so as long as the zeppelin attacked from behind, the crews manning them would be unable to track their hunter.

A lookout positioned in the dirigible's bow notified the bridge that the *Patoka*'s crew was scrambling to battle stations. The zeppelin had been detected. The ZR-1's skipper acknowledged the information and ordered an acute course alteration to reposition his craft. Even though traveling at full speed, the world's largest flying machine swiftly banked sharply to starboard. By flanking the U.S. Navy ship from behind, they could also neutralize the effectiveness of at least one of the *Patoka*'s portside forty-millimeter-gun crews, and possibly both, because of their inability to rotate completely to fire across their own deck. The portside gun crews would be sitting ducks with their backs to the dirigible. Therefore only two ZR-1 machine guns would be trained on them, while the zeppelin's four other gun crews could target the only real threat, the starboard antiaircraft gun crews. Following their destruction, the *Patoka*'s bridge and any exposed personnel would be next.

In short, because of what the *Shenandoah* brought to the mix, the *Patoka* was hamstrung by her own arsenal—and by now, both sides knew it. Adrenalin ran high aboard the zeppelin as the distance separating the two vessels dissolved.

Aboard the ZR-1, additional offensive weapons were also being readied. Orders were given to open the twin bomb bay doors for a low-level, near-simultaneous release of four of their eight five-hundred-pound bombs. At this altitude, it would be like shooting fish in a barrel. They would be sure to hit their target, quite probably sinking the lumbering support ship on the first pass. The mission was proceeding with clockwork precision, exactly as planned.

As soon as Commander Robinson saw the aircraft turn, he ordered the *Patoka* to shift course to starboard in response, in order to bring his guns to bear. But it was impossible for the cumbersome supply ship to react quickly enough. As soon as the *Patoka* started to turn, the ZR-1

reversed its starboard bank and veered sharply to port. Robinson groaned audibly. He had fallen into the zeppelin's trap. His change of course had been what navy theory had dictated, and his wartime experience had validated—and it was just what his attackers had hoped for. Robinson hadn't anticipated that the huge aircraft could respond that fast. His ship certainly couldn't. The airship's decisive maneuver now placed the ZR-1 on a seventy-degree angle to centerline of the *Patoka*'s path. On this devastating course, the zeppelin would cross above her from the starboard and behind: the perfect position for attack. Seconds away from the flyover, Commander Robinson looked skyward and swore out loud as he saw the zeppelin's bomb bay doors opening. Game over. The art of war had just been transformed, right before his eyes.

The victorious skipper bent over the bombsight himself, as the gigantic zeppelin crossed unchallenged above the *Patoka*. He then smiled broadly and ordered the twenty-five-man crew of the ZR-1 to stand down. They had proved their point. With the mock attack over, the crew abandoned their battle stations, and the gun turret and bomb bay doors were closed. Then Lieutenant Commander Zachary Lansdowne radioed a brief message to Commander Robinson, his fellow U.S. Navy officer on the ship below: "USS *Shenandoah* requests permission to dock."

Lansdowne was the most experienced zeppelin pilot in the U.S. Navy. In fact, while assigned to the British military after the war, he had participated in the first successful dirigible crossing of the Atlantic. It had been a four-and-a-half day trip from Great Britain to Mineola, Long Island on the English zeppelin R-34. Considered a speedy crossing at the time, the accomplishment helped spur dirigible construction in both countries. A graduate of the Naval Academy, Lansdowne had received the Navy Cross for assisting the Brits in this joint achievement and was subsequently rewarded with this impressive command.

Built at the Lakehurst Naval Air Station in New Jersey, the huge ZR-1 was the U.S. Navy's first dirigible—the USS *Shenandoah*. Her name meant "Bright Star," and it certainly fit. Based on German zeppelin designs obtained as spoils of war, the *Shenandoah's* operating priorities were speed and altitude. And in keeping with the prevailing attitudes in America, she had to be the largest airship ever built. However, beyond her colossal size, the ZR-1 had several marked improvements over her Teutonic siblings. She was powered by six brawny Packard V-8 engines—a combined eighteen-hundred-plus horsepower, the most ever put aloft on a single aircraft. Her entire interior framework, including circular ribs ninety feet in diameter, and the more than 680-foot-long horizontal strakes that defined her outer structure, were made of duralumin. Duralumin, also used in thin sheets as the outer skin covering, was a composite of quenched, age-tempered aluminum, copper, magnesium, and manganese. It was lightweight, strong, durable, and tear-resistant. The one major fault of duralumin was its susceptibility to corrosion, but its pluses far outweighed this single drawback.

The *Shenandoah's* biggest advance over existing German and British zeppelins was her use of helium rather than hydrogen. While hydrogen, the lightest element, provided the greatest lift per cubic foot of volume, it was exceedingly combustible when exposed to oxygen. Helium, totally inert and only slightly less effective as a lifting force, was the perfect substitute.

There was one problem: helium was scarce and sources rare. Fortunately for the United States, the majority of the world's supply of helium was trapped in natural deposits under American soil. Even so, the *Shenandoah* required more than two million cubic feet of the precious gas, nearly exhausting the country's reserves. Her prodigious appetite launched a nationwide effort to unearth more helium.

The *Shenandoah* was constructed using twenty individually sealed gas compartments within her rigid frame. These compartments were linked by a complex plumbing system that allowed helium to be transferred, or "valved," from section to section to adjust the attitude and altitude of the craft.

The dirigible's suspended control pod housed the ship's bridge, as was the case with her closest relative, the "gas bag" soft-sided blimp. Blimps, however, could only carry personnel in the control pod, whereas the main tubular structure of the hard-sided dirigible contained numerous cabins. These cabins served as sleeping quarters, toilet facilities (heads), galley, and offices for the crew of twenty-four that manned the dirigible. They were linked by narrow walkways that in most sections were open to the cavernous interior latticework that formed the structural framework. In many ways, the sailors that manned her lived like construction workers on the girders of high-rise building skeletons.

Another striking difference was that unlike blimps, a dirigible, with its structured shell, could withstand considerable damage to its outer skin and still remain aloft. In fact, repairs were often performed in-flight aboard the *Shenandoah*. It was not uncommon for harnessed crews to climb on top of the huge cylinder in mid-flight and then lower themselves over the sides to perform inspections and repairs.

On this midsummer day, Lieutenant Commander Lansdowne had two missions to fulfill. First, he was to test the dirigible's effectiveness attacking a ship at sea. With this brilliant surprise attack on the *Patoka*, he had proved the *Shenandoah*'s military worth beyond a doubt. In time, Lansdowne's air-to-ship tactics would ultimately become the benchmark for American military lighter-than-air craft battle strategy. Lansdowne himself would become the toast of many flyboys.

The other objective Admiral William Moffett had for Lansdowne and the *Shenandoah* was to overturn one of the most prevalent criticisms of dirigibles—to prove that they could operate effectively away from their home base. Moffett had been responsible for the clandestine refit of the USS *Patoka:* the stern-mounted docking tower as well as all the equipment necessary to properly service the *Shenandoah* at sea. If Lansdowne's men proved the validity of Moffett's concept today, the consequences would be global.

Dirigibles, unlike airplanes, used relatively small quantities of fuel to take off or stay aloft, and consequently they could remain on-station for extended periods of time. While they could carry extraordinary fuel loads and cruise for many days, even weeks, they were still hampered by having to return to a naval facility to refuel. In fact, in the few months since her completion, the refueling of the ZR-1 had never been attempted anywhere besides her home at the Lakehurst Naval Air Station. Being able to refuel at sea would remove that constraint and make it much easier for the giant airships to control the skies.

To accomplish Moffett's objective, Lansdowne's second order of the day was to dock the *Shenandoah* at the *Patoka*'s new fantail tower. Aware of the high stakes, Lansdowne turned the craft in a wide circle to burn off some speed and once again aligned the *Shenandoah* astern of the *Patoka*.

Aboard the *Patoka*, a chagrined Commander Robinson released his crew from the battle stations, and all hands proceeded to their positions for the docking procedure. Their well-honed drills—which, before today, had only been dry runs—were finally to be tested. A hundred men swarmed the aft section of the ship, while several swabbies climbed to their assigned places on the tower.

Robinson kept the ship at speed and pointed west-northwest, directly into the wind, hoping to stabilize the ship. Even the slightest rock or roll at sea level made the top of the 125-foot-tall tower vacillate precariously. Fortunately, the swells were small.

From the starboard catwalk on the *Patoka*'s bridge, Commander Robinson signaled to the *Shenandoah* that his crew was ready to proceed. As Robinson peered intently through his binoculars, the *Shenandoah* began its approach. While the rate at which the ZR-1 was closing in was only about as fast as a brisk walk, the prospect of stopping something so incredibly large was unnerving.

The airship edged closer, and a hundred-foot-long hawser was eased out directly from its prow. The heavy line streamed in the wind next to several dangling shorter lines that were permanently secured near her nose. Then, as the ZR-1 closed to within seventy-five feet, a rogue wave rocked the *Patoka*, causing the tower to swing wildly side-to-side, like the needle of a metronome.

As the ZR-1 crept closer still, a single aviator, visible in an opening in the bow of the titanic vessel, turned and signaled to someone inside.

Abruptly, the *Shenandoah*'s nose angled upward. At first, Robinson thought it was a sign that the *Shenandoah* was aborting the pass, but that was not the case. Instead, all six of the V-8s went into full reverse, sounding like a distant swarm of angry hornets. Almost instantly the leviathan slowed to the same speed as the *Patoka*.

"Unbelievable!" Lowering his binoculars, even the once-skeptical Robinson had to marvel at the aircraft's maneuverability.

As the spire swung past the dangling lines, one of the sailors on the tower was miraculously able to hook the primary hawser. The forward observer in the bow of the dirigible quickly fed that line out, which was in turn led down the inside of the tower and around a winch onboard the deck of the *Patoka*. Slack was carefully maintained on the line until the ship's rocking motion mercifully decreased. Two static lines were then captured by the crew waiting on deck and looped around deck cleats. Care was taken to maintain slack in these lines as well. The sailors queued up and passed the lines hand to hand. From Robinson's point of view, it looked as if they were setting up for a lopsided tug-of-war with the giant. As the shipboard winch spun, the *Shenandoah* was slowly and steadily reeled in to the top of the tower, where at last it came to rest. Mission accomplished.

Aboard the *Shenandoah*, Lieutenant Commander Lansdowne ordered all engines to idle. The floor beneath them, which had been angled slightly upward, had passed through horizontal and was tilted ten degrees down, a sign that the thirty-six-ton aircraft was being secured. Extreme care needed to be taken at all times to prevent airships from unexpected or excessive slant, as they were notoriously fickle and slow to respond to attitude corrections. Injuries could easily occur when the angle became too acute. Ten degrees was as steep as Lansdowne cared to see, so crew and ballast were quickly shifted aft so as not to exceed that angle. In addition, the stern-most engine was rotated so that it pointed downward, and the throttle engaged. This action effectively pulled the stern down toward horizontal equilibrium. Once the initial inclination had been balanced and the ship leveled, Lansdowne had some of the gas in aft compartments valved forward. Shortly thereafter, the colossus reached a controlled equilibrium and dutifully trailed the *Patoka*—Robinson's gigantic new toy balloon.

With docking successfully completed, the skipper ordered all engines shut down. In the eerie quiet that followed, the dirigible crew could suddenly hear orders being shouted on the deck of the *Patoka*, 125 feet below. Lansdowne smiled broadly and, picking up the intercom, congratulated his men for a job well done. He then radioed his thanks to Commander Robinson.

Lansdowne ordered his executive officer to assign a skeleton crew to remain onboard on anchor watch. Then, straightening his uniform jacket, he climbed the ladder from the control pod straight up into the cavernous belly of the beast. Making his way forward along the ten-inch-wide internal catwalk, he passed several of his men, who congratulated him as they clung to the framework so he could pass. Several of them fell in behind him as he marched toward the bow. With the control pod well forward of amidships, this meant a sixty-yard walk along the narrow bridge, but in their euphoric state, the men barely noticed the distance.

As Lansdowne neared the prow, the internal walkway curved steeply upward, matching the shape of the nose until it was again necessary to climb a ladder. When he reached the forward observation platform, just inside the peak of the bow, he was greeted by two airmen manning lines on either side of a complex framework. Lansdowne nodded and they released the lines, which let an eight foot by three foot hinged vertical slice drop down from the duralumin skin. A strong breeze buffeted the skipper, and he grabbed at his hat. To control the trailing aircraft, the *Patoka* was maintaining eleven knots into a five-knot headwind, and the resultant wind whistled through the narrow opening at a gusty eighteen miles per hour. Once lowered, the hinged framework served as a horizontal gangway, complete with rope handrails. From 125 feet below, it looked like the narrow mouth of a giant sperm whale had just opened.

A hush of anticipation fell over those gathered on the ship's deck. Two sailors perched on the tower across the abyss saluted enthusiastically as Lansdowne appeared. With all the confidence of a circus acrobat, he strode across the gangplank. When he reached the tower safely, he saluted the *Patoka*'s flag and barked smartly, "Request permission to come aboard!" The awaiting throng erupted in cheers and the ship's horn blasted out an earsplitting welcome.

The USS *Shenandoah;* dirigible ZR-1. Note the control cab suspended far forward of the nearly seven-hundred-foot-long airship. The other pods are the engine nacelles. Each contained a 300-horsepower Packard engine. There were six engines originally: one at the stern of the control pod (this one was eliminated later as unnecessary), two each just forward of the U.S. Navy insignia, two just aft, and a sixth engine suspended far aft.

The USS *Patoka* in 1924: The *Patoka* was a fuel oiler. She is shown here with her recently outfitted and unusual stern tower. With the exception of several battleships, the *Patoka* was one of the largest ships in the U.S. Navy.

The ZR-1 prior to her maiden flight. Note the suspended control pod.

The *Shenandoah* under construction.

The ZR-1 *Shenandoah* after successfully mooring to the *Patoka*.

Navy Lieutenant Commander Zachary Lansdowne climbing from the *Shenandoah's* bow.

Chapter 7

Saturday—August 9, 1924

6:10 AM Hawaii Time

The weekend of the big InterService Regatta dawned bright and beautiful. *Another Saturday in paradise,* John thought as he left his house just after sunrise. He had packed a small overnight satchel the evening before so as not to disturb his sleeping wife.

As Rodgers made his way toward the piers, he saw Byron Connell bicycling towards him on his new red balloon-tired Columbia. He had a light gray, navy-issue, rucksack made of heavy canvas slung over one shoulder. John could tell his sailing partner was looking forward to the upcoming races. Byron's ever-present grin was as bright as the bike.

"So, you ready?"

John grinned back. "You bet!"

Byron slowed to match John's pace. "Boy, two days' racing is exactly what I need right about now. Just being out there with the wind and the sea always recharges my batteries."

Rodgers nodded. "Same here. For me, it's the competition. Racing sailboats is like playing chess in three dimensions against multiple opponents. There's no time to think of anything else."

Byron grinned again.

"OK, you go on ahead and prep the plane. I've got to stop in and eyeball the duty rosters, then I'll meet you and we can get out of here."

"Aye, aye." At this, Byron stood up on his pedals and sped off toward the bulkhead.

After checking in at his office, John repaired to the piers. Sparky Stantz was there, waiting for him by the two-seater biplane he had serviced in preparation for the flight. As John approached, the young man snapped to attention and saluted smartly.

"Good morning, *sir*!"

This was odd. While Sparky was one of the top enlisted men in John's charge, and certainly the best radioman, he wasn't especially known for his crisp military bearing. Something was up. Rodgers returned the salute, and handed him his bag to be stowed.

Tilting his head to the side, he eyed Sparky warily. "Well Mr. Stantz, what's the status of our plane?"

"Right and ready, *sir*!" responded the chief radioman, grinning from ear-to-ear. This was stranger still. As Sparky secured the bag, John made a mental note to ask Wild Bill later what was up with his buddy. At that point, Connell pulled his head from the port engine nacelle.

"We're prepped and ready, sir. Who's got the duty?"

"I'll take it this morning, Byron. Your turn Monday."

"Aye aye."

Without further preamble, the defending champions of the annual InterService Regatta clambered aboard the seaplane, John flying, and Byron in the forward cockpit.

They taxied out across the harbor, then John spun the plane around and goosed the throttles. Their takeoff run pointed them back toward the Koolau Mountains. Heading directly into the brisk, twenty-mile-per-hour trade winds, they were quickly airborne. John maneuvered the plane in a lazy extended turn to the right over Halawa and Moanalua, and then a few miles later, a slow left turn as they banked past downtown Honolulu and headed up Nuuanu Valley.

As John and Byron flew over the jungle, they were treated to views of waterfalls on both sides. These ribbon-thin cascades fell hundreds of feet, only to disappear entirely into the lush undergrowth. The verdant valley was alive with every shade of green imaginable. A single, small winding road climbed beneath them, but was mostly obscured by the luxuriant canopy of magnificent monkeypod, koa, and sandalwood trees rising above the dense flora beneath.

As they proceeded, the mountains began to close in, the trade winds growing stronger as the valley narrowed. Having risen gently for eight miles from the outskirts of Honolulu town, the tropical gorge now led sharply up to a breathtaking precipice: a huge notch in the mountains known as the Nuuanu Pali. This dramatic pass was walled on both sides by vertical lava-rock columns rising twenty-five hundred feet above sea level.

Flying in these mountains never failed to thrill Rodgers. The macabre history of the place intrigued him as well. As they approached the pass, he shouted to his copilot, "Hey Byron, ever heard of the Night Marchers?"

"Something to do with a local battle, sir?"

"Yeah, in 1795 King Kamehameha united these islands. When he conquered Oahu, his warriors chased the defenders up to that cliff down there. They didn't have much choice—death or captivity. As I understand it, most of them jumped, or were pushed. Folks here believe their ghosts haunt the Pali—the Night Marchers."

Byron was duly impressed. "Helluva jump."

Generated by the abrupt updraft from the windward side of the island, plump, moisture-laden clouds stretched across the top of the Pali. Today, as usual, the pass itself was clear, creating a unique tunnel: jungle below, lava-rock walls to the sides, and wind-swept clouds above. As John and Byron approached, flying 2,000 feet above sea level, their hull barely skimmed above the treetops, while their upper wings just grazed the underbelly of the clouds.

The ever-present trade winds funneled into the pass, causing strong, tricky air currents that buffeted the plane as they negotiated the tunnel. Fortunately, today's conditions only hinted at the furious headwinds that often roared through the pass.

As they cleared the pass, the roller-coaster ride eased and the ground fell away. In a heartbeat, they went from flying at treetop level to almost fifteen hundred feet above the jungle below.

Byron gasped. "Jeez!"

Rodgers laughed. "Spectacular, huh? Never gets old. And look out there."

About five miles straight ahead, the azure blue of the Pacific stretched to the horizon. The axe-shaped Mokapu Peninsula and its dormant volcano bisected the center of the stunning seascape.

To their right, they could see the tall ironwood pines of Kailua. Visible too, were thousands of gently swaying coconut palms. Beyond the trees, Kailua Bay opened broadly to the Pacific. Several tiny, uninhabited islands dotted the spectacular bay—home to many species of wild waterfowl.

To their left lay the large lagoon known as Kaneohe Bay. Eight miles long and three miles wide, this body of water was more tranquil than Kailua Bay, and contained numerous shallow tabletop reefs. From the air, these colonies of microscopic creatures looked like patches of gold punctuating the brilliant aquamarine blue.

John sighed, savoring the idyllic view from his cockpit. "That's something, isn't it? Did you know the writer Robert Louis Stevenson once pronounced this the most beautiful bay in the world?"

Byron grinned, "I can sure see why, sir."

The site of the weekend regatta, Kaneohe Bay was also the home of the Kuwaahoe Military Reservation, a 344-acre fledgling military base. Only a few buildings defined the facility, most of them grass shacks and ramshackle huts. As they made their descent toward the bay, John and Byron could see that the lagoon was already dotted with a half-dozen sailboats of various sizes, cruising gracefully in different directions, with no apparent destination.

Byron laughed, "I bet they're really clipping along today—those guys must have their hands full."

John nodded, "Uh-huh. Looks easy from up here, doesn't it?"

Rodgers banked the biplane to the left and then to the right as he glided into a casual approach. They lined up on the virtually indistinguishable seaplane runway, heading almost directly into the early morning sun and straight into the prevailing east-northeast trade winds. The landing area was protected from wind-blown waves by a very shallow reef adjacent to the hilly promontory that jutted out into the Pacific, connecting the

Mokapu Peninsula to Oahu. Both the reef and the volcanic hillside were windward of normal trade winds, which tended to keep the natural landing area glassy smooth.

Touchdown was simple. Once the plane had slowed, John taxied her to the makeshift pier and ramp that served boats and the occasional visiting seaplane. Sailors quickly secured the plane while John and Byron gathered their gear. A small crowd, excited by the plane's arrival, had gathered to greet the aviators. As they came ashore, a dozen or so military types greeted them with salutes and some good-natured kidding about their "fluke" win the year before. These were the men they'd be competing against during the next two days. After brief introductions to teams they hadn't met before, the defending champs were hustled off to a utilitarian warehouse dormitory. The sailboat races would get underway as soon as official racing protocols had been observed.

The skippers' meeting was held an hour later, outlining the regulations, course, and placement of the race buoys. John had Byron read through the "Notice of Race," the official document that outlined the rules. Byron observed, "Nothing we don't know, here. It's the same as last year. Six races, three each day, with one 'throw-out.' All we need are five good ones." There were eight teams of two. Every crew was assigned a different boat for each race, making the competition as fair as possible. The boats, two-man wooden scows, were all similarly constructed with a single mast and two sails: an oversized main and a jib. The boats had a three-foot-deep dagger-board keel, a transom-hung rudder, and little else. They were light and fast.

John was impatient for the meeting to be adjourned so that they could get out on the water. Once it was over, Byron ran ahead to cull a good set of sails, while John went straight to the boats to inspect the one they'd been assigned for the first race. The regatta was off and running.

6:00 PM Hawaii Time

Raring to go for their long-awaited double date, Sparky Stantz and Wild Bill Bowlin leaped from the Waikiki trolley and raced each other to the pristine white, six-story Moana Hotel. This was *the* quality Hawaii hotel.

The turn-of-the-century building was an example of exquisite classical architecture. The thirty-five-foot tall Ionic columns of the *porte cochere* defined and protected the curved carriage entrance. The colorful fuchsia bougainvillea plantings against the white building, along with the gray-white trunks and emerald-green fronds of the royal palm trees, completed the stunning picture. Under perennially brilliant blue skies, with the golden sand of Waikiki beach and the turquoise surf of the Pacific as its backdrop, the Moana Hotel was as close to perfection as anything Sparky and Bill had ever seen.

The eager young men ran up the half-dozen steps to the Moana's generous porch and entered the elegant foyer. From there, they sailed full-steam through the lobby, heading toward the beach. Freshly shaved and showered, they'd imagined they would blend right in with the well-heeled civilian tourists surrounding them. But the two twenty-six-year-old seamen stood out in the crowd like twin beacons in the night.

True, they were wearing civilian dress shirts, like the majority of the other men at the hotel that evening. And it was not out of line for the fair-skinned Midwest boys not to have much of a tan; that was the case for most of the visitors sitting on the outside lanai of the well-known beachside restaurant. No, it was their extremities—the ultra-close-cropped hair and shiny black military oxfords—that gave them away. Sparky and Bill knew their cover was blown when the charming local hostess smiled and asked them, "Where can I seat you, sailors?"

It was beautiful anywhere beneath the famous sprawling banyan tree, but they requested a seat close to the small beachside stage. The hostess found them a table down front, just to the left of the performance area, angled toward the setting sun. There they were, on the lanai of the swankiest hotel in the Pacific, watching the brilliant tropical sun slip toward the horizon. They had just over twenty bucks between them, and if Sparky could be believed, they had dates with two of the most beautiful women in Hawaii. Pretty good for two boys from Indiana. Life just didn't get much better.

A four-piece band was performing on the small, slightly raised platform beneath the wide canopy of the banyan tree. At the moment, the band was playing a lilting Hawaiian melody, and singing in falsetto. Bill whispered to his buddy,

"Sparky, sounds like that guy's yodelin'!"

"Nah, it's prettier than any yodelin' I ever heard, but look how he's holdin' his guitar—it's sittin' flat across his lap! I've never seen a guitar with a crazy metal face like that. And what's he's playing it with? Looks like some kind of bar he's slidin' up and down the strings."

"That sound is somethin' else. Gotta write the folks back home about this."

At the table to their right, two slightly older, athletic-looking Hawaiian men sat with two equally striking women. All four seemed to be totally absorbed in the music. When the band finished the number, the lead singer announced that they would be taking a short break. As the musicians accepted their applause and exited, the two beautiful women excused themselves and rose to leave their table. Their escorts stood politely. As he adjusted his chair to allow the women to pass, Wild Bill happened to catch the eye of the taller of the two men. Bill nodded and offered a friendly "Hello," which was subtly, but warmly acknowledged.

A waitress wearing a fragrant plumeria flower lei approached the table, and the sailors ordered iced tea, as their options for legal liquid refreshment were sharply reduced by Prohibition. Carried away by the surroundings, and feeling rich beyond his means, Wild Bill offered to buy a round for the neighboring table. Surprised by the gesture, Sparky turned to look at the men, then asked Bill, "Do you know them?"

Bill shrugged, "Nah. I just felt like it. They seemed nice. Say, when do our girls come on?"

"I'm not sure, but Lei said their show was at sunset, so it can't be too long."

The two sailors leaned back, basking in the tropical ambiance, taking it all in. The assorted clouds along the horizon were beginning to reflect the colors of the setting sun, and the gentle evening trade winds made the eighty-four-degree weather feel as perfect as it could be. As they watched, a sleek schooner glided toward the nearby Ala

Wai boat harbor entrance and Sparky said, "Now that's my kind of sailing! I wonder how the Skip and Lieutenant Connell are doing in their regatta."

"I wouldn't worry 'bout them," grinned Bill.

The sky continued changing colors, turning to a golden orange, streaked with pinks and light blues by the time the waitress reappeared, carrying a tray with assorted glasses and bowls. She placed a carved koa bowl of macadamia nuts in the center of the round table, then set straw coasters and two iced teas in front of the sailors, deftly balancing the remaining drinks on her tray. Each of the tall glasses was topped with a slice of pineapple and a paper straw. Smiling conspiratorially, the waitress then turned to the neighboring table. Clearing the old glasses, she replaced them with new drinks, and informed the two Hawaiians of their benefactor. The man Bill had spoken to earlier lifted his glass and toasted the sailors with a hearty, "Mahalo, braddahs. Alo-ha!" His companion followed suit with a simple, "Mahalo."

Sparky and Bill raised their glasses and said, "Aloha."

This exchange was interrupted by a powerful jungle drumbeat from offstage. As the audience grew quiet, a powerfully built man wearing only a multihued *lavalava* ran barefoot onto the lanai. He carried a flaming torch and a large conch shell. He set the torch in a stage-side receptacle, then leaped up the two short steps onto the platform. Facing right, he lifted the spiraled shell to his mouth and blew into it, emitting a pure, deep-throated tone. Turning left, he blew another bass blast. Then, tucking the shell under his arm, he leaped from the platform and grabbed the torch. Holding it aloft, he ran through the startled audience to the periphery of the lanai, where he lit the black tiki pots atop a pair of crossed bamboo stalks. The man continued his performance until a dozen or more torches burned brightly beneath the banyan tree. By the time he finished, the band had reappeared and two slender, golden-brown *wahine* had joined them onstage. Sparky nudged Bill and whispered excitedly, "There they are—that's them! Lei's the one on the left. The other one is Lani." For once Bill was speechless.

The young women wore burnished, amber-brown coconut-shell tops and knee-length grass skirts slung low across their hips. Both dancers had thick, shiny black hair that hung loose almost to their waists. Gorgeous *haku* lei encircled their heads.

The bandleader introduced the next song, a ballad. He told the audience that the girls were going to act out the story in their dance. The rhythmic swaying of the dancers' hips, and the graceful, expressive gestures of their arms and hands enthralled the two boys from the Midwest.

A second melody followed, and the young women danced while the bandleader explained the meanings of their movements to the tourists. All in all, they danced six numbers. At last the bandleader called for the crowd to recognize the Akana sisters. Bill and Sparky shot to their feet, applauding wildly. The women gave a traditional hula bow, blew kisses to send their aloha to the audience, and left the stage.

Bill asked anxiously, "Should we go find them?"

Sparky reassured him. "No, Lei told me that we should wait at the table for them while they change." The sailors sat back down and only then began to sip their neglected iced teas, now lukewarm. The sky was almost completely dark, but the flickering tiki torches provided a subtle, romantic light.

Before long, Sparky spied the young women making their way across the lanai. "There they are!" They were wearing simple cotton dresses and had tied their long hair back in sleek ponytails. The *haku* lei were gone, but each girl sported a single white plumeria flower behind her right ear. Sparky and Bill watched as the sisters wove through the audience, toward their table. They were surprised when the girls stopped first at the adjacent table to greet the two Hawaiian couples with hugs all around.

Feeling more than a little jealous as he watched "his" girl embrace the men, Sparky caught Lei's eye. She smiled and pointed in his direction while saying something to the taller man. The Hawaiians then escorted the dancers to Sparky and Bill's table. The boys from Indiana jumped up as the group approached.

The warmth with which Lei greeted him quickly melted any doubts that Sparky may have been feeling. Lani, too, seemed to glow from within as Sparky introduced her to Bill. Lei then turned to the others and said, "Samuel, Duke. This is my friend Sparky, and his friend, Bill." Warm handshakes were exchanged with a chorus of "Aloha."

Samuel smiled. "We sort of met them already. They were kind enough to buy us a round of drinks."

Bill replied, "Our pleasure."

Lani eyed Bill with a thoughtful smile at this tidbit.

Studying Bill and Sparky, Samuel said, "Do you two know how to surf? Maybe we can *kokua*?"

Not understanding, the sailors exchanged a quick look. "Uh, no," they mumbled.

Duke laughed, a warm rumble. "Eh, no worries! *Kokua* means we help you, give you something back—a mahalo for the drinks." Turning to Lani and Lei, he continued, "Tomorrow's Sunday. Bring these two *malihini* down here after lunch. We'll see if we can't get 'em up on a wave."

Sparky grinned. "Wow, that would be great!" and then glanced at Lei to make sure his response had been appropriate. She flashed him an encouraging smile. It was all set.

Duke grinned.

"'Kay den, we'll see you on the beach tomorrow afternoon."

Samuel leaned in. "Ladies, I'm sorry, but we've got to go. We have a dinner reservation and we're late already. See you tomorrow. Aloha!"

Taking turns, Lei and Lani hugged the large man and his even larger companion. With parting "Alohas" for all, the two Hawaiian men collected their dates and waved goodbye.

Still standing somewhat awkwardly, Sparky and Bill pulled out chairs for the Akana sisters. When the foursome was seated together at the table, there was a moment of silence, a bit of shyness in the air. Clearing his throat, Bill broke the ice.

"So. Nice guys, huh?"

"Yeah. Yeah, they were nice," echoed Sparky.

Lani and Lei exchanged a look only sisters could understand, before bursting into laughter. Catching her breath, Lei asked, "Do you know who those guys are?"

Blank stares, and then Sparky shrugged, "No."

Toying with the boys, Lei said, "I'll give you a hint. They're both just back from Paris."

Still in the dark, Sparky said, "Paris? Hmmm . . . that's no help. What do they do?"

It was Lani's turn to play with them. "They were mining for ore."

"In Paris? That doesn't make sense."

After another round of giggles, Lei finally let them off the hook. "Sparky, that was Duke and Samuel Kahanamoku. They just won silver and bronze medals at the Paris Olympics."

Lani chimed in, "Duke may be getting older, but that was his fifth Olympic medal! Their finishes gave the U.S. first, second and third in the hundred-meter freestyle. That young kid, Johnny Weissmuller, finally broke Duke's old record."

Bill let out a low whistle. "And those guys are going teach us how to surf ?"

Sparky just shook his head. "They're never gonna believe this back home."

Kaneohe Bay facing north, as viewed from the Nuuanu Pali. The Mokapu Peninsula is out of the picture, to the right.

The Moana Hotel, with Diamond Head in the background.

The Moana Hotel's Grand Ballroom in 1924.

The Waikiki Beach side of the Moana Hotel.

The trumpeting of a conch shell has become a traditional part of torch lighting ceremonies.
Pictured here is performer wearing a colorfully printed *lavalava*.

A Dobro guitar being played. This was the progenitor of the Hawaiian steel guitar. This uniquely Hawaiian instrument was an acoustic guitar, designed and constructed in a way that made it reverberate with a distinctive twang when the steel strings were plucked and properly massaged with a metal slide.

Johnny Weissmuller and Duke Kahanamoku: The gold and silver champions in men's hundred-meter freestyle in the 1924 Olympics. This was the first medal earned by Weissmuller and the fifth over three Olympics for Kahanamoku. Although a poor-quality photograph, this rare moment captured between two cultural icons makes it worth including.

Duke Kahanamoku

Chapter 8

Sunday—August 10, 1924

1:12 PM Hawaii Time

John and Byron cruised back and forth across the bay in the last scow they would sail during the course of the weekend regatta. They were tuning the speedy little boat as they awaited the start of the sixth and final race.

They had performed exceedingly well in two of the three Saturday races. However, in the third race, they had been pushing hard in the brisk winds, and while jibing—turning with the wind directly behind them—the boat had snapped a shroud, toppling the mast and the entire rig. Neither of them had been hurt, but they'd had to take a DNF (Did Not Finish) for that race. The disaster had left them mired in the middle of the competition on Saturday, a status that galled the defending champions. They'd sailed well in their two races this morning. With the DNF as their "throw-out," they were now tied for first, but they could not afford any further missteps—not if they wanted to win. John and Byron had their hands full, and they knew it.

The wind was picking up as all the sailboats jockeyed for the best possible start positions.

"Can we rake the mast a bit more?" John knew the scow would go upwind better if the mast was angled back slightly from vertical.

"Aye skip. Run her up into the wind and let the sails flog."

John pushed on the tiller until the boat was aimed straight into the breeze. She slowed immediately with the wind on her nose, and the sails flapped like an unencumbered flag. It would be easier to adjust the tension on the forestay and shrouds—the triangulated lines that held the mast in place—without the wind pushing against the sails.

Byron eased the turnbuckle at the base of the forestay and then took in the slack, first on the port and then on the starboard shrouds.

"How's that, skipper?"

"Looks good to me." Easing the tiller to turn the boat sideways to the wind, John began pulling in the mainsheet—the aft line that ran through a block and tackle on the boom to control the mainsail. As the mainsail began to fill, Byron retrieved the flopping jib sheet and pulled it in until both the fore and aft sails were set at the same angle. As the little boat accelerated, John pulled the mainsheet further in. Byron followed suit on the jib. As they hardened up on the sails, the power of the wind forced the boat to heel over and pick up even more speed. Responding to the boat's tilt, the sailors shifted their weight to the windward side, trying to flatten her a bit. John adjusted the tiller so that the scow was soon scooting along, heading upwind.

"Can you give me more cunningham?" asked John. Moving inboard to the base of the mast, Byron pulled on a small block and tackle, which tightened the leading edge of the mainsail, making it more aerodynamic. Additional minor adjustments were made, and the twin sails were soon hard and flat, shaped like a Roman warrior's breastplate. Pulled in tight as they were, the sails were positioned almost directly fore and aft, and the boat clawed its way even further into the wind.

On top of the pure excitement of the sport, the physics of sailing appealed to John. He was fascinated by its close relation to flying. As they sat hiked out over the starboard side, John studied the two sails. The wind behind the sails curved inward, hugging the backside of the canvas. Because that air had to travel further, it sped up and filled in what would otherwise be a vacuum as the boat moved forward. The increased speed of this laminar flow caused a lifting effect, not unlike the way the wind worked with the curved-wing shape that allowed an airplane to fly. When countermanded and directed by the keel and rudder, the boat put this force to good use. The ever-tapering gap, sandwiched between the two sails, forced the wind to speed up even further as it funneled between the canvas, rocketing the boat forward ever faster.

John felt the water pressure tugging on the tiller, trying to force the boat to turn upwind.

Byron called, "The slot looks better. How's she feel?"

"Slight weather helm—perfect." It had to be.

"Wind looks steady. Maybe ten to twelve knots. More wind than this morning, but almost the same as yesterday afternoon."

"As in the *third* race yesterday afternoon?"

John grinned. "Sure hope not!"

As they approached the committee boat, John yelled, "Sail number twenty-eight: Rodgers!" The fishing craft that served as the regatta's official start and finish boat acknowledged the hail. The committee boat was securely moored at the starboard end of the imaginary start/finish line, while a small, white-flagged buoy marked the opposite end. John understood that while the race committee always tried to align the start line as perpendicular to the wind and the first upwind or windward mark as possible, minor wind shifts could skew the line so that one end or the other was more advantageous. They needed to determine which end was favored, as a fast start would be critical if they wanted to nail this race. John and Byron went to work.

John looked at his chronograph. "Let's run the line." Knowing how long it took to sail between the committee boat and the opposite buoy would help him decide the best position for their start.

At the end of the dash, Byron yelled, "One minute, ten seconds."

"OK. Heading up." John turned the scow straight into the wind until the sails flapped out of control. This maneuver all but stopped the boat. As the sails fluttered and banged "in irons," John mentally triangulated the course to the first buoy and made his choice. "Looks like the committee boat end." Byron nodded in assent.

Seconds later, a horn sounded and the officials raised a yellow pennant: ten minutes to the start. At the same time, the course for the race was posted on a chalkboard at the stern of the fishing boat. It read:

A, B, C

2X

Byron called, "A, B, C, twice around." The boats would race counterclockwise, twice around a triangular course defined by the orange race buoys A, B, and C. Buoy A was located almost directly into the wind from the committee boat, while C was almost straight downwind from them. B was the wing mark, well out to the left side of the course, defining the third corner of the triangle.

The waltz of the swans began as the skippers alternately sped and spun their boats, jockeying for the best position behind the line. The pace increased with a second horn blast and the raising of a blue flag: five minutes to go.

The tension ratcheted up, and the activity onboard the tiny crafts intensified with the countdown. Attention to detail was paramount. The scows were alternately tacking and jibing, trying to get into position without painting themselves into a corner.

The blue flag dipped. One minute. The pace aboard the little ships grew frenetic. Besides continually trimming the sails for abrupt course changes, Byron was now counting down to the start. With thirty seconds to go, the other skippers began to reveal their start strategies. Two of the boats had opted for the port end of the start line, possibly to avoid the confusion that was developing at the starboard end. The remaining six boats were racing on slightly convergent upwind courses, angled behind the start line, all aiming for the exact same spot next to the committee boat—the extreme starboard end of the line. John noticed that one boat was leading out well in front of the group charging the line.

"Thirty-four's early. He'll have to slow or turn down to keep from jumping the start." If a boat crossed too soon, it would either be disqualified, or have to sail around and start again. It was a sure way to kill any chance for a win.

All those competing knew the rules of racing forbid a boat from barging—coming in on too broad an angle and forcing its way in at the start line. In addition to being illegal, this particular foul was considered extremely bad form, and sailors were quick to lodge an official protest if they felt they had been barged. However, it was both legal and advantageous for a boat to find a hole in between the approaching boats and turn upwind on a "proper angle" before a collision occurred.

John and Byron were alone on a port tack. They were running at near full speed, parallel to the start line, but several boat lengths below it, heading toward the committee boat end. And they were on a collision course with boat number thirty-four.

"Twenty seconds."

Most all of the other boats were sheeting their sails in tight as they screamed down toward the start line several lengths behind number thirty-four. Just when a collision seemed imminent with boat thirty-four, John turned quickly to his right behind them and then spun the boat hard to the left, tacking over onto starboard, directly in front of three boats charging down at the committee boat end of the line—and now their stern.

Shifting their weight quickly to the opposite side of the boat and simultaneously sheeting home the sails on the new tack, John and Byron accelerated. Byron was still counting down. "Ten . . . nine . . . eight . . ."

Seven seconds before the start, John and Byron had the sails fully sheeted and taut as a snare drum. Their scow was sailing at top speed on a perfect forty-five-degree angle to the line. The boat was heeled hard over, with both sailors hiking out over the starboard rail. One last boat was diving in from their starboard, running a convergent course with no room to spare, while the other three were tucked in behind John and Byron, sailing the same angle but trailing them to the line, closely bunched.

This last boat seemed to be trying to force their way in before John could shut the door. John was certain they wouldn't be able to make it without fouling.

"No room! No barging! No room!" John hailed the encroaching vessel at the top of his lungs. "Four . . . three . . ." counted Byron. As the two identical scows converged, the offending skipper finally saw he was in trouble. If he held his course, he would T-bone John. And if he tried turning left and downwind behind John, he wouldn't be able to miss the trailing threesome and would most likely collide with one of them—not great options.

The gun sounded and the red start flag was raised. The barging boat had no choice but to make a drastic turn to the starboard, straight up into the wind. Luckily, he just missed hitting either John or the committee boat, but not by much. However the radical shift was so sharp that they overshot their turn. In no time at all, they were wallowing dead in the water, facing into the wind on the wrong side of the committee boat. As they tried desperately to salvage their situation, the rest of the fleet screamed past the start line and were soon several hundred feet ahead of them. John and Byron were out in front.

Byron crowed, "Jeez, that was close—what a start!"

They skimmed across the water at a bracing clip. The small fleet all aimed upwind at a forty-five-degree angle toward their goal. John held the lead position and blanketed the wind from the boats beneath and behind. Blanketing effectively slowed and "dirtied" the flow of air for the trailing scows, allowing John and Byron to inch further ahead. As the trailing competition fell back, one by one they swung their boats starboard, turning through the eye of the wind and onto a port tack to try and escape John's covering position and get to "clean air."

To counter this strategy, once the closest competitor to them had tacked, John called to Byron, "Ready about . . . helm's alee!" And then he slammed his sailboat over to the opposite tack as well. This maneuver kept John and Byron between the wind and the nearest competitor, constantly blanketing his wind. As the boats weaved their way up the course, the move was repeated several times. With each tack, John and Byron were able to put a little more distance between themselves and the trailing boat. The remaining fleet continued to separate, trying to evade John's covering position.

By now, it was tough to tell who was ahead, because several of the boats that had trailed earlier had sailed well over to the opposite side of the bay and had gotten a favorable wind shift. There was a considerable distance between them, and they were sailing very different angles in stronger wind. Byron pointed towards the group.

"Skipper, they've caught a break. The wind's swung around and given them a lift." John knew it had been a gamble to get this far to the left side of the course, but they couldn't defend against all of the boats. Just then the wind shifted again, forcing them to sail even further left. Not what they wanted. John made his choice.

"Let's get out of here. Ready about. Helm's alee." And they tacked onto port. This put them directly on a converging course with the other boats.

"Uh, sir?"

"Byron, they're all on a starboard tack, but the port tack is favored now, right?"

"Aye, sir . . . ?"

"I think we can beat the odds here, even though they have right-of-way. If we get lifted enough, we'll be sitting pretty. If I'm wrong . . ." He didn't need to finish. Seeing what his commander was up to, Byron grinned. "Let's go for it, skip. I love a good game of chicken!"

Heading up the course, John and Byron continued on their port tack while the majority of the fleet bunched tightly on starboard. Since everyone was sailing at forty-five-degree angles to the wind, the convergent courses would intersect at ninety degrees, a recipe for disaster. John knew that whoever got to the point of intersection and crossed ahead would have a distinct advantage to win the race. He also knew that if he didn't cross ahead of the fleet, he would have to bear off and duck beneath all of them as the competitors' hulls were all overlapped; there was no safe way to weave between them. Ducking behind them all would probably put them in last place—not an option.

As they raced up the course, Byron tried to sight and calculate the angles, while John focused on sailing the boat as fast as he could. The entire regatta could shift on this single confrontation.

The distance was closing quickly when John felt the wind velocity increase, which leaned the scow over further. Beneath the hull, their keel bit into the water, slightly increasing their angle of attack, and allowing John to steer slightly higher upwind and closer to the mark. Holding on for dear life, Byron shook his head. "It's gonna be close . . . !"

As they converged, the leading boat in the starboard-tack fleet began yelling to John for right of way: "Starboard!" Then, louder still, "Starboard!" This was the appropriate hail, although it was sometimes used to try to intimidate the port-tack boat.

In this confrontation, John had three choices: tack, duck, or cross. Tacking before he reached the oncoming boats would safely put him on a starboard tack but in an untenable position, running parallel to and beneath the gaggle of approaching boats. Ducking would send them behind the sterns of the entire group and probably cost them the race. Crossing was the most dangerous call. Because they were on port tack, if they forced any one of the converging boats to deviate from their proper course to avoid a collision, they would foul out of the race. This was no place for the timid. Undaunted, John responded with, "Hold your course!"

Through clenched teeth, Byron murmured again. "It's gonna be *close*."

John could feel the keel digging in, making it possible for him to sail slightly higher into the wind. He was able to keep the speed up, and with less than two boat lengths to go, he breathed, "Got 'em!" Seconds later, they sliced past the onrushing fleet with less than five feet to spare. Byron's face split in an enormous grin, and they both whooped and hollered. The race was certainly not over, but it had been a critical strategic triumph.

Rounding the first weather buoy fifteen seconds ahead of the nearest opponent, John and Byron knew they had just won two of the three elements of a sailboat competition: the start, and the race to the first upwind mark. They had established a commanding lead. Now they had to hold onto it. That was the third element—the rest of the race.

The next leg was a broad reach out to B buoy, the wing mark. On a broad reach, the apparent wind was hitting the sails at approximately ninety degrees. This was the fastest point of sail for these boats, and John and Byron had their charge literally humming. The spray shot out to the sides from the flattened bottom with fire-hose intensity. By the time they approached the second buoy, the two aviators had their boat skipping like a stone.

Turning the boat downwind and jibing the sails over to the other side at the wing mark required teamwork and precise timing to keep the boat from tipping over.

"Ready to jibe. . .Jibe ho!" Their innate skill and hours of practice made it look easy as the sail abruptly slammed across to the opposite side.

The competition had caught up some on the downwind run to C, the leeward buoy, because while sailing downwind they could blanket some of John and Byron's wind. John had nevertheless stayed between the second-place scow and the next mark, jibing and covering from ahead. Once they rounded C, they turned and headed back toward A, the original windward mark. As they worked upwind, tacking back and forth on forty-five-degree angles, John stretched out his lead once again, this time rounding the buoy just over a minute ahead of the second-place boat.

"Trim for speed," John commanded as he eased the tension on the mainsheet. Byron immediately eased the jib sail to counteract the wind now coming from abeam, and the boat accelerated. Retracing their course, they sped along on the broad reach, hooting with exhilaration. Carving their turn smoothly at B, they owned the run all the way to C. After passing that mark, they turned and trimmed the sails to windward for the final upwind leg to the finish line. By this point, they were unchallenged, crossing well ahead of the second-place boat.

Slowing their boat, the triumphant aviators slid behind the committee boat, hailing the traditional, "Thank you, Race Committee!" They received waves and "You're welcome!"'s in exchange. "All *right*!" grinned the sun- and wind-burned Rodgers.

"Yeah! That was some sailing, skipper. Good job!"

"Hey, thanks to you. Helluva great jibe at the last wing mark." And the two sailors continued to replay the highlights of their thrilling victory as they sailed gracefully back to the pier.

John and Byron had become the first-ever repeat winners of the regatta, easily outdistancing the second-place crew—a Marine Corps team that had put up a good fight. The triumphant defenders had already planned to wait and fly back to Pearl Harbor early the next morning, so that they could participate in the post-regatta luau and awards ceremony that evening. Now they had a reason to party.

Once they had dropped and bagged the sails, Byron ran to get some drinks. When he returned, he had a beautiful redhead in tow. As John saw them approach, he just smiled and shook his head. The young lieutenant never failed to amaze him. Give Byron five minutes and he'd come up with a gorgeous woman—sometimes two. At least he had a date for the evening's festivities.

That night, they had a great time. Enjoying the revelry, the victors both consumed a fair amount of bootlegged bathtub gin. It was a terrific end to an exhilarating couple of days.

Shortly after 9 PM, John wandered away from the boisterous group, back to their temporary quarters. A community phone was on the wall in the hallway—one of the few phones in all of windward Oahu, and the only link from the sprawling facility to the outside world. Picking up the heavy Bakelite receiver, John adjusted the mouthpiece to his height. He cranked the handle, which jangled bells and elicited a perfunctory response from the operator. John gave her the five-digit phone number for his house and asked her to place the call. The last ferry to Ford Island on Sunday nights was at 8:45. Ethel was sure to be home. The connection was much faster than he'd expected. *Modern technology!*

To his surprise, there was no answer. After ten rings, he clicked the receiver to bring the operator back on the line. John checked to see if she'd dialed the right number, and asked her to try once more. Again, the connection went through, and once again, there was no answer. Puzzled, he hung up. *Oh well.* He shrugged and went back to look for Byron. They had a victory to celebrate.

Kaneohe Bay

By 1924, telephones were in use throughout the Honolulu area, but many outlying areas had yet to be connected by the relatively new devices. On Oahu, phone service was limited to operator-assisted calls.

Chapter 9

Monday—August 11, 1924

6:00 AM Hawaii Time

As the sun rose, John made his way down to the makeshift pier, where Byron was already preparing their seaplane for the half-hour flight back to Ford Island. To vary the scenery, the route they had selected would follow the nearly deserted beaches of the windward shoreline.

"Morning, Byron. How goes the preflight check?"

"Looking good, sir. Engine, fuel levels, wing surfaces, static cables, active controls—all at the ready."

"How about the bilges—any water?"

"No sir, she's shipshape and ready to go."

"Let's head out, then—you've got the duty today."

Donning helmets and goggles, they clambered aboard. John cranked the engines, which started right up, and they taxied out into the beauty of Kaneohe Bay at dawn.

In the sheltered lagoon, takeoff was simple. As they gained altitude, the wind whistled past their ears, while the roar of the engines and heavy chop of the propellers whipped the air. Leveling off at three hundred feet, they headed east over the northern end of the Mokapu Peninsula. Turning right, they flew between the mountainous end of the peninsula and the pair of large rock islands just off the coast. Startled by the plane, several dozen split-tailed Frigates lifted off from their rock-island rookery and soared above the aviators. Byron shouted, "Sir, we were lucky! One of those critters hits us, it could do serious damage—they must have a wingspan of over six feet! They remind me of—what-do-you-call-em's? The prehistoric flying dinosaurs?"

John hollered back, "Pterodactyls, yeah, it's the skinny wings. Who knows what we'll see next? If it were four, five months from now, I'd tell you to keep your eyes peeled for whales. This is their favorite winter watering hole."

Once through the narrow opening, Byron swung slightly back to the right. In no time at all, they were flying over the brief outcroppings of lava-rock cliffs that bordered Kailua Beach, and soon after that, the wide, shallow reef that protected Kailua Bay. Long, lazy rollers broke on the uninterrupted three-mile stretch of sand, the spume glistening pink and gold in the early morning sun.

About a half-mile out to sea, the light aqua hue of the shallow water suddenly turned a sparkling indigo where the ocean floor dropped off. John called over his shoulder to Byron, "How 'bout those colors? You know, if you'd told me when I was a kid that water could be this many different shades of blue, I'd never have believed you."

"Where'd you grow up, again, sir?"

"In Maryland—along the banks of the Chesapeake Bay. That water went from drab green, to slate gray, to blue-black. Nothing like what we're looking at this morning."

Beyond Kailua was a thin strip of sand, two miles long, called Lani-kai; and then the much longer, graceful curving crescent of Waimanalo Beach. This view was the reason they'd picked the Windward route home. Watching as the early morning sun spilled color across the sand below, John shook his head and called back to his pilot, "That's got to be the most beautiful damn stretch of shoreline in the world."

"Aye, sir."

Ten miles later, they rounded Makapuu, the southeasternmost tip of Oahu, and headed west toward Koko Head Crater. Passing Makapuu Point, the Pacific darkened to an even deeper shade of blue as the ocean shelf dropped off sharply into the deepwater channel between Oahu and

Molokai. The wind increased markedly, and the ocean surface sparkled like a brilliant gemstone in the tropical morning sun, whitecaps riffling the surface all the way to the horizon.

"Looks a little rough today, sir. Glad we're not down there in a scow."

"You got that right, and not just because of the chop. That undersea chasm you see, the Kaiwi Channel? Currents down there can really rip along. It's called the Molokai Express for a reason—get caught in that sailing between Oahu and Molokai, and it'll ship you straight out into open sea. Next stop, Japan."

"Jeez."

It was smooth going in the clear, early morning air. They made good time, flying past Kahala, Diamond Head, Waikiki Beach, Honolulu; soon, Pearl Harbor came into view. On the east side of the harbor, they could see dozens of warships docked in the deepest loch, some three abreast. John saw two huge battleships, several heavy cruisers, and innumerable destroyers, all suckling from assorted fuel barges. There were even some foreign naval vessels in their distinctly lighter shades of gray, queued for their turn at the trough.

Byron laughed. "Fleet's in, no question about it."

"They're just back from maneuvers. Arrived Saturday. I bet it was crazy in town these past two nights."

"Glad we ducked that bullet, sir. Better to have been where we were."

"Roger."

John was thinking of more than just missing the hordes of drunken sailors in port. His time in Kaneohe had been immensely restorative. The regatta had cleared his head, and the glorious morning flight home had lifted his spirits. With the new day came renewed hope for a fresh start. He was ready to do whatever it took to fix things up with Ethel.

Byron banked the seaplane and turned into the wind to line up their approach. Soon they were staring down the buoyed-off landing zone. As Byron cut power, the engine noise subsided, and they could hear the wind whistling over the wings and through the guy wires. As they neared the surface, Byron expertly pulled back on the yoke to slow the descent and level the craft. Still, when the seaplane hit the harbor surface, she bounced back into the air like a flat stone skipping over water. She then settled, and the force of the water dragged her quickly to a near-stop. Her nose dropped and the wake caught up with her, casually lifting first her stern and then her bow as it rushed by. Byron delicately eased the throttles forward to maintain control and they turned toward the familiar piers.

Once they had docked, John left Byron to secure the plane, and headed off to stow his gear. His building appeared to be deserted. He checked his chronometer—not quite 0700; the staff would not yet have reported for duty. Entering his office, he thought about calling Ethel. He'd been worried when she hadn't answered the night before. He reached for his phone, and then thought better of it. Ethel was a night owl. Even if she had managed to catch the last ferry home, she would probably have read late into the night before dropping off to sleep. Waking her up with an early morning phone call would most definitely not be the best way to start repairs on their marriage.

Dropping his bag on his chair, John checked the messages on his desk. Nothing. He was relieved, at least, not to find a message from the base hospital. Leaving his office, he called across the tarmac to Byron, who was coming up from the dock on his bicycle.

"Spare those wheels for an hour?"

"She's all yours, sir," Byron shouted back, and rode the bike over to his commanding officer.

John mounted up. Pedaling hard, he quickly traversed the mile to his manicured front lawn. As he braked to a stop, he noticed the front door inside the screened porch was closed. This was unusual. They always left that door open when they were at home. In fact, most times it stayed open even when they weren't. Life on this island base was safe.

Ignoring the kickstand, John dropped the bike on the lawn. The Golden-Plover-in-residence skittered nervously away from the front of the house as Rodgers double-timed it the length of the walk and bounded up the steps to the porch. At the front door, he tried the handle and was surprised to find it locked. He bent down to the milk box, tilted it, and retrieved the hidden key. Sliding it roughly into the lock, he opened the door and entered.

On alert, now, he moved into the main hall, where the sight awaiting him stopped him in his tracks. *My god, we've been robbed!*

The living room was bare. The navy-issue furniture and curtains remained, but all their personal items were gone. In the dining room, the table and chairs that had come with the house were still there, but the hutch that he had built was gone, along with the good china and silver that had been displayed inside it. All the pictures and wall hangings had been removed. Frantic at what might have happened to his wife, he called out,

"Ethel . . . ? Ethel, you here? You OK?" Nothing.

John's head was spinning as he stumbled down the hall toward their bedroom.

"ETHEL! *ANSWER ME!*" Silence.

Rounding the corner into the once-familiar surroundings, he saw that their bed had been stripped. The top of Ethel's bureau, ordinarily littered with her personal effects, was empty. He threw open her closet to find only a couple of empty hangers dangling forlornly. *What the hell . . . ?*

Bewildered, he staggered back down the hall into the living room. Then he saw it. A small white envelope perched on the otherwise naked mantle. "John" had been written in Ethel's elegant, country-club copperplate.

John opened the letter. He couldn't read a word of it. *Shit.* He had left the bag with his glasses back in his office. John squinted hard at the message, but still couldn't make any of it out. Cursing out loud, John stuffed the letter into his pocket. He marched out of the house, across the porch, and down the steps. The screen door slammed behind him. Picking up the red bike where he had let it fall, he jumped on and pedaled furiously back to his office.

After returning the salute of the lone sailor standing early guard, John reentered his office, locked the door, and rustled through his bag. Extracting the forbidden glasses from a shirt pocket, he sat down in his desk chair and pulled out Ethel's note. Smoothing the paper, John was dismayed to note that even with glasses he still had to struggle to make out the words. It wasn't just the poor light, either. His eyes were definitely getting worse.

The letter offered a brief, one-paragraph explanation: Ethel had decided to leave. It was over between them. She had arranged for movers to "take what was hers" and had enclosed their invoice for John to handle. She had sailed Sunday evening on the *Lurline,* bound for Los Angeles. Her attorney would be contacting John shortly. She had signed off with a simple "E."

Stunned, John forced himself to read the letter again and again. The whole scene felt surreal. The word "divorce" had not been specifically mentioned, but Ethel's reference to an attorney made it obvious.

John was forced to confront the stark truth: his marriage was dead, and along with it, quite possibly his navy career.

The SS *Lurline:* This ship, capable of carrying fifty-one passengers, entered service between California and Hawaii in 1908. At the time, it was the epitome of luxury and speed.

Ford Island circa 1924.

Chapter 10

Tuesday—August 12, 1924

8:55 AM Hawaii Time

Fort Street was a busy thoroughfare at almost any time of day, but just before nine on a weekday morning, traffic was at its peak. A Honolulu trolley car clanged twice to announce its approach. Stepping from the curb, a slight, middle-aged Japanese man prepared to seize his opportunity to cross the congested intersection. As the trolley braked to let off passengers, he stepped cautiously from the curb, acknowledged a passerby with a polite nod, and hurried across the street. Well dressed in a dark business suit and top-quality wire-frame bifocals, the gentleman stopped in front of a storefront office not far from the corner. A modest sign painted on the door's glass window in gold leaf identified the business. It simply said "Optometrist," and in smaller letters below, "Masahiro Mikami."

Taking a key from a small Japanese silk pouch, Masahiro Mikami unlocked his place of business. He turned the brass doorknob, and entered to the happy tinkle of the small bell hanging on a coiled spring above the wood-framed door. He reversed the cardboard sign that hung in the door window from *Closed* to *Open*. After turning on the light, he pulled the chain that turned on the four-bladed overhead fan and opened the old-style, double-hung office windows. Immediately a cool breeze drifted in, noticeably freshening the interior space.

It was a small, neat two-room affair fronting Fort Street. Dainty hand-sewn white curtains dressed both the windows and the door, and billowed gently in the trade winds. Evidence of his late wife's industry, they provided a modicum of privacy for the front room.

Adjusting his glasses, Masahiro walked down the corridor that led to his sanctuary—the back room that doubled as examination room and office. It was a modest space, functional and clean. His daughter saw to that. In the back wall, a well-worn panel door opened to a small courtyard, a space shared by several neighboring businesses. Only a small hook-and-eye lock secured this entrance. A tiny bathroom was off to the side. Masahiro flipped the hook and carefully wedged the screen door open. When satisfied that he was taking full advantage of the trade winds, he returned to his favorite room.

A large black-and-white eye chart, somewhat yellowed with age, dominated one wall of the office. A white glass-fronted cabinet containing instruments of optometry stood next to the chart. Across the room, a well-worn brown leather cushioned chair awaited patients, while Masahiro's wheeled stool rested in the middle of the room. A tidy roll-top desk and straight-backed wooden chair were positioned against one wall.

The front doorbell tinkled merrily, and a beautiful young Japanese woman soon appeared in the passage between the offices. This wisp of a girl filled the hall with a warm, gentle presence. She spoke in lilting but carefully enunciated English.

"Good morning, Father. I brought you the newspaper and some manapua," she said, laying the pastry box and paper on his desk.

Akiko Mikami was the center of her father's life. Exquisitely petite, Masahiro's only child had long, silky jet-black hair and soft brown almond-shaped eyes. She possessed a radiant smile, but it appeared all too infrequently. This morning, in her delicate pure white blouse and knee-length pale green cotton skirt, she was the very picture of a young Japanese woman in the Honolulu of 1924.

Masahiro's wife, Hiroko, had died two years before. While "Masa"—Hiroko's affectionate nickname for her husband—was a loving father, his deeply ingrained samurai upbringing kept him from demonstrating emotion of any kind, let alone physical affection. He offered brief, formal thanks.

"*Domo*, Akiko." His demeanor would have given no clue, but Masahiro Mikami was worried about his only child.

At her mother's insistence, Akiko had attended college at the University of Hawaii, graduating with honors in education. In the 1920s, this was an unusual accomplishment for a woman, let alone one of Japanese ancestry. Masahiro had not approved. Although he hadn't actually forbidden Akiko's pursuing the degree, he hadn't expressly consented, either. He had worried that university life would cost Akiko a measure of innocence, and irrevocably distance her from Japanese culture and values.

Hiroko had no such reservations. She was grateful to the country that enabled her daughter to achieve a worldly success unthinkable for a young girl back in Japan.

"We are *Americans* now," Hiroko had gently insisted whenever Masa had voiced his concerns.

In the end, Masa had been proud of his daughter, now twenty-six, but the Mikami family would not be not allowed to celebrate Akiko's accomplishments for long. Five months before Akiko's graduation, Hiroko had become gravely ill. Shortly after they diagnosed the cancer, the doctors pronounced her condition terminal. Masahiro and Akiko were heartsick, but Hiroko refused to give in to the disease. She fought tenaciously, and even managed to attend Akiko's graduation ceremony, although it was the last time she would leave the house.

As Hiroko's health declined, Akiko was never far from her side, putting her own life on hold to serve as Hiroko's full-time nurse. Devastated by the protracted suffering of his beloved wife, Masahiro had retreated into his work, leaving the burden of caregiving squarely on his daughter's shoulders. It was a role she had been more than willing to accept. The cancer ravaged Hiroko's body for more than two years, until at last, mercifully, she passed. Only Akiko had been with her at the end.

Months after Hiroko's death, Masa had finally emerged from his own mourning enough to see the wreck his daughter had become. He was forced to admit that as physically painful as the long battle had been for Hiroko, it had devastated Akiko emotionally. In addition to the understandable grief over the loss of her mother, she seemed to be struggling with demons he could not understand.

He proposed a traditional marriage match as a way to lift Akiko out of her depression, but something had gone awry during the courtship, and the relationship had ended awkwardly, only making matters worse. Akiko had never divulged the details, and Masa had been reluctant to probe. Finally, he had simply resigned himself to a life of bearing witness to his daughter's grief.

But Akiko had proved stronger than Masa imagined, and as time passed little by little her darkness seemed to be lifting. The beautiful smile that had disappeared for so long was beginning to return.

In his office, Masahiro heard the cheery entry bell ring once more, followed by a brief murmured exchange in the front room. Akiko appeared in the doorway, accompanied by a tall man casually dressed in shirt and slacks. Bowing formally, she announced, "Father, this is Mr. John Rodgers. He would like you to check his eyesight." She bowed slightly once again, and then withdrew as Masahiro invited Rodgers into the sanctuary.

Twenty minutes later, Masahiro escorted John as far as the passageway between the two rooms. Akiko was waiting to show the handsome patient out. Addressing his daughter in Japanese, Masahiro said, "We'll have to order Mr. Rodgers special lenses from the mainland." Turning toward John, he spoke in heavily-accented English, "They should be here in one month. Thank you, Mr. Rodgers. Akiko will take care of the transaction. Aloha." Masahiro then bowed respectfully, and retreated to the back room.

Akiko said, "Mister Rodgers, how may we contact you when the glasses are ready?"

John hesitated. "It's kind of difficult to reach me. I may be moving."

"Ah, I see. Well, if you would prefer, I am sure they will be here by the end of September. Why do you not return on October first? They will certainly be ready by then."

"That'll be fine. Do I pay you now?"

"If you like." And with that, they settled up.

John bid Akiko goodbye, then paused at the doorway. As she watched, he scanned the sidewalk traffic casually before opening the door and exiting the little shop. Akiko was intrigued. What could he have been looking for—or who? Akiko peeked out from behind her mother's curtains. She whispered, "Aloha, *Mr. John Rodgers*"—and smiled.

Across the street from the optometrist's office, a uniformed figure drew back into the shadows as Rodgers walked away. Stunned, Lieutenant Byron Connell shook his head in disbelief.

Fort Street, downtown Honolulu

Chapter 11

Wednesday—August 13, 1924

10:50 AM Hawaii Time

The windows were wide open to the trade winds in the second-story office at the Schofield Barracks headquarters building in central Oahu. A tall, angular officer paced incessantly as he dictated to his aide. Despite the tropical heat, the officer seemed cool and in control. His uniform was custom tailored, as would be expected of the son of a wealthy U.S. Senator. He wore the single gold star of a brigadier general on his collar and a great number of multicolored ribbons on his breast, including the Distinguished Service Cross and the Distinguished Service Medal. General Billy Mitchell was a war hero. He had commanded the American air wing in France during the First World War, to great success and notoriety. His experiences there had shown him the capabilities of the airplane as a military tool, which had led him to become a staunch proponent of air power.

However, General Mitchell had recently been banished to this Pacific outpost because army brass was tired of his antics. This reassignment had been the result of Mitchell's willful disobedience of direct orders, which he had ignored while attempting to sink the *Ostfriesland*, the old German battleship, in an incident that had become legendary. Mitchell had done it to prove his point about the potential of air power in front of a large assemblage of congressmen, high-ranking army and navy officials, and most significantly, the press.

His orders were to drop only five-hundred or one-thousand-pound ordnance; instead, he used two-thousand-pound bombs and was barely able to get them into the air. He had also been ordered to release the bombs from 5,000 feet and instead had obstinately had them dropped from under 1,000 feet to assure accuracy. Worst of all, he further alienated himself from the brass by taking his case to the press after the demonstration, an anathema in any military organization. This penchant for speaking his mind in public, especially when he differed with his superiors, had helped seal his fate. Probably the only thing that saved him from further punishment was his record as a war hero and brilliant tactician.

General Mitchell had embraced the Army Air Corps and had become its most passionate supporter. Believing in the future of airpower, he had fought for a separate branch of the service that would unite all military air forces. His idea had merit and was not without precedent. England had already developed an air ministry that oversaw all military aircraft, the Royal Air Force.

However the U.S. military elite were not so sure that following England's lead on this issue was the best course of action. The army and navy already had air divisions, wings they were developing to meet their own specific needs. They were troubled by the prospect of an outside agency intent on taking control of their aircraft. In addition, many military leaders didn't share Mitchell's opinion of the future importance of the airplane. Much of the conventional wisdom was that planes were good for surveillance, and could possibly be used for support of ground troops, but beyond that, they were of little consequence. According to popular opinion, wars were won on the ground or at sea, not in the air.

General Billy Mitchell entertained much more grandiose ideas for airplanes. He envisioned bombers and attack fighters—planes that could sink ships and cripple tanks. This idea put the outspoken Mitchell on a collision course with many of his superiors. The powers that be had reassigned him to the Pacific to get him out of their hair and away from a press corps that loved his obstreperous opinions.

Incapable of retreat, General Mitchell spent his detention expanding his crusade. While stationed on Oahu, Mitchell observed the growing tension between Japan and the United States. Disputes about the Washington Naval Treaty and Japanese-American trade sanctions and tariffs had produced a precarious stalemate and fostered distrust.

Mitchell traveled to the Philippines, where he met with General Douglas MacArthur and observed the strengths and weaknesses of that island territory. Mitchell then sailed to Japan. The Japanese were skeptical of his visit and most unwilling to divulge the clandestine armament that was taking place—with good reason. On his own, Mitchell became an unauthorized spy. He pretended to photograph the industrious population, while he was actually collecting data on their growing military might. What he saw was a country designing and building airplanes at a prodigious rate. It seemed that Japan was every bit as convinced as he was that the airplane could be a decisive factor in war, and that bombers would be critical.

General Mitchell continued to pace the floor in his small Hawaii office. The heavy carpet muffled the sound of his boots as he dictated the synopsis of his 324-page report. He was on a roll, and the words spilled out effortlessly.

> "Increasing friction between Japan and the United States will take place in the future there can be little doubt, and that this will lead to war sooner or later seems quite certain. The United States must not render herself completely defenseless on the one hand thinking that a war with Japan is impossibility [sic], and on the other by sticking to methods and means of making war as obsolete as the bow and arrow is for the military rifle. Japan knows full well that the United States will probably enter the next war with the methods and weapons of the former war . . . It also knows full well that the defense of the Hawaiian group is based on the island of Oahu and not on the defense of the whole group of islands. It is my belief that Japan is a serious threat to American security and that they will probably attack the U.S. at two places.
>
> "First at Pearl Harbor, Hawaii. Attack will be launched as follows: bombardment attack to be made on Ford Island at 7:30 AM. The Japanese bombardment of Pearl Harbor would include 100 planes

organized into four squadrons of 25 planes each. The objectives for attack are:

1. *Ford Island, airdrome, hangers, storehouses, and ammunition dumps;*
2. *Navy fuel oil tanks;*
3. *Water supply of Honolulu;*
4. *Water supply of Schofield;*
5. *Schofield Barracks airdrome and troop establishments;*
6. *Naval submarine station;*
7. *City and wharves of Honolulu.*

"*A subsequent attack will be made on Clark Field, Philippine Islands at 10:40 AM. Japanese pursuit aviation will meet bombardment over Clark Field, proceeding by squadrons, one at 3000 feet to Clark Field from the southeast and with the sun at their back, one at 5000 feet from the north and one at 10,000 feet from the west. Should U.S. pursuit be destroyed or fail to appear, the airdrome would be attacked with airborne machineguns [sic]. The Japanese Air Force would then carry out a systematic siege against Corregidor.*"

Pausing momentarily, Mitchell collected his thoughts. His many years of playing to the press had taught him much, and he wanted his summation to have the ring of an historical pronouncement. When he was sure of himself, he dictated his conclusion:

"*If a nation ambitious for universal conquest gets off to a flying start in a war of the future, it may be able to control the whole world more easily than a nation has controlled a continent in the past.*"

He was nothing if not prophetic.

11:22 AM Hawaii Time

Twelve miles away, alone in his Ford Island office, a bespectacled Commander John Rodgers bent over a large map of the eastern Pacific that overhung his desktop on all four sides. Several smaller charts were scattered on top, as well as a large straightedge, a compass, a set of parallel rulers, and a pair of dividers. John had already managed to plot the rhumb line from San Francisco to Honolulu in pencil. It confirmed that the more northerly course he proposed was indeed 180 nautical miles closer than if they were to leave from San Diego.

As he studied the prevailing wind charts, John was gratified to observe that his preferred plot also established that the strong late-spring trade winds should give them a significant tailwind boost. In fact, those trades should blow from directly astern for the majority of the trip. As was his custom, he had meticulously lettered the huge maps with his precise calligraphy and added the projected wind angles.

There was a rap at the door. John quickly removed and pocketed his wire-rimmed glasses. "Come in."

Lieutenant Byron Connell stepped smartly into the office. "Morning, sir. Reporting as required. Just took my flight physical. Fit and fine!"

John nodded absently.

"It looks like you're getting a head start on our project, sir."

"Yeah, but I can still use your expertise, Byron. Can you corroborate the northern course heading?"

Transferring the plot using the parallel rulers, Byron confirmed the course as 240 degrees. "Looks right to me."

"Thanks," John said unenthusiastically.

"Hey skipper, what's got you worried, here?"

"Aw . . . I'm anxious about our range. Even if we leave from San Francisco, it's a hell of a long trip. The trade winds should help, but I don't want to have to count on them."

Byron shrugged. "Well . . ."

John studied his friend. "You know what? Let's worry about that later, once we know the flight characteristics of the new planes."

"Aye, aye, sir. I gotta run, I've got the duty this afternoon. And skipper, don't forget your flight physical is this afternoon at four."

"Yeah, and I've got paperwork I need to address." John tilted his head toward the pile of papers stacked on his chair.

"Aye, sir."

As Byron was leaving, he surreptitiously slid a folded piece of paper onto the stack. The office door closed, and knowing no one would dare enter without knocking, John reached for his glasses. After putting them back on, he lifted the stack from the chair and sat down to review it. The folded note on top caught his eye. Curious, he unfolded it, then stared in shock. His secret was out. The block letters were written in Byron's familiar script:

E

C K L

H I J O M

D E Q N A B G

G L K M Z B L P

This year's eye examination chart.

John realized he had nothing to fear; Byron would not reveal his secret. Now, however, he needed to memorize this document.

Brigadier General Billy Mitchell

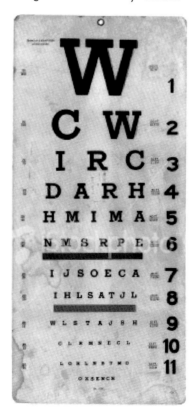

A period eye chart

Chapter 12

Monday—October 6, 1924

11:50 AM Hawaii Time

Late this Monday morning, Commander John Rodgers was on a crowded bus, heading into town to pick up his new glasses. An older, muumuu-clad local woman, sporting a *lauhala* hat and a fragrant plumeria lei, had just lumbered aboard. When John courteously stood to offer her his seat, her raucous reply, followed by a rich belly laugh, caught him by surprise. "Eh, watchu t'ink—I too ol' fo' stan' up?"

Red-faced, he stammered, "No, no of course not, I just thought . . ." but she interrupted in her island-style pidgin English.

"Das' OK, you get mannas! Somebody wen' raise you right . . . 'Kay den, I goin' sit—oddawise I goin' get hot . . ." and she eased herself and the large bag she was carrying into the seat John had offered.

"Good t'ing we get da trades today, yeah? Oddawise no can do notting. Eh, you look like one say-la man. You stay from da base?"

"Uh, well, yes." John was wearing civvies for his appointment.

"Dey good-kine guys, da Pearl Habah say-las. I get two *hanai* dottas—my sistah's keeds, I take um in fo' bring um up, you know, cuz sistah no can—anyway . . . dey like two nice Pearl Habah say-las," she volunteered.

Unable to get a word in edgewise, John simply allowed himself to enjoy what was clearly a performance designed to entertain everyone on the bus.

"Eh, I Aunty Momi . . . I ev'rybody's Aunty Momi. Ho—try wait, try wait!" She reached into her prodigious bag and produced a large mason jar, which she proceeded to open as she continued full steam ahead.

"Heah, get pickled green mango—try 'um!"

Nothing would do but for John to accept a taste of the homemade treat, which Aunty Momi then proceeded to share with the other passengers nearby.

"Watchu t'ink? Ono, yeah? From my tree. Ho, dat tree so choke wit' mango . . . !"

For the rest of the ride into town, the irrepressible Aunty Momi held court from her seat, regaling all who would listen with stories of her adventures growing up in Waikiki, and how it had changed over the course of her lifetime. Her uninhibited monologue was punctuated with a rich, infectious laugh. Before long, all onboard were in much better moods than when they'd gotten on.

When they reached the end of the line at the Oahu Railway Terminal, John jumped off the bus and helped his new Aunty step safely down to the street. He bid her "Aloha" and received a warm hug in return, as if they had known each other all their lives.

"'Kay den, I goin' see you bumbye. Get mo' pickled mango. T'anks, eh, fo' da seat. You one nice say-la, yeah?"

As he watched her bustle off down the sidewalk to the Waikiki trolley car waiting at the end of the block. John smiled, shaking his head in amazement. *Just one of the things I love about this place.*

John walked the two blocks to Masahiro Mikami's place of business, checking up and down the street, fervently hoping not to run into anyone he knew. He stopped two doors away from his destination, pretending to be interested in the seersucker suit in the tailor's window. Once he was certain the coast was clear, he slipped furtively into the optometrist's office.

The bell tinkled cheerily as he entered. A familiar lilting voice greeted him before the door was fully open. "Aloha, Mr. Rodgers. I, ah, we have been expecting you. Your lenses have come in, and my father has already framed them."

John gazed down at Akiko Mikami. She was even more beautiful than he had remembered. He took a moment to collect himself, then managed, "Aloha, Akiko. And it's John. Please."

Akiko's smile filled the room. She approached John as if he were an old friend. John marveled at the way she seemed to float rather than walk.

"Mr. Rodgers, um, John, I am so sorry but my father just left for a luncheon appointment. He will be back about one-fifteen. I am afraid you will have to come back, as he must adjust your frames and check your corrected vision. You may, of course, wait here if you would like. I was just going to go out for some lunch, though. Would you care to join me?"

This was the second time that morning an unusual woman had rendered him nearly speechless. Glancing at his chronograph, he realized he'd arrived right at lunchtime—12:05. Embarrassed, and assuming Akiko was just being polite, John tried to demur.

"Oh, uh, no, that's OK. I'll just go and, uh, do some shopping." Even to him, it sounded pretty feeble.

Akiko laughed lightly and shook her head. "Shopping? No, I do not think so. You are going to accompany me for lunch."

Her smile could have melted an iceberg.

"Well, if you're sure . . . ?"

"I am not taking no for an answer, Mr. . . . . I mean, John."

John hesitated for a second and Akiko giggled, "Well then, if we are going to go, let us go." Effectively ending any further discussion about it, she indicated the door. The tiny bell tinkled brightly as John opened and held it for her. As she stepped past him, she flipped the *Open* sign to *Closed* and moved the *Back At:* hands on the cardboard clock face to 1:15.

"Do you like Chinese food, John?"

John nodded, and the two started up Fort Street. They turned right on King Street and entered a small Cantonese restaurant. The tiny place was nearly empty, and the sole, ancient waiter pointed them toward a booth near a curtained window. They slid in and sat facing each other. The little booth was too small for John's long legs and he bumped against Akiko's under the table. The accidental contact was not altogether unpleasant.

"Sorry, clumsy of me," he managed to stammer. Akiko blushed, which only unnerved John even further.

There ensued an awkward pause. Akiko was the first to recover. After studying him, she asked simply, "Is 'Rodgers' your real name?"

The question caught John off-guard. "Well, yes. Why would you ask that?"

"Well, Mr. John Rodgers, before I answer you, I must warn you that I am very observant. Shall I go on?"

Despite her advisory, John was intrigued. He nodded.

"It is obvious from your haircut and the way you carry yourself that you are in the service. The Naval Academy ring on your right hand confirms that and tells me which branch. I wondered though, if you were in the military, why you would come to a commercial optometrist unless you were trying to hide your eyesight problems. I would guess that is because you are a pilot," Akiko pointed at his wrist. "Only pilots wear fancy watches like yours.

"So, you see how I would conclude that in an attempt to keep your eyesight problem a secret you might use an alias. Yes?"

John didn't know quite how to respond. He had been laid bare in one fell swoop. As long as he and Ethel had been married, she'd never been able to read him like that, not that she had ever tried. It was a little disconcerting.

"No, I mean yes. I mean Rodgers is my real name." He paused briefly. "As to everything else, I would have to say, guilty as charged."

"Well, Mr. John Rodgers, not to worry. Your secret is safe with me." And again she disarmed John with her smile.

The old waiter reappeared, and Akiko asked John if he would like her to order for them both. He nodded affirmatively, and she ordered a traditional Cantonese dish of chicken with vegetables, and a bowl of steamed white rice.

As they waited for their food, Akiko deftly drew John out with questions that probed so gently he found himself telling her things he'd never have dreamed of sharing with a relative stranger. She caught him off guard again and again, but her candor was enchanting, and her genuine curiosity, both attractive and disarming.

She extracted from him tales of his childhood in Maryland, and his decision to follow his family's tradition of naval service. He spoke of his love of flying, and made her laugh with stories of his cousin Cal's picaresque cross-country flight. John discovered he loved to make Akiko laugh.

When their meal arrived, John was further surprised as she took over, pouring his tea and serving him his food from the family-style serving bowls. But this was her way, and he followed her lead. Akiko never missed a beat as she continued peeling away the layers of John's reserve. She managed somehow to make him feel safe, even as he revealed more and more of himself.

Halfway through the meal John observed one special detail: because of his time in Hawaii, he had become, if not expert, certainly competent with chopsticks. Somehow Akiko had tactfully arranged for a knife and fork in case he needed them. Realizing they were not necessary, she had unobtrusively slid them off to the side.

As the meal was drawing to a close she threw John for a loop. "How long have you been divorced?"

"Excuse me?"

"John, your ring finger still showed signs of a wedding band when you first came to our office. It seems to have tanned up nicely now."

John could only shake his head. "You're amazing, Akiko!"

"Thank you," she said simply, and waited for the answer to her question.

John could feel his guard go up; this was sensitive territory. And yet, he found himself wanting to tell her. He took a breath and plunged in.

"My wife, uh, well, she left me a couple of months ago. She's filed for divorce, but because she's in California and I'm here, it may take a while to get it finalized."

Akiko toyed with her rice. "Well then, are you dating anyone, John?"

"Uh, no. I didn't think—I mean I haven't—"

"Do you like me?"

"Akiko! My, you are a very direct young woman."

Laughing softly, she said, "Young? I am almost twenty-seven. I am already an old maid. As for being direct, I have to be, or all the good ones like you, Mr. John Rodgers, will get away."

John was struck dumb. He had never before known a woman as forthright as this tiny dynamo. He wasn't sure how to proceed in the face of Akiko's unaffected honesty. She certainly shattered the stereotype of Oriental inscrutability. There was another pregnant pause.

Once again, Akiko rescued him. "John, this is a new era, and I am the product of the times. I am a modern woman in many ways. I see this surprises you." She grew serious for a moment. "As I have learned, life is short." Then she smiled. "And so I would like to ask you something. Would you join me for a beach picnic on Sunday?"

John just stared at her for a moment. And then, surprising himself, he blurted, "Sure, I'd love to."

"Good! Meet me in front of the office Sunday morning at ten."

John was beaming. "What can I bring?"

"Just that smile . . . and a swim suit and towel."

"Anything else?"

Grinning like a conspirator, Akiko leaned forward and lowered her voice. "If you can find a bootlegger, how about a bottle of wine?"

"I'll try."

"Now, let's get back to the office before my father finds out about this."

"Would he be concerned because I'm *haole*?"

Akiko replied, straight-faced, "Oh no, it won't bother him that you're Caucasian. But not being Buddhist, now that might make a difference." And then she flashed him that magical smile.

Half an hour later, John bid Masahiro and Akiko goodbye and closed the office door, to the cheerful tinkle of the little bell. He immediately removed the new glasses from their protective case and slid them into the breast pocket of his shirt. He then dropped the bulky cardboard case in the public trash receptacle in front of the shop.

For the first time in months, John was happy. There was a spring in his step as he walked back down the street. He shook his head, amazed at how one afternoon in the presence of a charming woman could so change one's outlook on life. Sunday couldn't come soon enough. He was smitten.

The Oahu Railway terminal

This was Honolulu's hub for all train, trolley, and bus transportation. The railway serviced the western and North Shore areas of Oahu. During the twenties, it was a big deal for a family to take a train ride into town.

A Honolulu Rapid Transit trolley crossing the River Street Bridge.

River Street defined the westernmost end of the Chinatown section of Honolulu. Trolleys ran from the Oahu Rail Terminal eastward through Chinatown, downtown Honolulu, and to Waikiki. Separate spurs traversed some of the more densely settled areas of town. Buses and sampans were common in less populated areas.

Commander John Rodgers, in civilian garb

Chapter 13

Tuesday—October 7, 1924

5:40 AM Pacific Time

"Turn left five degrees to new heading: two, five, five," commanded Zachary Lansdowne as he looked out into the pitch-black night from the control pod of the *Shenandoah*.

"Aye sir. Turning left to two, five, five" replied the pilot.

"Trim elevator. Nose up two degrees to assist ascent."

Spinning the vertical wheel, the Chief Petty Officer, whose sole job was controlling the elevators at the rear of the craft, called, "Roger. Nose up two degrees."

The huge dirigible wasn't responding as quickly as Lansdowne had hoped. They were maintaining 6,000 feet, a thousand feet above their normal operational maximum altitude. "We need more altitude. Incline pods four and five to max elevation and valve gas from bags fifteen and sixteen to three and four."

Multiple responses came back as engine pods four and five were rotated and helium was pumped forward to push the zeppelin even higher.

"Altitude?"

"Climbing now through six, one, zero, zero, sir."

Lifting his binoculars to stare out at the moonlit mountainscape, Lansdowne asked, "Rate of ascent?

"Steady now at one hundred feet per minute."

"Not enough. Increase rpms to thirty-five hundred."

"Aye sir, thirty-five hundred on all engines."

"How many bags are at operating maximum?"

"Sir, six bags now at maximum inflation. Three, four, eleven, twelve, thirteen, and fourteen."

"OK, increase one, two, seven, eight, nine, and ten to maximum."

"Roger, sir." The noncom spoke into his microphone, requesting the additional bags to be inflated.

Knowing that with the increased altitude the helium would expand in the individual bags, Lansdowne cautioned "Let's keep an eye on them though. We don't want them pushing on the framework."

"Close monitor on all full bags. Over."

Clicking off the variables, Lansdowne asked, "Air speed?"

"Sir, down to forty knots with the headwind."

A second call sounded throughout the control cab. "Sixty-three hundred feet and still climbing steady at one hundred, sir."

Not enough.

The control pod, which was angled slightly upward, suddenly rocked hard to port, and the framework in the giant dirigible creaked and groaned in protest. A chief petty officer called out, "Wind now gusting at twenty-five knots."

Lansdowne ordered, "All engines ahead full. Increase elevation to four degrees. Fill remaining forward gas bags five and six, but I want all available men monitoring their expansion. We can't afford a failure. Not now."

Multiple "Aye sir"s echoed through the control pod.

"Four degrees up and holding, sir."

"Sixty-five hundred feet and climbing. Climb slowed to seventy-five feet per minute."

Zachary Lansdowne clicked off this information. He knew that, all things being equal, as the ship rose and the air thinned, the ascent would slow; thus the reason for the extreme measure of topping off all twenty gas bags. There was danger in filling the bags to their maximum, however. The helium bags would continue to expand as the surrounding air pressure decreased with the higher altitude. This left the bags vulnerable to puncture from the internal framework. Even worse, the bags could actually overinflate enough to bend the superstructure and compromise the integrity of the entire ship. Consequently, all crew within the main cylinder were watching the bags closely, their hands on the corresponding valves, ready to dump helium if necessary.

"Wind increasing. Gusts to thirty from due west."

"Speed?"

"Steady at forty-two knots, sir."

"Altitude?"

"Sir, six, seven, five, zero. Climb slowed to fifty feet per minute."

Barely above the height of the pass. Zachary knew he needed more altitude.

Again, the huge zeppelin rocked as the wind pummeled her massive silhouette, shaking the gigantic ship like a toy balloon. However, this time the wind pushed them up. The ship rocketed skyward in the updraft, making all aboard feel as if they were in a speeding elevator.

A nervous response to the radical climb followed. "Sixty-nine hundred feet, and rising." All aboard knew that it was dangerous to ascend too quickly, especially at this altitude. The risk of overinflation was on everyone's mind.

Zachary held his balance on the sharply angled floor. He stared out into the night through binoculars, straining to see the approaching mountains.

"Sir, emergency dump from bags three and four reported."

Calmly Lansdowne acknowledged, "Roger." He knew that some gas might have to be released at this altitude. He was glad it was just two bags. If too much gas was released, the ship would have trouble controlling her descent. A number of zeppelins had crashed in the Great War when they had released too much hydrogen and then dropped from the skies in horrendously protracted, deadly falls.

Another voice was heard. "Sir, I can see some lights ahead. Ten degrees off our starboard bow."

Swiveling his binoculars, Zachary commented, "That'll be Truckee. OK gentlemen, let's level her out at 7,000."

"Sir, nosing down to level flight. Maintain altitude at seven, zero, zero, zero."

"Speed steady now at forty-five knots. Heading two, five, five."

Continually buffeted by the wind funneling over the mountain pass, the giant made modest progress. Except for repeated orders, the ship's crew was mum. All aboard listened intently as the creaking of the framework exceeded even the sound of the multiple engines and propellers.

Still glued to his binoculars, Lansdowne ordered, "Change heading to two, eight, zero."

"Roger, new heading: Two, eight, zero."

Moments later, the huge silver behemoth glided in relative silence over the tiny mountain town of Truckee on the California-Nevada border. The *Shenandoah* then slipped westward through the infamous Donner Pass and soon began a gradual descent to a less perilous altitude. She had crossed the Sierra Nevada Mountains safely during the night—an unbelievable accomplishment.

At sunrise, the long morning shadow from the *Shenandoah* stretched ahead across the hills and valleys like a giant messenger announcing her arrival. It had been an exciting two days. Traveling at an average speed of fifty-one knots, the *Shenandoah* had flown nonstop from within view of the Atlantic at Lakehurst, New Jersey all the way to California. Now, in the early morning light, her crew was relieved and exhilarated to catch sight of the Pacific Ocean at last.

While there was considerable excitement aboard the ZR-1, only polite congratulations were exchanged. Strict shipboard discipline precluded a more exuberant reaction. The skipper smiled, then turned his focus back to the controls of the great craft. Another enormous challenge lay ahead.

The gigantic dirigible was completing the final hours of an epic flight: the first nonstop transcontinental crossing of the United States by a lighter-than-air craft. The ZR-1's flight had been a runaway promotional success for the navy. Only a few airplanes had previously succeeded in the ambitious endeavor, most by stopping innumerable times for fuel and repairs. The press and the public had followed the historic flight with zeal. All across America, people had traveled miles just to catch a glimpse as this marvel of modern aviation passed overhead.

The *Shenandoah* was right on schedule for an early morning landing at Crissy Field, outside San Francisco. In preparation for her arrival, a tower nearly identical to the one back in Lakehurst had been constructed in a remote corner of the air base. Admiral Moffett had also sent a small team of sailors ahead by train—men who were experienced in corralling the ZR-1. They had spent the last few days prepping an additional two hundred swabbies for the complicated docking procedure.

The shiny silver *Shenandoah* cruised majestically across the outlying farmland, enthralling the Californians who had risen early to see her sail by. The image of the dirigible soaring majestically above at the astonishing speed of sixty miles per hour was one that few of her earthbound observers would ever forget. The weather was idyllic. The temperature was cool but the air was clear, and the wind, nearly still.

Onboard, Lansdowne put down his binoculars and ordered a gradual descent. "Steady on course. Ten-degree dive. Normal plane."

"Aye, aye. Ten-degree dive. Normal plane," repeated the pilot, setting a complex series of events in motion.

The operator spun the elevator control wheel, activating a complex system of cables and pulleys. An extraordinarily long set of cables snaked from the suspended control pod up into the bowels of the beast, all the way back to the twin elevators at her tail, some two football fields aft. In response, the trailing edges of the elevators dropped. This redirected the air stream, raising the dirigible's stern and angling her nose downward. But this maneuver alone would not achieve descent.

At the same time, two sailors in the control pod turned on matching sets of spigots that led to multiple pairs of pipes, each almost a thousand feet long. The pipes ran fore and aft from the control pod, the entire length of the ZR-1, and connected the twenty separate lifting chambers in a maze of convoluted plumbing. Once opened, pumps initiated the complex procedure of valving helium aft from some of the forward compartments.

This job was one of the most critical onboard. If not enough gas was shifted relative to the new angle of attack, the dirigible would skid like a car on ice with its wheels turned too sharply, except that the skid would be in a vertical plane. If too much gas was shifted, the craft could easily continue beyond the intended ten-degree incline, and if the dive wasn't stopped in time, the crew would soon find themselves unable to stand on the sharply angled deck. If steep enough, they could actually be thrown forward. And if the dive continued unchecked, the zeppelin would eventually find itself in a deadly headstand, something to be avoided at all costs. Although this catastrophic situation was rare, it was not without precedent.

As the craft angled downward, the engines were throttled back slightly so that their sixty-knot speed would not be exceeded. An observer on the ground would have barely noticed the ten-degree incline unless they viewed the craft in profile from a considerable distance away. However, onboard the *Shenandoah* the sensation was both immediate and acute. The ten-degree shift felt like the steepest of hills, making even simple movement difficult. Anticipating this situation, the designers had installed handholds throughout the vessel.

Thanks to the skills of the finely honed crew, the *Shenandoah* maintained her controlled dive and continued her descent without incident. She reached 150 feet in altitude at the outermost edge of the field and leveled out. By this time Lansdowne had slowed her to less than ten knots. Had the wind been a factor, this maneuvering speed would have had to be faster, but the stillness of the air allowed a slower, safer approach. Using only the rudder, they performed a perfect small flat turn to starboard—a kind of controlled skid—to line up on the tower. Once the massive flying cylinder was perfectly aligned, Lansdowne throttled her down to a near-stop.

Several hundred feet in front of the tower, below the giant's nose, two hundred sailors stood by in orderly team formations ready to obey the megaphone signals from the officer in charge. Several mooring lines were played out from the bow of the *Shenandoah*. The lead man on each of the mooring teams grabbed and passed a line through many hands in a classic tug-of-war configuration. While the men couldn't possibly have moved the monster, the idea was for them to help it maintain its position. Soon all the lines were in gloved hands, and Lansdowne gently bumped the ZR-1's throttles in an attempt to edge closer to the tower. The foremost prow-mounted line was captured by the ground crew and was soon snaked up the tower and secured to a winch. Following docking signals from the officer below, Lansdowne cut the *Shenandoah*'s engines to idle and the winch took over. Shortly after that, the huge dirigible was firmly secured flat and level, and the first successful nonstop transcontinental flight had been completed to the navy's credit. Lansdowne nodded with satisfaction: *Moffett would be pleased.*

The USS *Shenandoah* in flight over the San Francisco Bay area in October 1924.

The *Shenandoah* flying above California, October 1924. This first nonstop crossing of the United States helped to unite the nation and reinforce Americans' belief that their country could accomplish anything.

The USS *Shenandoah,* with the Golden Gate in the background before the construction of the famous bridge.

The *Shenandoah,* moored at NAS North Island San Diego, where it subsequently docked after stopping at Crissy Field, October 1924.

Chapter 14

Sunday—October 12, 1924

10:20 AM Hawaii Time

Although the Honolulu Transit Company buses ran on a restricted schedule on Sundays, they were almost always full of sailors heading through town and on to the white sands of Waikiki Beach. This Sunday was no different. Sitting near the back of the crowded bus, Byron regaled John with his plans for the day, which included a surfing lesson in the waves off Waikiki Beach.

"Why don't you come with me, John? We can take the trolley. It'd be fun."

Although John's pending divorce was not public knowledge, Byron was aware that Ethel had left. He had been concerned about his friend. "Hey, if you don't want to surf, there's always iced tea under the banyan tree at the Moana Hotel . . . ?"

John smiled and shook his head. "Thanks, Byron, I appreciate the offer, but actually I've got a better one," John replied. He knew he could trust his best friend to be discreet.

Surprised, Byron grinned. "Why, you sly old fox. What haven't you told your old pal?"

John shrugged more nonchalantly than he felt. "Oh, nothing really. I just have a date with a girl I met. We're heading who-knows-where on a picnic with who-knows-who. Maybe it's a church luau. Anyway, we'll probably be surrounded by forty of her closest friends and family."

"And her name is?"

"Akiko. She's Japanese, but she's not like any Japanese girl I've ever met."

"Hmmm . . . sounds as if my friend is interested."

Slightly embarrassed, John was glad the bus was slowing for his stop. He stood, ready to amble down the aisle. "OK, see you later."

"Roger, sir. But I'll want a complete report."

John stepped off the bus and headed in the direction of Masahiro Mikami's office. He was early as usual, but found himself walking briskly, anticipation quickening his steps. The sun was out in full force and the trade winds were almost nonexistent, making it feel hotter than normal. When the trades died in October, Hawaii could be oppressively hot, but this morning seemed especially beautiful—at least John thought so.

He carried a small gym bag containing his swimsuit, a plain white bath towel, a bottle of illicit homebrew red wine, and a corkscrew. His eyeglasses were in the inner pocket of the bag.

As he approached the optometrist's, he was struck by how quiet the street scene was. The normal hustle and bustle of a working weekday or the crush of Saturday's shoppers was missing, and the sidewalks were deserted. Sunday morning church services, he guessed.

There was no sign of Akiko at the office. He was, after all, almost a full half-hour early. Still, he had hoped . . . John smiled ruefully. He hadn't felt this jittery in years. This remarkable woman had turned him into a tongue-tied teenager. But he had to admit it felt good.

John checked his chronograph and then checked it again. He started to worry about his appearance and found himself looking at his reflection in the storefront glass. He was wearing a light blue, open-necked cotton shirt and casual slacks. He had on a pair of cordovan loafers and a matching belt. The few people he saw on the street were all clad in their Sunday finery. He hoped he was dressed properly for whatever Akiko had in store for them. Setting his gym bag on the sidewalk, John glanced at his watch once more and then looked back at his reflection. He adjusted his shirt and inspected his hair.

"Aloha, Mr. John Rodgers," came the lilting voice. "You look just fine. Please come in," And then Akiko opened the front door of the office, to the tinkle of the overhead bell.

"I didn't see any sign of life so I didn't even think to knock," said John. "How long—I mean did you know I was out here?"

"Of course. I told you I was observant," she said with a knowing smile.

Once again this unusual woman had thrown John off-balance.

"I was just, uh, well, you know, making sure." He stopped, at a loss to explain himself. Akiko had him off the hook in no time.

"I am glad you wanted to look good for me, and I am glad you were early. Now we can catch an earlier bus."

"Where are we going?"

"I want to take you to one of my favorite places—Kailua Beach on the Windward side. Have you been?"

"Well, no, not really. I mean I've flown along the Windward coast many times but I've never actually been to Kailua."

"Good. I would like to share it with you."

Akiko slung a beaded natural-canvas beach bag over one shoulder. As she lifted the wicker picnic basket that had been sitting on her desk, John immediately offered to carry it. He opened the door for Akiko and then followed her out. Only as they left the office did John notice Akiko's attire. He had been so mesmerized by her personality that he had been oblivious to what she was wearing.

Akiko had dressed in a charming yellow print sundress that showed off her petite figure exquisitely. A finely woven, wide-brimmed straw hat framed her face like a halo. She had on the barest of sandals with virtually no heel. All in all, she was a delightfully pretty package. And John felt like an ungainly giant walking next to her.

They were in luck. After only a brief wait, one of the quaint sampan buses that served as transportation to the outlying regions of the island pulled up to the stop. Akiko giggled. "Fortune is smiling on us this morning. Our sampans are not known for their punctuality."

The odd contraption, built on a small flatbed truck, was brightly painted, with a cab in front for the driver and a semi-enclosed cabin in the back for passengers. John offered his hand and helped Akiko up the fixed steps centered at the rear of the rattletrap vehicle. They moved quickly into the cabin and took seats on a bench that ran the length of the bus, facing an identical bench on the opposite side. Given the absence of the trades this morning, John was glad the sides of the sampan were open to the elements, although isinglass windows could be rolled down in case of inclement weather.

At first, Akiko and John had the passenger compartment all to themselves. The sampan stopped twice to pick up passengers as it puttered its way along Bishop Street and headed out of town up Nuuanu Avenue. Joining them first was a taciturn farmer who nodded a greeting but was mute during the trip. At the second stop, John climbed down the rear steps to assist an older Hawaiian couple. It was then he heard a boisterous "Aloha!" from none other than Aunty Momi. Putting down her enormous potluck basket of food, she embraced John as if he was a long-lost family member.

"Mistah John! So glad fo' see you. Eh, I tol' you we goin' meet again. Dis my husband Harold." At this, her somewhat reserved companion's weathered face wrinkled into a warm smile, and they shook hands. Never one to let the conversation lag, Aunty Momi confided energetically "We go Kailua town fo' see his family. Ho, is one *beeg* family, too! *Auwe*—plenny *keiki* deah, dat place *choke* wit' keeds!"

As she climbed up into the back of the sampan, John tried to introduce Akiko but Aunty Momi beat him to it. Reaching out she gave Akiko a hug. "Howzit? Ho, you stay cute, yeah? You call me Aunty Momi. You know Mistah John long time? You treat him nice. He stay one good sayla-man. My girls, Lei and Lani, dey datin' good sayla-mens too." And Aunty Momi's rich pidgin discourse continued unabated as the sampan started its long uphill climb through the valley.

Noticing the picnic basket next to Akiko, she asked "So, Mistah John, you folks goin' go fo' one potluck?"

"No, we're going to picnic on Kailua Beach."

Aunty Momi was instantly curious. "Get good-kine stuffs fo' *kau kau*?"

Akiko smiled. "No, just a little chicken, some fruit, some snacks." At the mention of fruit, Aunty was on high alert.

"Eh! You no get bananas, yeah? Nevah bring banana ova da Pali. Banana ova da Pali stay bad luck—serious-kine *pilikia*. Pretty girl, no wan' bad luck."

Akiko looked quickly at John, then back at the animated matriarch, who was already off on another tangent.

The sampan soon left the city behind and started the gradual climb up through Nuuanu Valley. The road became lined with banyan trees sporting long hanging tendrils that occasionally brushed the roof of the bus. The temperature cooled as the canopy of trees overhead began to close in, and soon they were tunneling along through dense vegetation. With the sun still dappling through the trees, a light, misting rain began to fall, giving off a comforting aroma. The circuitous trail meandered up the valley, often paralleling Nuuanu Stream. At one particularly abrupt S-turn, a place called Morgan's Corner, the stream displayed itself as a beautiful waterfall. Here, the stream tumbled over ancient, moss-covered lava rock and musically cascaded into a pond guarded by flaming red torch ginger and giant dark green elephant-ear plants. Even Aunty Momi was silent, mesmerized by the beauty.

As they continued on, John found that the jouncing ride, combined with the ever-increasing incline, from time to time pushed Akiko up against his side. Neither seemed to mind. Aunty Momi didn't miss a beat. In stentorian tones she announced, "Eh—you stay lovahs, yeah? Ho, young love da bes'."

Akiko blushed, shook her head and giggled.

Trying to conceal his own fluster, John demurred. "Oh no, Aunty Momi, we're just friends."

Aunty Momi didn't buy it for an instant. Shaking her head, she repeated firmly, "I know um when I see um."

John felt naked. There was no hiding from Aunty Momi. He and Akiko just looked at each other and burst out laughing.

As the bus neared the summit, the road seemed to flatten, and the vegetation thinned somewhat, allowing the riders glimpses of the sheer cliffs towering on either side of the valley. The steep, vertical walls undulated like a washboard on its side, each recess having been formed by its own waterfall and untold eons of erosion. The perpendicular bulwarks were covered in greenery that grew all the way to the top of the 3,000-foot peaks.

As the sampan approached the Pali lookout, the driver slowed the vehicle to a crawl. Several hundred feet from the top, the gentle breeze dramatically increased in strength. Without warning, heavy gusts of wind began to rock the rickety little bus. At the summit, the road narrowed to a single lane and took a sharp ninety-degree right-hand turn. Before they had a chance to enjoy the view, the ground on their left dropped off completely, and a rock wall was only inches away to their right.

John nudged Akiko. "Now I understand the stories of horses balking at this stretch."

Aunt Momi chimed in, "Dey wen' call dis da road dat could neva be built."

John was curious. "Aunty Momi, I've heard the wind can be so strong up here that it can tip cars over, and even blow them over the cliff. Is this true?"

She nodded emphatically. "*Auwe,* can! I wen' lose one cousin ovah da cliff, was t'ree yeas ago. But not so bad today. No worries today."

The road—more trail than road at this point—hugged the vertical wall as they slowly descended. The impossibly steep cliffs could intimidate even the most composed driver. This precarious path hugged the cliffs, with switchback after switchback, and the occasional pullout so that approaching vehicles could pass. It appeared to John that because of the precipitous grade, the rule of the road was that cars going up took precedence over those coming down.

As the little sampan bumped and juddered its way down the mountain, the passengers could see the occasional ribbon waterfalls that cascaded often a thousand feet or more in narrow, moss-covered channels. These often spilled onto the road, scattering rocks and turning the asphalt wet and slippery, adding to a driver's anxiety.

Once they'd made it through the narrow pass, the windy gusts subsided, dwindling almost immediately to a pleasant breeze. And after innumerable switchbacks, the road widened to two lanes, and the steep decline gentled into a more manageable downhill. The trees again formed a tropical canopy. Enormous vines seemed to be everywhere.

John chuckled. "Tarzan would have felt right at home here."

The cacophony of birdcalls was audible over the wheeze of the sampan's four-cylinder engine. Occasional shafts of sunlight filtered brilliantly through the tall trees as the little bus rumbled along over the moss-covered road. At this point, the stagnant humidity and almost total lack of breeze contrasted sharply with the weather they'd experienced at the top of the pass. The earth itself gave off the fragrant aroma of rich humus. John was amazed to find a tropical eden so close to the twentieth-century city of Honolulu. He felt intoxicated by the beauty of this mountain jungle.

Twenty minutes later, the sampan rambled into the coconut tree–dotted village of Kailua and shuddered to a stop. Having perched on the low bench for too long, John gladly unfolded his lanky frame and climbed down the rear steps. He turned to help Aunty Momi, who trundled out, still talking. He then held his hand for Akiko, who was tiny by comparison.

Harold and the mute farmer climbed down, and alohas were exchanged all around. As Aunty Momi bustled down the path, she called back over her shoulder, "Akiko-girl, you take care Mistah John. He good sayla-man. Good sayla-man like my Lei and Lani's. 'Kay den, I see you bumbye. Aloha!"

It was a glorious afternoon. The sun and breeze seemed to caress Akiko and John as they walked the half-mile to the beach, a lovely stretch of powder-fine, silver-white glistening sand. The beach was dotted with coconut palms, shaded by innumerable tall ironwood trees, and nominally protected from the wind by the knee-high *naupaka* plants. The hardy *naupaka* grew well on the small dunes fronting the ocean, and the plants were covered with thousands of tiny, mildly fragrant white flowers. Akiko eyed the expanse critically, and said, "Here," pointing to a place on the grass about a hundred feet from the water.

She produced a blanket from the wicker basket, and John spread it out on the chosen site. Then it was a question of where to change into their bathing suits. This produced an interesting problem. Looking at the possibilities that surrounded them, John chuckled and pointed to a nearby stand of coconut trees.

"I think that would be the *wahine* dressing room?" Akiko followed suit, pointing to a sizable dune in the other direction.

"And that would be for the gentlemen?"

Laughing a bit sheepishly, they retired to their respective corners.

As they returned to the picnic blanket after changing, John had a hard time forcing himself not to stare at Akiko's elfin figure. Her smooth, hairless skin enthralled him. The snug one-piece suit hugged her tiny frame. She had let her long black hair hang loose, and watching it waft in the ocean breeze ignited John's imagination. He set aside those thoughts as best he could.

Akiko opened the cornucopia of goodies she had packed for their lunch. She paused to look at John, then gingerly removed a glass jar which contained a mixed-fruit salad. It was a colorful mélange of mango, grapes, pineapple, and . . . Aunty Momi's forbidden fruit. John did a double take, and then teased Akiko, feigning horror. "Uh-oh, bananas! Bad luck's on its way!"

Akiko didn't respond in kind. She lowered her eyes.

"I am so sorry. I didn't know." She seemed near tears. Her reaction caught him completely by surprise. He tried to reassure her.

"Akiko, I was only kidding. It's just a local superstition, it doesn't mean anything." She looked up to meet his eyes, and gave a little nod.

"Yes, of course." Then, breaking the spell, she busied herself with the rest of the food. She had prepared small pieces of boneless chicken, cooked *mochiko* style; some sushi rice, and some almond sugar cookies. As she spread them out on the blanket, John opened the wine and then realized out loud that he had forgotten to bring any glasses. Trying to cheer Akiko, John said, "Aha—now there's the bad luck! We'll just have to make do. Here." And he offered her the bottle.

Somewhat nonplussed, Akiko nevertheless smiled gamely and accepted the bottle. "Cheers!" she took a tiny sip of the wine and then passed it back to John. The woman never failed to amaze him.

After lunch, Akiko took a Brownie box camera from her beach bag and asked John if she could take his picture. Somewhat embarrassed, John nevertheless agreed. Akiko aimed the black cube and happily snapped his portrait. John then reached for the camera and nodded for Akiko to pose. Looking into the small eyepiece, John saw Akiko's silky hair blowing in the breeze, framing her delicate features. She was a vision of loveliness, an image he hoped never to forget. He pressed the shutter.

Returning the camera to her bag, Akiko suggested they stroll along the beach, and they ambled toward the shoreline. Sensing John's reluctance to talk about personal matters, Akiko tried a more oblique line of questioning.

"When we last saw each other, you spoke of your love for flying. What else does Mr. John Rodgers enjoy?"

Her question prompted him to tell her about his passion for sailing and sailboat racing. He found himself describing the similarities between flying and sailing, and discovering connections he hadn't been aware of before. He was surprised at his ability to articulate the reasons he loved both. As he spoke, he revealed more and more of himself, without realizing it.

At last he caught himself. "Akiko, now I want to hear about you. I've met your father. Tell me about your mother."

Akiko tucked her chin down and replied quietly, "My mother died two years ago."

John stammered, "I'm sorry, Akiko. I didn't know. Would you like to tell me about her?"

She gave him a look he couldn't read, and said simply, "It is a story for another time perhaps. Not now, not today." Then she smiled and continued, "You have spoken a little about your family—the funny cousin, Cal? Please tell me more. Please talk to me about your ancestors."

John obliged, giving Akiko some insight into his family history. While he downplayed their powerful social status, Akiko nevertheless recognized that he came from a distinguished background. She could sense that John felt honor bound to measure up to his forebears.

They fell silent, and walked further down the beach in silence. For the first time since he'd met her, Akiko seemed lost in her own thoughts. Suddenly she stopped and turned to John with a question that stunned him. "You would never hit me, would you, Mr. John Rodgers?"

Looking at the delicate beauty before him, he was at a dead loss for a long moment, and then did the only thing he could think of. Reaching out and folding his arms around her, as tenderly as he knew how, he whispered into her ear, "Never, Akiko. *Never.*" They stood together for a moment, then she looked up at him, her eyes wide with childlike vulnerability. He bent down and kissed her, softly at first and then again warmly. She pulled away briefly and studied his face as if to memorize it. Then rising up on her tiptoes, she wrapped her arms around his neck, and kissed him passionately.

A sampan bus on a Model-T frame. Sampans, as they were commonly called, served the areas of the island that weren't otherwise accessible via the urban Honolulu Transit Company's network of buses and trolleys, or the more rural sugarcane trains that served the north and west shores of Oahu. Sampans, independently owned and operated, weren't known for being on strict schedules or specific routes, and they would often take passengers right to their door. The cabins were built with a longitudinal curved roof, higher in the middle for headroom, while the passengers sat on facing benches on either side. A fixed set of steps was centered in the back to facilitate entrance and egress. The sides were open to the elements, although isinglass windows were at the ready if the weather became an issue. They were normally rolled horizontally and secured to the sides of the roof with simple leather ties.

Although a less-than-ideal reproduction, this is a rare image of 1920s sampan.

Kailua Beach, facing north. It's hard to capture the beauty of this lovely stretch of sand in period photographs, but at least you have the sense of what they looked like in the 1920s.

Kailua Beach, facing south

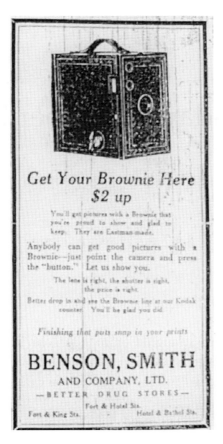

Advertisement for a "Brownie" camera as it appeared in the 1924 *Honolulu Advertiser*. This compromised image was enlarged from archival microfiche.

Chapter 15

Wednesday—October 22, 1924

4:42 PM Hawaii Time

Still in uniform, a distraught Commander John Rodgers raced for the first taxi in the queue just outside the Makalapa Gate of Pearl Harbor. Jumping in, he barked, "Town—as fast as you can."

For the past fortnight, John had been to hell and back. The day after his glorious beach picnic with Akiko, he had received a deeply disturbing letter from Los Angeles. It had been from his wife.

Ethel knew just how to pull John's strings. In the note, she blamed John and his career for the failure of their marriage. She asked for money, as well as for assistance with some of the business details of their separation. John was beside himself. For quite some time, he had blamed himself for the deterioration of their relationship. Reading and rereading Ethel's bitter words, he was increasingly convinced that there must be something he could still do to save the marriage. Divorce was a failure, and John was not a man to fail—not himself, not his career, not his status as the scion of the Rodgers family. As he considered his situation, he was filled with guilt for his attraction to Akiko. Despite his genuine feelings for her, he convinced himself that if he was going to have any shot at salvaging things with Ethel, he would have to distance himself from Akiko. He needed to write two letters.

The first was a heartfelt apology to Ethel. In this letter, he said he understood the hardships his career had caused her. He offered to compromise his future in the navy by requesting a less-demanding post back in Maryland so that she could resume the life she had so desperately missed; something he never imagined he could have done before. The letter was as sincere and conciliatory as he could make it.

John then wrote a short note to Akiko, trying to explain his painful situation. He begged Akiko to understand why he could not see her anymore. It was a much harder letter to write. It took him five tries.

John sent Ethel's letter as a telegram, along with the money she had requested—more than she had requested, actually. He asked that she wire her response, as a letter could take well over a week—a long time to hang when the stakes were so high.

John addressed Akiko's note in care of Masahiro's shop. Mail service on Oahu would get it to her in the next couple of days. He had to steel himself before he could push the envelope into the mail slot marked "Local."

Now, as he leaned back in the rear seat of the taxi ten long days later, John studied the two envelopes in his hand. The fatter of the two was from Ethel. Her response had arrived at last: an official application for divorce. He put on his glasses and pulled the pages out to read them yet again. Ethel had already signed the legal document, and her signature had been notarized. There was a blank for his signature and a place for his notary. She had also enclosed a stamped return envelope addressed to Thomas John Weigand, Esq., Attorney at Law, at a Los Angeles address.

Clipped to the top of the front page of the sheaf was a short, handwritten note.

> *John,*
>
> *It's over. Get it through your head.*
>
> *Please sign and return the documents.*
>
> *Ethel*

Sighing, John folded the papers and replaced them in the envelope. It *was* over. He knew that now. He would sign the documents tomorrow, knowing full well that the act would signal a major shift in his life. Dealing with the social inferences, his family's inevitable disapproval, and moving into different quarters were the least of his concerns. Looming ahead of him like a guillotine were the career-threatening consequences of divorce. But these were small hurdles compared to his present task.

Putting the envelope on the seat next to him, he turned his attention to the second letter. It was smaller and addressed in delicate, precise penmanship. He carefully slid the rice paper out and caressed it before rereading the message.

> *My dear Mr. John Rodgers,*
>
> *I received your letter and wanted to thank you for your kind words. I will do my best to understand and respect your wishes. You are a very special man. I only wish I could comfort you.*
>
> *Aloha,*
>
> *Akiko*
>
> *PS: Please accept this photo as a remembrance of a truly wonderful day.*

A scallop-edged black-and-white photograph was clipped to the back of the note paper. It was the photo John had taken of Akiko on Kailua Beach—an eternity ago.

She stood against the backdrop of the curving bay, her dark hair caught forever as it wafted in the ocean breeze. It was the portrait of an angel. On the back was an inscription:

To my Mr. John Rodgers

Fondly, Akiko

John carefully slipped both the photograph and the note back into the envelope and placed them in the inner pocket of his uniform coat, next to his heart.

Fifteen minutes later, the Morris-Markin taxicab sputtered to a stop on Fort Street outside Masahiro Mikami's optometrist shop. It was shortly after five o'clock, and the *Closed* sign was already hanging in the door. John quickly paid the driver and unfolded himself from the rear seat, ignoring the running board as he jumped down and sprinted to the front door. He knocked politely and tried the doorknob, but the shop was locked. Trying to slow his racing heart, he stood up straight, put on his uniform cap, and adjusted his tie in the reflection of the glass.

From inside the darkened storefront came Akiko's voice. "Mr. John Rodgers, are you preening yourself *again?*"

The door opened quickly to the cheery sound of the familiar bell and there she was. Akiko studied him gravely, her dark eyes shining. He couldn't read her expression. The flustered navy commander stood frozen, suddenly uncertain how to proceed. At last he managed to stammer, "Akiko. I wanted, that is, I, uh, I wondered . . ."

Rescuing him, Akiko interrupted, "Please come in, Mr. John Rodgers. Come inside."

"Is it OK? I mean, is your father . . ."

"My father has left for a business meeting. Please come in and sit down. I am glad you have come."

As Akiko slipped gracefully into the chair behind her desk, John nervously perched on the edge of the small rattan sofa designated for waiting customers.

"Akiko, these last ten days have been the worst of my life. I thought I was doing the right thing—what a husband is supposed to do. I believed I had to do everything in my power to try and make my marriage succeed. Please believe me when I tell you I'm sick about how I've treated you."

"Mr. John . . ."

"Akiko, please! I just want to apologize. You're the last person I wanted to hurt."

Pausing, to be sure he had finished, Akiko said gently, "John, I know that. And I knew I would see you again. Let me tell you why.

"Life sometimes gives us great difficulties. Sometimes we can deal with them and sometimes they are too much. You asked me about my mother. Let me tell you now. She was a strong person, a wonderful mother. I was her only child and she doted on me as I grew up. It was she who convinced my father to put aside Japanese tradition and let me go to college. But while I was pursuing my degree, she came down with cancer. At first I refused to accept that she was dying. I tried everything I could think of to make her better, to ease her pain. I thought if I tried hard enough she could overcome the disease. But she did not. I thought I could make the pain go away. But I could not. She only grew worse."

A tear formed in the corner of Akiko's eye as she continued, "Along the way I finally saw through my own grief, and recognized the pain she was in. She knew she could struggle no further, and begged me to understand. Up until then, I had been too close to see that the fight was lost. She begged me to let her go, to help her go. There was nothing else for me to do." The tear escaped and slid down her porcelain cheek. Ignoring it, Akiko continued, "You, too, have been struggling to save something that is already dead. You are here today to tell me your marriage is over, is that not right?"

"Akiko, how do you . . . ?"

"I knew that your marriage was over. From our first meeting, it was clear to me that it had been a long time since a woman treated you as something treasured and special.

"If we are strong, we can deal with the pain of letting go of something that has been important to us. I know you are a strong man, and you are a good man, Mr. John Rodgers. You can live with this pain. That is why I knew you would come back."

"Akiko, I don't know what to say. Thank you."

A quiet moment passed between them. Then the shadow of a mischievous grin appeared on Akiko face. "But as for accepting your apology, I will not let you off that easy."

"Akiko, what can I . . ."

"Mr. John Rodgers, it is dinnertime, and I am hungry. A gentleman would surely want to offer a lady dinner to make amends."

A 1922 Morris-Markin Taxi, forerunner of the Checker Cab

Chapter 16

Monday—January 26, 1925

6:55 AM Eastern Time

Three months had passed since the *Shenandoah*'s triumphant cross-country adventure, and she was now back at home base. The sunrise at Lakehurst Navy Air Station painted the sky a clear, crisp, cyan blue. The huge dirigible, and the equally large docking mast that secured it, cast immense shadows that disappeared into the short scrub pines surrounding the seaside airfield. It was a bitterly cold January morning in New Jersey, but the air was still and calm: perfect conditions for the daunting maneuver ahead. The 170 sailors gathered in groups on the sandy soil two hundred feet below the floating *Shenandoah* wore warm winter clothes and heavy leather work gloves. They stood waiting for orders as they held the half-dozen lines that dangled limply from the ZR-1. A heavy-duty diesel-powered tug idled beyond and to the right of the tower.

As the post-dawn sun glinted off the bright duralumin skin, all below were focused on the craft, even though many of the men found it difficult to look directly at the shining silver leviathan. The ground crews were as silent as if they were attending a funeral; serious work was at hand. In previous dirigible operations, men had gotten tangled in mooring lines and had been plucked from the ground, plummeting to serious injuries and death. Just over a year before, the prow of the airship had been seriously damaged in a dramatic mishap that occurred while it was attempting to disengage from the mooring mast in heavy weather. It wasn't surprising that today the tension in the icy air was palpable.

In the suspended control pod aboard the *Shenandoah*, Lieutenant Commander Zachary Lansdowne paced nervously. He wanted this maneuver accomplished before any wind came up. He had his crew fire five of the six Detroit-powered engines, but without engaging the propellers. Once the Packards reached their normal operating temperatures, he gave the go-ahead to his executive officer, who then signaled to those below that the *Shenandoah* was ready to cast off.

On the ground, the teams of men responded by taking up the slack in the cables. Once this was done, the hawsers holding the airship to the mooring mast were cast off, leaving a cadre of around a hundred men holding on to the largest balloon in the world. At this point, the slightest breeze could easily turn the 680-foot-long giant into a runaway freight train.

As soon as the zeppelin drifted well clear of the mooring mast, Zachary ordered two of the outboard engines to be engaged. Simultaneously, the cable that was secured to the rear of the tug drew taut and the tractor crept forward using all of its extraordinary torque. Nothing much happened at first. While the multiple ground crews could do little to actually move the ZR-1 on their own, they pulled for all they were worth to try and direct it. When it seemed that no outside force short of a hurricane could move her, the *Shenandoah* started inching forward trailing the mighty tug.

Lansdowne deftly alternated the two outboard engines, first throttling up the portside pod to nose the craft to the right, then increasing speed on the starboard nacelle to slow the turn and edge the airship farther forward. The ground crew had to take care to simply steer—avoiding any excess downward pull on the bow lines. Because a lighter-than-air craft is always in a constant battle to maintain level trim, even minute weather and barometric pressure differences between the bow and stern can be of considerable concern. A ship this long could quickly rise or drop at either end, especially when not at speed or altitude. It was vital to keep the *Shenandoah* from nosing toward the ground. It was not unheard of for a tethered airship to nosestand, tipping as much as eighty-five degrees vertical—a deadly possibility to be avoided at all costs. Fortunately, the air remained calm, and the enormous craft stayed level as it proceeded at a walking pace across the several hundred yards of broad, flat, sandy expanse towards Hangar #1.

Fifteen months before, Hangar #1 had been the construction site for the ZR-1. It was the largest freestanding structure in the world, and the only building capable of corralling the *Shenandoah*. At 966 feet long, 350 feet wide, and 200 feet high, its size defied comprehension. Except for the side-wall frames, the entire interior of the cantilevered building was without internal support. The floor area was mind-numbing; over ⅓ million square feet.

Each of the unimaginably massive twin doors of the hangar stood 177 feet tall, and weighed as much as a navy destroyer. They were free-standing affairs that traveled on multiple rails. It took two large motors a full twenty minutes to slide one of these giant barn doors open.

The hangar itself was so huge that it could actually rain indoors, which happened occasionally when the doors were opened and warm, humid air flowed into the cooler interior and condensed. When it did "rain," astonished new recruits were often told apocryphal stories of interior thunderstorms, which were often believed, to the amusement of their seniors.

The dirigible covered the half-mile distance from mooring mast to hangar in less than fifteen minutes, much to Lieutenant Commander Lansdowne's relief. Yet it took another half-hour to lower and properly align the great craft for entry into the cavernous vault. Extreme care had to be taken to keep the four tail fins from being damaged as the shiny silver bird of prey reentered its nest. It was not until two hours later, when the hangar was once again sealed from the outside, that Lansdowne could finally relax.

Safely ensconced in her hangar, the *Shenandoah* would spend the next several months being serviced and modified. In the past fifteen months, she had logged innumerable cross-country miles without significant downtime. She was due for a rest.

The changes Lansdowne had recommended included the elimination of the number-six engine, which was mounted at the stern of the control pod. It was virtually never used, as the noise, and particularly the vibration, interfered with safe operations inside the control pod. Besides, the other five outboard-mounted engines were more than sufficient to power the ZR-1. Other adjustments were planned, but the most important part of the *Shenandoah*'s dry-dock time was to assess and confirm the structural integrity of the craft.

Speaking over the ship's intercom, Lansdowne congratulated his crew and then relieved them. As skipper, he was the last man to descend the short ladder from the pod to *terra firma*. It would be more than five months before the *Shenandoah* would once again command the skies.

9:09 AM Hawaii Time

At Wheeler Field, near Schofield Army Barracks in central Oahu, Brigadier General Billy Mitchell was in the process of inspecting his modest fleet of airplanes when his aide ran up. The lieutenant snapped to attention, saluted crisply, and handed over a telegram addressed to Mitchell.

"Sir, this just came over the wire."

Mitchell unfolded the paper. His face darkened as he read the memo he'd been expecting.

When it had come time for Mitchell's annual review at the end of the year, his superior officer, Lieutenant General Mason Patrick had reached a breaking point with the brash young officer. Patrick had read Mitchell's 320-page tome describing in detail a hypothetical Japanese attack against Hawaii. Mitchell had predicted that the Japanese would come from the west through the Kolekole Pass of the Waianae Mountains and attack strategic areas on Oahu—military air fields and bases—specifically targeting the battleship fleet at Pearl Harbor. Patrick had dismissed the report as both preposterous and politically radical. In fact, before sending the report up the chain of command, he had scrawled a one word response on the last page: "Arse."

Even though Patrick had not agreed with Mitchell's premise, he might not have pursued the matter further had Mitchell not taken it upon himself to tout his theory to the press. The headlines that subsequently hit newsstands across America exacerbated the already strained relations between the U.S. and Japan. The reverberations reached all the way to the White House.

General Patrick's response to Mitchell's untoward showboating was evident in the assessment that appeared in Mitchell's personnel file: "This officer is an exceptionally able one, enthusiastic, energetic and full of initiative; but he is fond of publicity, more or less indiscreet as to speech, and rather difficult to control as a subordinate."

When Mitchell finished reading the telegram, his aide asked, "Sir, is there to be a reply?"

"No, no," Mitchell shook his head. "Lieutenant, good news and bad news. The good news is we've got new orders. We're heading stateside. Texas. Fort Sam Houston. The bad news is the sons of bitches have busted me back to colonel."

The *Shenandoah* and Hangar #1, Lakehurst, New Jersey

The *Los Angeles:* the ZR-1's next-generation sister ship, in a terrifying and death-defying near-vertical headstand.

General Billy Mitchell

Chapter 17

Thursday—February 18, 1925

1:20 PM Eastern Time

Seated at his office desk in Washington, D.C., Admiral Moffett closed the folder containing the report he had just finished rereading. The news was not good. Setting his jaw, he picked up the black desk phone and asked for a long-distance operator. He waited impatiently as the local operator relayed the number he had requested to her overseas counterpart. Whirrs and clicks followed, and then word that the connection had failed. The D.C. operator advised Moffett that she would call him back as soon as she could get through to Hawaii.

8:33 AM Hawaii Time

At his desk on Ford Island, John Rodgers heard the phone ring in the outer office. Moments later, his secretary appeared in the doorway.

"Long-distance for you, sir. Washington calling."

John picked up the phone immediately, "Commander John Rodgers speaking."

The overseas operator's voice sounded hollow and distant, as if echoing down a long pipe.

"Please hold for Admiral Moffett." And then a deeper male voice came on the line. "John, how are you?"

"Admiral . . . Fine, thank you. How can I help you?"

A short delay followed as the sound traveled 5,000 miles across the earth.

"John, I don't like to put off bad news. We've got some problems with your planes. The wings have to be totally redesigned to take the extra weight of the twin Packards, and the propellers aren't large enough to take advantage of the added horsepower. New ones will have to be designed and built. It'll cost us time."

John started to respond, but the signal lapse caused Admiral Moffett to speak over him. "I've got the team at Philadelphia working on the problems, but to be realistic, I think we'll have to delay the mission until July. I'm sorry, but that's our situation at this point." The pause that followed gave John time to reply.

"Sir, I'm sure you and the crew in Philadelphia are doing the best you can. We can adjust our schedules accordingly, but may I remind you, sir, we have to be careful we don't slip too much further. The prevailing trade winds generally weaken as we approach September. All of our calculations indicate that those strong trades will be critical to the mission."

The lag time continued to hamstring any real conversation. Eventually, Moffett responded, "OK John, but you need to know that it's not just the Philadelphia planes that are delayed. The Boeing plane up in Seattle has run into problems as well. It seems no one correctly estimated the stresses that the new engines' torque would deliver to the frame. They have to rebuild the entire fuselage to keep the engines from tearing the plane apart."

"Admiral, what you're telling me certainly differs from the reports I've received from Lieutenant Commander Strong. All he says is how well the build is going."

"I'm sorry about that, but I'm telling you what I know to be true. Strong has a tendency to stretch the facts."

John knew better than to push the issue. It was clear that the admiral had been politically maneuvered into a corner. He knew that Lieutenant Commander Strong had not been Moffett's first choice, nor, for that matter, would John have picked the brash young lieutenant commander to command the third plane.

Before Rodgers could respond, though, Moffett interjected, "Look, John, we'll deal with Strong later. Right now we need to get this mission back on track. Can you get me a revised schedule based on a mid-July start?"

"Yes, sir. Sir, one more thing."

"Yes, John?"

"Have you been able to get an answer on our city of departure?"

"Not yet. The question's been presented, but there are a lot of different opinions. Like you, I prefer San Francisco because of the reduced distance to destination. I think anything that will help us succeed is paramount. But the fact that San Diego has such a big naval base is influencing the decision. You know the game—political bullshit. A couple of maps might help those idiots see why we prefer San Francisco. I'll do what I can to get you an answer soon."

"Very good, sir."

"OK then, John. Get me that revised schedule and I'll keep you posted on the progress over here."

The line went dead. Rodgers hung up the phone, walked to the door, and instructed his secretary to schedule a meeting with the two crews, ASAP. Closing the door again, he returned to his desk. He reached into his jacket pocket and took out his glasses and the treasured photograph of Akiko. *God, she's beautiful.*

During the four months since Ethel had declared her intention to divorce, she and her lawyers had thrown up one roadblock after another. It had mystified John, as she had been the one to sue for divorce in the first place. As demoralizing as the long, drawn-out process had been, it would have been infinitely worse without Akiko.

Because he was still technically married, John had held himself back from pressing for anything more serious than a close, platonic relationship. Despite the evident attraction on both sides, the relationship had yet to be consummated. John was a man of honor, and Akiko seemed to understand. Even so, a profound bond was developing between them. Smiling to himself, he replaced the picture and began to prep for the upcoming powwow with his men.

An aerial view of the Naval Air Field in Philadelphia, facing west. In the mid-1920s, it was the birthplace of most all navy planes, and specifically the PN seaplane series. Note the Delaware River in the right of the picture which will have further significance later in the narrative.

Engine tests on the PB1 Boeing plane. Note the unusual "push-pull" arrangement of the huge 800-horsepower Packard engines, and the duralumin skin on the fuselage and floats. An extraordinarily rare photo of the PB1.

Chapter 18

Friday—June 19, 1925

4:02 PM Hawaii Time

"Commander, Admiral Moffett's on the line for you, long distance." It was just after 9 PM back east. Wondering what could be up, John lifted the heavy receiver.

"Commander Rodgers speaking. Hello Admiral."

After a brief pause filled with clicks and static, Moffett's voice came through.

"John, a couple things. First off, no delays to report. The planes are all being flight tested and should be ready to go as scheduled. Second: good news. We are a 'go' for San Francisco as the point of departure. Your concept has been approved as written; ships and all. We are still scheduling the shipment of the planes to San Diego for reassembly and testing, so you should stick with your plan to head out there in a couple of weeks. I'll let you know the details once the planes are crated up and on their way." Here Moffett paused. The silence stretched.

"Admiral? You still there, sir?"

"Yes, John, I'm here. Listen, there's something else we need to discuss. We can't afford to have anything take away from the success of this mission. You and your crews are going to be subjected to some fairly close scrutiny by the press, so we need to make sure that no one has any skeletons in the closet. I understand that three members of your crew are single and I'm not so old I don't remember what that's like. I need you to make sure they keep their noses clean. My sources tell me that Bowlin and Stantz are seeing two local Hawaiian girls—sisters. That might not play well here on the Mainland, if you know what I mean. The navy can't dictate who men can and can't date, but I want you to make sure they understand the importance of the situation. There's too much riding on this mission to risk it being compromised by tabloid gossip. Do I make myself clear?"

John was stunned that Moffett would know more about his crew's private life than he did. It suddenly occurred to him that Wild Bill and Sparky just might be the two "sayla-men" Auntie Momi had gone on and on about.

But John was more worried about his own situation. "Admiral, you need to know something. My wife has filed for divorce."

There was a long moment of silence, then Moffett said, "I'm sorry John. Any complications with the divorce? Anything you think I should know about?"

Of course there was something else: Akiko. *Should I tell him?* John made his decision.

"No, sir."

"OK, John. Then that's it. I'll let you know when we'll need your crews in San Diego. Goodbye."

The quick disconnect caught John unaware. He stood there still holding the receiver for a moment. Realizing the line was dead, he wondered if he had made a mistake.

John was all too aware of prejudice in America. He had, however, lived a very sheltered existence up to this point. Suddenly, bigotry was no longer an abstract concept. *What if the press gets wind of our relationship?* Scandal-sheet fodder for sure. How terribly unfair this would be to both Akiko and her father. And he had to admit, the thought of his own family's reaction concerned him as well.

As he contemplated his situation, John changed into civvies for the dinner date he and Akiko had planned. After Ethel's departure, he had been obliged to move into the Bachelor Officer Quarters on Ford Island,

and consequently, found himself living out of his travel bag more often than not.

He left his office with Moffett's admonitions echoing in his mind. Walking to the passenger ferry, he grew increasingly troubled. He debated with himself alone in the back of the half-empty bus to town. By the time he reached the trolley terminal, he'd come to the conclusion that he would have to call it off with Akiko. Interracial relationships were viewed with considerably more tolerance in the multicultural mix of Hawaii than they were on the Mainland, where prejudice against crossing race lines could be ferocious. *It's for her own good*, he assured himself. *It's not fair for me to put her in jeopardy.*

At his stop, John Rodgers jumped down from the King Street trolley. He left the late afternoon heat of the downtown sidewalk to step into the cool of the restaurant they had chosen for the evening. The charming little eatery, one of his and Akiko's favorites, was located in a two-story brick building in the narrow lane called Merchant Street. It was one block from the Honolulu waterfront harbor, and three blocks from Masa Mikami's office.

A number of interconnected wooden-bladed ceiling fans spun in syncopated harmony above his head. Stained-glass windows filtered the late afternoon sun, creating a colorful rainbow ambience. As John's eyes adjusted to the dimly lit space, he was greeted by the hostess, who immediately guided him to a booth in the back, where Akiko sat waiting.

Her face lit up at the sight of him, and John's heart sank. He thanked the hostess and slid easily into the high-backed green leather bench across from Akiko. The hostess placed menus on the table. Without opening his, John ordered iced tea for the two of them. Once the hostess had put their glasses on the table and left, John reached across for Akiko's hands.

"Akiko, we have to talk."

She was instantly concerned for him. "So serious! What is it, John?"

He stalled, putting off the bad news, "Several things. I received a telegram today from Ethel's attorney in California. They finally got all the papers filed and now it's only a matter of time before the divorce is final."

"But, John, that is wonderful! It has been such a long ordeal for you. And now you will soon be a free man!" Blushing, she stammered, "I mean, you will be, um, able to do as you like . . ." Unable to work her way out of the corner, she simply shrugged and giggled.

John felt awful, but he still couldn't bring himself to drop the bomb. "There's more. I got a call from Admiral Moffett. They've approved my choice of San Francisco for the point of departure. In fact they've agreed to the whole plan as I outlined it."

"Oh John, I am so happy for you. They saw that you were right."

"We still don't have a firm date, but I imagine we'll be leaving for California in a week or so."

"Ah, so soon? Tell me something, Mr. John Rodgers. All of your news is good, and yet your face is full of sadness. Why is that?"

John still had hold of Akiko's hands, but he couldn't meet her eyes.

"Akiko, I don't know how to say this so that you'll understand. I'm not even sure I understand it completely myself." He paused to steel himself, and could feel her hands grow tense in his. "I think we need to stop seeing each other. I'm concerned that if our friendship grows into something more serious that you'll end up being hurt. Your father could be at risk as well." Trying to remember the argument he had rehearsed, John plowed on, hating the words even as they tumbled from his lips, "Akiko, the mission I'm about to undertake will place me under severe public scrutiny; and as a result you could be subjected to a racial smear campaign. The American press can be spiteful; they'll stop at nothing to juice up a story. They don't care whose life they damage, as long as the story sells papers. I couldn't bear to make you vulnerable to that." John pleaded, "I don't want you hurt because of me."

The silence that followed seemed endless. Finally Akiko spoke. "I need an honest answer. Are you worried about me or yourself?"

The question stunned him. As usual, she had gone to the very heart of him. Gazing steadily at him, and refusing to let go of his hands, she continued, "What you are talking about does not frighten me. Let me tell you a story. Some time after my mother's death, my father tried to arrange a marriage for me with a 'good' Japanese boy. Someone who was, he thought, appropriate for me. I suppose the boy was handsome in his way—he certainly thought so. Nevertheless, what was important to my father was his traditional Japanese background. He was from an affluent and influential family that had just moved into our neighborhood from Hokkaido.

"Despite my own reservations, I felt it was my duty to respect my father's wishes, and this boy began to call on me. After we dated a few times, his true nature began to show itself. He had been raised in the samurai tradition and soon began to demand subservience from me in all things. I had to walk behind him, to say only what would please him." Akiko smiled ruefully, "The role of a traditional Japanese woman is not easy to assume for one raised as an American.

"One evening, when we were dining with friends of his, something I said irritated him—embarrassed him in front of them. He didn't say anything at the time, but I could see he was upset. Later that evening, as he walked me home, I asked what was wrong. He turned and hit me with the back of his hand—hard! Hard enough to make my nose bleed. Then, instead of being contrite, he blamed me for what had just happened, and demanded an apology."

"My god . . . !"

"That was the last time that I saw him. I never told my father, and I'm sure the boy's family never heard what happened from him; and that is just as well. Had it been known, the result would have been discord within our little community."

John was silent, horrified by the abuse she had described. Akiko shook her head gently.

"Do you see what I am trying to say? This was a case where supposedly everything lined up—the culture, the race, the religion—and yet it turned out to be a disaster for us both. I am sure he would have been miserable with me as well.

"What you and I have is more than many get to experience in a lifetime, and for me, that far outweighs the differences between us. I do not wish it to end because of what others might say or think. The risks you describe do not frighten me nearly as much as the thought of losing you."

John was ashamed of himself in the face of her clarity. If she could put everything on the line for him, how could he do anything but try to match her courage?

"Akiko, I'm sorry. I've been such an ass. Please forgive me." Shaking his head at his own idiocy, he told her, "I don't want it to end either. Whatever lies ahead, we'll meet it together."

"Are you sure?"

"Yes. Yes, I'm sure." He leaned across the table and kissed her on her forehead.

Akiko squeezed his hands lightly then withdrew hers. She gazed down and wrapped them around her glass.

John couldn't read her. He was suddenly apprehensive. Had his doubts offended her? Was she now having her own second thoughts because of his lack of faith? As he watched her anxiously, Akiko tucked her chin slightly. A long moment passed.

Finally: "So, then, Mr. John Rodgers, do you still want to see me?"

"Yes. Damn it, yes, Akiko!"

"Hmm. Then I guess now that you are about to be single, and because you will be going away from me for a while, perhaps I should tell you *my* news for today?"

John nodded, both relieved and curious. "Please."

Akiko continued, "My father took the train to Waianae this afternoon to visit my uncle, and he won't be home until tomorrow. I thought it might be an opportunity for me to see how the other half lives." Blushing ever so slightly, she said, "I have booked a room for tonight at the Moana Hotel in Waikiki. I wonder . . . do you think you might know someone who would be interested in spending the night there with me?"

Recognizing the significance of the offer, John was stunned. Collecting himself he said quietly, "Akiko, are you sure?"

"Yes, Mr. John Rodgers, I'm sure." Grinning mischievously she asked, "Now, who do you have in mind?"

"God, Akiko, I love you."

"I'm glad. Because I love you, too." It was the first time the word had passed between them. "Now let us finish our tea and leave. I understand that at the Moana, they will even serve you dinner in your room. Shall we find out?"

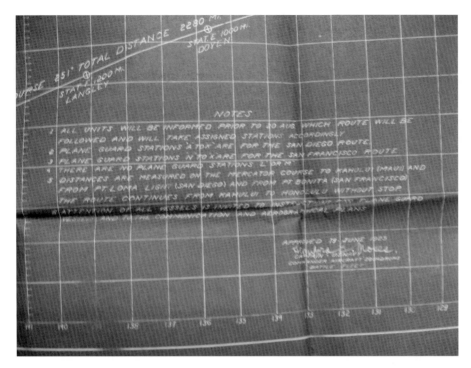

A portion of the actual chart submitted by Commander John Rodgers, which was approved and signed on June 19, 1925. The chart plotted two routes to Hawaii, one originating from San Diego and one from San Francisco. The decision to use the San Francisco course was dictated by the slightly shorter distance and the public relations coup that San Francisco's Diamond Jubilee celebration provided. On the chart, Rodgers proposed the placement of specific navy vessels at two-hundred-mile intervals along the rhumb line. Note the remarkably precise lettering that Rodgers employed (and was noted for), considering the deteriorating state of his eyesight.

Chapter 19

Sunday—July 26, 1925

1:05 PM Eastern Time

The *Shenandoah* was flying once again. Lieutenant Commander Zachary Lansdowne had been successfully performing surveillance missions with the scouting fleet in the Atlantic, occasionally being towed by the *Patoka* while moored to that ship's mast. Although not as much fun as sneaking up on an unsuspecting ship for a practice bombing run, it was surprisingly challenging duty.

Both Robinson's sailors on the *Patoka* and Lansdowne's aviators on the ZR-1 had gotten pretty good at catching the mooring mast. Despite their fabulous first success a year ago, this was still a relatively new operation, with a sharp and unforgiving on-the-job learning curve. There had been several close calls, and quite a few missed passes, especially when the wind was up, but overall, both crews continued to validate Moffett's concept with regularity.

Outfitting the huge zeppelin was never easy. In addition to the obvious logistical challenges, it was the point of greatest vulnerability for a dirigible. Consequently, the crews were always on the lookout for ways to speed up the process. Besides supplying the necessary food and supplies for a crew of forty, the *Patoka* was also responsible for replacing helium and pumping thousands of gallons of water and aviation gas aboard the *Shenandoah*. The water's primary use was as ballast. The ZR-1 would expel the water either to gain altitude or slow rate-of-descent. As a result, her water tanks, which held over eleven hundred gallons, needed to be topped up every time she docked. Then there was the element of danger: aviation-grade gasoline was considerably more combustible than ordinary automobile gas. During fueling, sparks from static electricity posed an ever-present risk. It was critical for the dirigible to be grounded at all times, lest an errant spark set off a major explosion.

Towing the dirigible was another thing. As big as she was, the *Patoka* certainly could have used more horsepower, because trailing the huge balloon was not as easy as it sounded. To begin with, the *Patoka*'s stately pace was problematic. Her top speed was only eleven knots when unfettered, and that was markedly reduced whenever they had the ZR-1 in tow. And the *Shenandoah* tended to drift when confronted with a crosswind, slowing the ship even further and making it more difficult for Commander Robinson to hold a proper course.

However, the real problems occurred when the *Patoka* wanted to proceed downwind with the *Shenandoah* in tow. If the breeze was stronger than the *Patoka*'s reduced top speed of about eight knots, the *Shenandoah*'s stern would swing out to as much as a ninety-degree angle from the ship. If the swing proceeded any further, it could seriously jeopardize the dirigible, possibly tearing off the nose section—and if the fuel lines were compromised, there was significant potential for fire and/or explosion. As a result, it became standard procedure to avoid towing in conditions with the wind coming from astern. Unfortunately, that could not always be avoided. And today, as the *Shenandoah* prepared to disengage from the *Patoka* with a strong and variable breeze, the tension onboard was palpable. Everyone knew this maneuver was going to be touch and go.

"Time?"

"Sir, confirm thirteen-oh-five eastern."

"Sir. We have topped off the water ballast and disconnected the hoses."

"Good. Weight?"

"Sir, 9,055 pounds, sir."

Repeating the numbers for the sake of the log, Lansdowne responded, "Confirming nine, zero, five, five pounds of water ballast. Gas bags?"

Another voice called, "Sir, eighty-four percent full, and balanced on all twenty bags."

Absorbing these numbers, Lansdowne said, "Eight, four percent full. Fuel load?"

"Sir, we have completed refueling at 16,070 pounds, and all tanks have been vented and secured. Hoses not yet retracted."

"Reading one, six, zero, seven, zero pounds fuel. Correct?"

"Aye, aye."

"Compliment?"

"Aye, skipper. Thirty-nine souls."

"*Patoka*'s heading?"

"Due north, sir."

"Attitude?"

"Sir, bubble down one degree and steady. Forty-five degrees starboard trail."

Lansdowne did not like those last numbers. It meant the *Shenandoah* was canted to the right of the stern of the *Patoka* at a considerable angle. "Confirm four, five starboard trail. Let's get those fuel lines retracted, pronto!"

"Aye, sir. Working on it."

"Wind?"

"Sir, six knots from the northwest, but gusty." And with that report, the *Shenandoah* rocked sideways like a huge cradle.

Lansdowne's voice was calm in the face of potential disaster. He ordered, "Props disengaged. All engines start."

From within the control pod, several voices called in sequence, "Ignition. Start. One, running at idle." Then, "Two, running at idle." And so it continued until all five engines were started.

The wind pummeled the monstrous airship again. Suddenly, two tense voices chimed in. "Sir, wind gusting to twelve from the west."

"Trail now eight, zero degrees starboard."

Again the huge ship pitched from the increased side wind.

Keeping his own nerves under control, Lansdowne asked, "How are we doing on retracting those fuel lines?"

"Sir, forty yards to go."

"As quick as you can, mister."

A third voice was heard. "Sir, attitude exceeding ninety degrees starboard trail." It was as if the stern of the *Shenandoah* was vying with the *Patoka* to take the lead.

"Radio Commander Robinson aboard the *Patoka*. Request immediate left turn to two, seven, zero."

"Roger, request *Patoka* change heading to two, seven zero."

Aboard the *Patoka* Commander Robinson received the flash request, but had already anticipated the maneuver and had ordered the helm of the *Patoka* hard left. Getting the long vessel to turn quickly enough was another thing.

Back aboard the *Shenandoah* Lansdowne asked tersely, "Hoses?"

"Almost there, sir." With the reply, an even more powerful gust lifted the dirigible's stern, precipitously increasing the downhill angle of the floor.

Immediately, "Sir, bubble down six degrees and increasing."

"Engage propellers. Reverse one-third."

A panicked call overrode the responses from the throttle controllers. "Swinging past one-twenty. Sir, one-thirty, no, one forty!"

"Fuel lines?"

"Sir, almost . . ."

Watching the fueling officer closely, Lansdowne saw his relief before he heard the report he'd been waiting for.

Lansdowne shouted, "Disengage! All lines clear! All engines, full reverse!" The massive *Shenandoah* slowly backed away from the *Patoka*'s tower. But she was still in danger.

"Sir, the *Patoka*'s stern is swinging straight for us!" Because the huge mother ship was now free of the tethered craft, her turn to port was accelerating, and the 125-foot tower on her stern was heading directly toward the ZR-1. As the *Shenandoah* backed away, the giant tower seemed to be chasing her.

Lansdowne called, "Blow ballast one through four." Immediately four tons of water cascaded onto the extreme stern of the *Patoka* and into the Atlantic. The dirigible rose slightly. It was enough. As the

Patoka completed her turn, the tower swung beneath the rising nose cone, missing it by only a few yards. Disaster had been averted.

9:20 AM Hawaii Time

The original nine months' wait had stretched into eleven, and John Rodgers was still in Honolulu. Niggling production problems had continued to plague the new planes. But now with the window of opportunity quickly evaporating, it seemed that the mission was moving forward at last.

In Hawaii, Rodgers' and Snody's crews had trained together for months, devoting themselves entirely to the project. The teams included a pilot, copilot, navigator, mechanic, and radioman for each plane. All had been cross-trained to be able to cover at least one other position. And to a man, they were in the best physical shape of their lives as a result of a workout plan Rodgers had implemented. Then they'd had to wait.

Now, the day before he was to sail for California, John stood silently at the open window of his room at the Moana Hotel. After their glorious first night together, five weeks before, the Moana held special significance for John and Akiko. He had invited her to share a romantic farewell weekend with him there.

As Akiko showered, John stared down at the busy scene four stories below. Down on the beach, the Waikiki tourists fresh off the cruise ships stretched out on the sand, trying to darken their skin. Assorted naturally bronzed Hawaiian beach boys and surfers starkly contrasted the pale visitors. A number of the fairer guests wisely took shelter in chaises beneath the multitude of brightly colored beach umbrellas.

Wrapped around John's waist was a luxurious white Turkish towel with an elegant "M" embroidered on it. The summer trade winds were at their glorious best, and John let the breeze cool his body, still damp from their morning's lovemaking. Only crumbs remained on the large silver breakfast tray that covered most of the small room-service tabletop. John lifted the coffee pot and poured the last of the rich dark brew into one of the dainty china cups, sipping absentmindedly.

The previous month had been a blur. His pending divorce had become public knowledge on base, as had his relationship with another woman—a Japanese woman. He had been too preoccupied preparing for the mission to pay much attention to the rumors circulating, but from time to time he allowed himself to wonder if his career might be in jeopardy. At this moment, however, he didn't care. His focus was elsewhere.

John had to admit he felt more confident in the potential success of his mission than he had been at the outset. He had realized early on that Admiral Moffett had put himself and the U.S. Navy on the line for this mission, and that meant John's head was on the chopping block. But Admiral Moffett had been enormously supportive, offering John all the backup in Washington, D.C. he needed. And John had needed it, as he had some major problems to solve. Big problems necessitated big ideas.

One of his ideas involved communications and tracking. Rodgers knew that joint task-force maneuvers were scheduled for the waters off Hawaii in the late summer. Consequently, there would be a large assortment of ships in the eastern Pacific. Destroyers, cruisers, multiple fuel and supply ships, and even Moffett's newly reconfigured ship, the revolutionary aircraft carrier *Langley,* would be participating. John asked Moffett if the ships might be available to assist in their mission, and when John outlined his idea, Moffett had heartily agreed.

John's course was a straight-line plot of 240 degrees from San Francisco to Honolulu. A plane's radio transmission range was just over a hundred miles; so John had envisioned placing ships approximately two hundred miles apart all along their intended course. Such positioning of navy ships would allow the seaplanes to be in continual radio contact as they leapfrogged signals along their path. Secondly, the ships would serve as visual guides, keeping the planes on their rhumb-line track to Hawaii. And third, should they run out of gas, or if disaster should strike any of the three flying boats, refueling or rescue would be relatively close at hand.

Rodgers had been frustrated as one delay after another postponed the mission. As he had told Moffett at the start, the best-case scenario would be to attempt the flight in late spring or early summer to take advantage of the strongest trade winds. That had been the original plan, but for reasons beyond Rodgers' control, the mission had been pushed back a number of times, and their scheduled departure date was now August 31. This date pleased Admiral Moffett, as it coincided with San Francisco's Diamond Jubilee, the city's seventy-fifth anniversary celebration, and would mean greatly increased press coverage. It was, however, of considerable concern to John—the trade winds were known to decrease in strength and consistency as the fall approached.

After several construction delays, the two new planes built in Philadelphia were finally finished. Designated PN9-1 and PN9-3, they were expected to arrive in San Diego in a week and a half—not a day too soon by John's calculations. Before being shipped from the East Coast, the new planes had proved their capabilities in in-flight testing. One plane had even been airborne for twenty-eight hours, thirty-five minutes, and twenty-seven seconds, a new endurance record. However, that was still an hour-and-a-half short of what would be necessary to accomplish the mission. And the test had been accomplished with only a pilot onboard a totally stripped aircraft. John knew that the planes would need to perform better than that to succeed. More testing would take place in California.

Meanwhile, in Seattle, Boeing's newfangled plane, the PB1, had been hampered by a series of delays in construction and testing. As a result, the PB1's skipper, Lieutenant Commander Strong, had persisted in pushing John for a later start date. He wanted to go in mid-October. John was increasingly irritated by Strong's inability to recognize the importance of the summer trade winds to the success of the mission. It was generally assumed that the new Boeing seaplane would be faster than the PN9s, and with greater range. John wondered if Strong's stalling tactics were really necessary, or just an attempt to garner the spotlight, should the PN9s fall short of the goal. Rodgers tried to be fair. He worried that his own opinions were being tainted by Strong's letters; the tone of the lieutenant commander's correspondence bordered on braggadocio.

While John wanted to keep an open mind, he couldn't shake the fact that Strong had some well-placed Washington, D.C. contacts and seemed to be using them to gain prominence in the press. One reporter had picked up on the planned mission and reported it as a race between the old guard—Rodgers—and the new navy as represented by Strong and his crew. A timely newspaper article had mentioned Rodgers only in terms of his famous forbears, while prominently featuring Lieutenant Commander Strong's picture, implying that Strong was in charge. John struggled with this misrepresentation, while Strong denied having anything to do with it. For his part, Admiral Moffett remained mute on the situation, believing any press was good press.

John was brought back to reality as he felt Akiko's arms encircle his waist from behind. Naked, and fresh from the shower, she pressed her small breasts against his back and leaned her head sideways against his broad shoulder blades. She smelled deliciously of the Moana's fragrant coconut shampoo. John folded his arms on top of hers and rocked gently.

"Akiko, I love you. I'm going to miss you."

"Well, Mr. John Rodgers, you'd better miss me. It's not often I sneak away to spend a weekend with a strange man."

Spinning her around John held her shoulders and looked deep into her eyes. "I meant what I said last night. You are the most important thing in the world to me. When we get back, I'll be finally divorced, and then we are going to get married."

Looking down thoughtfully, Akiko said, "We have much to discuss before that can happen. If you complete this flight of yours, the success will assure your career, and then the last thing you will need is a Japanese wife."

"But Akiko, you're as American as I am."

"That may be, John, but not everyone is going to look at it that way."

"I don't care. I love you. Nothing can change my mind. Listen carefully, young lady. I'll say it again. I love you! And if you'll have me, and your father will allow it, we're getting married right after this mission."

There was a brief moment of silence before Akiko gazed up at John. Her eyes were bright with unshed tears. "I could not want anything more."

The *Patoka,* towing the ZR-1 at a difficult angle. The huge dirigible was subject to even minor wind disturbances and was therefore never towed in a tail wind.

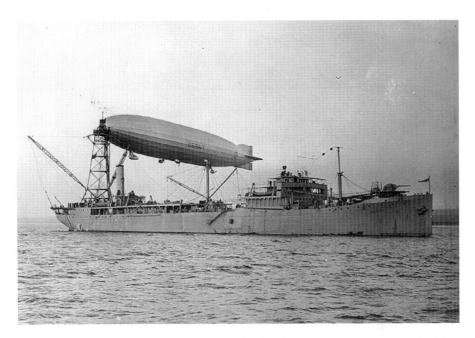

This picture illustrates what happened when the *Patoka* did not tow the *Shenandoah* fast enough, or if the wind changed direction suddenly. This is a dangerous angle and could have caused serious problems if it had become any more acute.

Even at anchor, problems could occur, as the dirigible would swing with a wind change well before the ship could respond. Although of dubious quality, this image captures such a dramatic moment.

The Moana Hotel

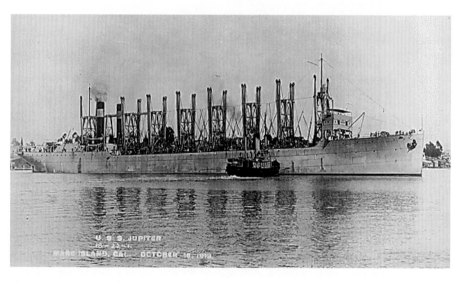

The USS *Jupiter,* a coal transport. At the conclusion of the Great War, she was transformed into the nation's first true aircraft carrier, the USS *Langley.*

She had been rechristened in honor of James Langley, an early proponent of American aviation. It was an enormous ship (as shown here in comparison to a typical U.S. Navy destroyer), although not as big as the massive dreadnought battleships. She was one of a kind, with a totally flat fore-to-aft landing platform and complete lack of superstructure. The flight deck seemed poised on multiple legs above the ship's hull, which made her look top heavy. In fact, her landing platform was so high above the water line that it was doubtful any waves would ever break there.

Chapter 20

Monday—July 27, 1925

8:22 AM Hawaii Time

The date of departure dawned bright and temperate. Moored against a Pearl Harbor pier, the USS *Aroostook* emitted a thin column of charcoal-gray smoke from one of her twin stacks. The *Aroostook* was a strange looking warship, one of a small handful of seaplane tenders that serviced the U.S. Navy. In a former life, she had been a coal-fired transport freighter, but eight years ago she had been reborn. New diesel-fueled boilers and a complete refitting had transformed her into a reasonably modern, unique warship. The *Aroostook* normally carried a single patrol seaplane off her stern, but today she was unburdened aft. She would play a crucial role in monitoring the return nonstop attempt: she would be the primary ship for refueling or recovery should one or more of the planes fall short of the mark. In one hour's time, the *Aroostook* would sail for San Diego, serving as the personal transport for Rodgers, Snody, and their crews.

The new twin PN9 aircraft to be used for the attempt were also on their way to San Diego. The construction and testing of the redesigned planes had finally been completed at the prestigious naval aircraft factory in Philadelphia. The planes were securely wrapped in oilcloth and loaded on a freighter. The freighter was en route—scheduled to transit the Panama Canal the next day, and then head north for the rendezvous in Southern California.

The *Aroostook*'s skipper, Commander W. R. Van Auken, strode out on the bridge. Seamen were scurrying about on the wharf below, their sleeves rolled up and their gray jumpsuits stained greasy black from manhandling the huge tar-soaked hawsers that secured the ship to the pier, and the fuel-oil hoses that gave the ship her lifeblood.

Many wives and girlfriends had come to the quay to bid farewell; a number were crying. Already, most of the off-duty sailors onboard lined the rail, jostling for position and waving goodbye. Chief Petty Officer Kiles Pope's wife, Lilly, held an infant balanced on one hip, while a toddler clung tightly to her petticoats. Little Bobby, the oldest, and three progressively smaller Pope offspring raced around the wharf in a rambunctious game of tag.

Not far from Lilly Pope's brood, two young Hawaiian beauties waved up at the ship, giggling at the wolf whistles coming from above. Wild Bill and Sparky leaned over the ship's rail, paying special attention to Aunty Momi's *hanai* daughters, Lei and Lani. Uniform regulations at a Hawaiian departure were somewhat lax, as the multiple flower lei both sailors sported attested.

A black Model-T Ford taxicab slid to a stop near the gangway, and Commander John Rodgers jumped out from the rear seat. He bent to retrieve a huge navy-issue sea bag. Throwing it over his left shoulder, he wrapped his right arm around the waist of the petite Japanese woman who'd also exited the cab. He lifted her clear of the car and kissed her long and hard. Her hat, half crushed by the passionate embrace, slipped off her head and dangled from a bright orange ribbon. Enthusiastic whistles rained down on them from the ship's deck. The loudest came from John's crew. Lowering Akiko gently to the ground, Rodgers looked up and acknowledged the razzing with a good-natured wave.

Then it was time for goodbye. John took Akiko's hands and gazed steadily at her. "I love you, and I'll write as soon as I can."

"I'll write you too. But, just please come home safe to me."

"I will . . . Now I've got to go." A quick kiss, then John headed for the gangway. As he reached it, he stopped and turned for one last look.

Akiko stood waving a small yellow scarf, and watched as John sprinted up the gangway. Blinking back tears, she whispered, "I love you, my Mr. John Rodgers."

3:37 PM Hawaii Time

The ship left Pearl Harbor, rounded the famous Diamond Head Crater at the end of Waikiki Beach, and headed east-northeast, bound for Southern California. Within hours, most of John's crew was bored. They had been kept so busy during the past several months in preparation for the upcoming mission that unstructured leisure time felt odd. Suddenly, the two PN9 crews were simply idle passengers on a ship. By nightfall, Sparky Stantz was miserably seasick. It took him a full twenty-four hours to get his sea legs; he underwent a fair amount of testosterone-laden teasing as a result.

Even though the two crews knew each other well and got along, it was only natural for good-natured competition to surface on the small vessel. With time on their hands, the men wagered on everything from who could reassemble a radio fastest to who could eat the most peas. The rivalries were mostly friendly, though, and John took care to see they stayed that way. Morale and teamwork would be crucial to the challenge that lay ahead of them.

By the third day at sea, Wild Bill Bowlin and his inseparable partner in crime, Sparky Stantz, had wrangled their way into both the radio and engine rooms. The tiny quarters of the radio room were impossibly cramped for both them *and* the sailor on duty, but they managed. During their extended visit to the communications hub, Sparky and Bill even tried to rewire one of the radios so that it would have a longer range, before the officer of the day intervened and good-naturedly tossed them out. Looking for more mischief, they were soon belowdecks, traipsing about the intricate and convoluted piping of the steam boilers and the attendant machinery. While the elaborate bowels of the engine room were considerably more spacious than the radio room had been, the noise was deafening. By the latter part of the day, they were both wearing earplugs and coveralls that were splattered with oil. To their delight, their creative curiosity was not only tolerated but actually appreciated by most of the *Aroostook*'s crew.

At John's urging, Lieutenant Kiles Pope spent much of the trip befriending the launch and retrieval team—a good group to know if you ever needed them. He learned a good deal from these specialized seamen that manned the seaplane gantry. These were the men responsible for off-loading waterborne aircraft in the open ocean, and the safe recovery of same. These men were also schooled in the tricky art of refueling a plane as it floated in the open ocean. Pope watched, fascinated by the procedure. First, a crane was swung out to the leeward side of the ship on a ninety-degree angle. Then a buoyed line from the end of the gantry was played out. The crew of a seaborne plane would capture and secure that line to their bow. The crane operators above on the *Aroostook* would then reel in the line until the plane was amidships, being pulled on a parallel course with the ship. A messenger line would then be tossed to the crew on the plane. As they pulled in this line, a fuel hose would be attached to it. Once the hose was secured onboard the plane, fueling could begin. This was a difficult enough procedure in calm waters, and Kiles wanted to learn all he could about doing it in rolling seas, at the same time hoping he would never have to use this knowledge.

Lieutenant Allen Snody and Lieutenant Arthur Graves—the command pilot and copilot of the second seaplane's crew—honed their navigation skills along with Byron and John, taking several independent sextant sights each day and comparing their results. In addition to plotting the ship's progress, these four men also closely monitored the prevailing strength and direction of the wind and currents. John compiled copious notes on all these variables and then shared his findings with the crews of both planes.

From the start, the *Aroostook*'s skipper, Commander Van Auken—or "Van," as he preferred—was quite cordial with his guests onboard. But he became especially friendly with John during the course of the crossing.

Van was an avid student of naval history, and he considered the Rodgers family to be the closest thing the U.S. had to military royalty. Van loved having the opportunity to discuss the nuances and little-known details of John's famous predecessors' naval victories, over coffee in the officers' mess.

"During the War of 1812, I understand the British dispatched an entire regiment to your ancestral home in Maryland and burned it and your family's inn to the ground."

"Whoa . . . Well, yes."

"It's true then? They did it in revenge for your great-grandfather's many victories on the open seas?"

"That's what I've been told."

"John, this is amazing. They actually burned your family's home before they torched the White House!"

John chuckled ruefully. "I'm not sure they actually went after ours first, but it was all a part of the same mission."

Van's good humor and lively personality belied his bookish background. Over the course of their conversations, John came to like and respect the man, and a solid friendship was formed.

Because the *Aroostook*'s operations were so closely tied to aircraft maneuvers, Van Auken was personally excited for the crews he was transporting. He fully understood the ultimate goal and what it could mean for the navy's future. Plus the *Aroostook* was to be assigned an important station along John's rhumb line during the mission. They were to be located at station "V," eighteen hundred miles from San Francisco. This position was fairly close to Hawaii, and would be critical if the planes ran low on fuel in the final portion of their flight. Although any of the vessels along the route might be able to refuel the planes, the *Aroostook* was obviously better equipped and more familiar with this difficult procedure. More importantly, the *Aroostook* was the primary recovery vessel should one of the planes have to be rescued from the sea.

As Rodgers prepared for the feat of navigation ahead of him, he struggled with the *Aroostook*'s impressive but ungainly set of nautical charts. The ship's extensive compendium of maps had to be overlaid one on top of the other on a large chart table—a luxury John would not have when onboard his new plane. The PN9's navigation station was basically an open cockpit in the nose of the plane to facilitate taking sextant sights.

There was a countertop of sorts in the cubbyhole that the navigator could access by bending forward, but it was small and cramped. There was no way John would be able to use normal charts, but he had an epiphany. He approached Van with his idea.

John suggested that normal marine charts—for that matter, almost all maps—ran horizontally west to east. Since he would be flying from east-northeast to west-southwest he would have to lay a patchwork quilt of multiple large rectangles diagonally across his miniscule chart table. This would be virtually impossible. Therefore he wondered if they could lay the direct rhumb-line course horizontally, and instead, angle the longitude and latitude. Furthermore, John suggested that this map should be created in one long piece, designed to unroll left to right, not unlike ancient papyrus scrolls. With a map of this type, he could easily plot his course in a compact space.

Van immediately recognized the brilliance of the idea, and had his crew assist in manufacturing just such a map. With Rodgers' input, Van had his machine shop produce the rollers, then ordered his staff to cannibalize several of the extra charts that all naval vessels carried. By the time the USS *Aroostook* approached San Diego harbor, Commander John Rodgers was the proud owner of a chart the likes of which had never before existed.

One of Admiral Moffett's innovative ideas implemented during the First World War was the conversion of the USS *Aroostook* to be a seaplane tender. As such, she was uniquely equipped to launch or retrieve seaplanes from her stern. She was similarly capable of refueling seaplanes that were still in the water.

The USS *Aroostook*, arguably the U.S. Navy's most famous seaplane tender. A small seaplane is seen on the aft deck in this photograph.

A brass sextant

A sextant is used to measure the angle of elevation of a celestial object in comparison to the horizon for navigational purposes. Making this measurement is known as "taking a sight." The angle and the time of the sight, if observed and computed accurately, can be used to calculate location on a nautical or aeronautical chart.

Chapter 21

Monday—August 3, 1925

9:52 AM Pacific Time

Upon their arrival in San Diego, the PN9 crews had received their new billets and set up shop. But there was little more to do until the planes arrived, so Commander Rodgers had issued all the men two-day passes. Wild Bill and Sparky did not waste any time taking advantage of the opportunity. Early this morning, they had climbed aboard the coastal train and headed north to San Juan Capistrano, a sleepy beach town south of Los Angeles.

The brass bell clanged loudly as the 280,000-pound Pacific Southern locomotive slowed to a stop at the small coastal train station. Its sooty black coal smoke drifted away quickly in the midmorning sea breeze. The swarthy locomotive wheezed intermittently, spewing bursts of steam.

The summer sun was bright and the day was already warm. Dressed in casual civilian clothes, Wild Bill and Sparky jumped down from the Pullman-Standard Suburban coaches. Almost immediately, they were greeted with bear hugs and a deep baritone "Aloha!" from their friend, Duke Kahanamoku. Duke had moved to Southern California earlier in the year, and the guys had stayed in contact. Duke led the boys to a well-worn Model-T pickup truck. They tumbled their gear into the back, where Duke's prized koa wood surfboard was already secured. The three of them squeezed tightly into the cab.

"So how're the waves here?" was Sparky's first question.

"Surf's up, braddah—at least today! We're going to the break at the entrance to Newport Beach harbor."

"Great!"

Duke continued, "It doesn't usually get this big over here. There must be a storm out at sea, because last night the swells started growing, and they were even bigger this morning."

The animated conversation continued for the relatively short drive to the beach. Duke wanted to know the latest from home, and the guys filled him in as best they could. The topic of the Akana sisters came up, and Duke, ever the big brother, wanted to make sure the young ladies were being properly treated. The boys' words tumbled out, but the grins and their obvious affection told Duke all he needed to know.

They arrived at the harbor entrance and were thrilled with the size of the waves.

"Whoa, brah! I'm amazed. They're even bigger than this morning—this is the biggest surf I've seen since I got here!" Duke yelled as he parked the truck on the edge of the breakwater.

The surf which normally curled calmly over the shallows on one side of the harbor's ship channel, was breaking in a continuous wave all the way across the mouth. The harbor's entrance was effectively closed out by the huge eight-to-ten-foot swells. Closer in, the white, frothy foam churned down the channel in relentless rows. This seemingly spent surf traveled all the way into the breakwater, only to explode in magnificent fury on the jagged boulders, throwing white spray high into the air.

Despite the gorgeous Southern California day, this was storm surge. This surf was a far cry from the beautiful long blue-green rollers of Waikiki Beach. It was obviously too much for less-than-expert surfers. Indicating the powerful waves pounding behind him, Duke said, "Guys, I'm sorry but I'm not sure you're ready for this."

Wild Bill and Sparky nodded in unison, not wanting to appear chicken, but grateful for his assessment. They both knew they'd have to be crazy to try even swimming in these conditions. Bill piped up, "But you go, Duke. We've got to see this!"

Duke untied his famous surfboard, lovingly named *"Papa nui."* It was humongous, measuring sixteen feet long and weighing 114 pounds. Sparky grabbed one end of the giant laminated plank and helped Duke negotiate the uneven rocks of the breakwater wall. As they walked, Duke told them to be on the lookout for two of his friends who were planning to meet them here. Duke laughed, "It'll be tough to miss them. I think they're the only two other surfers in all of California, and they'll be bringing their boards." With a long look at the imposing swells, he continued dubiously, "But this may be too nasty even for them."

Then, without further hesitation, Duke slid *Papa nui* on top of the next boiling peak. Instantly, he was horizontal on top of the surfboard as the wave started to recede from the rocks. With the strong and practiced alternating strokes of an Olympic freestyle champion, Duke glided expertly out into the ocean's fury.

It wasn't too long before he had knifed through several of the powerful curls two hundred yards out, turned, and readied himself to catch a wave. He didn't have to wait at all, as the next swell was the largest they had seen. Paddling powerfully then rising quickly to his feet, the golden-skinned Hawaiian hurtled down the face of a twelve-foot wave. Crouching slightly, with his left foot forward, he carved a lazy S as the wave collapsed behind him. Duke rode the angry foam of the dying wave out before dropping prone onto the board and heading back out for more.

Wild Bill and Sparky hooted and hollered their approval from their wet, slippery perches. Duke continued to put on a private show for the Indiana natives until several curious local residents made their way out onto the rocks. Within a half-hour, a small crowd had gathered to watch the water wizard perform his magic.

Suddenly, one of the locals pointed out to sea beyond the breaking surf. A fairly large commercial fishing boat was wallowing slow and low in the water, obviously struggling. It seemed to be trying to limp into the harbor.

The talk on the breakwater became animated, as the stormy harbor entrance seemed certain suicide for the heavily laden vessel.

"Those guys'll never make it," Sparky hollered to Bill over the crashing surf.

Bill nodded and called back, "Yup, they're in trouble, all right."

"Look, there are a lot of men onboard!" yelled someone from the crowd. It was true, there appeared to be more than two dozen souls huddled, hanging onto the rails.

And then, catastrophe. A rogue wave swamped the gunnels of the boat and rolled her over sideways as if she were a piece of driftwood. The wave continued roiling through, and when next the spectators could see it, the fishing boat was upside down in the turbulent foam.

Cries went up in unison from the shore, but Duke was already streaking out to the wreckage. He reached the closest body and tried to pull him up on his surfboard, but it was obvious that it was too late: the back of the fisherman's skull had been smashed. Duke focused on the next closest, two men fighting to stay afloat but certainly not good swimmers. He paddled quickly to the first and manhandled him onto *Papa nui*. Duke was broadside to the surf as he reached the second man. As he pulled that fisherman aboard, a giant wave smashed into the three of them, tossing them like popcorn in a popper. Luckily, Duke was able to keep the men on the board, and they attempted to ride with the flow. As the wave subsided, Duke regained control and headed for the far end of the breakwater near the public beach. He knew there was no way he could land these men safely on the rocky wall where the crowd had gathered.

Sparky, Wild Bill, and some of the crowd realized what he was doing and scrambled along the rocky breakwater back towards the beach. Bill shouted to someone to get to a phone and call for help. In short order, the two sailors had waded into the churning undertow just as Duke managed to reach them. The aviators quickly pulled the two terrified, waterlogged survivors from the surf.

Before the foursome had their feet on dry land, Duke had turned around and was already heading back out. He paddled like a man possessed. He knew there was little else that could be done in these conditions. Certainly no one could swim out, and there was no boat that could chance the wave-ravaged channel.

When he again reached the wreckage, three hundred yards out, Duke ignored the dead bodies bobbing in the spume, and focused on the survivors clinging tenaciously to the overturned hull. He was able to load another couple of men onto his board and paddle through the violent spindrift, once more passing them to his two pals in the shore break.

Before the disaster had occurred, Duke had been just about to come into shore for a rest. Now his shoulders were crying out in pain—pain he had to ignore.

Paddling out for the third time, he thought he might have more success if he took only one person at a time. This would allow him to make quicker, less taxing trips. He reached the scene again and shouted his plan to the desperate fishermen. Selecting a man with an obviously broken arm, Duke loaded him onto the board and paddled back like a dervish. His decision had been the right one, and with only the weight of one other onboard, he was able to surf most of the way back to shore.

A fourth trip began as more and more people gathered on shore watching the Herculean effort. An ambulance and the police had arrived and were assisting the survivors as they were brought in. They were able to do little else but watch the rescue effort. At this point, Duke's two surfing pals pulled up. Without wasting a second, they unloaded their huge surfboards and joined the rescue.

By the end of the day, Duke had personally saved eight men, and his surf buddies had rescued another two apiece. Twenty-nine men had gone into the water and seventeen had perished, but twelve survived due to what the Newport Beach police chief called "the most superhuman surfboard rescue act the world has ever seen." Duke, who had moved to California hoping to break into films, had become a celebrity faster than even he could have dreamed.

When the hoopla died down that day, Duke, Wild Bill, Sparky, and Duke's two surf buddies eventually loaded up their surfboards and trundled back to the house Duke was renting. A small party ensued, but exhaustion soon prevailed, and one by one they collapsed into well-deserved sleep.

Baldwin Pacific 4-6-2 locomotive #2467. These powerful locomotives were the most popular workhorses for many of the United States western railways in the 1920s. Its 4-6-2 designation indicated that it had four leading wheels arranged in a "truck" for stability, with six large coupled driving wheels and two trailing "bogeys."

The Railway Station at San Juan Capistrano

KAHANAMOKU HELPS SAVE 13 IN LAUNCH

Hawaiian Swimmer and Others Go to Their Rescue With Surf Boards—Five Are Drowned.

LAGUNA BEACH, Cal., (Æ).— The Hawaiian swimming star, Duke Kahanamoku, and his fellow surf-board experts, today were the heroes of the beach here, credited with saving the lives of thirteen persons, when the gas launch Thelma capsized last night.

Five of the launch party were drowned before the swimmers could reach them, but the bodies were recovered.

The launch was starting on a fishing trip when it turned over. Kahanamoku and others of his party saved all who could keep themselves afloat until help came, bringing them ashore on their surf boards.

A *New York Times* article from the day after the rescue. The story was picked up by the Associated Press and made headlines across the country, even though the number of those rescued was incorrectly reported—only twelve survived. It also spurred the acceptance of the surfboard as more than just a Hawaiian oddity, but rather as a lifeguard's tool.

Duke Kahanamoku with *Papa nui* ("Big Board") on Waikiki beach

Duke Kahanamoku: hero and winner of five Olympic medals

Chapter 22

Wednesday—August 5, 1925

10:05 AM Pacific Time

At last, the long-awaited prototypes had arrived. Standing at the navy piers in San Diego Harbor, Commander John Rodgers, Lieutenant Commander Allen Snody, and their crews supervised the off-loading of several large wooden crates containing the disassembled components of the twin PN9s. Large portions of the wings had been detached from the fuselages for shipment, leaving only the center stubs in place. The missing sections, floats, and braces had been packed separately and were quickly unloaded and moved to the ramp area, where the reassembly would take place.

Shortly thereafter, both fuselages were carefully deposited in the calm water of the harbor, and then towed to the dock next to the launching ramp. A large, wheeled dolly was backed down the ramp and immersed in the water. The main body of John's plane was pulled stern first onto the dolly and secured to it. A small tractor made short work of pulling the craft up the ramp. A second dolly was submerged and the same procedure was repeated for Snody's fuselage. At that point, the eager crews scrambled to remove the oil-soaked canvas pieces, which had served to protect the aircraft during their journey.

Once the tarpaulins were removed, the planes that greeted the men appeared ungainly, unfinished, and just plain ugly. Perched high on the wheeled dollies without wings or propellers, they did not look like machines the men would want to bet their lives on. Loose wires hung everywhere, and protective grease covered almost all exposed surfaces.

Undaunted, John withdrew two thick assembly manuals from a manila envelope. Handing one to Snody, he said, "OK guys; let's put these ladies back together."

The two crews set to work. Snody gathered his men separately, while Byron called to Kiles, Wild Bill, and Sparky: "Let's get the wings on first. We'll feel better when she looks more like an airplane." Wielding pry bars and hammers, the four of them tore into the crates.

Meanwhile, John rolled up his sleeves and set up a couple of sawhorses and a crate lid to serve as his workbench. He focused on the manual, silently thanking his lucky stars for the large print, the bright outdoor sunlight, and his intimate knowledge of the PN series of seaplanes.

It was a surprisingly simple task for these skilled men to attach the wings; the hardest part was getting the tension correct in the multiple crossed cables that secured the upper wings to the lower ones. The control cables were easier to reconnect, and soon Byron was sitting in the cockpit talking to Kiles, who was lying prostrate over the upper starboard wing. Pulling on the control wheel, Byron called, "Fully back."

"OK, got it." Followed by, "Try, full forward." And in no time the aileron controls were completed.

Compared to wheeled planes, seaplanes were notoriously overbuilt in order to withstand the additional stresses of water takeoffs and landings. They also had to be strong enough to be hoisted onboard a ship in the open ocean, if need be. These planes had to be sturdy. But sturdy meant heavy, and weight was the enemy.

All day long, the crews fussed over their respective planes, and as day lengthened toward night, John stood back to survey the progress. Each plane was nearly fifty feet long, distinguished by the blunt, rounded nose and broad boat shape of its flattened V-shaped lower hull. Both the hull and fuselage were made of steel ribs covered with sheet duralumin—the same rugged, lightweight material used for zeppelin exteriors—and painted drab gray.

Viewed from the front, the bottom of the hull was twice as wide as the narrow, slab-sided cabin that was perched above it. When seen from the side, the hull was unusual in that it had a double step. The bottom of the hull ran horizontally from the rounded bow halfway to the tail, before notching up eight inches. It continued horizontally for seven more feet before it stepped up again, whereupon it angled upward at fifteen degrees all the way to the stern.

The twin wings visually dominated the biplane. Consisting of ash stringers and wooden ribs that were holed to keep them light, their surfaces were tightly wrapped with a heavy fabric that had been water-proofed with dull gray dope paint. The lower wing was sixty-seven feet wide, and bisected the top of the fuselage at the midway point. It carried two distended outboard floats suspended from the wing tips, one or the other of which would touch the water if the plane rocked in the swells. The floats acted to keep the plane upright, much like an outrigger can keep a canoe from rolling over in the surf.

The upper wing was slightly longer and stood a full eight feet above the lower one. It was mounted on six pairs of vertical struts. Multiple cables crisscrossed the wings for strength and stability. The men had tuned the tension in these cables so that the loads would be distributed evenly when flying.

The twin Packard V-12 power plants were mounted twelve feet off the centerline of the plane on either wing. The twin-bladed propellers were enormous: thirteen feet in diameter, hand-hewn wooden sculptures that came uncomfortably close to the fuselage. They were made of ash, with finely buffed metal-clad edges and tips.

Each of the PN9s had twin open cockpits for the pilots, positioned side by side, eight feet forward of the wings. Both of the pilot cockpits had small framed–glass windscreens designed to provide a modicum of protection from the wind. A third, smaller, open-air navigator's cockpit was located right at the nose. It was fitted with a compass mount and an integral half-moon sight. Further aft were two even smaller open-air cockpits for the radioman and the flight mechanic. Two main access hatches were positioned well aft of the wings and steps, one on each side. Two small porthole windows had been installed on either side of the fuselage, one forward, and one aft of the wings—more to provide light in the cabin than for sightseeing.

The rudder and elevator were attached at the rear on the severely narrowed fuselage. The whole tail assembly was made of wood and fabric and was strongly secured with triangulated struts and cables both above and below the horizontal winglet. Painted on each side of the aft portion of the rudder were three vertical stripes—red, white, and blue.

Studying the plane alongside his commander, Byron Connell nudged John. "She looks a bit better now. She's some little baby, isn't she?" And, just like that, the moniker stuck. Soon everyone in Rodgers' crew was calling their plane *Baby*.

Sunset found the aviators tired but gratified, ready to give in to the growing darkness. They'd managed to get the planes completely assembled, but the checks would have to wait until tomorrow. As the ten men ambled across the field toward their quarters, Allen Snody asked, "Skipper, your plane's Number One, and ours is Number Three. What happened to Number Two?"

This question had been lurking in the back of everyone's mind. They all turned to hear John's reply.

"Three planes were built. PN9-2 was the first completed. She was the only one ready to fly before they had to be shipped to us. Subsequently she became the test plane; the one that set the flight endurance record."

Wild Bill chimed in, "Yeah! She flew for over twenty-eight-and-a-half hours."

Snody countered, "But where is she now? Why didn't they send her instead of Number Three?"

John knew how superstitious pilots could be about airplanes. He had hoped to avoid this question but his men deserved an honest answer.

"After her endurance flight, Number Two was declared unfit to fly and was cut up for scrap."

John paused as the men absorbed that information, and then he continued. "Her frame was found to have multiple failures. The backbone of the plane had been severely weakened, apparently by numerous improper welds; so much so that she was damaged beyond repair."

Bill muttered, "Holy shit!"

"Gentlemen, this information's not public knowledge, and I expect you to keep it that way. The press would have a field day with this tidbit if it ever got out, so this will not be discussed beyond ourselves. Understood?"

Hearing no dissent, John continued. "Know this, though, I have been assured that the structural problems have been addressed and should not be an issue with Numbers One and Three."

Snody spoke quietly. "Sir, are you saying that neither of our planes has actually been test flown yet?"

"That is correct." Rodgers raised his chin, hoping to project a confidence he was far from feeling. "And men, that's exactly what we're going to do."

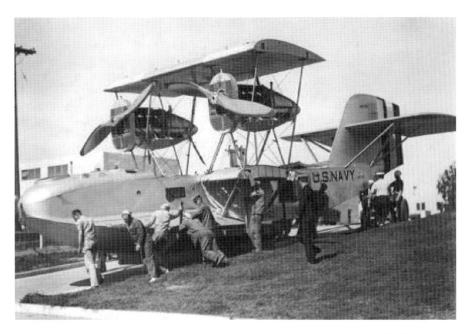

The PN9-1 *(Baby)* upon arrival in San Diego (wings not yet attached).

Rodgers' PN9-1 heeled over in its typical ungainly posture. This was the normal condition of both Rodgers' and Snody's planes at rest. The significant exception was prior to their transpacific flight when they were fully loaded with fuel. At that time the excess weight caused the wing floats to be nearly swamped. The generally awkward stance illustrated above differed markedly from the PB1, which normally floated straight and level.

Outrigger canoes in Polynesia come in two basic types. There are those with a single outrigger, or *ama* (on these canoes, the *ama* acts as a buoyant float if the canoe leans toward it, and as a weight if the canoe leans away from it). Shown above is a double *ama* canoe. The *ama* here are buoyant on both sides. The double *ama* canoe traditionally leans on one *ama* or the other when in calm waters. When in waves, this positioning of the *ama* will allow the canoe to maneuver with greater ease.

Byron Connell, unknown officer, John Rodgers, Allen Snody

Chapter 23

Thursday—August 6, 1925

6:10 AM Pacific Time

John was up at sunrise, anxious to test fly *Baby*. He, Connell, and Pope suited up early, and when they couldn't find Bowlin and Stantz after a cursory search, the three of them met up with Snody and his crew and headed down to the pier. There they found the cowling off the port engine, and Wild Bill bent over it, deep in concentration. Hearing them approach, Bill straightened up and said, "Mornin' skipper. Thought I'd get a head start and check her fluids."

Rodgers nodded. "Good man. Where's Stantz?"

"He's onboard fussin' with the radio."

With that, a chipper Sparky Stantz poked his head out of the cabin door. "Mornin', sirs."

Rodgers chuckled to Byron and Kiles, "Well, I guess we don't need to wonder if these guys are up for a test flight."

Four hours later, both planes had been checked over thoroughly and preflighted. Shortly after 10:30, the planes taxied out to the bay's seaplane runway, an area off to the side of the main channel.

Prior to takeoff, pilots of ground-based planes will normally stand on their brakes and spool up their engines to maximum rpm to clean out their carburetors and make sure that they are running properly. This is impossible for seaplane pilots. Instead, they are forced to alternately throttle up in short bursts, and then quickly shut down, hopscotching erratically as they taxi to their takeoff position. Rodgers and Snody thus shuffled their charges to the designated area, and prepared to embark on their respective maiden test flights.

In the pilot's seat, with Byron next to him, John turned *Baby* into the wind—and without a moment's hesitation, jumped on the throttles. Despite the surge of power, the plane was slow to respond, initially trundling along as sluggishly as a tugboat. Then, as *Baby* started to gather speed, her nose rose upward out of the bay while her tail stayed in contact with the water. The real shift occurred when the craft eventually reached planing speed. At that point, *Baby* leveled out, rising up on her steps as a water-skier might. With the combined screaming of 1,000+ Detroit horsepower, the Packard-powered plane started to show her stuff, skipping madly over the wavelets, her speed increasing dramatically. Finally, *Baby* lifted free of her second step. With only the forward half of the hull still touching the water, John pulled back on the yoke and the plane leaped skyward, breaking her tensile bond with the water and catapulting them into the air.

Baby climbed quickly, and John soon eased the throttles back a bit. He put the plane in a bank to port and proceeded to ascend in a lazy turn. As they reached five hundred feet, he looked over his left shoulder in time to see Snody's PN9-3 scud across the bay and lift clear of the water's surface. Both planes seemed to be performing admirably. Encouraged, Rodgers called to his copilot, "Looks like we may be good to go after all."

"Roger, sir!" came the enthusiastic reply.

Two hours later, earthbound once again, the two planes plowed slowly toward the floating dock. Once they'd been secured, Byron and John surveyed *Baby*'s exterior from the top of the wings to the bottom of the keel. Meanwhile, Kiles concerned himself with adjusting the control cables, taking any slack out of them and checking the pulleys for freedom of movement. Sparky and Wild Bill busily set about reviewing the cooling systems, as *Baby*'s instruments had indicated both engines were running too hot.

Bill Bowlin soon reported to John and Byron that there was, indeed, a problem with the radiators. With the exception of one minor pinhole, the hoses were intact, but both radiator cores were leaking severely. It seemed that the radiators had not been properly isolated from the violent torque and vibrations that the massive engines imposed on them during takeoff. When John inspected the recalcitrant radiators himself, it was clear that the mounts were woefully unsatisfactory and had caused the brass cores to separate in several places.

While stretched out headlong beneath the starboard radiator mounts, Rodgers heard Allen Snody call from the other plane, "Commander, we've got a real problem with our radiators."

John immediately climbed down off *Baby*'s wing and walked across the floating pier to Snody's plane.

"Permission to board?"

"Yes sir, come onboard. Take a look at what we're dealing with. I think this could be serious."

John was dismayed to see that the damage to Snody's radiator cores was even worse than what *Baby* had sustained.

"The problems are identical. We've obviously got a design flaw here. The mounts just aren't isolating the radiators from the vibrations."

As Snody peered over John's shoulder, he said, "I think the problem could be more complicated than just the mounts. These monster engines put out so much torque. I just don't know . . ."

John nodded. He was worried. A nonstop flight to Hawaii was out of the question with a compromised radiator. This was a problem serious enough to ground the planes. In fact, the radiators in both planes had been so severely damaged that they might not be able to be effectively repaired.

John pulled both crews together to discuss the problem.

"OK, guys. The way I see it, we've got two problems. First, the radiator mounts need a total redesign. Second, the radiators themselves have been significantly damaged. We may need replacements if they can't be repaired. Any ideas?"

Lieutenant Snody spoke up first. "Sir, let me and my crew work on redesigning the mounts. I know a couple of guys that work in the machine shop of the shipyard. I'm sure they could help."

"OK."

Byron was next to volunteer. "Kiles and I can hit up the base procurement office. Maybe we can find some new radiators there."

Wild Bill chimed in. "Sir, those are good ideas, but we should work all the angles. Why don't you let Sparky and me go talk with some of the supply types from the base motor pool? Let's see if they can help us repair or replace the radiators." Winking conspiratorially, he added "Sometimes we noncoms can get more done than you officers."

Rodgers smiled in spite of himself. Bill had a point. "Alright Mr. Bowlin, see what you and Sparky can do. Gentlemen, I have to admit I'm concerned that simply repairing the cores may not be a satisfactory solution. Rebrazing the cores could cause more problems than it fixes; it might weaken the surrounding flanges, and that's not something we want to risk."

John was forced to confront the fact that the cooling-system issues were a major setback. He was aware that the radiators had been one of the biggest causes for the delay in the delivery of the planes, but he thought the problems had been resolved. When he got back to his quarters, he decided to take a chance on catching Admiral Moffett. He knew Moffett had been scheduled to arrive in California this week. Using the public phone in the lounge at the bachelor officers' quarters, John was able to get through to Moffett's suite at the Olympic Hotel in San Francisco.

"Admiral, this is Commander Rodgers."

"Hello, John. How are things going? Is everything on track?"

"Sir, the planes are here and assembled. We test flew them today, but we have a serious problem with the radiator mounts. They are woefully inadequate. The design doesn't isolate the radiators well enough, and all four of them failed as a result of the beating they took during the test. We're designing new mounts, so that's not the problem. The real issue is the amount of damage the vibration inflicted on the radiators. Between the cores and the tank flanges they are in pretty bad shape."

"How can I help?"

"Well sir, I'm concerned that we'll need replacements."

"They can't be repaired then?"

"Possibly, but with the abuse they've taken and the torque that the new engines produce, I sure wouldn't trust them."

There was a long pause, then Moffett said, "We've got a gut buster here, John. There aren't any spares. I thought this issue had been addressed after we lost Number Two, but apparently that's not the case. I'm sorry, but it's impossible for Philadelphia to redesign and build another set of radiators, then ship them across the country in time."

"Alright, sir. I knew it was a long shot, but I thought it was worth asking. We'll figure something out."

"Keep me informed."

"Yes sir." And the line went dead.

The PN9-1: *Baby* before takeoff. Note that the plane seems tail-heavy. She would stay this way until she reached enough speed to climb up on the forward step. Once up on the step, she would plane like a surfer, which in turn increased her speed until she finally became airborne.

Credit: National Archives

The PN9-3: Lieutenant Snody's plane, identical to *Baby*

Chapter 24

Saturday—August 8, 1925

9:15 AM Pacific Time

Two days had passed, and neither Snody nor Rodgers had been able to secure replacement radiators. To make matters worse, John had received a message the day before from Lieutenant Strong, saying that the initial test flight of his crew's new Boeing plane had resulted in serious damage to both of their radiators as well: a disheartening coincidence. Strong had already tried brazing the cores, a solution that Rodgers had discarded as only a temporary fix. Nevertheless, after two days, their attempts at securing satisfactory replacements had come up empty, and John had been forced to agree that the only viable solution for the mission was to remove the radiators and re-braze them at the navy machine shop on base. Future PN9s would have the luxury of time to solve the problem on a permanent basis, but for now, they were forced to make do.

Just before eleven o'clock, the re-brazed radiators were delivered. Bowlin and Stanz were still out researching alternatives when they arrived, so Snody's crew set to work reinstalling them, with Kiles Pope and Byron Connell assisting. This time, they used more substantial heavy rubber motor mounts. These new mounts were originally designed for securing boilers to a destroyer's keel and were too large for the space available on the planes, but were easily shaved to the correct dimensions.

Once installed, with all hoses in place and clamped, the radiators were pressure tested for leaks. They held; so far so good. Next, they needed to be vibration tested.

For the testing, stout lines secured the seaplanes forward and aft directly to either side of the floating pier. Additionally, two longer spring lines were run, one from the bow to a cleat even with the tail, and another from the aft end of the fuselage forward to a cleat opposite the nose. These crisscrossed lines took up the slack and served as backups. Once sure that *Baby* was safely tethered, John climbed aboard, leaving Byron and Kiles to monitor the reins. He took a seat at the controls and tested them, even though the plane wasn't going anywhere. John pointed left at Byron and called "Clear prop!" followed by "Ignition!" The portside aeromarine starter began to whine like a slow siren, and the left-side engine sputtered briefly, then roared to life. To the men present, the sound was deafeningly beautiful. Not many in the world had ever heard the thunder of that much virtually unbridled horsepower. John idled it back quickly. He repeated the start sequence, this time indicating the starboard power plant. The second Packard engine fired immediately. Just as he had done with the portside engine, John pulled back on the corresponding throttle, and craned his neck to check the lines. Byron gave John the thumbs-up, then spun his index finger in the air. Acknowledging the go-ahead, John eased both throttles forward until the engines reached 2,500 rpm, fifty percent of their redline, and held them there.

Baby fought against her restraining lines and rocked in her harness as her props chewed the air, but she remained well tethered. Once assured the lines held fast, all eyes moved to the bronze sculptures directly behind the spinning wooden propellers. Hopes were swiftly dashed by a formidable leak from the portside that the prop wash was blowing aft. The starboard side held out a bit longer, but soon, it too was losing water at a prodigious rate. Byron slashed his forefinger horizontally across his neck to signal "Cut!" In response, John shut down the ignition and closed the throttles, and the mighty engines shuddered to a stop. He climbed out onto the wing and was soon joined by Byron and Kiles. A quick inspection was all it took to see that their problem was far from solved. Disheartened, the trio climbed back down onto the dock.

The focus shifted to Snody's plane. It had been similarly secured to the opposite side of the floating dock. John hoped that Snody's repairs would fare better than *Baby's* had. After an identical test, Snody's port engine seemed to hold. However, frustration soon set in as his starboard engine started leaking like an open spigot. Disappointed, John ordered Snody to shut both engines down. The group's morale sank to an all-time low.

Slumping with discouragement, John turned away from the group only to be surprised to find they had a visitor. Standing alone on the edge of the pier stood Colonel Billy Mitchell. *How long has he been there? And for that matter, what's he doing here in the first place?* Keeping his questions to himself, John approached the army maverick, saluted, and extended his hand. "Colonel."

Accepting the handshake, Mitchell said, "Good to see you again, Commander." Nodding his head toward the planes he observed, "Looks like you have some problems."

"Cooling systems."

"Well, I'm not surprised. Those planes weren't designed for engines that big."

A frosty silence followed. The tension in the air was palpable. John finally responded, "Nothing we can't handle."

"Let's hope so, Commander. Let's hope so."

With that, Mitchell stepped back and saluted again. "Good luck with your race." As Rodgers returned the salute, Mitchell turned and walked off.

John swore under his breath. *Race? It's not a race, damn it.*

No sooner had Mitchell disappeared from view, than the crews were interrupted by a car horn blaring wildly. They all looked up as a navy vehicle careened across the tarmac at breakneck speed. Wild Bill was at the wheel hooting and hollering, true to his moniker, while Sparky half hung out the passenger window like a golden retriever, grinning from ear-to-ear. They screeched to a stop. Jumping from the car and saluting, Bowlin bellowed, "Sir, Chief Mechanics Mate William Bowlin, and Chief Radioman Otis Stantz reporting as ordered. Sir, mission accomplished!"

The antics of these two seldom surprised John. He knew better than to ask how they'd wangled the car. "Out with it, Mr. Bowlin!"

"Sir, you know our friend, the Olympic swimmer Duke Kahanamoku—the guy we visited on our pass? Anyway, Duke seems to know everyone, so we got in touch with him, explained our radiator problem and asked for his help—what'd he call it, Sparky?"

"*Kokua.*"

"Yeah, his *kokua*. So, he *kokua*'d us! He contacted a lady friend who works in Los Angeles for a company there called Flexo. They custom make some of the biggest and best truck radiators in the world. We got her our requirements; Strong's too; dimensions and such, and she's promised completion of six heavy-duty radiators built to our specs by the twenty-fifth."

Sparky interjected excitedly, "We know that's too long for delivery here, 'cause we have to be in San Francisco before then, so I contacted my Uncle George. He's an ex-navy man, Chief Petty Officer. He owns a small orange grove in Anaheim, and he's volunteered to truck them straight through to San Francisco for us, soon as they're finished."

The entire group was amazed and delighted. Much backslapping ensued; Bowlin and Stantz were the toast of both crews. At last, Byron said, "Well, now all we have to do is find a way to patch these sieves so that we can make it to San Francisco."

John didn't want to spoil the celebration, but he couldn't help thinking the same thing. He had no way of knowing if they could make it that far. Seaplanes had never gone that distance before, even in perfect condition. Now they were going to try to limp these two compromised aircraft all the way to San Francisco without overheating the engines. Nevertheless the problem only strengthened John's resolve. He had to find a way.

Period air-mail stamp, featuring an aviation radiator.

Pacific Coast Hwy
South Laguna - 1925
from the Howard Wilson collection

The Pacific Coast Highway in 1925. The new radiators for the three airplanes were trucked all the way to San Francisco on this road.

Chapter 25

Friday—August 21, 1925

6:11 AM Pacific Time

The last two weeks had been busy ones for the crews. Each time they took the planes out for a test flight, they would end up spending a day and a half repairing them. However, minor repairs were the least of their worries. The real demons were the radiators, and an unanticipated problem with excessive fuel consumption.

In addition to the radiator leaks, the planes were far from meeting their minimum required miles-per-gallon ratio. Nor had they come even remotely close to the fuel efficiency of the ill-fated PN9-2. Both crews tried everything they could to get the most from every drop of petrol. They rebalanced the props, modified the lubricating systems so there was no unnecessary friction, gapped and re-gapped the points and sparkplugs, boosted the voltage from the battery and generator, rewired where they could to avoid any power drain, and adjusted the carburetors over and over. John had gone so far as to send telegrams to the contractors in Philadelphia and the engine builders in Detroit, asking for help. But there was no quick fix. The advice from the creators was only moderately helpful, but to date the planes still hadn't met the minimum miles-per-gallon requirements John knew they would need to attempt the crossing. Nevertheless, the teams kept at it.

Knowing they would have new radiators for the transpacific trip was a relief, but they still needed to get the planes to San Francisco without damaging the engines. So Wild Bill Bowlin and Kiles Pope had tackled the cooling system problems with vigor and ingenuity. They each approached the problem from opposite angles.

Kiles had attacked from the inside. He recalled how, years before, his father had added oatmeal to the family's Model-T radiator to keep it from leaking: a homespun solution to a common problem. The concept had later been improved on with a commercial product called Liquid X. Instead of oatmeal, it contained tiny lead particles suspended in a base solution. As the liquid tried to escape, the minute lead pieces would collect at the holes, filling them and plugging the leaks. The idea worked surprisingly well, and the suspended lead, however toxic, was even touted to prevent further leaks.

Kiles had managed to find some Liquid X at a local garage, and had poured some into all the radiators. It seemed to have stemmed the leaks in the re-brazed radiator cores during their testing, but only time would tell.

Wild Bill had approached the problem from the outside, with something called a "swamp cooler." He told John these contraptions were often used to cool farm tractor engines in the heat of the Indiana summer. Bill modified and mounted a two-gallon can of water from the upper wing between the engines on both planes. From the bottom of each can, he led two small copper tubes which gravity fed to the top of the radiators. Each tube had a small shut-off valve that could be reached from the open cockpit. If the pilot saw that the temperature was climbing on one or the other of the engines, he could open the appropriate valve and let water trickle over the front of the radiator. This water would soon evaporate, helping to cool the engine. It was a simple but seemingly effective fix, and so far the temperatures had held on the test flights. Rodgers' most immediate concern was whether or not they could make it to San Francisco without major incident. The men on both planes had done their best to mask whatever anxiety they were feeling, but they all knew the fate of the mission hung on their ability to keep their engines cool enough for the duration of this flight.

Leaving San Diego in the early morning light, the temporarily repaired twin PN9s flew westward over the main ship channel and straight out to sea. As they thundered along, they startled the local outbound fishing fleet less than two hundred feet below. Powered by the combined 2,100 horsepower of the four Packard V-12s, the wooden propellers sliced the air like huge blenders. Once clear of the harbor entrance, Rodgers banked to starboard. Snody, who was flying slightly astern and off John's starboard wing, followed suit.

The crews had stowed and secured their possessions aft, along with all their tools and spare parts. Normally, a transit crew would have moved equipment to their destination by truck, but John had insisted they fly with the gear. He wanted to simulate the weight of the extra drums of fuel they would be carrying on their transpacific flight to figure how many miles to the gallon the planes could get when fully loaded.

John had Byron relieve him at the controls, so he could attend to other duties. He busied himself with fuel-usage estimates, observing the Southern California coastline and trying to calculate their mileage.

Both crews were excited as the planes headed north, but their high spirits were edged with tension. They felt that they'd done everything humanly possible to get the planes to San Francisco without overheating—but everyone aboard was well aware that should the temporary radiator fixes fail, the engines could overheat in a matter of minutes. If that happened, it would most assuredly kill the mission, and quite possibly themselves.

The pressure was on politically, too. In a matter of days, the navy brass would join Admiral Moffett to witness the start of what the press had christened the "Race to Hawaii," scheduled smack in the middle of San Francisco's weeklong Diamond Jubilee. Admiral Moffett had made it very clear to John that any further delay would be a public relations nightmare for the navy.

During the flight, conversation was virtually impossible, due to the incessant, earsplitting drone of *Baby*'s huge propellers. The crew probably wouldn't have said much anyway, as they were all focused on willing the twin temperature gauges to remain in the green. John's eyes were seldom far from them or the fuel gauges. For the moment, his only concerns were that the fuel mileage be good and, more importantly, that their improvised radiator fixes would hold.

Several hours and too much fuel later, San Francisco Bay came into view. This in itself was a victory. As far as they knew, they were the first planes to fly nonstop from San Diego to San Francisco. The planes approached the city from the southwest and lined up on the infamous Alcatraz Island. John indicated to Snody that he should land first. After a quick buzz of the landing area, Snody turned into the eighteen-knot wind. He pulled back on the throttles and his plane slowed and dropped. Leveling off at twenty feet over the water, Snody tried to ease the plane down, but the large surface area of the dual wings fought him to stay aloft, and they glided over the water for what felt like an interminable amount of time. This phenomenon was known as flying in ground-effect: when the air between the plane and water acts like a cushion that doesn't want to compress. Snody slowed to where he was close to stalling the plane. The hull of the dull gray craft finally dropped and skipped along on the water. From there, the friction slowed the seaplane plane further and allowed the PN9-3 to slice into the surface. Cutting a frothy trough, they plowed through the whitecapped water, throwing a wide wake with their metal hull. As the plane slowed to a stop, it crabbed to the right off a wave, causing the craft to lean onto its portside wing float and simultaneously lift the starboard one free of the water. Ungainly as it looked, at least the craft was safely down. Snody accelerated and started the tilted plane on its long taxi to the piers.

Then it was Byron's turn. Swinging around from the racetrack pattern he had been flying, he duplicated Snody's approach. As he decreased speed, the small white marker buoys raced to greet them. *Baby*, too, fought to stay airborne, but Byron's deft handling of the throttle and the yoke forced her to yield. The first touchdown was harsh as the plane bounced off a wind-swept wave. The shock knocked the swamp-cooler bucket free. It banged against the elevator and was gone in an instant. At that point, *Baby* was traveling at almost fifty knots. She plowed through the water, spray shooting out from each side until Byron reined her in. She rocked to a near-stop before he revved the engines to bring her up to taxi speed. Simultaneously pressing on the right foot pedal and easing the left throttle, he nosed the canted plane towards the piers. The breeze was brisk, making the long taxi difficult. They had to crab their way to the landlubbers waiting for them on the dock.

Thankfully, up until the swamp-cooler had been jettisoned, the flight had been surprisingly uneventful for both planes, save for the slight increase in vibrations everyone had noticed. All four radiators had leaked, but not one of the engines had approached red line temperature. While the jury-rigged radiators would never have been able to withstand the stress of a transpacific mission, they had gotten the planes safely to San Francisco. All things considered, it had been a successful trip.

John had plenty of other things to fret about now. The limited trials they were able to perform in San Diego had shown him that the estimated range of the planes was still not what the designers had projected. And, after his initial calculations of their fuel consumption on this trip, it was obvious that even his conservatively revised figures were too optimistic. In fact, as of now, it appeared that even if the planes could get off the water with a full load of fuel onboard, not shake themselves apart over the long haul, and not overheat, they would still run out of gas at least four hundred miles short of the Hawaiian Islands. And four hundred miles was a long way off, out on the open ocean. Yes, they could still land and refuel if necessary, but that would be a huge step down from their projected goal of a nonstop flight. John thought that maybe with some further carburetor adjustments and some divine assistance, they might be able to cut into that number somewhat, but it was doubtful that they could reduce it significantly—unless they had a strong tailwind.

Consequently, Rodgers was counting more heavily than ever on the trade winds. John figured if they could luck into twenty-plus knot tailwinds for the entire trip, they might just make it.

Liquid X, a radiator stop-leak: a petroleum-based concoction that contained microscopic motes of lead. It fixed leaks when the suspended lead particles clogged a hole in the treated radiator. Advertising for the product touted it as preventative as well. Despite the poor quality of this photograph, it is worth having an idea of what this bizarre product looked like.

Chapter 26

Sunday—August 23, 1925

1:51 PM Pacific Time

At last, the day both press and public had been waiting for arrived: their chance to meet the three intrepid crews of what was now being reported as a great transpacific "race." The summer sun shone brightly on the many who had gathered in Chrissy Field near downtown San Francisco for the eagerly anticipated Sunday afternoon festivities.

It was a warm day by San Francisco standards, but the cool breeze off the bay kept the temperature pleasant. A temporary platform had been erected in front of a large navy-blue suspended backdrop. Stars-and-Stripes bunting festooned the backdrop and draped the platform edges on three sides. A dozen chairs and a podium stood onstage, awaiting the distinguished speakers to come. Both the American flag and the Department of the Navy flag were prominently displayed. The navy band was seated to the right of the platform, and was entertaining the gathering with lively Sousa marches. It might as well have been the Fourth of July.

A sizable contingent of VIP civilians and press filled the first few rows facing the podium and the bay beyond. Brightly colored hats and parasols adorned the well-heeled ladies in this section, while most of the men wore natty sport coats and ties. Behind the seated throng, almost a thousand others in somewhat more casual attire had gathered on blankets spread out across the grassy meadow. Excited children laughed and darted between the groups, as parents tried in vain to keep them in check. Anchored close offshore, somewhat obscured by the stage backdrop, were the two identical PN9s. They, too, had been draped with red, white, and blue bunting for the occasion.

At two o'clock, the host of the event, San Francisco Mayor James Rolph ushered California Governor Friend William Richardson and an assortment of navy and army brass, politicos, and specially invited guests up onto the platform and their assigned seats. Anticipating action, the press crowded to the front, and several flashbulbs popped. The navy band struck up a stirring rendition of "Stars and Stripes Forever." Excitement mounted, as the crowd focused on the ceremony to come.

Behind the temporary dais, the mood did not match the exuberance out front. Dressed in their finest uniforms, Moffett, Rodgers, Snody, and their crews nervously awaited the pending introduction. All was not well.

A grim-faced Admiral Moffett, with an anxious aide lurking in his shadow, asked angrily, "John, how could this happen?"

Commander John Rodgers was clearly annoyed as well. "Admiral, Lieutenant Strong telegrammed last night that they had to land at Coos Bay, near Marshfield, Oregon. He said they were experiencing another overheating problem, but he assured me it would be a simple fix, and that they'd be airborne at first light, arriving here no later than 0900. When they didn't show this morning, I had Chief Stantz try to raise them by radio. We've contacted every port of call between here and Coos Bay, with no luck. No reports—either of his progress, or a downing."

"We need them here, damn it!" Moffett exclaimed to no one in particular. "We're going to look foolish with only the two planes here. How do I explain this to the press? Hell, it's already after two o'clock!"

John bit his tongue. It was inexcusable not to radio in—and it was just like Strong. Rodgers was sure Strong's ego would never let him publicly announce that he couldn't arrive as planned. The new plane had been designated Patrol plane, Boeing, first edition, and it had been built specifically for the transpacific mission. John wondered if something untoward might have befallen the PB1 aircraft. He hoped that wasn't the case, for many reasons. For one, the press would go berserk in the event of an accident, and Colonel Mitchell would have a field day, sabotaging all the good that Moffett was trying to accomplish for the navy. If Strong was OK, but arrived too late for the ceremony because of some malfunction of his aircraft, it would still be a black eye for the navy.

The patriotic music finished with a flourish, and the audience applauded as the bandleader took his bow. On cue, Mayor "Sonny Jim" Rolph stepped up to the podium and adjusted the microphone to address the audience.

"Distinguished guests, ladies and gentlemen! May I please have your attention," his amplified voice blared from the multiple loud speakers mounted next to the platform. With or without Lieutenant Strong, the official ceremony had begun.

Rolph welcomed the crowd, presented those seated on the dais, and gave a surprisingly short address. He then introduced Admiral Moffett, who joined Rolph at the podium, and shook the mayor's hand. Polite applause riffled through the general audience, as few on the lawn knew anything about Admiral Moffett or his involvement with the popular mission. Moffett had expected this response, and turned quickly to the task at hand. He thanked the crowd, and paid obligatory homage to the VIPs on the platform. Then, to the astonishment of Rodgers and the two crews, Moffett launched into a pitch that was pure P. T. Barnum.

"And now, ladies and gentlemen, we come to the moment you have all have been waiting for! Please allow me to introduce the brave navy aviators who are going to risk their lives attempting an incredible feat of great daring, which, until today, was considered absolutely impossible."

At this, the crowd roared. Moffett was right; they had come to see the so-called flyboys. Their excitement was palpable. Most people in America had not yet driven a motor car, let alone flown in an airplane. Flying was still considered a dark art, and these San Franciscans had flocked to Chrissy Field this afternoon to see the men who dared tempt the gods.

Moffett began with the noncommissioned officers, introducing them one by one. Wild applause followed each presentation as the men stepped up to salute the admiral, then lined up across the stage behind him.

When nine clean-shaven American aviators stood at parade rest behind the admiral, he wound up for the big finish.

"And now, to lead this brave cadre of men, I am proud to have the honor to introduce to you the courageous officer who has agreed to command this mission. Ladies and gentlemen, I give you Commander John Rod . . ."

At that moment, a deafening roar drowned out everything else as a huge, sparkling silver plane suddenly zoomed from behind the platform's backdrop. The crowd reacted with a collective gasp as the shining giant thundered past, only a hundred feet over their heads. Ladies fainted and babies shrieked. Everyone started pointing and yelling. Terrified children raced back to the relative safety of their parents' blankets. All eyes were riveted on the incredible apparition.

To the crowd's delight, the shiny plane banked ninety degrees sharply to the left, practically standing on its wing edges. In unison, the spectators rose to their feet. The bright summer sun glinted off the mirrored finish forcing many to shield their eyes in order to keep watching. Excited "Oohs" and "Ahs" emanated from the throng as the powerful plane circled, completely circumscribing the outer edges of the crowd, then reversed its bank and turned toward the bay. Once it was far enough out, the craft completed its turn and headed straight for the gathering again. Eschewing the officially designated landing area, the big seaplane leveled out, dropped low over the water, and seemed to be heading straight at the park. At the last minute, it flared out, skipped smoothly, and then settled dramatically in for a shoreline landing. The crowd burst into applause. Still showing off, the aircraft then taxied a bit too fast for safety and sidled up to the pier in one smooth, straight and level motion—right between the two drab gray PN9s that were leaning clumsily on their portside floats. The festive red, white, and blue bunting with which they had been draped was blown half off by the prop wash of their larger sister when she eased past them and moored close in. The dislodged bunting on the PN9s exposed more of the drab gray paint and only added to their slightly pathetic appearance, especially next to the glistening newcomer.

The crowd raced to the water's edge to ogle the spectacular new seaplane. Even the VIPs from the platform scrambled down for a closer look.

Strong's plane dwarfed the other two planes in every way possible. She was seven feet taller, ten feet longer and her biplane wings were fifteen feet wider than the PN9s. She stood out like an Amazon between two lowly handmaidens. Her huge engines were rated at 800 horsepower apiece, and were unusually mounted fore and aft of the cockpit, in a pull/push tandem design that few in the crowd had ever seen before. This in-line design feature made the craft look sleeker and more modern than the PN9s. Plus, having the weight of the engines directly over the center line of the plane meant that unlike the awkwardly listing PN9s, the PB1 rode level in the water. As a result, her two outboard floats appeared to be superfluous. The four-bladed propellers were stainless-steel affairs that gleamed in the afternoon sun, far outshining the twin-bladed wooden props on her two siblings. The plane exuded power and purpose.

The most startling difference was her shiny silver color. The mirror-like finish of the fuselage was the result of a freshly buffed and shined duralumin skin, and the part that was fabric had been painted with a reflective metallic silver paint that made the plane literally sparkle. Her tail was emblazoned with a larger-than-life "PB1." No question about it, she was a star—the largest seaplane in the world—and her crew basked in the glow of her reflected glory.

Once the plane was secured, five smartly dressed aviators dropped to the dock and saluted the crowd in unison, eliciting another roar of ecstatic applause as the press and the populace went crazy. This hotshot crew of leather-jacketed, testosterone-laden aviators was exactly what the frenzied audience had been waiting for; not the crisply pressed, uniformed teams that had been previously introduced. Any thought of completing the formal presentation was abandoned when the navy band rose from their seats and marched to the shore playing "Anchors Aweigh."

In no time at all, Lieutenant Commander James Strong, his copilot Lieutenant Rico Botta, and his noncom crew of three were mobbed. Tall and handsome, Strong and Botta looked as if they'd come straight from Hollywood central casting. The press ate them up. Cameras flashed and primitive moving-picture machines cranked film at a prodigious rate as reporters vied for the attention of the demigods, bombarding them with questions.

Lieutenant Commander Strong was a thirty-five-year-old Naval Academy graduate who came from old West Coast family money. He was a shade over six feet tall, broad-shouldered, and square-jawed. His short-cropped dark blonde hair was partially covered by his navy cap, while his ice-blue eyes were hidden behind the jaunty aviator goggles he sported. With his disarming smile and undeniable sex appeal, Strong epitomized the ideal navy flyboy.

Lieutenant Botta's background was remarkably different. Australian born and raised, he had migrated to the States after college. At twenty-six, he had enlisted in the U.S. Navy and soon progressed to Officer Candidates School. His bright mind and aeronautical background quickly moved him to the top of his class and up the ranks. When answering questions about the extraordinary new plane, his strong Aussie accent was an instant hit with the press, and the ladies in the crowd.

Reporters also crowded around Admiral Moffett, congratulating him for arranging such a spectacular entrance. Although initially reluctant to take credit for Strong's blatant showboating, Moffett recognized the incredible marketing opportunity Strong's spectacular arrival had created, and decided to let the press make their own assumptions.

Byron nudged John as they stood with Snody and their crews, far from the melee. "Well, John, there's your Lieutenant Commander Strong. I told you he was a prima donna. But damn, just look at their plane; she's a modern beauty! Talk about spit and polish."

John was not as enthusiastic. "I'm not so sure, Byron."

"What do you mean?"

"I think the basic design may be flawed. A seaplane handles differently on the water than a wheeled one does on the tarmac, and I wonder if the designers took that into account. Look, when a seaplane taxis, it has to be able to run up one engine faster than the other in order to turn at low speeds. In-line engines can't do that."

Byron responded, "You know, you're right. A seaplane with the engines in tandem like this one, acts like a single-engine plane." Studying the design of the bobbing plane, Byron continued thoughtfully,

"Although their plane is a 'pretty boy,' it could be tough to maneuver on the water. I wouldn't want to have to line her up for takeoff in any kind of a crosswind."

Kiles snorted, "Pretty boy. Hey, that fits—PB1 . . . *Pretty Boy!*"

Gesturing over his shoulder toward the crowd, Byron observed wryly, "I don't know if it fits the plane, but it sure seems to fit the crew."

Airman's Runway at Chrissy Field: the army air base where Rodgers and company departed from.

The large building to the right was the enlisted men's housing; the smaller cottages were officers' quarters.

Mayor of San Francisco: James "Sonny Jim" Rolph

California Governor: Friend William Richardson

PLANE FOR FLIGHT TO HAWAII TO BE READY AUG. 28

From the beginning, the Boeing PB1 plane was the odds-on favorite to successfully complete the transpacific crossing. This almost unreadable article was printed in *The Honolulu Advertiser*. The article names Lieutenant Commander Strong as the pilot of the "giant mystery plane" and describes the PB1 as fifty percent larger than the PN9 sister planes that would accompany it.

Boeing's PB1: built especially for the transpacific mission, it was notable for the push-pull mounting of its engines, shiny silver color, huge four-bladed props, and its considerably larger overall size when compared to the PN9s. It is seen here sitting deep in the water, under a full fuel load.

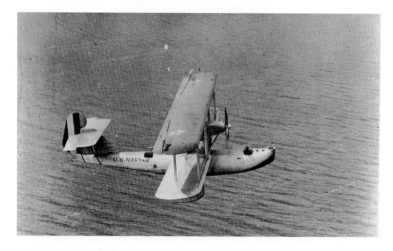

The PB1 (Pretty Boy) in flight. Everything about the PB1 seemed more modern. In fact, however, there was a serious design error. The single water-bound rudder of a fuselage-displacement plane cannot effectively control it at taxi speeds without help. In this case, it is too small in relation to the length of the hull. Turning assistance is needed in a seaplane whose main flotation is the fuselage itself. The hull will tend to proceed in a straight line, ignoring the modest effect of a single rudder—unless outboard forces help it turn. For the most part, the navy had recognized and corrected that problem by mounting single-engine seaplanes on two outboard pontoons—each pontoon has its own rudder, rather than one large fuselage with a single rudder. This plane, however, was built by former lumber company, Boeing, who may not as yet learned that lesson.

Lieutenant Commander James H. Strong: from an article in *The Honolulu Star-Bulletin*. John Rodgers was not even mentioned in the paper on this day.

Chapter 27

Friday—August 28, 1925

9:52 AM Pacific Time

Ironically, the army had extended base hospitality to the three navy crews, billeting the enlisted men in the noncom barracks at Chrissy Field and putting up the officers in small cottages on the grounds. However, the Olympic Club quickly became the temporary unofficial headquarters for Admiral Moffett and his teams.

This morning, Moffett had summoned Rodgers for a private, one-on-one meeting. Anticipating a routine briefing, John reported to the Admiral's suite. The high-ceilinged main room was spacious—furnished with a secretary desk, sofa, leather arm chair, and a large, round table with four chairs. Moffett was seated at the table, which was covered with a mountain of paperwork. Without looking up, he gestured absentmindedly for Rodgers to sit.

John waited as the Admiral leafed through the pile. At last, Moffett looked up.

"John, I need a status report, as I'm sure you know; but first, I want to make something absolutely clear."

"Sir . . . ?"

"I know that among your crew and Snody's men there are some noses out of joint after Strong's stunt the other day. Am I right?"

"Sir, I'm afraid that's affirmative, but . . ."

Moffett interrupted, "I'm not interested in explanations. Hell, it's only human. That son-of-a-bitch stole your boys' thunder, but the point is, the press ran with it. That's the best ink we've ever gotten. It's good for the mission, good for the navy, and that's all that counts—for the moment.

"Don't worry, Strong's blatant disregard for teamwork will go on record, but for now I need you to rise above any petty annoyance you may harbor against Lieutenant Strong and his crew. I want you to tell your men and Snody's team in no uncertain terms to do the same. It is critical that we present a united front. Is that clear?"

"Yes sir, will do sir."

"Good man. Now about that status report."

"Sir, the crews have actually worked quite well together this past week, regardless of any ruffled feathers."

"Good. Glad to hear it."

"Believe me, sir; with only seventy-two hours to go before final takeoff on Monday, we're all very much aware that we're under the gun. There's still a lot that has to happen before then."

"Give me details."

"Sir, the six new radiators arrived yesterday afternoon, and they look great. Bowlin has rallied all three crews, including Strong's, and they began installing them last night. We expect that the new radiators, combined with what we've learned about improving the mounts, will correct our overheating problems."

"Good."

"With the admiral's permission, it's not all good, sir. Fuel consumption is a challenge. My calculations continue to be anything but encouraging. Neither of the two PN9s has been able to come close to the fuel efficiency of the other test plane—the one that had to be scrapped. We've talked with the Packard engineers and they've shipped four new carburetors designed to run leaner. They should be here today or tomorrow, but that won't leave much time to adjust the jets. Strong's plane burns more fuel than ours, but is able to lift more fuel, so mileage may not be as big a problem for them."

"Any more negatives?"

"Frankly, sir, at this point, our real concern is the constancy of the trade winds. As I've said from the first, the trades are critical. If they drop off, we'll be in serious trouble."

"OK, John. I appreciate your candor. We're all hoping for twenty-knot trades." Moffett paused, "John, I'm aware that you know how important this mission is, but I can't emphasize it enough. We have got to pull out all the stops. Hopefully, once you install those new carburetors, they'll give us the added range you need. But whatever it takes, I need you to get those planes to Hawaii. There's a lot riding on your success."

"Yes, sir." *Not to mention both of our careers.*

1:47 PM Eastern Time

A staff car pulled up in front of the Army–Navy Club in Washington, D.C., brakes screeching. Even before it had stopped completely, a young army lieutenant jumped from the vehicle, ran up the front steps two at a time, and disappeared into the venerable building. Dressed in a stiffly starched cavalry uniform, complete with leather cross belt, riding breeches, and high-top brown boots, Billy Mitchell's aide headed straight for the stairs without stopping at the front desk. Moments later, he knocked at the door of the Colonel's temporary residence. When Mitchell opened the door, the junior officer saluted sharply and held out a Western Union envelope.

"Sir, this just in for you."

Mitchell returned the salute. He accepted the telegram and motioned for aide to enter.

"Thanks, Lieutenant Smith." He glanced at the envelope and chuckled. "Let's see what's up in California."

Closing the door, Mitchell opened and read the full-page message—unusually long for a wire. When he had finished, he turned to Smith.

"You say this just came in?"

"Yes, sir. The information is up to the minute."

Mitchell chortled, "It seems the navy's party in San Francisco is about to end." He held up the telegram, "I don't believe these guys! According to this, they still don't know if the planes can even take off with a full load of fuel, let alone make it to Hawaii."

Mitchell read through the telegram again and turned to his aide. "Call the press. I want to talk with them right away. We need to take the lead on this."

Two hours later, Mitchell held court for a large gathering of the D.C. press corps. Like so many rats, they had taken to following this pied piper, gobbling up every morsel he tossed their way. As he had before, Mitchell railed against "this foolhardy race," stating yet again that the navy was ill-prepared for an undertaking of this magnitude.

"The navy can't compete against the modern aircraft of the Army Air Corps, so instead they are having an intramural contest." As the reporters feverishly scribbled Mitchell's juicy, attention-grabbing quotes, he continued, "When this race fails, as it is sure to do, who will be there to pick up the pieces?" Ever the politician, Mitchell went on to say he hoped the contest would not end in tragedy: "America is still recovering from too many terrible losses experienced in the War."

He concluded his tirade by attacking the personalities involved, audaciously suggesting that although Admiral Moffett was a war hero, that didn't necessarily mean he would always make good decisions. Then Mitchell took aim at what he believed was Moffett's irrational obsession with dirigibles.

"Moffett can't even see that those bags of hot air will have no place in a modern air corps." All fodder for the next day's headlines.

4:54 PM Hawaii Time

As Masahiro Mikami's last customer of the day prepared to leave the optometrist's office, Akiko walked her to the door. Outside, the brisk trade winds felt good, mitigating the late August heat. Akiko bid her aloha, and flipped the sign in the door to *Closed*. She changed the tin hands on the "We will return at" sign to read "8:00 AM." As she went back inside and closed the door, she heard the chimes from the Kawaiahao Church clock peal five times. *Seven o'clock in San Francisco.* She wondered if John had eaten dinner yet.

Alone in the quiet front office, she sat at her desk and took an envelope from the pocket of her dress. Eagerly she removed the three-page letter that had arrived from John the day before. Unfolding it, she caressed the pages he had touched, before allowing herself to read them yet again. Akiko glowed as John's words of love and tenderness filled her heart to overflowing. She couldn't imagine life without him.

In his letters, he had shared with her the pressure he was under, from Admiral Moffett, the navy brass, the press, Colonel Mitchell, the three crews, and worst of all, the frustrating delays. He had also kept her informed on the status of his divorce, which was nearly finalized. She prayed for his safe return to her arms, and the life they would begin together.

As Akiko contemplated the happiness that lay ahead of them, a wave of dizziness came over her, catching her by surprise. It quickly passed. Puzzled, she mentally reviewed her day, wondering what might have caused the odd sensation. She was surprised to discover that she had somehow forgotten to eat lunch.

Masahiro stood in the doorway between the offices, watching his only child daydream. Akiko started from her reverie to find him looking at her. Embarrassed, she bowed her head and quickly hid the letter in her lap. Masahiro pretended not to notice. Without a word, he walked to the cabinet-sized RCA radio that had been a gift from his late wife. Standing four feet tall against the wall, the radio occupied too much space for Masahiro's taste, but it reminded him of Hiroko and the affection they had shared. He seldom listened to it anymore, but today he twisted the wooden knob and turned it on. Akiko heard the familiar buzz as the radio tubes warmed up. She ached for any news of John, but had not dared to turn on her father's radio herself. She had not yet told Masahiro about her relationship with John, and had worried that her sudden interest in his mission would raise unwelcome suspicions.

The signal came in just as the announcer intoned, ". . . and here's Miss Billie Holiday with her latest hit." The brilliant jazz singer's voice dripped sensuality as she sang words that touched Akiko's heart:

> I was blue, just as blue as I could be
> Every day was a cloudy day for me
> Then good luck came a-knocking at my door
> Skies were gray but they're not gray anymore.
>
> Blue skies
> Smiling at me
> Nothing but blue skies
> Do I see.
>
> Bluebirds
> Singing a song
> Nothing but bluebirds
> All day long.
>
> Never saw the sun shining so bright
> Never saw things going so right
> Noticing the days hurrying by
> When you're in love, my how they fly.
>
> Blue days
> All of them gone
> Nothing but blue skies
> From now on.
>
> I should care if the wind blows east or west
> I should fret if the worst looks like the best
> I should mind if they say it can't be true
> I should smile, that's exactly what I do.
>
> Blue days
> All of them gone
> Nothing but blue skies
> From now on.

Akiko let herself float along on the music, waking from her trance as the song ended. Studying her thoughtfully, Masa said, "I wonder if they'll have any news about Mr. Rodgers?" Akiko felt her cheeks flush. She wondered how much he knew—or had guessed.

The sound of a rooster crowing came from the speaker—the trademark opening sound effect for Arakawa's General Store commercials. As the announcer enthusiastically pitched a wonderful new fabric that had just arrived from the Mainland, the advertisement gave Akiko time to try and collect herself. By the time it was over, she felt ready to take a stab at casual conversation.

"There may very well be news of Mr. Rodgers, Father. I read in the paper this morning that the planes will be leaving San Francisco for Hawaii this coming Monday." Her words tumbled out. "Father, it is such a very long way to fly. I hope they will all make the journey safely. Mr. Rodgers is such a nice man, do you not think?"

Catching herself, Akiko blushed and stopped, wondering if she'd said too much.

Masahiro simply grunted his assent.

"And now the news . . ." crackled from the radio. "A fire at a Kakaako warehouse was extinguished shortly after seven this morning. The Fire Department responded . . ." and the announcer droned on. Akiko listened intently to every word, determined not to miss any mention of John.

"And, in San Francisco today, Navy Commander John Rodgers and his band of brave naval aviators were hard at work on their three seaplanes in final preparation for the start of their big race on Monday. If all goes well, by this time Tuesday evening, they could be enjoying a hero's welcome. And, in sports . . ."

Masahiro switched off the radio and reached for the door.

"Let's go, princess."

Believing her secret was still safe, Akiko tucked John's letter back into her pocket, turned off the office lights, and followed her father outside.

The Olympic Club in downtown San Francisco, commonly frequented by military types. It was usually occupied by visiting navy crews because of the proximity of the navy's piers and the lack of adequate billeting on base.

A present-day picture of the Chrissy Field enlisted men's quarters (with part of the ramp for the Golden Gate Bridge in the background).

Console radio, circa 1925

The Honolulu Advertiser for August 28, 1925: The excitement begins to build in Honolulu as a modest headline (second from right and enlarged, although of poor quality) indicates that Snody's plane will be marked with a yellow tail and Rodgers' plane will have a yellow bow. The Associated Press article goes on to say: "Commander J. H. Strong's plane, being much larger than the other two, will be easily distinguishable and will not be marked by color." This type of report was commonplace and was subtly indicative of the opinion that Strong's plane was the one to watch.

See 'em better
with BINOCULARS!

Get a CLOSE-UP look at the daring actors in the dramatic ending of the great Trans-Pacific Flight next Tuesday. Hundreds of times in the next few months or years you'll find good Binoculars invaluable.

Bausch & Lomb, $40.00 to $90.00

Wollensak Binoscopes, $5.00 and $7.00

Wollensak Pocketscopes, $1.00, $1.50, $2.00

HONOLULU PHOTO SUPPLY CO.
Oldest and Largest Photo Shop in Hawaii
Eastman Distributors

1050 FORT ST.   NEAR HOTEL ST.

An ad from the August 28, 1925 *Honolulu Advertiser* for Honolulu Photo Supply, which was located on Fort Street near Masahiro Mikami's Optometrist shop. The ad mistakenly features wheeled aircraft, rather than the seaplanes that were being used for the actual flight.

236

Chapter 28

Saturday—August 29, 1925

7:27 AM Pacific Time

As the crews had hoped, the new radiators were easily installed on all three planes. While considerably more robust than the originals, they were also heavier. Looking to eliminate any extra weight, the aviators decided to jettison the swamp coolers. The men figured that with the more substantial new radiator cores, they could forgo the extra weight and wind resistance of the jury-rigged devices. Liquid X, on the other hand, was deemed a simple, effective preventative. They added it to all six cooling systems. The new, leaner-running carburetors then replaced the older ones on the twin PN9s.

The three planes had finished their static tests, running the engines to maximum rpm while still earthbound—and incredibly, no leaks had occurred. Now, as the crews prepared to board their planes for flight tests, Byron Connell found John scowling at *Baby*, deep in thought.

"Sir . . . ?"

"Dammit, they're riding too high, they're just too damn light. Byron, the planes haven't been fitted with their extra drums of fuel yet. In order for us to get a true indication of how the planes'll manage under mission conditions, we need more weight."

"Yeah, guess you're right, skip."

Rodgers surveyed the local sailors standing around—some who had actually assisted the teams, along with a good number of rubberneckers. He grinned at Byron.

"Let's see who's up for a free ride."

Rodgers quickly found fifteen eager souls—five for each plane to serve as live ballast. The extra weight still did not equal the full weight of the fuel load they would eventually be carrying, but at least it was a closer approximation for the test.

John squinted up at the sky, encouraged by the stiff breeze that was blowing.

"Byron, what've we got in store weather-wise today?"

"Sir, I can't say for sure what's coming up, but right now we've got winds from the east at twenty-five knots." He added, "Feels like home."

"Roger. If these conditions hold into Monday, I'll be happy. Then let's just hope our trades pick us up along the way."

John and his crew fired up *Baby* and led the three-plane procession away from the cove. As all three pilots alternately goosed and pulled back on their throttles, the planes plowed and coasted towards the designated takeoff area.

Lieutenant Byron Connell was at *Baby*'s controls, with CPO Kiles Pope on his right, half-hidden behind the twin transparent-glass windscreens. Commander John Rodgers occupied the navigation station in the extreme bow, his head and shoulders visible above the fuselage. Chief Mechanics Mate Wild Bill Bowlin was stationed further aft at the amidships cockpit, while Chief Radioman Sparky Stanz was below, secured at the radios. *Baby*'s five volunteers sat on the corrugated floorboards just aft of amidships, across which lines had been tightly strung for them to hold on to.

As she floated on the water, waiting to take off, *Baby* was buffeted by the substantial, wind-driven whitecaps on the bay. Byron hollered to John above the din of the idling engines.

"Wind's holding, sir—the sheep are in the meadow this morning!"

It was difficult to be heard over the engines' roar, so John simply nodded in assent and gave Byron a thumbs-up, followed by the signal to turn

Baby straight into the wind for takeoff. Byron complied, maneuvering the craft into a starboard turn. When *Baby* was lined up and ready, John pointed to the sky with a spinning motion, and shouted, "Let's go!"

Byron throttled up both enormous engines, and *Baby's* growl intensified into a thunderous roar as she plowed forward, slowly gathering speed. The force of the powerful prop wash from *Baby's* huge twin blades blew the tops off the whitecaps behind her. As she accelerated, though, it was hard to tell if the new carburetors were actually delivering additional horsepower. As John had feared, the extra weight of the human ballast seemed to hamper momentum. He signaled Byron to push the throttles to the stops. The engines screamed in response. Soon *Baby* was hurtling across the bay.

The engine noise and vibrations were extraordinary. Between the pounding that the duralumin hull was taking as they crashed through the waves, and the forceful horizontal waterfall of spray that thrummed along the sides, riding in the plane felt like being inside a giant bass drum. For the wild-eyed volunteers, unable to see outside, the beating continued for what seemed like an eternity. They huddled inside the cramped cabin, hanging onto their ropes for dear life, cursing themselves for ever having volunteered, as the relentless abuse seemed sure to tear the craft apart. All aboard concentrated on willing the plane into the air.

But *Baby* fought valiantly. At the four-mile mark, she finally lifted up onto the step, but she was hindered by a series of growler waves that slowed her slightly, pulling her back down. The water refused to ease its grip. The plane struggled mightily for another couple of miles, pitching through the whitecaps, to no avail. At last, John signaled Byron to cut the throttles. *Baby* plowed like a road grader as she slowed down. They U-turned to starboard and taxied back toward the cove.

Meanwhile, six miles away, Snody cranked up his plane and started to accelerate. Just as *Baby's* run-up had been, Snody's was way too long. It appeared that he was experiencing the same problem getting his aircraft up on its step with the added weight. At one point, the spray completely enveloped the right side of the plane as it porpoised through one particularly large wave. The starboard engine took the brunt of it and sputtered momentarily, but continued on. As Snody approached the same four-mile marker, his craft suddenly rose up on her step, and as she did, she leveled and quickly gathered more speed. She continued to accelerate incrementally for two more miles, and then, while skipping over a couple of wind-driven waves, she inched into the air. It seemed that Snody willed the plane forward, flying in ground-effect, as the air compressed between the lower wing and the water's surface. For several excruciatingly long minutes, the plane tenuously skimmed just above the waves, then at last she was truly airborne. Snody banked his plane to port, and began to circle in a holding pattern as he waited for the other planes.

Back on *Baby*, John turned to watch as *Pretty Boy* prepared to take off. She seemed to be experiencing troubles of a different kind. By now, Rodgers and crew had taxied to within a mile of the takeoff area, and could clearly see that Lieutenant Commander Strong was having a difficult time lining up the plane. Just as Rodgers had predicted, the shiny silver behemoth was completely at the mercy of the brisk easterlies. It looked as if Strong was trying unsuccessfully to rein in a headstrong horse. After twice being blown off his desired upwind angle for takeoff, Strong seemed to give up and simply let the stiff breeze turn him to face downwind. At that point, he gunned the engines to accelerate. Byron shook his head incredulously.

"Sir, what the hell is he up to?"

Rodgers shrugged, "Looks to me like Strong's hoping to gain some kind of control with the airborne rudder. It's a risky move."

As they watched, Strong, now traveling at considerable speed, turned hard to port. This maneuver heeled the plane dangerously on its starboard float, which promptly dug into the swells. *Pretty Boy* slowed, and Strong countered by giving her some more gas. As luck would have it, the plane was on a crest when he did. Instead of taking a nosedive, the PB1 somehow spun out, turned 180 degrees, and faced straight into the wind. At exactly that instant, Strong corrected the rudder and poured gas to the engines. *Pretty Boy* came to strict attention and began to furrow the designated runway. The noise from the combined 1,600 horsepower was beyond earsplitting. The huge four-bladed props threw a massive amount of spray aft as the plane gained speed. At three and a half miles, it climbed to its step. *Pretty Boy* gained more speed and finally lifted off at almost the same spot as Snody's plane had. While it had taken more effort than John had expected, at least two of his charges were in the air. Now only *Baby* was water bound.

In the time it had taken Strong to lift off, Byron had positioned *Baby* back at the headwaters. Byron looked at John for the order, and once again Rodgers gave the wind-it-up signal. Byron eased the throttles forward, and the whitecaps slapping at the bow intensified as *Baby* accelerated. Struck by an idea, John ducked into the fuselage and yelled for the crew and volunteers to move further forward to help get *Baby* up on her step. Barreling down the bay, the craft did seem to climb onto her step more easily this time. It was almost as if she was embarrassed to be the only one still stuck in the water. Once she began planing, *Baby* accelerated nicely past the five-mile marker. Then, as she skipped across some wave tops, Byron pulled the yoke back and *Baby* broke free. They climbed to a modest one hundred feet, and the crew began their flight checks.

Inside Snody's craft, however, all was not well. As soon as the men's ears had adjusted to the greatly reduced noise level, all onboard were alarmed by a horrendous vibration in the starboard propeller. The rogue wave had obviously damaged either the engine or the prop. Nonetheless, Snody's call was to continue.

The three planes joined up in a loose formation and headed out through the Golden Gate, the channel that led from the bay into the Pacific Ocean. It was a spectacular sight, one that several alert photographers on shore captured. They knew the photos would be eagerly snapped up by the press, to run alongside the flight test results published in tomorrow's papers—publicity that would continue to ratchet up the pressure to succeed.

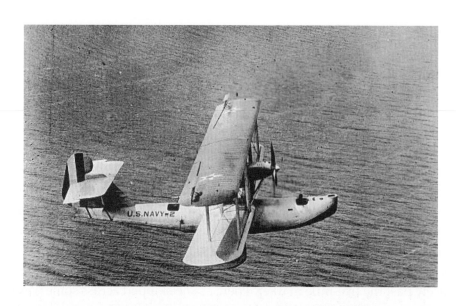

Boeing Aircraft's PB1 *(Pretty Boy)*

The PN9-1: As ungraceful as *Baby* appeared in the water, she was a beautiful plane to fly. This picture clearly shows Rodgers and crew in their various open-air cockpits: Rodgers in the bow, Connell and Pope behind the small windscreens, Bowlin in the mechanics cockpit (between the engines), and Stantz further aft, almost hidden by the engine struts.

NAF Philadelphia's PN9-1 *(Baby)*.

The pending transpacific attempt begins to get more press, as illustrated by the August 29, 1925 *Honolulu Advertiser* headline. The successful test flight was covered nationwide in this Associated Press article.

The August 29, 1925 edition of *The Honolulu Star-Bulletin:* This is a second-section article that outlined the flight mission and delineated the positive effect it would have on the island territory of Hawaii. The far-right-hand column reflects on the beginning of Japan's massive military buildup. Japan announced that it was building four new heavy cruisers, four torpedo boat destroyers, and a compendium of submarines and support vessels. Although claiming to conform to the spirit of the Washington Naval Treaty, the growth of the Japanese navy was a precursor of events to come.

Chapter 29

Sunday—August 30, 1925

10:39 AM Pacific Time

The bright midmorning sun streamed into the bedroom of Ethel Rodgers' small but elegant art deco apartment in Burbank. She had opted to stay in Southern California, at least until her divorce was settled. She had told her family in Maryland it was because her attorney was in Los Angeles, but the truth was that Ethel was not yet ready to face the social stigma her split with John was sure to cause back home. She stirred and peered groggily at the alarm clock on her bedside table. *God, how did it get to be so late?* Closing her eyes, she lay back and rubbed her throbbing temples. It had been a heck of a party the night before, and she was paying for it now.

Ethel's feet had barely touched the ground before she grabbed a pack of Luckys and a "strike anywhere" match from her nightstand. She stifled a smoker's cough and lit a cigarette to start the day. Slipping into some elegant mules and a scarlet silk wrap, Ethel teetered unsteadily down the hall and opened the front door to her garden stoop. Gingerly shading her eyes, she picked up the hefty Sunday newspaper. Exhaling heavily, she trundled back inside.

Her efficiency kitchen was small, and today it looked the way she felt. Ethel shifted some dirty dishes in the porcelain sink, searching for a passable teacup and saucer. Finding them, she prepped her percolator and listlessly went through the motions of preparing her morning coffee. At last, steaming cup in hand, she eased herself into one side of the two-person dine-in nook. Ethel normally enjoyed the cheery, sunlit alcove. This morning, however, she reached up and closed the red-and-white checked cotton curtains.

Taking a long drag on her cigarette, she unrolled the newspaper on the table. Immediately, the photograph of three seaplanes passing the Golden Gate headland caught her eye. The caption read, "Race to Hawaii starts tomorrow," followed by the headline, "THREE NAVY SEAPLANES TO ATTEMPT THE IMPOSSIBLE." The story continued: "Led by Commander John Rodgers, three navy seaplanes will start their race to the Hawaiian Islands tomorrow."

Ethel frowned and stubbed her cigarette out on the photo. She made a mental note to phone her attorney in the morning. *Just in case.* She then crumpled the front page section, tossed it into the rubbish, and retreated back to her bedroom.

2:01 PM Eastern Time

The late summer heat in Lakehurst, New Jersey was stifling in the midday sun as Lieutenant Commander Zachary Lansdowne climbed from the staff car and crossed the flat expanse toward the *Shenandoah's* two-hundred-foot-tall mooring mast. He had his marching orders. The navy needed to make the *Shenandoah* more visible to the general public Their prized airship was the second part of Admiral Moffett's two-pronged public relations campaign for naval aviation—John Rodgers' transpacific mission was the first. The *Shenandoah* was slated to embark on a tour across the Midwest. Harvest time was always the occasion of many state fairs, and the appearance of the silver behemoth sporting the U.S. Navy logo would be a powerful marketing asset. Moffett wanted Lansdowne to crisscross the country, displaying the navy's aerial flagship at as many state fairs as possible along the way. The admiral had even issued a flight invitation to a civilian photographer to record the journey.

As Lansdowne approached the tower he was met by Lieutenant Joseph B. Anderson and Rigger CPO Mark Donovan. They both saluted, and greeted the commander.

"Good afternoon sir."

"Sir."

"Gentlemen. Come with me."

Anderson was a young, bookish sort whose assignment to the *Shenandoah* as the ship's aerologist was a perfect fit. Aerology is the branch of meteorology which concerns itself with the weather and air currents, especially at altitude. His assignment to the giant airship was considered a plum position for his unique specialty. It was his first appointment of any merit since becoming an officer, but he was both competent and knowledgable.

Rigger Mark Donovan, a slight, wiry, noncommissioned officer, was a hardscrabble jack-of-all-trades. He had been posted to the ZR-1 since her maiden flight, and knew the physical ins and outs of the enormous airship intimately. His tasks aboard the *Shenandoah* centered on the twenty gas bags and the surrounding structures. Donovan was notorious for his gymnastic skills when negotiating the fantastic internal framework of the zeppelin. More than once Lansdowne had marveled at the rigger's acrobatic maneuvers within the cavernous interior. No one aboard knew the craft better.

Lansdowne led his two subordinates to the elevator at the base of the mast. After they had entered the enclosed cage, he nodded toward Donovan. "Take us up."

"Aye, sir." Donovan shut the collapsible gate and pulled back on the throttle-like controller. The elevator slowly began its ascent.

Lansdowne was a strict, no-nonsense man. While considered fair and even understanding to his men, he was not known for casual conversation, so it did not surprise either of his companions that there was no conversation during the ride up.

As the elevator reached the boarding platform almost two hundred feet up, Lansdowne opened the gate himself and saluted the ship's unseen flag, which was more than two football fields aft. Then he stepped briskly across the narrow gangplank and into the bow of the giant craft. Saluting again and requesting permission to board, his men followed suit.

The threesome descended the narrow duralumin steps. The forty-five foot staircase curved in concert with the exterior shape and consequently was interrupted by several landings as the curve flattened and they neared the keel walkway. Above them, the yawning interior seemed otherworldly, with huge silken bags filling most of the interior. The sacks moved mysteriously with unseen air currents, seeming to breathe in and out like great silver lungs, making the ship feel like a living creature. These airbags were filled to ninety-one percent capacity with precious helium, about six percent more than normal, in preparation for the upcoming extended trip.

The sailors continued along the ten-inch-wide catwalk that ran for over two hundred yards along the interior keel. Halfway along, they reached the tiny living space—just 144 feet square—known as the "lounge," where Lansdowne beckoned the men to sit with him.

He turned to Anderson. "First: I need a thorough assessment of the weather patterns along our intended route—the whole route. The Secretary of the Navy, Curtis B. Wilbur himself is requesting it." Shaking his head, he continued, "He basically wants us to predict the weather for the next four weeks.

"He's allowed us to put this trip off because of unpredictable summer turbulence, but he's fed up with the delays. Now that September is upon us, he's asking that we get on with the tour. Thank God Admiral Moffett understands that thunderstorms must be avoided at all cost. He'll stand by whatever decision we make, but I am sure he's being pressured as well."

Anderson nodded.

Then Lansdowne turned to Donovan. "Second: I need to make a personal inspection of the entire aircraft to make sure she's shipshape. Donovan, I want you to take me everywhere from the external topside catwalk that runs the length of the ship, through the entire framework of girders, rib by rib. I want to check the fuel and water systems myself, and inspect over and around each and every gas bag. I want to scrutinize the control cables, and I even want to climb out into each of the suspended engine gondolas. I need to be sure the *Shenandoah*'s ready for anything."

11:22 AM Pacific Time

Time was running out for the teams. With less than twenty-four hours to go before the planned start, all three planes were being meticulously taken apart and rebuilt. Every item needed to be checked and double-checked. Luckily, the crews were assisted by a cadre of swabbies that Moffett had recruited. Rodgers had no idea how they would have managed without the extra help. All hands worked feverishly as the deadline approached. Along with the standard mechanical prep, each plane seemed to have her own specific problems to troubleshoot.

Snody's crew had spent most of the morning with their starboard engine. The beating that it had taken on their long takeoff run the day before was their primary concern. The engine had to be thoroughly cleaned after its saltwater bath. The crew had replaced all ignition components with spares. Unfortunately, the two-bladed propeller on the starboard side had sustained significant damage, and there was no spare. The abuse had distorted the normally circular mounting holes on the propeller hub into ovals. The crew removed the huge prop and shimmed the holes as best they could. They then rebalanced the prop before reattaching it to the plane's engine, but its condition was still questionable.

Strong's crew had embraced *Pretty Boy*'s nickname, and after they had secured their spare fuel tanks and stowed their basic supplies they set about on a different tack. Boasting that he wanted *Pretty Boy* to make a good impression on the Hawaiian *wahine,* Strong had his crew washing, waxing, and spit-polishing their silver pride and joy.

Onboard *Baby*, Rodgers had more practical concerns. The flight tests Saturday had not gone well. The new carburetors had not improved the rate of fuel consumption, as had been hoped. Taking some personal initiative, Wild Bill had tracked down the owner of the local San Francisco Packard dealership the night before. Interrupting the man's dinner at a swank restaurant, Bill had pleaded for assistance with the carburetor conundrum. The car dealer, well aware of the imminent "race," had agreed to send help first thing in the morning, even though it was a Sunday. As good as his word, the owner and his chief mechanic had shown up before dawn, both attired in workmen's coveralls, and had spent all morning adjusting the carburetor jets.

To make matters even more complicated, *Baby*'s port radiator had sprung a small leak during the multiple engine run-ups necessary for the carburetor adjustments. Wild Bill added more Liquid X, which seemed to solve the problem. He topped off the starboard radiator, just to be safe, but the fact that they had sprung yet another leak had them all anxious.

Kiles had also discovered a surprising amount of corrosion on the cable fittings that controlled the ailerons and rudder. Not wishing to take any chances, Byron and Kiles were now busy replacing the entire set.

One of Rodgers' greatest concerns was air-to-surface communications: the radio equipment onboard had never been fully tested for maximum range. To address this issue, Sparky took matters into his own hands. He was in the process of installing a long retractable antenna that could be spooled out like a fishing line below and behind the plane once it was airborne. This was a technique he had employed successfully in the past. If it worked as it had before, the antenna would increase the radio's range.

In addition to the course, the alignment of the ships along the rhumb line, and the all-important trade winds, John continued to worry about his eyesight. Onboard, there would be little chance for the privacy he needed to slip on his glasses. To make matters worse, the cramped forward navigation station in *Baby* was badly lit, making it all the more difficult to see properly.

At long last, all the supplies had been carefully weighed and properly secured onboard each of the three planes. By now, *Pretty Boy* was the undisputed, albeit untested, heavyweight champion. Fully loaded, she had grown from 12,700 pounds net weight to almost 23,000 pounds gross. However, the additional weight was not considered a major problem, as the plane was supposed to be able to handle up to 24,000 pounds. For both the press and the general public, *Pretty Boy* was the odds-on favorite to win this race.

By comparison, Rodgers' and Snody's identical planes fell into the middleweight division, each tipping the scales at a modest ninety-one hundred pounds dry. They would both need to carry 1,350 gallons of fuel and fifty gallons of oil. By the time all the supplies and emergency gear had been loaded onboard, their gross weight had ballooned to over 19,300 pounds apiece—an impossible weight for the PN9s to get aloft.

John called Byron Connell and Allen Snody over for an emergency confab.

"Gentlemen, we have a serious problem. Look at how our planes are riding in the water."

Sure enough, both PN9s were floating nose-down, their wing-tip floats awash with the extra weight. Rodgers continued: "We're looking at an extremely dangerous situation. If one of those tips digs in on a wave when we're at speed, we could easily ground loop. If the bow digs in, we could pearl dive, or even flip."

Snody and Connell looked at each other. John was certainly right. Byron was the first to speak.

"Skip, there's no way we can cut back on fuel . . ." He trailed off as Snody volunteered, "What if we pitched everything that isn't absolutely essential? Would that do it, John?"

Rodgers nodded grimly. "Do we have a choice? The situation calls for drastic measures. We've got to get those planes up, and I think that's the only possible solution. Let's get to work and ditch anything that's not absolutely critical to the mission."

Both teams were gathered and instructed to jettison any nonessentials. Personal gear was the first to go. Clothing, toiletries—anything that could be bought or replaced once they reached Hawaii—was removed and weighed. That number was then subtracted from the plane's earlier weight.

The first elimination round didn't do the trick. Estimated flight time was thirty hours, so unnecessary food and excess water were off-loaded next. When they had finished, only a few sandwiches, a little coffee, several oranges, and some drinking water remained. Again, they recalculated the weight. John shook his head.

"Still too heavy. What else can we do without?"

Next, the distress radio, emergency generator, extra batteries, and all the parachutes were dumped on the pier. Another calculation was made.

"Nope, not yet."

Then, all the safety gear was jettisoned. The men figured that since they'd be in seaplanes after all, the life rafts and even the life jackets could be considered superfluous.

At last, John estimated that the planes weighed in at only 475 pounds more than when they had flown their test flight with the extra bodies the day before. As sunlight faded, the crews finished up under temporary lights and gathered around their commander.

"Whaddaya think, Skip?"

"Have we missed anything?"

"Nothin' else left to ditch, sir."

Rodgers studied the anxious faces surrounding him.

"Gentlemen, good work. We've done all we can do. We've pared to the bone and they're as light as they're gonna get. Let's call it a night."

Sparky spoke up with the question that was on everyone's mind.

"Sir, are we good to go for tomorrow? Can we make it?"

Rodgers answered with a confidence he was far from feeling.

"We're as ready as we'll ever be. Now, get some sleep, we'll need it. It's going to be a long trip." As he watched his men disperse into the night, he muttered to himself, "And pray for tailwinds."

D. Thompson, Rico Botta, James Strong, L. C. Sullivan, R. Davidson

The Honolulu Advertiser, August 30, 1925: Again, the press anoints the Boeing PB1 as the plane to watch as the start draws near. Pictured on the front page of the Sunday edition is Lieutenant Commander James Strong's crew. There is absolutely no mention of Commander John Rodgers, Lieutenant Snody, or the PN9 planes.

Kiles Pope, Byron Connell, John Rodgers, William Bowlin, Otis Stantz.

Pictured above is the crew of the PN9-1 prior to leaving for Hawaii. Kiles Pope is standing in the navigation station cockpit (not his normal position). Significant features include the two small prop-wash-driven generator propellers (located between and aft of William Bowlin and Otis Stantz), the curved-glass windscreens, and the multiple guy wires angled between the wings. All of these elements would become crucially important to the mission. Note the thirteen-foot hand-carved wooden propellers and the vertical distance of the upper wing from the lower one. Although the bow of Rodgers' plane appears dark in this photograph, it was actually painted navy yellow to differentiate it from Snody's plane, which had a yellow tail.

Interior view of the *Shenandoah*'s keel while she was under construction. Note the ten-inchwide catwalk that ran the entire length of the ship—well over two football fields.

Viewed here while still under construction are several of the innumerable gasoline tanks located within the ZR-1, which fed the six Packard V-8 engines that powered the airship. Note the worker's feet hanging off the edges of the narrow catwalk.

Chapter 30

Monday—August 31, 1925

5:04 AM Pacific Time

Today was the day. John awoke well before sunrise. It was still dark out as he shaved and went through his routine morning ablutions. When he had finished, his first official order of business was to check the weather report. While never one hundred percent reliable, the forecast looked promising. The messages relayed from the flotilla of navy vessels already on-station along the intended flight route reported light but steady winds from the east-northeast. Almost afraid to say it out loud, John whispered to himself, "Trades. . . !"

Rodgers gathered his gear and exited his room, leaving his suitcases at the door to be collected and shipped to Hawaii. He then made his way to the Chrissy Field officers' mess, picking Byron up along the way. Admiral Moffett had invited all of the men to share a private early-morning breakfast there.

Even at this early hour there was a gauntlet of reporters and photographers lining the way to the mess hall, pushing and shoving to start coverage of the heroes' big day. Flash bulbs bounced light wildly off the white walls, momentarily blinding the two aviators. Questions came at them rapid-fire.

"Commander, do you really think you can carry enough gas to make it?"

". . . what if you have to refuel?"

". . . which plane do you think will win?"

John fielded as many as he could, and then begged to be excused, as the admiral was waiting. A chorus of enthusiastic "Good luck!"s followed them, but even before John and Byron had entered the mess hall, the press surged in the other direction. Lieutenant Commander Strong, Lieutenant Botta, and the PB1 crew had appeared in the hallway. Now the reporters geared up into a *bona fide* feeding frenzy. It was clear *Pretty Boy*'s crew was the main attraction. As the door closed behind him, John caught the gist of the questions peppering Strong and his men.

"How long will it take you to get to Hawaii?"

". . . do you think the other planes will be able to keep up?"

". . . will you have to wait for them if they need to refuel?"

". . . can the other two go the distance?"

John sighed and followed Byron into the dining room.

Moments later, the men took their places around a U-shaped table with Admiral Moffett at the head. On his right sat Rodgers with Snody and Connell; Strong and Botta were on Moffett's left. The rest of the crews occupied the remaining ten seats. All three teams were anxious to get to their planes, but given the unswerving support Moffett had provided from the get-go, the men felt obliged to honor his invitation. To John especially, the meal seemed interminable. He felt like a caged wild plover yearning to get into the air and on his way back to Hawaii.

After the plates had been cleared, Admiral Moffett dismissed his aide, and the waiters. Then he stood to address the men. Sensing their mood, Moffett kept his remarks brief.

"I want to thank all of you personally for your dedication and perseverance." Turning towards Rodgers, he added "And I want to apologize for the innumerable delays." Then he surveyed the faces around him, deliberately pausing for emphasis.

"Gentlemen, naval aviation sits at a crossroads. Its very existence may be in your hands. The importance of this mission cannot be overstated.

"Many think what you're about to attempt is folly—an impossibility. Well, I believe otherwise, and I know you all stand with me on this. Yes, our plan is audacious, but that's the beauty of it. If you gentlemen succeed, your triumph will silence our critics and assure the future of naval aviation.

"Our goal today is to set a long-distance flight record, and to do it with *navy* aircraft, flying over the loneliest stretch of ocean on the planet. I want you to know whether or not you complete the mission nonstop does not concern me. Certainly we all hope it can be done without any of you having to land, but if you are forced to refuel at sea and are then able to continue, it will demonstrate the skill and ingenuity of navy aviators. I will still consider the mission a success. Questions?"

Lieutenant Commander Strong stood. "Admiral, do you wish us to maintain pace with each other throughout the crossing?"

The question behind the question was crystal clear to all: could Strong and his crew go out ahead in the faster plane and come in first to claim the glory?

Moffett shot a look at Rodgers, lowered his eyes and then addressed the group, "The press has labeled this mission a race. Let me assure you, it is not. It is my fervent desire for all three planes to arrive in Honolulu together. That said, although I abhor the idea, if one plane runs low on fuel and must stop, the others should continue on. If, on the other hand, one plane needs to maintain a faster speed than the others for the sake of fuel efficiency, then so be it. As I've said, I'd prefer you to arrive together if possible, but each of you, with Commander Rodgers' assent, will have to make those decisions as situations arise en route." At this, *Pretty Boy*'s crew could scarcely contain their delight.

Moffett continued, "One last thing: don't be misled: those reporters and photographers glad-handing you this morning will be only too happy to trumpet your failure this evening. In either case, you will be tomorrow's headlines across the country. Let's make sure it's because of your victory.

"Gentlemen, I thank you. I applaud your courage, and I wish you all a safe journey. Good luck and God speed."

At that, the room was called to attention. Moffett saluted the aviators, and then made his way around the table, shaking each man's hand.

The teams quickly filed out of the mess hall. Several members of the press were still outside, but most had already headed off to the planes. As John and Byron ran down the front steps of the officers' mess, Byron joked, "I'm glad we're finally getting underway. I don't know about you, skip, but good as it was, I had trouble chokin' down that chow."

John grinned. "Yeah, me too!"

The crews piled into the official cars waiting to transport them across the field to the planes. The day was bright, sunny, and free of the customary San Francisco fog. This was a good sign that the winds would be up soon. As the motorcade approached an intersection near the waterfront, a delivery truck ran a stop sign and nearly T-boned the car Rodgers was in. Sitting next to John, Wild Bill quipped nervously, "Well, I sure hope that's the worst thing that happens to us today." The men arrived at the water's edge and proceeded to the staging area to await the scheduled start. As they had a little over an hour to kill before being ferried out to the planes, a good deal of nervous pacing ensued.

During that hour the winds came up, and occasional flecks of white dotted the bay. The local breeze was slightly onshore. Though it was the wrong direction for a tail wind to Hawaii, if it kept up it meant that the planes could take off to the west, in the direction of their intended route, gaining a few precious extra miles.

By 9 AM, hundreds of boats of all kinds dotted San Francisco Bay. The navy had sent several warships, which were now anchored in the harbor. In addition to the astounding number of private boats, an equally impressive crowd lined the wharfs, the meadow, and the surrounding hills. The San Francisco Diamond Jubilee was in full swing, and many in the crowd had taken the day off to witness the historic spectacle. Hundreds of children still on summer vacation frolicked amid the throng. American flags flew proudly everywhere.

Admiral Moffett had already repaired to the USS *Gannet* when the air show began. From Washington, D.C., Colonel Billy Mitchell had urged the air corps to make its presence known, and the army responded by staging an impressive aerial display. More than two dozen planes from right there at Chrissy Field participated, thrilling the crowd with formation maneuvers. Moffett fumed silently as he watched the army planes strut their stuff. He couldn't help but resent their trying to horn in on his headlines. He only hoped that the size of his navy planes and the enormity of their mission would take center stage.

The press was everywhere. Onboard the *Gannet,* they almost outnumbered the invited guests. A blow-by-blow account of the start was being relayed to a local radio station for broadcast—a first for San Francisco. At precisely 9:15 AM, the three seaplanes were towed out to the designated launch area to save every last drop of fuel. At the mercy of both wind and current, they bobbed awkwardly from the pre-positioned anchor buoys. Downwind from the planes, a fireboat shot two streams of water high into the air, and a vivid rainbow accompanied the spray from the boat's twin cannons—hopefully, a good omen.

By 9:45 AM, John began to worry. The breeze that had greeted them earlier had dropped to under six knots. The waters within the protected cove of the bay had flattened, and all traces of the whitecaps that made takeoff easier had disappeared.

At exactly 10 AM, the crews climbed into a waiting powerboat that sped them across the water toward the aircraft. Seeing this, the crowds immediately began blowing horns and ringing bells. A couple of flares arced skyward, popped, and drifted slowly down. The air crackled with anticipation. The speedboat slowed to a stop next to the first drab-gray, heavily laden PN9-1. The crews exchanged salutes and handshakes and Rodgers and his team climbed aboard *Baby.* They immediately began to flight check the plane. Noting the time, Rodgers made his first entry in the flight log.

Snody and his crew were next as the motor boat sidled up to their PN9-3. Once onboard, they, too, busied themselves with their preflight checklists, paying a fair bit of extra attention to the starboard propeller.

The PB1, *Pretty Boy,* was moored on the far side of the fuel barge, closer to the USS *Gannet* and the rest of the spectator fleet. As the speedboat pulled up alongside their plane, Strong's team stood in unison to climb aboard their shiny silver aircraft, and a roar of applause, horns, and sirens began. Lieutenant Commander Strong saluted in the direction of the *Gannet.* He then doffed his flight cap and waved it high above his head to the assembled throng. Botta and the rest of his crew followed suit. Team *Pretty Boy* milked the moment for all it was worth, and the crowd ate it up.

By 10:30 AM, as Rodgers looked out across the bay, he continued to fret about the lack of wind. Taking off into a decent wind would have helped the heavy planes become airborne at slower actual speeds. In addition, a wind-whipped surface would have made it easier to break the water's tensile hold on the hull. Now, unfortunately, the breeze was barely perceptible, and glassy patches dotted the entire bay. The conditions could not have been worse for takeoff.

At 10:55 AM, a large powerboat ferrying Admiral Moffett and his entourage pulled up next to Rodgers' plane. He gave John two barographs so that he could prove the distance traveled—a world record if they made it without having to land to refuel—and two letters. One was for Admiral McDonald, commandant of the 14th Naval District in Honolulu; the other, for Wallace R. Farrington, the Territorial Governor of Hawaii.

Despite his anxiety to get underway, John advised Moffett that they needed to postpone takeoff, in hopes that the wind would pick up. Moffett accepted the decision, but both of them knew there was a limit to how long they could wait. For safety's sake, the planes needed to be in the air no later than 3 PM. With the two-hour time difference between San Francisco and Honolulu, a 3 PM departure meant they would arrive around 7 PM Hawaii time, the next day. Any later and they would have to land in the dark. Moffett wished the crew well once more, returned a final salute, and sped back to the *Gannet*.

Final checks were underway onboard the planes, when a navy lighter ferried a five-pack of hot meals and a thermos of coffee out to each plane. With nervous energy running high, the men had been burning calories at a prodigious rate. They eagerly wolfed down the food despite the large breakfast they had eaten earlier.

By noon, although still in a festive mood, the large audience was growing restless. The appointed takeoff time had passed, and the planes had not even started their engines. Most of the spectators were unaware of the reason for the delay. As time passed, the bolder among those on the water edged their boats nearer to the planes, hoping to see what the holdup was. Wakes from the assorted powerboats set the planes to rocking, making it difficult for the aviators to execute last-minute preparations.

When John's chronograph read one o'clock, he realized they had run out of options. The wind had not picked up as he had hoped, but he knew that wind or no wind they had to go now. He signaled to the other planes. They had already decided the launch order. *Pretty Boy* with her greater range and fuel capacity would lift off first, and then fly a lazy holding pattern as she waited for her sister aircraft. Snody's plane had achieved slightly better fuel mileage than *Baby* during their test flights, so he would be up next. As soon as Rodgers could get *Baby* airborne, the three planes would proceed in formation through the relatively narrow opening of the Golden Gate to the sea, and then directly onto the rhumb-line course.

Five minutes later, *Pretty Boy*'s crew cast off her anchor lines, and the plane drifted away from the mooring. Boats crowded in for a closer look at history in the making, and several had to be sternly warned away. Anticipation ran high. As the crowd watched with bated breath, all was suddenly quiet.

Two of *Pretty Boy*'s NCOs appeared, straddling either side of the PB1's massive nacelle, poised for action. Then the silence was broken by a loud bass voice: "Ignition!" At that, the electric starter caused the forward engine's flywheel to begin a whine that sounded like a muted police siren. The huge four-bladed propeller spun in slow-motion, thrilling the crowd. The engine coughed and caught, and the roar of the monstrous forward-facing Packard V-12 threw the crowd into a frenzy. The procedure was repeated for the aft pusher engine, and soon the din was overwhelming. Each engine packed more than 800 virtually unmuffled horsepower. None watching had ever been so close to such pure, unbridled mechanical power. The spray shooting from the enormous props soaked several of the boats that were close on the plane's stern, and they hurriedly retreated to drier vantage points.

The big silver bird cast off and swam powerfully away from its mooring ball. At first, Strong tried to thread his way through the flotilla, but as the PB1 reached taxi speed, the multitude parted before her like the Red Sea. Strong struggled to keep the massive seaplane online as she crabbed diagonally in the current. He throttled up, hoping to use momentum to gain more control. In response, the plane leaped forward, straightening a bit.

Pretty Boy approached the USS *Gannet,* anchored off her starboard side. Eager to show off for the VIP gallery onboard, Strong sped his craft close alongside. He waved proudly for the cameras, momentarily distracted as they passed in review alongside the navy ship—too fast. When Strong next looked where he was going, a large commercial tour boat loomed squarely in his path. It had exited from behind the shadow of the warship while Strong played to the navy brass. Several of the guests onboard the battleship screamed to warn him, but it was too late. All watched, helpless in the face of the pending calamity.

Strong pushed hard on *Pretty Boy*'s rudder pedals to try and get her to turn in time, but his efforts were in vain. The small, water-bound rudder simply cavitated, causing a whirlpool of water and a hollow of air to form behind the inadequate blade. Not only was the plane not turning, its forward momentum continued unchecked. The tour boat's skipper pushed his throttle to the maximum in a last-ditch effort to avert a collision. While the tour boat was far too heavy and sluggish to respond significantly, it did move a little. For a moment, it seemed that if *Pretty Boy*'s rudder could catch, she might be able to turn enough to sidestep disaster.

Cameras on the *Gannet* and other boats nearby had already been focused on the PB1 before, but now that a collision seemed imminent, the photographers began snapping shots like mad. They couldn't advance their film fast enough.

And then it happened. *Pretty Boy*'s portside wings slammed into the stern pulpit of the tour boat. The impact spun the plane like a top, skidding it to port and aft of the boat. The collision crushed the first few feet of both shiny portside wings, and severely damaged the port wing float. *Pretty Boy,* although still afloat and intrinsically stable, wouldn't be flying anywhere anytime soon. The sturdy tour boat, on the other hand, had escaped virtually unscathed. No one onboard had been hurt.

Admiral Moffett was momentarily stunned in the face of what was sure to be a public relations nightmare. His military training, however, enabled him to recover quickly and shift into damage control. He would deal with Strong later. For now, he had two other planes to get into the air. Standing in the conning tower of the *Gannet*, he commanded the radio operator to raise Rodgers and Snody. "Tell them to proceed as planned, and get airborne as soon as possible."

Rodgers was still reeling from the disaster and its potential impact on the mission when Sparky relayed Moffett's message to him. John looked across the water at Snody and got a thumbs-up from him, indicating he, too, had copied the message. Snody immediately let loose from his anchor ball and soon drifted safely clear of the spectator fleet.

While most of the horrified onlookers were still fixated on the PB1 collision, Snody fired his engines in sequence. Although the PN9s engines were a third smaller than the PB1's, they were still impressive. The engines caught without fanfare, and once the fickle crowd realized that the second plane was about to take off, all attention shifted to the PN9-3.

Snody taxied out to the starting point. Once the engine's operating temperatures were in the zone, he spun the plane about to face what little breeze there was and punched the twin accelerators. Snody traveled smartly down the intended seaway, but as had happened with Saturday's test flight, the overloaded seaplane seemed to take forever to get up to full speed. One mile, two miles, three miles, and then finally she started to skip. The velocity increased incrementally along the intended path, but the smooth water and lack of headwinds conspired against liftoff. While the starboard prop was functioning, the noise it was making was worrisome. Plus, the unbalanced vibration it produced as the PN9 strained to get up on its step made the entire plane rattle violently. Four miles, five miles, and still Snody couldn't break the bond. At the six-mile mark, he had exhausted his run. He gave up, and pulled the levers back to taxi speed. Snody had his radioman raise Sparky.

"The prop is holding. We just couldn't quite lift off. Smooth water. Too much weight aft. Request permission for a second run."

Damn! Rodgers swore under his breath. The six-mile taxi back and the second run up would cost Snody precious fuel. Nonetheless, John radioed his assent. Knowing that it would take Snody the better part of a half-hour to taxi back, Rodgers had his crew cast off from their ball. Once clear, he signaled Byron to start up *Baby*'s port engine. It fired immediately, and Connell slowed it to a modest idle. However, when he tried to engage the starboard starter, it spun but the engine wouldn't catch. Byron let the engine rest momentarily and then pushed the button again, but with no luck. He repeated the sequence several times to no avail. This was a first. In all the tests, neither engine had ever failed to start.

Frustrated, Byron double-checked that the ignition, the spark arrest, and the choke were properly positioned, and then tried again. Again, the flywheel and inner workings of the starter sounded like a baritone siren, but after several tries, the starboard engine still wouldn't fire. Wild Bill signaled to Byron to cut the ignition to the obstinate engine. Once it was shut off, he and Kiles climbed out onto the starboard wing to see what could be done.

From his vantage point onboard the *Gannet*, Moffett groaned inwardly. His spectacular launch was quickly becoming a fiasco.

Byron hollered forward to John, pointing to the portside engine.

"Do you want me to shut her down as well?"

"No. It'll take more fuel to restart her than to let her idle for a minute."

Standing upright between the two starboard wings, Wild Bill fiddled with the carburetor on the recalcitrant cast-iron power plant while Kiles stood, holding the cowling open. In only a few moments, they'd worked their magic. They secured the louvered sheet-metal cover, and Bill shouted to Byron, "I think we're good to go. Close the choke and try 'er again."

As soon as Kiles and Bill were back inside *Baby*, Byron called out, "Ignition. Clear prop." This time, the starboard engine sputtered to life, and then ran up to speed. They immediately started their taxi, not wanting to waste any more precious fuel. As they proceeded, John noticed a small yellow smoke stream trailing from the starboard engine. *Should be bluish gray. She's running too rich.* He made a mental note to have Kiles and Wild Bill check it out once they were airborne.

As *Baby* approached her starting point, John saw that Snody had completed most of his return taxi. He was less than a mile away and headed towards them, parallel to, but well clear of, their intended takeoff route. John gave Byron his heading and the signal to go.

Byron eased the throttles forward gingerly to save fuel. As *Baby* increased her speed he massaged the throttles even further forward. The heavily loaded plane sluggishly plowed a wide furrow in the bay. She slowly picked up speed until she had climbed onto her step at the three-mile mark. The knot meter inched higher, but she still couldn't break free. At the four-mile mark, John left his perch and signaled for the crew to move below and forward.

While *Baby* skipped like a stone across the water, John untied two drums of fuel, and with Kiles's and Wild Bill's help, they managed to shift them further toward the front of the plane. Ordinarily unsecured ballast in a plane was a danger to be avoided, but John was prepared to do whatever it took to get *Baby* aloft.

The crew all squatted down facing aft and placed their backs against the upright drums. They remained motionless as Byron pushed the throttle levers as far forward as they could go. Right at the six-mile marker, the noise of the water beating against the fuselage suddenly stopped, and the boat became a plane. They flew in ground-effect briefly, then climbed carefully to fifty feet and executed a slow turn. They performed a long lazy oval, flying low over the bay, hoping that Snody would join them soon. If not, they would have to proceed alone. John returned to his forward crow's nest, while the rest of the crew secured the fuel drums back where they belonged. From his lookout, he could see the cheering crowds waving flags, hats, and kerchiefs as Snody started his second run.

Snody's crew had rearranged some of their fuel cargo forward as well. They had used the return taxi time wisely, and had jury-rigged a stout mooring line to hold their drums in place. They employed a trucker's hitch knot, which effectively acted like a block and tackle, allowing them to snug the heavy drums up tightly. They would return the drums to their original location once in flight, but for now they just needed to lift off.

At the starting point, Snody quickly came about and wasted no time. He gunned the engines. They accelerated down the chase in what seemed at first like a replay of their earlier attempt. The plane struggled mightily to break free of the water's surface as it careened pell-mell westward across the bay. After what seemed like an eternity, Snody's PN9 lifted off at exactly the same six-mile marker as *Baby* had. It was 2:55 PM, Pacific time. Five minutes to spare.

Snody inched skyward and banked left as Rodgers completed his low circuit and turned inside. Snody fell in, behind and to the right of John. The pair wing-wagged to the spectators and headed toward the Golden Gate. Because of the extra fuel they were carrying, the planes were unable to gain any more altitude and were forced to fly for the time being at a scant fifty feet above the wave tops. The audience below ooh'ed and ah'd, assuming the low-level flying was part of the show.

From a distance, the planes looked beautiful, but trouble was brewing. Aboard Snody's plane, the starboard engine was vibrating ferociously, worse than in any of her previous test flights.

A 1925 mobile radio broadcast facility

Packard's A1-1500 geared V-12 aircraft engines were used in the PN9 airplanes.
This engine developed just over 500 horsepower, at 2,100 rpm.

Packard's A1-2500 geared V-12 aircraft engines were used in the PB1 airplane. This engine developed over 800 horsepower at 2,000 rpm.

The USS *Gannet*: Admiral Moffett's observation boat for the start of the crossing. On the day of the event, it was packed with dignitaries and press.

Chapter 31

Monday—August 31, 1925

6:03 PM Eastern Time

In Washington, D.C., the telephone jangled twice before Colonel Mitchell's aide picked up. He quickly passed the receiver to his superior officer.

"For you, sir. An update from San Francisco."

The aide and one of Mitchell's favorite reporters were the only others in the room. They listened as Mitchell shouted into the phone, "Speak up! I can hardly hear you." There was a pause as the colonel strained to catch the information coming over the line. Shaking his head, he interrupted the caller at the other end.

"Wait . . . wait a minute! If I'm hearing you right, this is goddamned unbelievable! Run it by me again, slowly."

After another moment, Mitchell howled out loud.

"Son-of-a-bitch! That's what I thought you said. Good work. Thank you." Mitchell abruptly hung up the phone. Turning to his companions, he chortled, "Gentlemen, Lieutenant Commander Strong damn near tore the wings off that new plane, showing off for the navy brass—slammed her into a tour boat. Then to top things off, they barely got the two older planes into the air!" Shaking his head, he said, "These navy jokers just don't know what they're doing."

3:10 PM Pacific Time

After the initial fifteen miles of flight, both planes had been able to edge up to almost three hundred feet. Byron throttled back a bit, as Snody was falling behind, and consequently, they were not flying at their planned cruising speed. John came aft, where he and Sparky conferred over the roar of the Packards.

"Skip, Snody's radioed that they can't keep up. He claims they can't maintain seventy knots. Their starboard prop is shakin' real bad, and he's had to throttle back on it. He's afraid the plane'll fall apart if he doesn't. He wants us to push on 'cause he's not sure they can make it."

John frowned. "Not sure they can make it? Already? We've only just started!"

Sparky shrugged. "It's that damn propeller, sir. Nothin' he can do about it."

Rodgers nodded, making his decision. "OK. Tell them to give it their best shot. We'll continue on course at planned cruising speed." John turned and met a woeful stare from Wild Bill.

"I know, Bill, I know. But it's all we can do. It's up to us, now."

Poking his head forward into the pilot's cockpit, Rodgers updated Byron and Kiles.

"Maintain our planned cruise speed and heading. Snody can't keep up, so we're on our own."

Byron nodded, acknowledging the command, and with a feather touch pushed the throttles slightly forward. The balanced, rhythmic thrumming of the engines lulled the crew. As they passed the Farallon Islands, twenty-three miles off the California coast, John recorded the event in the ship's log. The rocky archipelago below was the last land of any kind before they reached Hawaii, more than 2,000 miles away.

3:15 PM Pacific Time

As he watched *Baby* slowly disappear into the distance ahead, Snody had his hands full. The vibration was bad. They could reduce it by lowering the rpm on the starboard engine, but if they did that there was no way the plane could maintain the cruising speed necessary to make it to Honolulu without refueling at sea. With the compromised prop, though, another takeoff would be out of the question. Nevertheless, Snody had little choice but to throttle back their airspeed even further. He slowed them to forty-five knots, but at that speed, they could barely stay aloft. Three hundred feet was the projected minimum functional altitude needed for the long antenna wire that had been spooled out after leaving the bay. Since they would need the antenna to assure adequate communication with the ships along their course, flying on the "deck" in ground-effect was not an option. Snody struggled to maintain the three hundred feet operational altitude as the PN9-3 trundled along, shaking like a wet dog.

3:57 PM Pacific Time

Baby's identical antenna wire whipped out lazily behind her. It was invisible from view onboard, but indispensable for transmission. John had plotted their 240-degree course on the uniquely scrolled Mercator projection map he and the crew of the *Aroostook* had created for the mission. According to John's calculations and Sparky's reading of the radio bearing from the coast, Byron was right on track. This was their rhumb line, along which the chain of navy ships stretched at two-hundred-mile intervals. The winds remained light from the aft. At John's suggestion, Byron slowly climbed to five hundred feet in hopes that the air currents aloft might be stronger.

Wild Bill and Kiles fretted over the starboard engine. Although the V-12 seemed to be performing well, and the yellow smoke John had noticed before takeoff had disappeared, they were concerned that the engine might still be running too rich. Little could be done about it in-flight without a dangerous wing-walk, so their focus was on the as-yet barely perceptible differences in fuel consumption between the twin power plants.

After they had proceeded one hundred miles from the coast, Sparky was able to reach the first ship in the chain by radio. That initial station, designated "N," was assigned to the destroyer, *William Jones*. She was waiting another hundred miles farther out, as planned. Although Snody was not yet within her radio range, Sparky was in touch with Snody's plane, and was able to relay their estimated position and pace to the *William Jones.*

An hour and twenty-six minutes later, Rodgers and crew approached Station N and the USS *William Jones.* They passed approximately five miles north of the warship and briefly caught sight of her profile despite the graying sky, low-hanging clouds, and the late afternoon sun. The radio signal was loud and clear onboard *Baby,* but Sparky was frustrated, as the radio-direction bearing seemed incorrect. Sparky took a visual sighting from the plane to confirm his suspicions. The radio bearing was supposed to point in the direction of the strongest signal; it should therefore have been pointing directly at the *William Jones.* Instead the radio bearing was fully fifty-five degrees off, and indicated they were further southeast then they actually were. This discrepancy, combined with the ebbing visibility, kept anyone on the *William Jones* from spotting the plane. Sparky reported his findings to Rodgers, who recorded the incident in the plane's log.

And then Sparky lost radio contact with Snody altogether.

5:04 PM Hawaii Time

It was late afternoon in Hawaii on this Monday, the last day of August. It had been an excruciatingly long one for Akiko. When she had first arrived at work in the morning, she hadn't been able to resist turning on her father's console radio, although she had never taken that liberty before. She had kept the sound as low as possible at first, but as the day wore on, she fiddled with the volume several times to make sure she didn't miss any reports. Between customers, she dusted and redusted the top of the console, anxiously listening for any word about the start of the historic race, to no avail.

Akiko was desperate for news of John. Her last letter from him had been a brief note, written almost two weeks ago. Until now, she hadn't realized how much she wished that her father had installed a telephone either at the office or at home. Masahiro tended to be old-school in that regard. For him, and for that matter for most of Honolulu, a phone was a luxury—an unnecessary expense. They didn't have a radio at home, so news of John's flight was only available via the newspaper or the office radio. Akiko was thankful that KGU, one of the two radio stations in Hawaii, would be following the story closely. Several times during the day, the regular local station announcer had promised that the station would soon begin hourly updates on the aviators' progress, but the workday had finished with no word.

As they closed up shop for the day, Akiko was surprised when Masahiro unexpectedly suggested that they go to dinner at a neighborhood restaurant. They walked together in silence. As Akiko daydreamed of John, she absentmindedly reached up to brush a drop of perspiration from her eye. *It's so still—no wind.* The realization stopped her in her tracks. *No trades!*

Masa turned to see what was wrong, "Akiko?"

"It's all right, Father. I'm . . . just a little hot, that's all."

They continued past Bishop Park and noticed a large crowd gathered near the Hawaiian Trust Co. Building. As they approached the throng, they saw that a huge blackboard had been erected by the Chamber of Commerce. At the top of the blackboard was printed, "Flight of the transpacific flyers." There was a map drawn below it with a list of all the aligned ships and their distances from San Francisco. In addition, there was a note that stated, "Takeoff: 2:55 PM Pacific." Akiko's heart skipped a beat. John was on his way. She fairly floated the rest of the way to the restaurant.

7:15 PM Pacific Time

Snody and his PN9-3 struggled valiantly along the prescribed route, maintaining three hundred feet. At that altitude, they were slightly more susceptible to rain squalls than *Baby* was, flying at five hundred feet. Because rainsqualls in the North Pacific rotate clockwise, Snody was forced to fly to the south as they encountered squalls en route. Although they were able to take advantage of the cyclonic breezes, it cost them dearly in terms of extra miles traveled, and pushed them further south of the rhumb line. Squalls, however, were the least of Snody's problems.

As they approached the *William Jones* on a slightly more southern course than Rodgers had, their radio failed. Snody wondered if the constant vibration had caused the problem, and he set his crew to work to repair it. They removed and replaced every vacuum tube, only achieving success after they passed just south of the destroyer. Flying low, they saw and were seen by all aboard the ship.

As they pushed bravely onward, the intense vibration persisted. Snody worried that the prop's wobble would eventually wear the mounting holes into ovals as before, further exacerbating the situation. If that happened, the prop could tear loose and rip free from its mounts. With the ferocious revolutions that the thirteen-foot prop was turning, it could easily slice right through the thin skin of the fuselage and enter the cabin. Not a pleasant thought.

But even worse than the starboard prop situation, the oil pressure of the portside engine was dropping precipitously, and oil was visible on the engine cowling. At first, the crew addressed the problem by siphoning some of their surplus oil into the motor using an oil line that they jury-rigged. That fix lasted about half an hour. Then the pressure dropped even further, and a large air-blown oil slick began to form next to the motor mounts. Snody realized this could be their death knell. If one or the other of his engines failed—and by now it was obvious either could do so at a moment's notice—they would be in dire trouble. Landing a seaplane in the open ocean was hard enough when everything was functioning properly; plus, the eight-foot swells surging below them were way too large to assure a safe landing, even with a healthy aircraft. Trying to ease the crippled plane down with only one engine was not an option. As capable as they all were, Snody and his crew now faced an impossible predicament.

5:46 PM Hawaii Time

Father and daughter sat quietly across the table from one another. Akiko was barely able to contain her desire to know how John was progressing. She tried to broach the subject delicately, without betraying her feelings to Masahiro.

"Father, after dinner, do you think we might stop first at the office before going home?

"The reason?"

Akiko was not sure, but she thought she detected an uncharacteristic twinkle in her father's eye, although his expression gave no other hint of levity. She stammered, "Um, well, I, I think I left something there." The excuse sounded feeble, even to her. She shrugged helplessly and admitted, "I'd like to see if we can tune into a radio report on Mr. John Rodgers' progress." She couldn't catch herself before adding, "I just want to know he's safe."

Masa studied his child. "This Mr. John Rodgers . . . he has become important to you over this past year, has he not?"

Akiko blushed and lowered her gaze, feeling foolish to have believed that she could hide her feelings from her father. It was time to confess.

"Yes, father, very important. More important than you know. He is a fine man, an honorable man. We love each other very much, and when he returns, we want to marry." There. It was out.

Masahiro was silent. While it pleased him to see his daughter glow with happiness as she spoke of the man she loved, he could see that serious problems loomed ahead for such a match. He had intuited that there was someone in his daughter's life and had even suspected that it was Rodgers. Like any caring father, he would have done anything to shield his child from pain. At last, he spoke carefully.

"Akiko, you must think about what you are doing. There are many walls you will have to scale in a marriage with this man. There are doors that people will try to close in your face. It will not be easy for either of you."

Akiko lifted her head and squared her jaw—an expression Masa had seen before, on his wife's face. "Father, believe me, we have thought very carefully about the challenges ahead of us. However difficult it may be, neither of us wants to face life without the other. We can meet anything as long as we are together."

Masahiro's stoic expression softened. "You are your mother's child, Akiko. I hear her determination in your words. I could never deny her anything once she set her mind on it. You are old enough to make your own decisions. From the little I have seen and heard of him, I believe this Mr. John Rodgers to be a good man. You deserve happiness in your life, my daughter, it is long overdue. If it is your wish to be with this man, then I want you to know your mother and I approve."

Akiko's eyes filled with tears of happiness and she rushed to her father's side, hugging him, as he remained seated. While uneasy with this public show of emotion, Masa patted her hand, and then bade her to sit back down. The tension of concealment now gone, Akiko proceeded to volunteer more than Masahiro probably cared to know about her relationship with John, but he listened patiently, inwardly reveling in his daughter's joy, even as he wondered whether her happiness could continue.

After dinner, on their way back to the office, they stopped by Bishop Park again. The crowd was larger, and the report on the blackboard had been updated. It now said the flyers had passed the first ship, the USS *William Jones*, at 5:40 PM. Akiko was thrilled, and even Masahiro had to admit he was excited. The times listed were of course Pacific Time—two hours ahead of Hawaii—but to have such an up-to-date report amazed them. A friend of Masahiro's from the Chamber of Commerce greeted them and advised Masahiro that he would be manning the board until 8 PM. He said they did not expect further updates until the next morning. Shaking hands, Masahiro bid him aloha and escorted Akiko back to the office.

When they arrived, Akiko went straight to the radio and had switched it on even before the door closed. She impatiently twisted the dial to the right wavelength, as the vacuum tubes hummed their warm-up song. Masahiro seated himself behind Akiko's small desk, while she knelt Japanese-style on the floor directly in front of the speaker, eagerly awaiting the evening news.

Sure enough, the report of John's mission led the newscast, although it was a cobbled "rip-and-read" report generated from earlier teletypes.

"Today's start of the big race to Honolulu appears to be ready to begin on time as three navy seaplanes attempt to fly nonstop from San Francisco to Hawaii." Masahiro started to say that this was old news, but Akiko's look shushed him. The announcer continued, "Led by Commander John Rodgers, the group seemed raring to get underway. If all goes well, they could be draped in lei, enjoying a hero's welcome by this time tomorrow evening. And in other news . . ."

The announcer droned on until Akiko was satisfied that there would be no further report on John. Close to tears with frustration and disappointment, she switched the radio off.

Masa comforted her as best he could. "We should go home. We'll hear more in the morning."

Akiko reluctantly agreed. "But may we please stop at the temple on the way?"

7:48 PM Pacific Time

Snody made his decision: eight-foot swells or not, they would have to land. The situation was dire; both the vibration of the starboard prop and the oil leak in the port engine had worsened. The plane was limping along in the air. Having reached the midpoint between Station N, manned by the USS *William Jones*, and Station O, which was the USS *McCawley*, they opted to try to make it to the latter. Snody radioed the *McCawley* to advise them of their intentions. The *McCawley* responded immediately and proceeded at flank speed back up the rhumb line in an east-northeasterly direction. Snody slowed the plane to a mere forty-five knots, barely enough to stay aloft. However, ship and plane were heading straight towards each other at almost sixty knots, quickly reducing the distance between them. The *McCawley* peppered the aircraft with radio chatter, assuring the aviators that the rescue ship would be with them momentarily. Remaining calm, Snody joked with his men that the *McCawley* seemed more worried about their predicament then they were. He teased his crew, "We're flying so slow John's plover would pass us!" The laughter onboard ceased abruptly when the port engine lost all oil pressure and died.

Snody immediately shut it down and slammed the starboard mixmaster full on. The plane crabbed violently to the left, and Snody fought with the rudder to keep his heading. The plane shook as the damaged starboard prop gyrated wildly. "Reel in the antenna. We're going in!" he shouted. They sent a desperate mayday; then Snody banked the plane around to head back into what little wind there was.

The crippled PN9 fell in a controlled dive. As low as it had been flying, it didn't have far to go before slamming into the first of many waves. The initial impact tore the starboard propeller off as if it was made of papier-mâché. Fortunately, the prop disappeared without further damaging the plane. Without its prop, the unfettered hub provided no real wind resistance, causing the Packard to rev uncontrollably. The engine screamed and certainly would have exploded if the next wave hadn't swallowed it whole. A blue-green wall of water slammed into the starboard wings, making the plane pirouette, then flinging it like a spinning, skipping stone over, under, and through the next set of waves.

After the crash landing, the plane somehow remained upright. Snody hollered, "Give me a roll call! Any injuries?" The crew responded. All were battered but alive. There were some serious bruises and a possible broken limb or two, but amazingly, nothing life threatening. Snody first thought he had somehow escaped uninjured, possibly because he had been well braced in the cockpit. Then he saw the gaping wound in his right thigh, bleeding profusely. He stanched the wound with his shirt and secured his belt around his leg as a crude tourniquet. Snody then grabbed a flare gun and fired it. The flare worked flawlessly; it was the only mechanical device that had that day. Then he surveyed the plane for damage.

Although badly beaten up, both wing tip floats were intact. That was good—they would keep the plane upright. In the cabin, the portside entry hatch had lost its door, torn off during the crash landing. However the rest of the interior was intact as far as he could determine. He took a deep breath. They were alive and would be OK as long as they stayed afloat. Then he noticed the water rising in the bilge.

The Farallon Islands, off the coast of California

USS *William Jones:* Positioned at Station N, it was the first ship on the rhumb line. Although seen by Rodgers and crew as they passed to the north of her, no one on the *William Jones* witnessed their passing. They did see Snody's PN9-3 some time later.

Chapter 32

Monday—August 31, 1925

7:49 PM Pacific Time

Once the PB1 fiasco on San Francisco Bay had been cleaned up and the plane safely ensconced ashore, Moffett ordered Strong to report to his temporary headquarters at the Olympic Club. The Admiral fully expected an embarrassed and contrite apology. What he got from the cocky young officer standing in front of him was anything but.

"Sir. Lieutenant Commander Strong reporting as ordered."

Moffett kept his focus on the paperwork on his desk, letting Strong's words hang in the air. Then, still not looking up, the admiral said, "Commander . . . ?"

Strong leapt right in. "Sir, I have completed a thorough assessment of the damage, and it appears that we can have my plane ready to leave for Hawaii in twenty-four to forty-eight hours."

Having already assigned a crack Aircraft Maintenance Officer to evaluate the plane, Moffett asked, "Is that what the AMO has determined?"

"Well, no sir. In my opinion he is being overly cautious. I know we can have the PB1 ready to go by Wednesday."

Moffett measured his words carefully, "Mr. Strong, how long did the AMO suggest would be necessary?"

"Sir, he said it would take at least a week."

"And you disagree with that conclusion?"

"Yes, sir, I do, sir."

Moffett's response to this was a noncommittal "Mmm."

Strong then blurted out, "Sir, if the damned patrol boats had done their job, this never would've happened. We did all we could to keep the spectator boats out of our way, but they mostly ignored our warnings. Those patrol boats were supposed to keep the taxi lanes clear. And then that stupid tour-boat operator . . ."

Moffett jotted some notes, and then interrupted in an ominously quiet tone. "Ah . . . so you believe the patrol boats failed to do their job properly?"

Believing that Moffett was agreeing with him, Strong continued more confidently. "Sir, yes I do. And Boeing's stupid in-line design, plus that pathetically undersized rudder, didn't make things any easier. You just can't steer that thing on the water."

"So, in addition, you're saying the plane's design was faulty."

"Yes, sir!"

There was a considerable pause before Moffett asked, "Is there anyone or anything else you'd like to blame for this disaster?" The sarcasm dripping from the commander's voice caught Strong completely off guard.

With no room to retreat, he straightened slightly and responded, "Uh, no, sir."

At last, the Admiral looked up from the desk. This time, when he spoke, cold fury edged his voice, "Let me get this straight, Commander. The patrol boats failed to do their job. The Boeing plane, which until this very moment you have raved about to both me and the press, has serious design flaws. And in your opinion, the Aircraft Maintenance Officer I personally assigned to check your plane, a top professional with a damn sight more experience than you, mister, *doesn't know what he's doing?*"

Strong swallowed hard.

Holding his hand up to preclude a response, Moffett continued. "Mr. Strong, do you not realize that I was standing right there as you sped irresponsibly alongside the *Gannet*, showboating for all you were worth? And now your only concern is flying 'your plane' on to Hawaii? I think not."

In the extended monologue that followed, Moffett's language was both blunt and colorful. When the Admiral had finished, a severely chastened lieutenant commander saluted and beat a scalded retreat, his future in naval aviation looking doubtful indeed.

When Moffett was again alone, he called downstairs for dinner to be sent up to his room. He was pacing the floor, still fuming, when a message was delivered: a telegram from the USS *McCawley*.

7:50 PM Pacific Time

At sunset, a few of the crew aboard the *McCawley* had actually watched the final seconds of the PN9-3 just before she dove into the sea. Those who had seen it doubted anyone could have survived the crash. The ship had been about two miles away at the time and the rough seas had prevented a visual sighting after the plane had slammed into the water. However, long faces were soon replaced with joyous cheers on deck at the sight of Snody's flare. An announcement over the ship's intercom scrambled a rescue crew and boat onto the davits. The *McCawley* was quickly on-site, and the recovery team's hours of drills paid off. They lowered the boat into the sea and it was off at full speed in no time. Within minutes, they had deftly maneuvered the craft next to the plane. While his men were transferred to the waiting boat and strapped into life vests by their rescuers, Snody retrieved his log book in its watertight recovery box from the forward navigation station. As he waded back toward the rescue boat bobbing outside the plane's doorless hatch, water began cascading in over the transom.

The little boat pulled clear as the Pacific claimed its victim. The PN9-3 was immediately awash, and the stern started to sink. It leveled out for a few seconds, and then the weight of the water pulled the plane inexorably down until only the air trapped in the hollows of the upper wing kept it afloat. In a matter of minutes, the waves finished her off, and she sank beneath the surface.

After Snody and his crew had been checked out by the ship's surgeon aboard the *McCawley*, a terse radio message was sent out. "Be advised: Prep-Negative Niner-Three crew safe. Plane sunk."

8:07 PM Pacific Time

Onboard *Baby,* Sparky picked up the sketchy report and relayed it to the crew: "PN9-3 crew safe. Plane sunk." John was silent as he speculated about the story behind the brief message. What had happened to Snody's plane? Had the prop ripped off? How had the crew been saved if the plane had sunk? John turned to Sparky. "Can you still reach the *McCawley?*"

"I can try, sir. But we're almost at the midpoint between her and the *Corry* at Station P."

"Well, see if you can get any more information from her. This message is crazy! Ask them what happened."

"Aye, sir." And Sparky set to work trying to raise the *McCawley* again.

John crawled past Kiles Pope, who had relieved Byron at the controls. He returned to his navigation station up in the bow to record the radio report. He needed to check his reckoning anyway. Taking a star fix with the sextant, he silently gave thanks that the sextant had an eyepiece that could be focused; he could use it without his glasses. He gathered the information necessary for his calculations, then withdrew into his dark, cramped navigator's warren. Out of sight of the others, he put on his glasses and set to work. He discovered to his dismay that between the poor light and the plane's vibrations, the glasses were not much help. Even with them, he had to squint to make out his own clearly printed block letters.

Aware of something moving to his right, John looked up to see the pulley moving on the simple clothesline that served as *Baby's* intercom. A wooden clothespin had a note attached. John pulled it off and strained to read Sparky's scribble: "Crew is safe aboard the *McCawley.* Minor injuries. Plane sank after all aboard rescued."

That much, he knew. The report continued: "Port engine failed. Difficult to maintain speed for a safe landing in heavy seas with damaged starboard propeller."

John sighed. *At least they're safe.* He printed neatly across the bottom of the page: "Advise rest of crew," and sent the note back to Sparky.

John pushed his glasses up on his forehead and massaged the bridge of his nose. Now they were truly on their own. And where were the trades they were counting on? Three-knot tail winds were not going to be enough. Once again he computed their rate of fuel consumption and compared that with their progress. The answer he came up with was not encouraging.

7:16 PM Hawaii Time

Once Akiko and Masahiro had returned home, Akiko paid a visit to the Kamakaiwi family, long-time friends next door. While playing on the floor with Kimo, their five-year-old son, Akiko listened to their living-room radio, which was perpetually on.

When the news came on, the updated report was confusing. It seemed that two of the three planes were not flying. First, the story said that Strong's plane had never left San Francisco, but offered few details as to why. The report continued with the fact that Snody's plane had crash-landed off the California coast but was expected to continue on after repairs were made. Only Commander John Rodgers was still on his way. The account was so cursory that when the station signed off the air, Akiko felt like pleading with the radio to tell her more. Frustrated, she politely excused herself and left.

Arriving back home, she quietly let herself in the unlocked front door. As she had expected, her father had already retired for the evening. Although Akiko was physically exhausted, her emotions were churning, and sleep was out of the question. Feeling slightly queasy, she removed a glass bottle of milk from the icebox, thinking it might soothe her upset stomach. She rocked the bottle several times to thoroughly mix the top cream with the milk beneath. Then she poured herself a glass of the cool white liquid and sat at the small kitchen table. Sipping slowly, she stared at the clock, willing its hands to spin faster. *If all goes well, by this time tomorrow, he'll be home.*

11:30 PM Pacific Time

As midnight approached, *Baby*'s crew shared lukewarm coffee from one of the metal thermoses. Rodgers relieved Kiles Pope at the controls, and Wild Bill took over for Sparky in the communications nook. Rotating this way, they had a rested pilot at the helm and fresh readings from the primitive radio directional finder. The subsequent radio signals, their own position plotting, and most importantly, John's own dead reckoning, led them to believe the plane was directly on the rhumb line. They would soon question that assumption.

At 11:55, they crossed Station P, manned by the destroyer USS *Corry*. In the pitch-black night, John thought he had seen lights from a ship well to the south. He had assumed that had been the *Corry*, but no one else could confirm the sighting. Although they were in radio contact with the *Corry*, she reported being unable to spot the plane. John was concerned because if the lights he had seen had been the *Corry*, then either she was considerably south of her designated station, or *Baby* was too far north. John was confounded, as the plots didn't jibe with either her reported longitude and latitude or the useless radio direction finder.

John conferred with Byron and they both agreed that if the *Corry*'s position reports were correct they should have flown directly over the warship. Why would she be so far south? Frustrated, John logged the facts into his book. The incident was left unresolved, and no other lights were sighted. On they flew, into the dark.

The August 31, 1925 *Honolulu Advertiser:* The PN9s are on their way. The Associated Press reported that the Boeing PB1 would follow in as few as forty-eight hours.

The USS *Corry:* At Station P, she was the second ship in line along the course.

Chapter 33

Tuesday—September 1, 1925

5:15 AM Eastern Time

It was still pitch black outside in Washington, D.C. when Billy Mitchell's alarm clock rang. As usual, the colonel was up before sunrise and had already showered. Grabbing a towel and dashing from the bathroom of his suite in the Army and Navy Club, Mitchell dove to silence the jangling noise. He then returned to the steam-filled room, wiped the mirror clear, and finished brushing his teeth. Toweling his buzz cut dry, he ambled back into the high-ceilinged bedroom to dress.

At exactly 5:30 AM, there was a knock on the solid oak door. When he opened it, Colonel Mitchell was greeted by his khaki-clad aide, Lieutenant Smith.

"Morning, sir!" was followed by a crisp salute.

Brusquely dismissing the salute, Mitchell said, "What's on the docket for me this morning?"

The aide withdrew a telegram from his brown leather valise. "Sir, I thought you'd want to see this first." As Smith proffered the familiar pale-yellow paper to his boss, Mitchell noticed a mischievous grin edging across his aide's face.

Mitchell snatched the telegram. A brief pause ensued as he digested the contents. Then, "Holy cow! The second plane *sank* . . . ?!" Mitchell crowed. "I knew something like this would happen! This is confirmed, then?"

"Yes sir. I got a call from the *Post* reporter not ten minutes ago. He got the same message. They're holding the presses to run the story in the late edition."

Mitchell barked, "Get him on the line! I want him to have my take on this. You're sure they've all been rescued? I don't want to come across as an ass if they aren't all safe."

"No, sir, Snody and all four of his crew are definitely aboard the *McCawley*, presumably heading back to the coast. I'll try to catch him now, I've got the number."

Mitchell nodded toward the black phone on the hotel room desk. "Call from here." As Smith picked up the handset and flicked the cradle twice to alert the hotel operator, Mitchell shook his head in disbelief and murmured to himself. "The damn thing *sank*!"

3:10 AM Pacific Time

The crew of the lonely PN9-1 had passed Station Q, the destroyer USS *Meyer*, an hour ago, with adequate radio communication but again, no visual sighting. And when John penciled in their position report, it once again failed to match the orientation indicated by the directional radio beacon.

Refreshed from a catnap, Byron Connell took over the helm. Both Byron and Kiles wore leather jackets, navy-blue woolen skullcaps, gloves, and the requisite navy-issue goggles to protect them from the wind blasting the open cockpit; the little screen offered only partial protection. Byron seemed both cheerful and optimistic. If willpower alone could have gotten them to Hawaii, he would have had them there in short order.

Sparky Stantz, on the other hand, hadn't slept a wink. He was too wound up. He jumped every time the radio crackled, even when Wild Bill was manning it. He couldn't stay away; he insisted on wearing his headset. The failed visuals and the faulty directional bearings were driving him crazy.

The continuing discrepancies had Rodgers worried as well. He repeatedly conferred with Sparky. A directional error as small as ten degrees could cause them to be more than four hundred miles off course by the time they ran out of fuel. Finding the forty-mile-wide island of Oahu in the great expanse of the Pacific was going to be tricky under the best of circumstances. John trusted his sextant over the unreliable radio beacons for accurate navigation, but that instrument depended on clear skies for proper sightings—and the weather was beginning to close in.

When not in the copilot's seat, Kiles Pope had been monitoring the fuel consumption with Wild Bill's help. Happiest when he had a mechanical problem to solve, Kiles was working on a way to cross siphon the fuel from the bottom of the auxiliary tanks without allowing air to seep into the line. If this were properly done, they'd be able to use every drop.

For his part, Wild Bill had mostly focused on the starboard engine. It was burning too much fuel. At 4:10 AM, he and Kiles approached John. Bill cleared his throat and said, "Sir, I, uh, think we need to fiddle with the carburetor jets on the starboard engine."

John shot Bill a worried glance. What his chief mechanics mate was suggesting called for an extremely risky operation. "Are you sure you want to go out there?"

Bill's cocky grin masked his trepidation. "Sure skip, no problem."

Rodgers turned to Kiles. "OK then, you're in charge of the jack lines."

Kiles went to work. He found a thirty-foot length of half-inch-thick, light-gray dock line that had survived the draconian off-load back in San Francisco. Kiles pulled up a section of the aluminum floorboards and secured one end of the line to a bilge crossbeam. He then wove and knotted the other end over Bill's shoulders, around his waist, and through his crotch, fashioning a crude boatswain's chair harness. Next, Kiles put on his gloves and held the line in each hand as he wrapped the middle section of the line behind his back. This mountain-climbing arrangement would allow him to feed out line to Bill as he needed it, while maintaining stabilizing tension in the line.

John motioned to Byron to ease the throttles a bit and slow the plane as much as possible. John then turned and signaled them to proceed.

Bill nodded to Kiles, then squeezed up through the mechanic's cockpit. In the pitch black of the night, the exhaust flashed blue, with occasional explosions of unburned fuel as it escaped aft. The crude fireworks gave an eerie cast to the plane and reduced their night vision. As Bill climbed over the sill and slithered out onto the wing, he felt as if the sixty-mile-per-hour wind was going to rip the clothes right off his body. He carefully crept aft behind the big twin propellers, making sure that the deadly blades did not slice him into luncheon meat or cut his safety line. He grabbed one of the many cables crisscrossing between the wings that served to hold them securely in place. He was reminded of the old sailors' adage: "One hand for the ship; one hand for yourself."

Bill then took two giant steps across the wing to the engine cowling. Once there, he moved the toggles downward on the cowling panel and pushed it into the teeth of the wind, holding the louvered metal door open with his left thigh. Flathead screwdriver in hand, he peered into the din.

While Kiles held the line taut in the cabin, John maneuvered sideways into the mechanic's cockpit, where he did his best to shine a flashlight over Bill's shoulder. Engulfed in the gaping maw of the engine compartment, Bill worked furiously. His struggle in the howling wind seemed to take an eternity. At last, giving a thumbs-up over his shoulder to the men inside the plane, he closed and resecured the cowling. Then, as he straightened up to turn around, Wild Bill's left foot slipped. The crew watched in horror as he fell face first onto the lower wing and started sliding aft.

4:22 AM Pacific Time

Outside the window of Admiral Moffett's Olympic Club suite, the San Francisco night lights twinkled like candles on a birthday cake. Inside, electric lights cast umber shadows over the round table in the suite. Moffett had not slept, unless catnapping with one eye open counted. From the reports coming in, it sounded as if Rodgers was flying an invisible plane. While the leapfrogging of the radio signals was functioning as planned, there had been no visual sighting confirmed since sunset. Moffett's staff was desperately trying to piece together the information trickling in as they attempted to solve the mystery. Reports from the radio beacons offered wildly inconsistent information concerning *Baby*'s whereabouts. Moffett also worried about the weather. News coming from the ships on-station had been disheartening. They reported fairly significant seas, which was odd, given the continued absence of the critical trade winds.

A phone rang on the far side of the room. Moffett's aide answered it and caught the admiral's eye, indicating the call was for him. Moffett strode across the hardwood floor and grumpily wrapped a large paw around the black receiver. Covering his left ear he listened intently. After speaking in gruff, muffled tones, Moffett returned the phone to its cradle.

Addressing the small group assembled in his suite, Moffett announced, "That was D.C. It seems our friend Colonel Mitchell is at it again. He's exploiting Strong and Snody's failures to call for congressional hearings on his proposal—the one that could effectively eliminate the navy's air arm. Worse, it seems his political cronies are climbing on the bandwagon and are going to help that son-of-a-bitch." Admiral Moffett rubbed his tired eyes and sighed. "We'd better get something positive to report soon."

7:25 AM Eastern Time

At the Lakehurst Navy Air Station, things had come down to the wire for the *Shenandoah*'s big cross-country public relations tour. Now everything hinged on the weather. The much-delayed launch had already been postponed for yet another day.

This morning, Lieutenant Commander Zachary Lansdowne and Lieutenant Joseph "Andy" Anderson stood waiting in the small office that served as the base weather station. This particular office was of supreme importance to the sailors that flew and supported the *Shenandoah*. It was here that all ground movement plans and launch decisions involving the great airship were approved. It was said that while only the likes of Admiral Moffett or President Coolidge could order the launch of the dirigible, even the lowliest swabbie in this office could countermand that order, if the forecast dictated.

After only a brief wait, Lansdowne was handed several reports recently compiled from weather stations east of the Rockies and north of the Mason–Dixon line. He set them on the counter to his right and in front of Anderson, and compared them to the similar-looking papers he had brought with him. The new set of sheets showed that some of today's barometric numbers were higher than the earlier reports had indicated, and some were lower, with no apparent trend. The readings confounded them both. When they had performed the same review the day before, they felt that the weather was too unstable and had postponed the launch. To their chagrin, the skies had remained gloriously clear all day, with no significant storm systems materializing anywhere along their intended route. While Lansdowne felt they had made the correct decision, the similar reports today tested his resolve. Nonetheless, after a brief discussion, he decided that the launch could wait one more day, and ordered the crew to stand down. Inwardly, Lansdowne wondered if he was becoming too conservative.

4:27 AM Pacific Time

Fortunately for him, Wild Bill still had the flathead screwdriver in his hand when he slipped and fell facedown onto the windswept lower wing. Because of the odd angle of the carburetor bolt he had been wrestling with, Bill had been holding the screwdriver blade down in his fist, like a killer in a bad melodrama. When he slipped, he'd had the presence of mind to dig it into the fabric covering the lower wing. The screwdriver cleanly penetrated the canvas-like material. Stiffened by the lead-based, nonporous dope paint, and stretched taut by the wooden ribs, the fabric held, saving Bill from sliding off the wing. While the thirty-foot length of safety line would have kept him from plummeting into the ocean below, had he slid completely off the wing, his safe recovery would have been doubtful.

Between his leverage from the screwdriver and Kiles's frantic pulling on the line, Bill was at last able to scramble back into the plane. Once safely inside the fuselage, he grinned sheepishly: "I think I'll cross wing-walking off my resume." Then he noticed Kiles Pope, pulling off his gloves, obviously in pain. "How're your hands, buddy?"

When Bill fell, Kiles's right palm had taken the brunt as the line ripped through his hands. Even with gloves, he had sustained a serious rope burn. Kiles stoically shook the injured hand several times as if to dismiss the pain, and spoke through gritted teeth.

"I'll be fine. Coulda been a lot worse."

John took a look at Kiles's hand and thought of the first-aid kit they had off-loaded back in San Francisco.

"Not much we can do for you now, Kiles, but we'll get you fixed up in Honolulu later tonight." Everyone on board nodded hopefully at that.

The good news was that, due to Bill's work on the carburetor jets, the starboard engine was now running much more smoothly. The rpms were up slightly, and it definitely sounded better. There were considerably fewer of the backfire "pops" that had resulted from the fuel mixture being too rich. However John would have to wait to see if the rate of fuel consumption improved. Right now he had another pressing concern.

The concept of placing ships every two hundred miles along the intended course for steady communication had resulted from John's epiphany about the maximum range of air-to-surface radios. Despite the incredible expense to the U.S. Navy for this outlay of men and vessels, John now wondered if he should have requested more vessels, at smaller intervals. The Pacific was a vast, lonely ocean, and it seemed to be getting larger as they flew on into the black night sky. With each unsuccessful sighting, John began to think that finding the ships along the rhumb line below was more luck than science.

Each ship's station was approximately three hours' flying time from the next in line. Flying over a seemingly endless ocean for three hours with nothing on the horizon for bearings was daunting enough. Missing a visual sighting of a ship meant facing six hours of the loneliest flying imaginable. Miss two, and the uncertainty stretched to nine hours. Missing three in a row was unthinkable; yet that is what had happened to *Baby* and her crew.

This geographic disorientation, coupled with the physical vertigo of flying in a dark, overcast night, might have made a lesser man question his calculations. But John refused to allow those doubts to enter his mind. He believed in his meticulously figured calculations. He just wished he could see them better.

After a half-hour, John had reason to be buoyed. The fuel mileage *did* seem to be improving and, more importantly, the wind had strengthened with the approaching dawn. For the first time since they left San Francisco, things seemed to be going their way.

And the crew had reached a milestone: they were halfway to Hawaii. Morale onboard rose. They cheered, and then adjusted their watches an hour to the local time. Kiles laughed, "If you can call Alaska Time local . . ." Byron countered, "Alaska? Hell, we're almost in the tropics!"

Soon thereafter, they had reasonable radio contact with the next station. The USS *Doyen* was on Station R. But as the first light of the new day peeked through the gunmetal-gray clouds, there was no sign of her below. They had missed four in a row: fifteen hours of flying and not one visual sighting. They could talk with the ships, but not see them.

The crew onboard *Baby* seemed to be getting used to the failures, dismissing them with gallows humor. Wild Bill joked, "Say, I bet the navy's using that new camouflage paint."

Sparky chimed in, "Yeah, the invisible kind."

"You gotta agree, it's mighty effective!"

All kidding aside, the men felt as if they had entered the dangerous realm of the unknown, described on ancient sailing charts with the words: *Beyond here be dragons.*

7:22 AM Pacific Time

The outdoor patio of the Hollywood Hotel was *the* place to be seen in Los Angeles, and the breakfasts there were excellent. Sitting at his table this morning, S. K. Alexander was a large man with a barrel chest that took a considerable amount of double-breasted worsted wool to cover. It was said that no one but his parents knew what the "S. K." stood for, as he always went by "Alex."

In the sea of freelance reporters in Los Angeles, Alexander was notorious for having one of the sharpest noses for a story. Digging dirt did not faze him in the least. Alex stared toward the entrance and checked his watch once more. Ethel Rodgers was late. He decided to wait a few more minutes and finish his coffee.

At last, Ethel appeared. Alex had met her at a dinner party they had both attended last month. While not particularly attracted to her, he had sensed a story, and had invited her to breakfast. He had chosen the time and the location carefully so that Ethel would not get the wrong idea. He folded his paper and stood to greet her.

Ethel made quite an entrance. She wore a burgundy sundress that showed a bit too much cleavage for this time of day, and a broad-brimmed straw hat with matching ribbon trim. She waved a long cigarette holder, and the ash from her Lucky Strike threatened to drop into some unsuspecting soul's eggs benedict as she sashayed through the tables. Her perfume arrived before she did.

Alex pulled out Ethel's chair and seated her. After brief pleasantries, coffee was served and they both ordered breakfast. Getting right to the point, Ethel batted her eyelashes and asked, "My dear Mr. Alexander, to what do I owe the pleasure of this invitation?"

"Call me Alex, please." Picking up the folded newspaper, he said, "Ethel, I've just been reading this article on the Great Transpacific Race. John Rodgers is your husband, isn't he?"

"My soon-to-be ex-husband, if my attorney can ever get our divorce finalized."

Alex pointed a stubby finger at the article, "Well, this race is getting to be a pretty big story, and I'd like to work some of the angles. Would you be willing to be interviewed?"

Caught off guard, Ethel scowled. Her southern belle upbringing made it difficult for her to accept the fact that Alex's invitation had nothing to do with her feminine charms. She recovered quickly, though, and her mind began racing to see how she might work the reporter to her advantage.

"Why don't you tell me what it is you want to know?"

His questions tumbled out. "What can you tell me about the planning that was involved? Whose idea was it? When did they first start working on it? Before you left Hawaii, what did your husband tell you about the mission that might not have been for general consumption? Things like that."

Enticed by the possibility of seeing her name in print, Ethel began to warm to the idea. "You know, Alex, I think we just might have a lot to talk about."

6:32 AM Alaska Time

At their backs, the sky turned a magnificent orange red as the sun rose, while the undulating ocean surface reflected the same palette of colors. The crew shared a spartan breakfast of white-bread sandwiches, cold coffee, and water. Morale was running high.

The twin Packards were purring now, and the winds seemed to be getting stronger. John was constantly engaged, checking on things. If he wasn't talking with Kiles or Byron at the controls, he was monitoring the fuel with Bill, making entries in their logbook, or conferring on the radio reports with Sparky. As it grew lighter, he went back to the plane's cramped navigator's nook to check the figures he had previously recorded in the dark. Tucked away by himself, he could put on the forbidden glasses to review his calculations. After several checks and rechecks, to his intense relief he was able to verify that they were still right on course.

Rodgers understood that keeping a huge warship on-station in the open ocean involved constant maneuvering within a fairly large area. Ships obviously couldn't drop anchor in the seemingly bottomless depths of the Pacific, and when the seas were as large as they had been, they needed to maintain a reasonable speed for both leeway and comfort. A ship would maintain position by sailing in a predetermined racecourse or rectangular pattern that might be five miles or more on a side. Variation in position, combined with even a minute miscalculation due to the inherent difficulty in taking a sextant sighting in the roiling seas, could easily have been the reason for the missed sightings. Nonetheless, Rodgers was glad to be able to vindicate his navigation.

The wind continued to increase, and was soon blowing at a stiff twenty-two knots almost directly behind them. Their air speed improved considerably. Soon they were traveling at eighty-five knots "over ground." *If only we'd had these breezes from the start.* Looking at the low, scattered clouds, John moved up to the cockpit and instructed Byron at the controls, "Let's drop *Baby* down to plan."

"Aye, aye. Dropping to three hundred feet," Connell replied, and eased the stick forward to their minimum cruise altitude.

John had turned his attention to Bill's fuel monitoring when Sparky spoke up. "I've got the *Langley*. From the signal, she should be straight off our bow."

At that, Kiles crowed from the cockpit. "There she is! Damn, she's a beautiful sight." Although the *Langley* was too far away yet to distinguish clearly, all onboard heartily agreed that the dot on the horizon was a sight to behold.

John raced forward to the navigation station to see for himself. Using binoculars, he focused on Admiral Moffett's brainchild. The USS *Langley* was the navy's first aircraft carrier, and had only been in official operation for nine months. As John surveyed the enormous carrier, many times larger than the destroyers they had passed unseen, he wondered if its size alone was the reason they'd been able to achieve a visual sighting this time. Looking at the planes lined up on her deck, he hoped that maybe one or two would launch and escort them for a while.

Onboard the *Langley*, Commander Kenneth Whiting would have liked to do exactly that, but it was not to be. Whiting had determined that although the wind was satisfactory for launch sequences, the seas were tossing the ship too severely to assure safe recovery of his aircraft. Almost as if he had read John's mind, he had his radioman send his apologies to that effect, adding the *Langley*'s good wishes for a successful flight.

As they closed on the carrier, John's crew gazed incredulously at the deck of the unique ship. It looked as if her entire compliment of 460 officers and enlisted was out on the flat, 540-foot-long superstructure. Considering the substantial heaving the ship was experiencing, it was a great tribute. Kiles yelled from the cockpit, "How the heck are those guys just standing there? There isn't a safety line anywhere!"

Several flares arced up off the deck in greeting as *Baby* flew straight overhead. Kiles rocked her wings in acknowledgement, and the mood, both on the flattop and in the plane was akin to New Year's Eve in Times Square.

The USS *Langley* had started out life in 1911 as a coal-bearing freighter named *Jupiter*. In 1919, she had begun a complete refit and reemerged several years later as something that looked like a floating billiard table with no visible superstructure, as seen in the dark, silhouetted photograph above.

The USS *Langley*. Note: her deck is totally flat and devoid of any superstructure.

The USS *Langley* was commissioned and put into service on December 1, 1924. She was America's first true aircraft carrier. Her success would change navy aviation forever.

Chapter 34

Tuesday—September 1, 1925

6:43 AM Hawaii Time

Akiko hadn't slept well. When she had finally dozed off the night before, she'd drifted into her worst recurring nightmare—at least that's how it had started. Her mother, wracked with pain, stood before her and begged Akiko to end her suffering. As she always did at this point in the dream, Akiko searched frantically for her father.

This time, however, there was no sign of Masa. Instead, when she turned, she saw John Rodgers. To her horror, he appeared to look right through her as if she wasn't there. Then the nightmare shifted, and she was all alone in a small, dark space with a group of strange men whose words were drowned out by some kind of horrible, mechanical din. Somehow she knew John was in this space, but she couldn't see or hear him. She tried calling his name, but the tremendous racket seemed to suck the sound from her voice.

Strange smells of hot metal permeated her dream, and she felt increasingly disoriented. The space started to spin and she shivered with fright. Then, suddenly she was alone in a room with her mother. Hiroko lay on a bed, evidently at rest, a peaceful expression on her face. As Akiko watched, her mother's eyes opened. She smiled and reached out, speaking words Akiko couldn't understand. In her dream, Akiko ran terrified from the room, tightly clutching a little square pillow.

She woke with a start, her head buried in her own pillow. She had broken out in a cold sweat and was shaking like a leaf. She curled into a fetal position to see if that would ease her churning stomach. It took her a few moments to become fully conscious. Looking at the clock, she saw that it was time to get up. Shaking off the nightmare, Akiko jumped out of bed, threw on a housecoat, and made her way down the hall to the bathroom. She felt terrible, as if she was coming down with something, but she was too excited to give in to whatever it was. John was coming home today!

After a quick bath, Akiko carefully applied just a touch of makeup and brushed her long black hair. She chose one of John's favorite dresses from the small closet—a simple, muted-yellow frock with white piping that accented her slender figure. She slipped it on and padded silently down the hall, barefoot.

To her surprise, when she entered the tiny kitchen, Akiko found Masa already dressed and seated at the kitchen table sipping his tea.

"Good morning, Father." She prepared herself a cup. Ordinarily she loved her morning jasmine tea, but today it tasted different. Puzzled, she set it back down. *It's just my nerves.*

"Why are you up so early, Father?"

Masa regarded her earnestly. "This is a big day, is it not? You must want to get to the office radio and hear what is happening with your Mr. Rodgers."

Touched by her father's thoughtfulness, Akiko wrapped her arms around him and buried her face in his neck. Masa grunted in response and said gruffly, "Now, stop that; stop that. We need to catch the bus."

Akiko tossed a small beaded purse over her shoulder and put on her favorite hat, the one with the bright orange ribbon that she had worn on her first beach date with John. Her hair, straight and shining, hung seductively to her small, round breasts. As they left the house, she slid her feet into a pair of simple, woven sandals and took her father's arm.

Traveling into town on the bus, Akiko filled Masahiro in on what little news she had heard last night at their neighbors' house. There had not been much additional information to report, but Masahiro noted that it seemed to comfort his daughter to review out loud the progress of the man she loved. Ever the patient father, Masa listened silently all the way into town.

Walking the two short blocks from the bus stop to the office was agony for Akiko. She wanted to run like the wind, but tradition dictated that she keep pace slightly behind her father. A newsboy stood on the corner waving *The Honolulu Advertiser,* Hawaii's territorial newspaper. The banner headline's typeface below the masthead was twice as large. It read, "PLANE IS FORCED DOWN." Beneath the headline was a four-column-wide picture of "Commander John Rodgers' flag plane PN-9 Number 1 in flight." The news hit Akiko like a body blow, and she had to will herself not to throw up. Masahiro quickly dug a nickel from his pocket and purchased a paper. Akiko huddled next to her father as they both read the report. Much to their intense relief, they immediately saw that the headline referred to Snody's plane—forced down three hundred miles from San Francisco. A happier subheading casually reported, "Rodgers' cruiser is expected to land in Honolulu today according to present calculations." It continued, "One lone naval plane is nearing the halfway mark and by all indications, will be successful in completing the greatest flight ever attempted." Akiko's knees buckled with relief, and she leaned heavily against her father. Somewhat at a loss, Masahiro comforted his daughter stiffly, and they soon resumed the short walk to the office.

Because Masahiro and Akiko arrived at the office early, they did not flip the office sign to *Open* when they entered. Akiko had the radio on almost before the jingle of the entry bell had stopped. She positioned herself in front of the console. A muted Louie Armstrong trumpet solo played, filling the time till the top of the hour.

Masahiro sat at Akiko's desk and read to her from the paper as they waited for the news broadcast to begin.

"Listen to how Honolulu plans to receive your Mr. Rodgers and his crew: 'Entire city to turn out for fliers. A typically Hawaiian welcome assured. The entire city is prepared to welcome the navy plane to Honolulu today with leis, whistles and flags.'

"And this, Akiko, also front page news: 'The approach of the plane . . . will be signalized by factory and steamship whistles. The plane is expected to fly over the harbor about two o'clock this afternoon. The Daughters of Hawaii will be asked to decorate the aviators with flower leis immediately after their arrival at the air station. A giant community luncheon will be given at the roof garden of the Young Hotel. This affair will be featured by the presentation of beautiful watches to each of the aviators. Due to the heavy traffic expected on the Pearl Harbor road today, those who are going to the harbor should start early.' An honorable welcome for brave men."

Akiko beamed. "Yes, Father!"

Further articles outlined good vantage points for viewing the conclusion of this epic flight, which military gates would be open to the public, and where to park. A small but prominent sidebar referred to the radio message that Rodgers had relayed to Governor Farrington yesterday after takeoff. It simply said, "See you tomorrow. Rodgers."

As the top of the hour approached, they focused on the radio. First came the commercial. This one was for cigarettes, and they patiently listened through the familiar closing refrain, "Call for Phillip Mor-ris!"

"Aloha, and good morning, Honolulu. Well, today we have exciting news to report. Two of the three planes bound for Honolulu are evidently out of the race. Information is sketchy, but it appears that Mission Commander John Rodgers and his crew of four are still winging their way westward to our island paradise. Our most recent reports have them still on course and on time. You may be able to see these brave men and their seaplane late this afternoon if you are on the Windward or southern coast of Oahu. Commander Rodgers, all of *Hawaii nei* wishes you a warm aloha for a safe arrival." And the report was over.

By now Akiko was shaking with anticipation. Without comment, Masa stood, walked to the door and flipped the office sign to *Open*. It would be a long day for his daughter.

9:56 AM Alaska Time

There were still a dozen oranges onboard, and Sparky distributed one to each of the crew. It was a meager brunch, but Bill managed to laugh it off. "Sparky, when Lei and Lani meet us tonight, the last thing I'm gonna be thinkin' about is food!"

Sparky just smiled. The thought of seeing his girl again excited him. He had been surprised by how much he had missed her. He wondered what Bill would think if he knew that his buddy had gone and fallen in love with Lani Akana. His let his thoughts drift to her lovely face and the image of her hips swaying gracefully as she danced. Ever since Lani had told him that in hula, the hands told the story, her supple fingers had entranced him. He couldn't wait to see her again.

The radio jumped to life. "Dog-dog-three-zero-three calling U.S. Navy patrol plane prep-negative-niner-one. This is U.S. Navy warship *Reno*. Come in P-N-9-1. Over." It was the destroyer next in line at Station T. Sparky donned his headset and acknowledged, "Prep-negative-niner-one reading you loud and clear." An immediate response came back, "Prep-negative-niner-one, we have you inbound at sixty-eight-degrees true, twenty miles out and closing. Lookouts posted. Over."

"Roger, dog-dog-three-zero-three. Six-eight degrees reciprocal. Twenty miles and closing. Prep-negative-niner-one, standing by. Over."

Sparky logged the entry and then scribbled a note, which he attached to the modified clothesline. He spun the wheel and sent the paper forward to John for posting in the log.

Kiles was at the controls and soon spotted the *Reno* on the horizon. She was right on line with their course, and heaving considerably in the heavy seas. As they approached, they could all see the oversized white "303" painted on her bow, Bill feigned surprise: "What's goin' on? Two ships in a row, right where they're s'posed to be?!" Sparky played along. "Yeah, that invisible camo paint must be wearin' off!"

Still flying at only three hundred feet, Kiles eased the plane up a little to assure that the long antenna wire they were dragging would clear. They flew over the *Reno* at four hundred feet, close enough to wave to members of the ship's complement and see them wave back enthusiastically. Kiles performed another wing-waggle as they passed over the gray Clemson-class destroyer, and flew on.

2:23 PM Eastern Time

By now, Zachary Lansdowne was becoming a permanent fixture in the Lakehurst, New Jersey weather office of Hangar #1. He continued to monitor the weather reports throughout the day hoping for confirmation of stable conditions along the *Shenandoah's* designated route.

The local conditions were ideal. In early September, weather this close to the Jersey shore was the best of the year. The ocean had warmed during June, July, and August, while the land was not as stiflingly hot as it could be during midsummer. As a result, in the fall, the temperature differential between the land and the water was considerably less, reducing the potential for gusting winds and sudden afternoon thunderstorms. It was definitely a pleasant time of year—in Lakehurst.

But the local weather was not what worried Lansdowne. Unlike the mellow late-summer Jersey shore conditions, the weather along his intended route across the Midwest was markedly unstable. The late summer/early fall in that region was known for dramatic weather shifts; conditions that gave rise to hurricanes, tornados, and violent thunderstorms. Cold fronts could blow in from the Canadian north and collide viciously with the warm remnants of moisture-laden cumulus. It was this unpredictable recipe for disaster that concerned Lansdowne.

10:29 AM Alaska Time

Rodgers checked in with Wild Bill again about the all-important fuel consumption rate and compared Bill's figures to his own. The news was not good: they were definitely going to run short on fuel. The wind had stayed above twenty knots for most of the past few hours, but the aviation gas was being used up faster than they had reckoned. According to John's calculations, at this rate they were going to fall 350 to 400 miles short of Honolulu. John advised Kiles and Byron to fly with a light hand and run the engines as lean as they could. But no matter what measures they took, they weren't going to make it without refueling.

John went forward to his cubbyhole, put his glasses on, and got to work. He logged the latest sighting and then referred to his scrolled chart. The next ship in line was DD-300, the USS *Farragut*. She was a twin sister ship to the *Reno*, and John hoped she would be as easy to locate as the *Reno* had been. All the ships involved in this mission carried enough aviation gas to refuel *Baby*. However, not all of them were equally skilled in the tricky maneuver of gassing up a biplane on the open sea. Rodgers would be happiest with a ship that had already mastered the procedure. As luck would have it, just two hundred miles beyond the *Farragut*, positioned within their range, was John's friend Commander Van Auken, and the seaplane-tender *Aroostook*—on Station V, four hundred miles east-northeast of Oahu.

Moffett had been very clear: if Rodgers was unable to fly all the way to the islands without stopping for fuel, the U.S. Navy wanted at the very least to set a distance record. With this in mind, John double-checked his math to see if they might somehow make it to the last boat in the rhumb-line progression. That vessel was the USS *Tanager*—a small minesweeper two hundred miles beyond the *Aroostook*, and only a tantalizing two hundred miles from Honolulu. However, John's calculations forced him to rule out that option. The *Tanager* was beyond their reach.

The solution was clear. They would rely on the *Aroostook* for refueling. John took it as providential that the *Aroostook* was the ship on-station in the perfect position to assist in a rapid refueling. Choosing the *Aroostook* also meant that once they reached the station, they would have up to thirty minutes of fuel to locate the ship and land. John felt that would be more than enough time.

John instructed Sparky to send a message to the *Farragut* as soon as they were in range. He wanted the *Farragut* to relay their plans ahead to the *Aroostook*. John dictated, "Unable to reach Hawaii. Fuel low. Plan to fly to Station Victor for refueling. Advise *Aroostook*. ETA Station Victor, 13:55 Hawaii Time." In other words, 2 PM. It was a push, but if they could refuel in as little as an hour, they might be able to make the additional four hundred miles to arrive in Honolulu shortly after sundown.

John noticed that the wind was turning more northerly. He consulted with Byron, and they decided to crab the plane ten degrees further north to compensate for the anticipated drift. John returned to his navigation counter to note this change in the log. Soon thereafter, Sparky passed a message up the line. "Message sent and received by *Farragut* on Station U. Their beacon indicates we are seven miles north of the rhumb line." This surprised John. They might have inched just north of course with his recent corrections—but seven miles? That seemed excessive. Nevertheless he climbed aft and had Byron adjust the heading back, five-degrees south.

Forty-five minutes later, they passed the *Farragut* without seeing her. By now, the crew had grown used to not seeing the ships on-station, so this was not as distressing an occurrence as it might once have been. What was disturbing to John was that the *Farragut* continued to indicate that they were still north of the rhumb line. The wind had clocked around a few degrees more, trying to push them even further north. At John's direction, Kiles, edged *Baby* an extra couple of degrees south.

John fretted in his navigator's compartment, taking still more sightings with his sextant, recording the exact time from his wrist chronometer, and plotting their coordinates. His figures were in considerable disagreement with those they had received from the *Farragut*. He was anxious to check in with the *Aroostook*, as he felt confident Van Auken would give him the correct information.

11:44 AM Hawaii Time

Discouraged at receiving no further radio news, Akiko left the office just before lunchtime. She quickly walked the couple of blocks to Bishop Park and the Hawaiian Trust blackboard. Once there, she was surprised by the size of the crowd gathered for the latest news on the aviators. She was too short to see the entire board over the taller heads in front of her, but soon, several gentlemen made way for her and she moved right up front. Someone had posted *The Honolulu Advertiser*'s latest extra edition on the display. The headline read, "RODGERS' PLANE LESS THAN 700 MILES FROM HONOLULU." Directly under the headline was another four-column-wide photo. This one had the five sailors of the PN9-1 lined up in their dress uniforms, with her Mr. John Rodgers in the center. She was so proud and excited, she found it hard to contain her emotions. Tears flowed freely down her cheeks.

Several well-thumbed copies of the paper were strewn on a folding table nearby. Helping herself to one, Akiko leafed through the entire paper, reading every relevant article. Two advertisements caught her attention.

The first was a large half-page ad for American Hawaiian Motors Company. On it were line drawings of the pride of naval aviation: the dirigible *Shenandoah* and the PN9. Beneath the aircraft were drawings of a racy-looking speedboat and a stately four-door phaeton convertible. The copy read, "SUPREME! On land . . . on sea . . . and in the air. For power, for speed, for reliable performance Packard is supreme. Today . . . Packard motors are carrying America's aviation banner to greater glory."

The second was a much smaller ad with a drawing of a more generic wheeled biplane. "Trans-Pacific Flight News will be broadcast from Radio KGU every hour commencing at 12 noon." Akiko abruptly put down the paper and raced back to the office radio.

12:16 PM Hawaii Time

Unbeknownst to the ship's skipper, the *Aroostook's* radio operator was nearing the end of a double watch. He had been covering for a sick friend, and was due to be relieved at 2 PM. When the *Aroostook* received her first signal from the PN9-1, it was garbled, but they were still a long way away. The exhausted radio operator did his best to align the radio beacon to get both better reception and a fix on the plane's position.

Commander Van Auken was informed of the radio contact, and within minutes he had amassed a considerable contingent of volunteers to stand lookout for the plane. Most of the ship's personnel had met and become friends with Rodgers and his crew during their passage from Hawaii to California. All were keen to see the aviators succeed. The barometer was dropping and heavy weather appeared to be closing in. Many standing watch carried foul weather gear, just in case.

By 12:35, no intelligible conversation had yet been passed, and a frustrated Van Auken marched to the radio operator's cubby. His appearance unnerved the exhausted radioman, and the curt instructions from his skipper only served to further fluster him.

Finally, at 12:47, contact was established. Several messages were exchanged, along with position reports. Had they been plotted at that moment they would have indicated that Rodgers was only slightly north of the rhumb line. The radio operator, however, was so flustered that he failed to properly align the radio beacon and did not fix their direction with it.

A sizeable rainsquall was bearing down on the *Aroostook* as 2 PM approached. Figuring that Rodgers should be close, Van Auken asked for the figures from the radio direction finder. These readings would indicate the relative bearing from both ship-to-plane and plane-to-ship. Generally speaking, the most important bearing for the *Aroostook* was the former: ship-to-plane. The other bearing, plane-to-ship, was called the reciprocal. However when Van Auken called the midshipman over, he said "Get me the reciprocals," indicating that he wanted both readings.

Anticipating a request for the directional reading, the sleep-deprived radio operator had aligned his equipment and checked it twice. The plane was at 0 degrees as seen from the ship. This meant that the plane was due north of the *Aroostook*. It also meant the reciprocal was 180 degrees.

Seconds after the operator had taken his reading, the midshipman stuck his head in the small cubical and mistakenly said, "The commander wants the reciprocal *now!*"

Because the midshipman had used the singular term, "reciprocal," the radioman assumed that Van Auken only wanted the bearing from the plane to the ship. He responded, "180 degrees true."

The midshipman ran back to the bridge and repeated to Van Auken, "Sir, 180 degrees true." The skipper and all on the bridge presumed this was the expected ship-to plane bearing and immediately turned to face south. As they scanned the horizon, the ship's intercom chimed four bells, indicating 2 PM and a mid-watch change.

Relieved in more ways than one, the exhausted radioman handed over the headset to his replacement and headed for his bunk. Sitting in front of the new sailor was the ship's log with the last entry printed in large letters. It was the 180-degrees notation that had been requested by the commander.

Van Auken gave terse orders, sending the midshipman back with instructions to radio Rodgers to execute an immediate ninety-degree right-hand turn and head north. Then, he ordered the *Aroostook* to perform a complementary turn and head due south at full speed.

A huge bolt of lightning flashed, and was instantly followed by a deafening thunderclap. The skies opened, and the rain began to pour down.

2:03 PM Hawaii Time

Visibility was nil. The rain hitting the plane sounded like hundreds of ball-peen hammers beating a mad staccato chorus. John stood impatiently next to the radio console, waiting for orders from Van Auken. The noise from the rain was so loud Sparky could barely hear the *Aroostook* over the radio, but after three confirmations, the directives were clear. Van Auken wanted John to head due north. Removing his headset, Sparky passed this news to Rodgers, who shook his head in disbelief.

"Due north, Sparky—are you sure? That doesn't seem right."

"That's what they said, sir, three times."

John shrugged uneasily. "Roger. Kiles, swing her around due north."

"Aye aye, skip."

The plane banked and turned ninety degrees to the right. The rain continued to beat a deafening rhythm on the single-walled hollow fuselage. John asked Sparky to reconfirm the orders one more time, but because of the din, Sparky was unable to hear any further directives. He wasn't even sure if the ship could read the messages he was sending.

John knew there were a multitude of reasons why they could be south of the *Aroostook*, but the order went completely against his instincts as a navigator. He imagined they could have underestimated the trade winds' drift. He guessed it could have blown them further south over the past six hours. It was also possible that the *Aroostook* could be at the northern end of their racetrack. John tried to convince himself that any of a dozen more variables could have contributed, as PN9-1 hustled through the rain—due north, speeding away from the *Aroostook*, which was now heading in the opposite direction.

2:12 PM Hawaii Time

Onboard the *Farragut*, a message was received from the *Aroostook*. It requested backup to assure a quick rendezvous with Rodgers' plane. Based on prior orders issued by Admiral Moffett, the *Farragut* had already been steaming at full speed down the rhumb line ever since Rodgers' plane had mysteriously slipped by them. A Clemson-class destroyer was reputedly capable of speeds approaching thirty-five knots, and the *Farragut* was proving it.

The skipper reviewed the message a second time, before ordering the ship to alter course to 230 degrees, ten degrees further south than he had been steaming. Even though they hadn't had a visual on the plane, his radio beacon had convinced him that Rodgers had passed to the north of them. Admittedly, the *Aroostook* was a full two hundred miles away, and that was a long way to fly a straight line in these windy conditions. And the wind had shifted, blowing more from the north-northeast, so he imagined it was more than possible that Rodgers had slid diagonally south of the prescribed course. Consequently, the *Farragut* raced onward toward the more southerly projected position of the PN9-1 as relayed by the *Aroostook*. They, too, were racing away from the PN9.

LANE IS FORCED DOWN

All Through the Night—Blazing A Path for Future Air Traffic

RODGERS' CRUISER WILL LAND TODAY ACCORDING TO PRESENT INDICATIONS

Lieut. Snody's Ship Forced Down 300 Mi. From Golden Gate Expected to Take-off Again For These Islands

COMMANDER JOHN RODGERS' FLAGPLANE PN-9 Number 1 in flight with full load and manned by the crew which is bringing her to Hawaii.

A September 1, 1925 first edition of *The Honolulu Advertiser:* The headline refers to the failure of Lieutenant Snody's PN9-3, while the text suggests that Rodgers was still on schedule.

The USS *Reno*

The USS *Farragut*. This picture may be helpful to understand the small size of the many destroyers that were called on to line the route between San Francisco and Hawaii.

The USS *Farragut* at top speed in calm waters

The *Farragut* rolling in heavy seas.

The *Shenandoah* at her mooring mast at Lakehurst NAS, New Jersey.

The *Shenandoah* with her five engines clearly visible. The control-pod gondola is well forward in this shot.

Bowlin, Connell, Rodgers, Pope, and Stantz.

The Honolulu Advertiser's 9 AM extra edition on September 1, 1925 reported Rodgers and crew to be only seven hundred miles from Honolulu. Considering their cruising speed of seventy miles per hour, they were scheduled to make their triumphant arrival around 7 PM Hawaii Time. Additional articles included good vantage points to witness the plane's arrival and the planned receptions for the crew. Also reported was the PN9-3 downing and immediate safe recovery of Lieutenant Snody and his crew by the USS *William Jones* three hundred miles from the California coast.

This advertisement appeared in both the September 1 and September 2, 1925 issues of *The Honolulu Advertiser* and *The Honolulu Star Bulletin*. Packard was obviously proud that their engines powered the dirigible *Shenandoah* and both the PN9 and PB1 planes. Similar ads with different copy ran simultaneously in many mainland newspapers and magazines (see next photo).

PACKARD

SUPREME—AIR, LAND AND WATER

Packard motors drove the giant Navy dirigible Shenandoah on its record-breaking flight of 8100 miles.

Packard motors enabled the sea-plane PN-9 to nearly double the previous world's record for non-stop sea-plane flight by traveling 2230 miles in 28 hours, 35 minutes, 27 seconds—with a starting load of nearly ten tons.

A standard Packard marine motor drove Rainbow III 1064 miles in 24 hours, a distance greater by 276 miles than any boat of any kind or size ever covered in one day.

Packard's quarter century of experience in the design and manufacture of motors is available to all in the Packard Six and the Packard Eight.

Ask The Man Who Owns One

Chapter 35

Tuesday—September 1, 1925

3:20 PM Pacific Time

Admiral Moffett received the relayed word that Rodgers would have to refuel. He was disappointed, of course, but by no means dejected. John had already set a world seaplane distance record, and by the time he reached the *Aroostook*, they would hold the record for nonstop ground covered by any type of aircraft.

Like Rodgers, Moffett was similarly pleased with the good fortune of the *Aroostook's* location on the rhumb line, as it would facilitate a fast refueling. Assuming a quick fill-up, John might even manage to arrive in Honolulu before dark, and the press would be sure to tout the accomplishment.

At the moment, though, reporters were demanding an update from Moffett. Resigned to delivering news of the forced landing, he chose the stairs to descend the three flights to the press conference meeting room. In the hall outside, impatient journalists milled about, rumors buzzing among them. Moffett strode past them into the meeting room and towards the small podium that had been set up. The press poured into the room behind him, pads and pencils at the ready.

Moffett tapped the round-framed, spring-suspended microphone to be sure it was on, then withdrew a plain white sheet of paper from his jacket pocket. Looking at the eager crowd before him, he unfolded it and began to read a short prepared statement.

"Gentlemen of the press, we have just received a radio message from Commander Rodgers stating that his plane is running low on fuel and will have to land at sea to refuel before resuming this history-making flight."

There was a collective gasp from the press, and some started to shout questions.

"Please . . . !" Moffett held up his hand for silence, indicating that he had not finished. The crowd simmered down to listen.

"The navy has anticipated this possibility, and the seaplane tender *Aroostook* is already in position approximately four hundred nautical miles from Honolulu, with a crew well trained in this operation. We expect that Commander Rodgers and his crew will be back in the air and on their way with minimal delay."

There was another surge of energy from the press, which Moffett again quelled.

"Ladies and gentlemen, may I remind you that Commander Rodgers and his intrepid crew have already set a world record for nonstop air travel. Even though they may have fallen short of the primary objective—a nonstop flight to Hawaii—they have nonetheless more than exemplified the 'can-do' attitude of naval aviation." Moffett then hedged his bet: "And they may still be able to reach Honolulu before midnight tonight."

Instantly hands shot up and questions were shouted out as the third estate pounced like a pack of jackals on fresh meat.

"Rodgers hasn't landed, then?"

"What's the likelihood of damage from a forced landing?"

"When will they come down?"

Looking at his watch, Moffett answered simply, "Soon."

Someone looking to bait Moffett with Billy Mitchell's incendiary rhetoric asked, "Level with us, Admiral Moffett. With the embarrassment of Strong's preflight crash, and Snody's plane sinking, is the U.S. Navy really committed to aviation? Or is this race just a stunt to get more money from Congress?"

Moffett clenched his jaw and answered evenly. "Rest assured our disappointments will be investigated, but no one expects perfection from a first attempt. That's why we started out with three planes. As far the navy is concerned, this mission was never a race." He couldn't resist the dig: "That's something you all dreamed up to sell more papers."

"Sir, did you really believe the dated technology of the PN9s would allow them to complete this mission? Weren't your real hopes pinned on the new plane?"

Moffett chose his words carefully. "If by 'dated technology' you're referring to the brand new twin Packard V-12s, which combined are able to produce over 1,000 horsepower; or the use of a thoroughly-tested design, capable of lifting off with a gross weight of 19,000 pounds, I think you may need to recheck your facts."

Having landed that point effectively, he continued. "And yes, we hoped the new Boeing plane would perform well, but the navy was smart enough not to put all of our eggs in one basket, so to speak. That's why I assigned Commander Rodgers, the best navigator in the U.S. Navy, to head up this mission, and fly one of the PN9s."

"Admiral, we understand the seas are pretty rough out there. Can we expect another sunken plane like the one Snody ditched?" The assemblage tittered at the question.

Initially ignoring the second part of the question, Moffett responded to the first. "Commander Rodgers' crew is comprised of the most experienced pilots in the U.S. Navy. Is it rough out there? Yes. And from the reports I have seen, an open ocean landing will not be easy. As far as the plane we lost, you must remember that Lieutenant Snody managed to land a damaged plane with only one engine. That's a formidable task in protected waters; almost impossible in rough seas. The miracle is that the navy was able to rescue all onboard that plane before it went under. Fortunately, Commander Rodgers does not have engine problems."

At that, Moffett thanked the reporters, indicating that the briefing was at an end. He marched out of the room, ignoring the questions that followed in his wake, and quickly retreated to the radio reports waiting in his suite.

3:42 PM Pacific Time

Ethel had downed a couple of shots of bootleg scotch while waiting for the evening paper to be delivered. She was eager to see what Alex had done with the information she had fed him over breakfast. This afternoon, however, the paper was late. Frustrated at the delay, she walked to an intersection not far from her apartment where she knew local newsboys hawked the latest edition. Entering a little hole-in-the-wall diner on the corner, she seated herself at a cramped booth with a view of the street.

The scotch had dulled her senses so that she didn't notice the faint odor of boiling lard that permeated the modest establishment. She examined the menu on her table and decided on a corned-beef sandwich and a Cherry Coke. When no one appeared to take her order, she stood and made her way unsteadily to the front of the diner. The hefty, apron-clad counterman barely acknowledged her presence, even as he wrote what she wanted on a slip of paper and called the order back to the kitchen. His sleeves were rolled up above his elbows, and she noticed a faded anchor tattoo on his muscular forearm. She returned to her booth, mumbling sarcastically to herself, "Another wonderful navy man."

Her shoes were beginning to pinch, so she kicked them off under the table and settled in to wait. Once the food came, despite her disdain for the ex-navy server, she had to admit the sandwich was pretty tasty. She finished the soda, too, and indicated she wanted another by tipping the empty glass and straw towards her new friend washing dishes behind the counter. Just as he approached with the second Coke, Ethel saw the paper truck speed by and a black-and-white bundle sail out of it onto the curb. A scruffy urchin emerged from the shadows, expertly popped the thin wire holding the package together, and picked up a stack of papers. Ethel jumped up and ran out the door, barefoot.

"Hey, lady!"

She called back to the puzzled counter attendant: "Don't worry, I'm not skipping out—I'll be right back!" Outside, on the street, she signaled the paperboy and for a nickel, bought a copy of what she was sure was going to be her moment in the sun.

Back at the booth, Ethel sat and stared at the front page. There it was, an article by S. K. Alexander, just below the fold. The story's headline read "TWO RACERS DOWN, ONE CONTINUES ON." Ethel sped through the article that continued on page four. The angle had shifted. Instead of touting the merits of the Boeing craft over the other two planes, the story focused on John and his crew. The fact that one plane had never even gotten off the ground and the other had sunk had clarified both the danger and enormity of the challenge. Now the message was all about the bravery of John's crew as they continued on alone.

During her breakfast interview, Ethel had not only impugned John's character, she had tried to claim ownership of the idea for the race in the first place—a fact easily checked and dismissed. Alex had quickly realized that he was listening to the ramblings of a disgruntled ex-wife. After Ethel left their tête-à-tête at the Hollywood Hotel, Alex had decided her information had no place in an article about a hero the public was clamoring to canonize.

Not even one measly quote! Simmering in the little booth, Ethel reread the article, then scanned the rest of the paper for anything more—any chance of her name appearing in print. *Nothing!* Cramming her feet back into her shoes, she crumpled the paper and left it on the table. As she slapped her money down on the counter and prepared to leave, the attendant asked, "Hey, lady, what about your paper?"

She fixed him with an icy glare. "Burn it!" she hissed, and stomped out the door.

2:03 PM Hawaii Time

Baby flew out of the squall, and the rain ceased as suddenly as it had began. It was nice to have only the roar of the propellers and engines again. The compass arrow was locked on twelve o'clock high as the crew headed north, searching for the *Aroostook*. The radio chatter continued as John muttered to himself, "Where are you, Van?" They were looking for any telltale sign of the tender—diesel smoke, anything.

After ten minutes of flying with no visual, Rodgers grew increasingly worried. Their fuel was alarmingly low. It didn't even register on the gauges. The last thing he wanted to do was run out of gas in midair. He knew something was terribly amiss. There was no way they could have been this far south of the *Aroostook*. Despite Van Auken's explicit instructions to fly north, John's navigator instincts took over. He called to Kiles, "Enough! Turn 'er around. New heading: due south."

"Aye, aye. Turning to new heading: one, eight, zero." And Kiles put *Baby* into a turn to the left.

John then hollered down to his radio man: "Sparky, send this message to the *Aroostook*: No visual. Fuel low. Check coordinates and reciprocals again. Have we passed you?" Sparky nodded and started the message. "No visual. Fuel low . . ." and then the engines sputtered. First the port propeller bobbled and ceased to spin, and a half-second later, the starboard one stopped cold. John looked at Sparky, who was already trying to send a Mayday. It was too late, though; they could only broadcast while the engines were powering the generator. And without the generator, they didn't have enough power to send a signal.

The seas climbed ominously toward them, as they all braced for impact. Because of their low altitude all Kiles had time to do was level the wings. They were about to perform the most perilous maneuver imaginable for a seaplane: an unpowered landing in high seas, while flying dead downwind.

2:13 PM Hawaii Time

Akiko had to hold on to both her hat and her skirt as she walked along Fort Street. The Hawaiian trades were brisk today. A smile came to her face. She knew how important the winds were to bringing John home. The past five weeks had felt like an eternity. She caught herself. *Is that all it has been—five weeks?*

She stopped at a small storefront restaurant that sold good hot meals— overflowing portions of simple local fare. Because of her excitement, she hadn't taken time for lunch and now realized she needed to eat something. Akiko ordered a teriyaki steak plate that came with a small tossed green salad, steamed rice, and chopsticks. She also ordered a cold Coca-Cola, paid for the meal and then sat down at a tiny table to enjoy it. Hungry as she was, Akiko only picked at the food in front of her. It was delicious, but she was just too anxious to eat. The Coke tasted good, though. She left the heaping plate on the table, paid the deposit on the Coke bottle and carried it with her back the two blocks to Bishop Park. Somewhat away from the crowd and safely ensconced under the shade of an enormous banyan tree, she found an empty park bench. Sitting near the Chamber's blackboard seemed appropriate today; it made her feel closer to John.

No new updates had been posted. She began to think leaving the office for lunch might have been a bad idea. She could have been back there listening to more up-to-the-minute information. Standing up, she tossed the Coke bottle into a trashcan nearby, and hurried back to the office. On the way back she got a terrible shock. A newsboy was hawking an extra edition. Its headline read: "FLIGHT DOOMED."

2:14 PM Hawaii Time

The sudden absence of noise was startling. All those onboard *Baby* heard now was the wind whistling through the guy wires, making them vibrate like taut guitar strings. They had only a few seconds before contact. While an ordinary biplane can glide efficiently because of its combined wing area, *Baby* was a seaplane, and a very heavy one, at that. Under the best of circumstances, her normal landing speed was fast. At least Snody had had one engine to land his plane. All onboard knew that without any power, this landing would be rough—and they only had one shot to get it right.

John barked, "Prepare for a crash landing!"

Kiles yelled, "Sparky, reel in the antenna!" but Sparky ignored him, hoping he could still send some kind of signal. Kiles scrambled into the cockpit next to Byron, while John dove forward to his open-air seat in the nose. Bill and Sparky braced themselves below, and everyone hung on.

A high wind was blowing off the tops of the waves, and the sea was littered with mare's tails of white foam. With Byron at the controls and Kiles backing him up on the other yoke, *Baby* skipped off the first wave and right over the second, hitting the third wave hard. The plane plowed right through it, throwing the crew forward in their seats like so many rag dolls. The fourth wave came fast, further slowing their forward momentum, and after several more bumps and bangs she was down. She had pulled to the right in the waves, and was leaning sideways to the wind. But she was upright, floating, and apparently intact.

John leaped from his forward perch, and stumbled through the rocking fuselage, to check on the crew. There were shaky thumbs-ups all around as everyone seemed to have come through unscathed. Rodgers turned his attention to his two pilots, "Well done, gentlemen."

Both waved off his praise, and Byron asked, "Are Bill and Sparky all right?"

"Yeah, just fine." As John ducked back in the fuselage, he shouted, "We need to check for damage."

The hull was secure. The only significant damage was that the forward support strut for the starboard wing-tip float was bent, pushing the front of the float upward on a thirty-five-degree angle—nothing serious. It wouldn't keep them from taking off again and continuing on to Honolulu after refueling.

John summed up their situation, "Well, it seems we're OK, and there's no question we have just set the world's distance record. Let's just make sure we're ready to get *Baby* airborne again as fast as possible as soon as we get some gas. Snody and his men got picked up in a matter of moments. I'm sure we'll receive similar service from our friends onboard the *Aroostook*."

"Any sign of her, skip?"

John searched the whitecapped seas. "Not yet, Sparky. Let's keep a sharp lookout." But they could see nothing but dark roiling seas and heavy gray clouds in every direction.

The plane rolled and bobbed erratically in the waves, forcing everyone to hang on to keep from being tossed about. Clinging to an overhead rib and leaning over the communications desk, John asked Sparky, "Is there any way we can get the radio to function?"

"Sir, the wind-driven generator's useless without the engines running."

"I know that, Sparky, but can you link the multiple starter batteries in some kind of series?"

"Skip, in order to send a signal we need more power than the batteries can provide, and we'd need some kind of broadcast antenna. Bill's reeling in my three-hundred-foot dragging line. It's useless in the water. The good news is that the batteries are fully charged and should allow us at least to receive signals. That doesn't take much energy. We'll still need to jury-rig an antenna, but it doesn't have to be as long as a broadcast one."

"Sparky, Bill, can you guys handle that?"

"Aye, sir," was the quick response.

John called to his pilots, still in the cockpit trying to keep the plane steady in the waves. Now in the relative quiet they could actually hear conversation from below. "Any sign of the *Aroostook* yet?"

"Negative on a visual, sir."

"OK then. Kiles, you stand watch. They should be here soon. I'll go get the binoculars from the nav station for you."

"Aye, aye, sir."

"Byron, do a thorough check of the plane—nose to tail. Check for any hidden damage. And make sure you double-check all the control cables. I don't want any surprises when we get this girl back in the air."

"Roger, skip."

Byron grinned. He knew what to check, and he knew Rodgers knew he knew what to check, but this was just John being his thorough self. Since Rodgers was heading for the bow, Byron started his recon from the stern.

The plane mamboed erratically as John lurched forward to the navigation station. As he stepped heavily into his navigator's cubbyhole, he heard the sound of broken glass underfoot. Fearing the worst, he leaned over and picked up the empty wire frames of his glasses. He slid his palm across the floorboards hoping to find one unbroken lens at least, but he had landed squarely on the spectacles, crushing both. *Damn, damn, DAMN!* Shaking his head in frustration he grabbed the binoculars from their hook, and bouncing off the fuselage ribs, he returned to the cockpit. Once there, he saw that Kiles had his hands full trying to steer the plane into the swells. John stepped up and sat in the copilot seat.

"See anything?" John asked perfunctorily, putting the binoculars up to his eyes.

"Nothing yet, sir, but honestly, I've spent most of the time trying to keep our girl pointing into the wind. Otherwise, the wind and waves'll sluice her around pretty bad." Kiles paused, "It must be pretty rough down below."

"Yeah. Bill's OK, but Sparky's pretty green around the gills."

"Sir, let's just hope we can get gassed up and out of here soon. Any word from the *Aroostook*?"

"Sparky and Bill are working on it," John said while scanning the horizon.

Down in the bowels of the plane, Byron worked his way forward, pulling up the floorboards and checking everything he could. Amazingly enough, *Baby* seemed totally unaffected by the hard landing. Entering the navigation station, he saw the shards of John's broken glasses. Byron then weaved his way back amidships where the crew's limited personal belongings had been stowed. There he retrieved his ditty bag from his canvas duffle, withdrew a small box and then cinched his sea bag shut. Retracing his steps, he opened the box, placed its contents on Rodgers' small map table and quickly ducked back out again.

3:07 PM Hawaii Time

The *Aroostook* had lost all radio contact with Rodgers. There had been a truncated message: "No visual. Fuel low," but that was all they'd had for the last hour. Van Auken was concerned but not frantic. He posted a double watch. The plane was no longer responding to any radio calls, therefore there was no broadcast signal on which to lock the radio beacon. Van correctly assumed that could be due to the fact that the plane was on the ocean's surface. He knew that they probably wouldn't have the power to transmit very far now that their long antenna was useless in the water. He imagined John's first order of business would be to rig a better antenna.

Van Auken was absolutely sure that they could not have passed the plane without a sighting regardless of the heavy seas. Plus the sky was clearing as they headed south and visibility was improving. Once the rain stopped completely they were able to see almost twelve miles to the horizon on either side from the top deck. So John and his crew had to be further south—unless they had already sunk.

3:26 PM Hawaii Time

Sparky had managed to complete the battery set-up to get the radio to receive, while Bill had likewise been able to rig an aerial. Now they could at least monitor the conversations between the *Aroostook* and the *Farragut*. Seconds later, the radio receiver was working, although the same could not be said for its operator.

The intense rolling of the plane made any job difficult, but for Sparky, trying to function in the closed, cramped quarters of the radio nook was fast becoming impossible. In addition to the sickening motion of the plane in the surf, the air in the fuselage was becoming foul from lack of circulation. Not only that, but the minute remains of aviation gas gave off noxious fumes. In a fairly short time, he became violently seasick.

Having completed his inspection, Byron saw Sparky's distress and opened the large main portside hatch. There were two hatches, one on each side of the plane, both located fairly high off the water. Even with the large swells there was little chance of any significant water coming aboard. Opening it significantly improved conditions in the dark, stuffy cabin.

Byron called to the suffering radio man, "Sparky, come over here and get some fresh air."

"Aye sir, thanks!" Sparky barely made it to the opening before spilling the contents of his stomach. Wild Bill hung onto his buddy's belt to keep him from pitching out the open hatch as Sparky gagged and vomited repeatedly.

John climbed down from the copilot's seat just as Byron and Wild Bill retrieved the spent chief radioman from the clutches of mal de mer.

"Everything OK, men?"

Wild Bill, trying to make light of his friend's predicament, smartly answered, "Aye, sir. CRO Stantz was just chummin' for some fish."

John shook his head. "Carry on sailor. We shouldn't be parked here for long." He then looked in Byron's direction and indicated the cockpit, "Kiles could use some help. And someone needs to act as lookout."

Byron nodded. "Aye, aye."

John continued, "I need to take some sightings to fix our position now that we have a working radio. At least we'll be able to hear the *Aroostook*. If they give us a fix on their latitude and longitude we'll know when they are close enough for us to fire a flare." At that point, a rogue wave slapped at the hull, almost knocking John off his feet. Righting himself, he proceeded forward to the navigator's station. Once there, he found a brand new pair of prescription wire-rim glasses waiting for him on the counter.

3:37 PM Hawaii Time

The radio crackled as a song was abruptly interrupted with a news flash. Akiko's head bobbed up from her work. "Ladies and Gentlemen, we have received a relayed message from the USS *Tanager* that Commander John Rodgers and his crew of four have radioed in with a progress report. They are evidently low on fuel and will most likely have to land at sea to refuel before they can complete their epic mission. Rodgers' last message was, 'Please keep good track. Gas is about all gone. Think it impossible to get in.'

"The *Tanager* is presently located approximately two hundred miles east of Oahu. 'Please keep good track' is generally considered a warning to stand by in case of an accident. Stay tuned to KGU Radio for further developments."

Akiko's eyes widened with fear. *Oh no—he's so close. Please, PLEASE bring him home safe!*

3:41 PM Hawaii Time

Van Auken had traveled almost thirty-five miles south of the rhumb line without a visual of any kind. He was confounded. *Where the hell are they?* Then he made a crucial decision. He needed help to find John, and he needed it now. Radioing the *Farragut*, Van plotted their position. The *Farragut* was now only fifty miles east of the *Aroostook*. Van laid out a search grid, working north and south parallel lines like a continuous dragnet as they edged west within the confines he had designated. He then had the radio operator again contact the minesweeper USS *Tanager*, which had been hovering at the final station on John's course. Commander W. Van Auken then ordered the *Tanager* to leave her post and join them in the search. Because she was just over two hundred miles away from the *Aroostook*, this would mean upwards of a nine-hour trip for the small vessel, but Van wanted all the help he could muster. He pulled out all the stops and contacted the aircraft carrier *Langley*. Once Rodgers had flown past the *Farragut*, the *Langley* had been officially released from duty and was now headed west for refueling at Pearl Harbor. Consequently, she was already heading their direction and was only 260 miles away. At her top speed of fifteen knots, she could be there before dawn.

The noon extra edition headline was dark. *The Honolulu Advertiser* reported that Rodgers, although still flying, was nearly out of gas and would most certainly be forced to land and refuel. Rodger's message is quoted, "Please keep good track. Gas is about gone. Think it impossible to get in."

This tiny image of the USS *Tanager* is one of the few existing pictures of the small minesweeper that was positioned at "Station W," two hundred miles from Oahu.

This afternoon extra edition of *The Honolulu Advertiser* had a different report.

Chapter 36

Tuesday—September 1, 1925

4:50 PM Hawaii Time

The weather in Hawaiian waters is notoriously changeable. As the afternoon wore on, the skies had cleared with no sign of squalls, and the fury of the wind and waves had abated considerably. The tropical sun shone warm and bright, and if not for the situation *Baby*'s crew were in, the day might have been considered pleasant. The pilots were getting the hang of holding the plane into the wind and swells. *Baby* was still rocking and rolling, but at least she had settled into a more consistent rhythm.

The team quickly established a system onboard the downed plane to keep things on an even keel as they waited for the *Aroostook*.

One man was needed full time to massage the tiny rudder that hung below the waterline. His job was to keep the plane heading into the wind and waves, both to prevent them from wallowing, and to slow their drift. The last thing they wanted was to float away from their last reported position. Byron and Kiles rotated every hour in this position.

One man was needed as lookout, and this job usually fell to the off-duty helmsman. He used the one pair of binoculars onboard, but only intermittently. Holding them steady took some practice. Plus, focusing too long through the glasses invited motion sickness.

A third was needed to man the radio. Since Sparky was still violently seasick, Bill was stuck below with this unenviable job. While Sparky rallied occasionally to try and give Bill a break, it didn't take long before he was overcome with nausea, and had to retreat to the hatch.

Sick as he was, Sparky still had the presence of mind to suggest the use of the kite antenna, a small box kite that trailed a thin wire. Although it ultimately proved less effective than the one Bill had strung up earlier from the upper wing to the tail, it did help to raise morale; the men thought it might be seen by the *Aroostook*. Unfortunately, it flew for less than twenty minutes before crashing into the sea, a useless wreck.

For his part, John focused primarily on keeping track of their position, calculating wind drift, current, and sextant plots. He also filled in at all the rotations, trying to keep everyone's spirits up.

John reckoned that they were 472 miles east-northeast of Oahu. He figured their drift at just over two knots in that same general direction. This was all good data. However, when he received the radio signal with the grid coordinates that Commander Van Auken had designated for the search, he realized the quick stop for refueling they'd hoped for was going to be out of the question.

6:55 PM Pacific Time

The San Francisco sun disappeared into the low clouds on the western horizon and the lights in Admiral Moffett's Olympic Club suite had to be turned on. It was getting late, and although Hawaii still had more than two hours of sunlight left, time was running out. The already grave situation was growing worse by the minute.

Admiral Moffett felt completely helpless. Three hours before, he'd received the report that the *Aroostook* had lost contact with Rodgers. No substantive information had come in since then. Pounding his fist on the hotel suite table, he railed, "Hell, Snody was picked up in minutes. What in Sam Hill is going on out there?"

In addition to his concern for the safety of Rodgers and his crew, Moffett also had to hold the attack dogs of the press at bay. Ever since his earlier emergency press conference, they had been incessantly nipping at his heels to find out what was going on. The newsmen had been aggressively grilling anyone coming in or out of Moffett's suite. The Admiral knew he wouldn't be able to hold them off much longer.

Desperate to take some action, a frustrated Moffett ordered a strong but unrealistic message radioed to the *Aroostook*. "Advise immediately expected rendezvous time with PN9-1."

As they waited for a response, Moffett's aide answered a knock at the door and a shore patrol sailor handed him the evening paper. When his aide delivered the paper to Moffett, the Admiral was startled by the headline: "CREW SAVED."

4:59 PM Hawaii Time

As the business day came to a close at the little optometry shop, no further information about John had been broadcast. Akiko was disappointed to realize that the radio news was not really "up-to-the-minute," as she had always supposed. Nevertheless, she hoped that the five o'clock report would offer an update on the situation at sea. Even if they'd had to stop and refuel, surely John should be arriving soon. Akiko was torn between waiting to hear the broadcast and walking to Honolulu Harbor to watch for his arrival. A third option was to take the trolley to Ala Moana Beach Park and join the welcoming crowd already gathering there. She decided to listen to the news first and then make her decision.

Weary from worrying about his daughter, on top of a long business day, Masahiro walked into the front office and seated himself in Akiko's desk chair without saying a word. He wanted somehow to comfort her, but aside from simply keeping her company, he was at a loss for what else to do or say. So he said nothing, and merely crossed his arms and closed his eyes as the five o'clock report began.

"More news on the incredible attempt to fly nonstop from San Francisco to Hawaii . . . after this message from our sponsor." As Akiko waited, she impatiently straightened the newspaper and the magazines on the end table. When the ad for Hawaii Territorial Bank finally finished, the announcer began, "Good news, Hawaii! John Rodgers and his brave crew have set a new world distance record for sustained flight. However, it appears they may fall short of their quest to make it all the way to our little island paradise nonstop. Low on gas, they plan to land in the ocean and refuel at a waiting U.S. Navy vessel. With any luck, these brave men might still make it here by sundown. All Hawaii will be watching our eastern skies tonight for the first signs of the heroes." The announcer then moved on to other news.

Masa opened his eyes and studied Akiko. "Well, daughter, the news is good, is it not?"

Akiko responded, hope shining in her eyes. "Yes, father. It appears so." *Please let him come home safe and soon.*

Masa was pleased to see Akiko brighten. "Shall we get some dinner?"

"Oh, father, I couldn't possibly eat now. I am going to go to the beach at Ala Moana to watch for John's plane as it clears Diamond Head.

"Hmmmm.·Would you like me to accompany you, Akiko?"

Akiko smiled and shook her head. "Thank you father, but I will be all right by myself."

"My child, if he does not arrive by sundown, I do not want you to spend the whole night alone on the beach, waiting."

Akiko was touched by Masa's concern. "Father, I will be fine. If he does not arrive by nine, I will take the trolley back to town and then catch the bus home, I promise."

"Well, promise me, too, you'll get something to eat. Do you have any money?"

"Yes, father. All will be well, really." With that, she kissed him on the forehead, picked up her purse and hat, and slipped out the office door to the tinkling of the little entry bell.

The sound faded quickly, and the room became still, despite the lazy jazz music emanating from the radio. The late afternoon sun shone through the windows, forming oblique waterfalls of light. Tiny dust motes spiraled through the rays in a slow dance, seeming to keep time with the plaintive saxophone. Masahiro sat in the desk chair worrying for his daughter; wishing that Hiroko were still alive to guide him in these matters.

At last, he donned his dark jacket and closed up the shop. As he walked the two short blocks to the bus stop he noticed a newsboy yelling "Extra!" He stopped dead in his tracks as he saw the headline: "RODGERS FORCED DOWN AT SEA."

6:42 PM Hawaii Time

The sun was low on the horizon when John called his crew together. He gathered them in an area next to the cockpit so all the men could hear the bad news at the same time. Byron was the first on hand. A look passed between them, and Rodgers said simply, "Thanks, Byron. I owe you one."

Once all were present, John began without preamble, "Men, we've got a problem, one that may delay our refueling. The radio chatter we've been picking up between the *Aroostook* and the *Farragut* makes it clear that the area they've delineated for their search is too far south. My most recent plot has us at 24 degrees 4 minutes north, 152 degrees 4 minutes west. We've kept our drift in check, thanks to Byron and Kiles, and my dead reckoning has us within four miles of where we landed, 468 miles east-northeast of Oahu. I'm sure the *Aroostook* will soon recognize their mistake and expand the search area, but for now we should plan on spending the night on the water.

"Kiles and Byron, the three of us should rotate helming and lookout duty." Taking a look at Sparky's pale face, Rodgers continued, "Wild Bill, can you handle the radio duties on your own for the time being?"

Sparky bravely protested, "Sir, I'll be fine. I just need to get my sea legs."

John knew all too well the debilitating effects of seasickness, but he had to respect his radio man's gumption. "OK, then, Sparky, you and Bill spell each other on the radio; but Bill, you keep an eye on him. Everyone clear?"

As the sun set, Kiles asked the one thing that was on everyone's mind. "Sir, just how far away do you reckon they are?"

It was a tough question with a bleak answer, but Rodgers faced it square on. "Fifty-one miles."

8:45 PM Pacific Time

The newspaper lay in a heap, the "CREW SAVED" front page face-down on the floor where Admiral Moffett had it flung two hours earlier, after realizing the elated headline referred to Snody's plane. An intensely frustrated Moffett had received no further word about Rodgers, and it was again time to update the voracious press. He retired to the bathroom, washed his hands and face, and brushed his short, buzz-cut hair. When the Admiral returned to the main room, his aide held his superior officer's navy-blue uniform jacket for him. Shrugging it on, Moffett squared his shoulders and buttoned the front closed. Checking a mirror by the door, he cinched his navy-blue tie and exited the suite without a word to anyone, slamming the door behind him.

Admiral Moffett descended the three flights of stairs once more and marched purposefully down the wide hallway. The hall was illuminated with evenly spaced electric brass and glass sconces. These cast ominous shadows, which measured his progress towards the press conference room.

Disgruntled reporters lounged all over the small ballroom, sitting anywhere they could, even on the floor. Seeing Moffett approach the podium, they leapt up and raced toward him, pushing and shoving for positions down front.

As Moffett took his place at the podium, the room quieted expectantly. "Gentlemen, I would like to thank you all for your patience. As you know, we have been busy coordinating a complex recovery effort." Here he paused, picking his words carefully. "I won't try to sugarcoat it. It has been a difficult few hours. As I indicated earlier, Commander Rodgers' plane was to land next to one of our vessels to facilitate refueling. Rodgers was in radio contact with that ship, the USS *Aroostook*—on-station as planned four hundred miles from Oahu—as they attempted to rendezvous. At 2:12 PM Hawaii Time, 4:12 Pacific, we received our last radio message from Commander Rodgers. In it, he indicated he was low on fuel."

A murmur buzzed through the room. Moffett raised his hand for silence, then continued. "We have not had any further contact with Commander Rodgers since that time. However, this is to be expected under the circumstances. Once on the water, it would be difficult to transmit a signal any distance.

"Let me assure you, the navy is doing everything in its power to locate Commander Rodgers and his valiant crew. Besides the *Aroostook*, we have called in the *Farragut*, the *Tanager*, and the *Langley* to assist in a coordinated search."

Here, Moffett was interrupted by several impatient reporters shouting questions.

"So, you're saying you know the plane is down . . ."

"Does this mean Rodgers and his crew have crashed . . ."

One particularly loud voice stood out in the confusion. "Admiral, does this mean you don't know where they are—or even if they've landed safely?"

"That is correct, for the moment. It's a big ocean out there, but I can assure you we have sufficient coordinates to confirm that they are within our search grid. With regard to where they came down, we know where they were when they were about to run out of gas. This will help us narrow the hunt. As I previously stated, the crew aboard PN9-1 is among the most experienced in the world. We are confident they were able to land the plane safely."

"But admiral, aren't the waves out there at least as rough as the ones that sank Snody's plane?"

Admiral Moffett answered bluntly: "Yes. Yes, they are."

7:27 PM Hawaii Time

To the relief of all the crew, the seas continued to diminish in size as the wind dropped after sunset. John and Bill had managed to slow their drift even further by rigging a bucket as a sea anchor, using the line that had previously served as the jack line. They attached this rope to a mooring cleat on the bow, and the bucket dragged out in front of the plane. They kept the plane pointed east into the wind, which meant that *Baby* basically slid backwards down the waves as they rolled slowly westward. Their ultimate island goal, Oahu, was now several hundred miles off their stern.

In the dark, hunger pangs set in, and the men broke out the ham sandwiches they had packed in San Francisco a lifetime ago. All were confident that a rescue would take place early in the morning, if not before. Their main concern for the time being was Sparky Stantz's seasickness. The dwindling swells had done nothing to alleviate his condition. They tried to get him to eat one of the sandwiches in an attempt to settle his stomach, but after only two bites he regurgitated again and accidentally dropped the uneaten portion overboard.

John grimaced when that happened, but said nothing, privately resolving to make a complete inventory of all remaining food and water. Fortunately, they hadn't consumed much during the flight. Taking stock in the tiny storage area amidships, John discovered they still had seven sandwiches, ten quarts of water, two quarts of coffee, one thermos of soup, and ten oranges. There were also emergency rations that hadn't been off-loaded back in San Francisco. Included in that kit was a three-pound tin of crackers and a six-pound can of corned beef. John felt considerably better to discover the supplies seemed relatively abundant.

Byron called back to John, "The sea anchor's helping to keep us headed into the wind. We still need to post a lookout, but if the breeze continues to drop, whoever's at the helm may be able to handle both duties."

"Roger."

John then disappeared down into the radio room to confer with Wild Bill and his miserable buddy. While Sparky tried to put on a game face, Rodgers could tell his main radio man was barely hanging on.

At 11 PM local time, Wild Bill picked up some increased radio chatter and was able to record new coordinates for the *Aroostook* and the *Farragut*, which he immediately passed on to Rodgers. In the semidarkness and without his glasses, John couldn't make out the figures Bill had scribbled. He quietly withdrew to his navigator's office, bumping against *Baby's* exposed ribs as he traveled forward. At his desk, John donned his new glasses and shined his flashlight on the figures. Dismayed at what he read, he squinted, not trusting his eyes, but the numbers did not change. He quickly applied an algebraic formula to verify his reckoning, and the numbers only confirmed his fears. *Dammit!* The *Aroostook* was now more than ninety-five miles away. The *Farragut* was even further.

11:25 PM Hawaii Time

Akiko removed her shoes at the front stoop, as was customary. She gently closed the screen door. Seeing the light on in the kitchen, she headed toward it, and found Masahiro seated at the table, a cup of tea in front of him. Without saying a word, Akiko picked up the ceramic teapot and topped off her father's cup. She then opened the cupboard and took out another cup for herself. Sitting down, she poured the fragrant amber liquid into the cup. She dabbed at her swollen eyes. She had obviously been crying.

Masa watched his daughter solemnly. "It is late, Akiko."

She bowed her head, "I know, father. I am sorry if I caused you worry."

Masa's impulse was to reach out and pat her hand, but he restrained himself. "I am glad you are home safe." When Akiko merely nodded, Masa volunteered, "I talked with the Kamakaiwi's just after ten this evening. The news hasn't changed."

"I know. There was a radio at the bus depot."

"Did you have to walk? Is that why you're so late?"

"No, I caught the trolley at nine, but when I got to the depot, I hoped I could find out more. I stayed there for a while listening. I didn't realize I had missed the last bus.

"Officer Baldwin recognized me there and offered me a ride home."

They drank their tea in silence. Ordinarily, Masa was not much of a conversationalist, but tonight he wanted to reach out to his daughter. He wanted to talk but he had no idea how to comfort her.

Akiko broke the silence. "I am sure they will be coming home tomorrow." She managed a little smile. "And now, it is late. I need to be pretty for Mr. John Rodgers. These puffy eyes will never do." And with that, she slipped from the room. Alone in the kitchen, Masa sighed. Hiroko would have known what to say.

Admiral Moffett (foreground) aboard the USS *Langley* during sea trials.

The USS *Aroostook:* note the flying boat on her fantail.

Chapter 37

Wednesday—September 2, 1925

4:56 AM Pacific Time

Admiral Moffett dozed fitfully, his body slumped in the wing-backed maroon leather chair in his suite. Those of his team who were on watch had strict orders to wake him with any substantive news, but there had been none. Messages relayed from the *Aroostook* and the *Farragut* were often received out of order. This disjointed information only increased the team's overall frustration and exhaustion. Those off duty had found perches in the suite to catnap until fresh news came in.

Just before 5 AM, the hotel phone jangled. Moffett snapped awake and picked it up before the second ring.

"What is it?"

"Long-distance person-to-person for Admiral Moffett. Will you accept the call?"

"Yes, yes—put it through!"

The operator obliged and a very faint voice came over the line. At the end of his tether, Moffett barked "Speak up—speak up, I can't hear you! Who is this, anyway?"

There was a slight delay, then, "Sir . . . sorry to phone you so early. This is Lieutenant Commander Lansdowne calling from Lakehurst."

The Admiral recognized the voice of the skipper he had assigned to steward the ZR-1, *Shenandoah*, on its public relations swing through the Midwest. The *Shenandoah*'s first stop was supposed to be at a fair in St. Louis. *Why the hell is he calling from New Jersey?*

"Zachary, is there a problem?"

"Sir, the ship's fine and the weather here in New Jersey is ideal, but we've been delayed for the past two days due to the forecast along our intended route, principally over the Delaware River Valley and eastern Pennsylvania. Conditions finally seem to have quieted down there, but now I'm concerned about the weather over the Ohio Valley. We had planned to leave here at first light this morning, but earlier reports from western Pennsylvania indicated the barometric pressure was falling there. I thought it prudent to delay our launch until conditions in the area stabilize."

There was silence as Moffett considered the options. "Are the reports that bad?"

"Sir, the reports are, at best, vague, but you had requested I confer with you if I had any reservations. That's why I'm reporting in."

Impatience edged the Admiral's voice. "Zachary, one of the reasons for this tour is to show people that the navy's ZR-1 can fly in most weather conditions. What exactly are you worried about?"

"Sir, with all due respect, late summer weather is notoriously unstable over the Midwest. I think it best to err on the cautious side, sir."

Moffett sighed. "Of course you're right. You're the skipper, Zachary. You know better than anyone if the conditions are safe. I want you to feel free to alter the course plans as you see fit. On the other hand, you also know what's at stake with this tour." Moffett paused briefly, and then continued, "I'll leave the final decision up to you."

"Yes, sir. At present I've scheduled our departure for seven hours from now, 1400 Eastern. If you don't hear from me, you'll know that we decided to proceed."

"Very well, good luck, Commander." Admiral Moffett replaced the receiver. He rubbed his face with a meaty paw, mentally reviewing the conversation. *Lansdowne didn't mention Rodgers.* He wondered if the news reports from the Pacific had reached back east.

6:10 AM Hawaii Time

By sunrise, the seas and winds had calmed considerably, rocking *Baby* in a steady, gentle rhythm. Even so, Sparky was still having a difficult time of it. John was on lookout. Standing on the lower wing, braced against a pair of the many guy wires that angled between *Baby*'s upper and lower wings, he scanned the endless early morning seas. A small tether ran around his waist and into the open cockpit.

From his limited vantage point, he could see almost five miles to the horizon in every direction. His navigator's mind quickly deduced what that meant. He could visually command more than seventy-eight square miles of open ocean. Yet there was no sign of a rescue ship. John also knew from experience that ships frequently sailed entire voyages between the West Coast and Hawaii without ever spotting another vessel until within sight of land, such was the enormity of the Pacific. When he reluctantly returned to the cabin to take his sunrise sight, he entered an observation in the flight log: *Few people fully appreciate the vastness of the Pacific. It is difficult to comprehend until you find yourself alone, floating on its surface.*

The lack of any sign of life discouraged the crew. They were understandably anxious to refuel and get home to Hawaii. They were, after all, less than seven hours' flight time from Honolulu. The occasional radio chatter they were able to monitor was both comforting and frustrating.

"Sir, we've just picked up some chatter from the *Aroostook*."

"What's the gist, Bill?"

"Well, sir, it's mighty nice to know they're out there, but they're not shifting the search area any."

"Damn."

"Yes, sir. It's all Sparky an' I can do to keep from shoutin' into the dad-blamed microphone. Wouldn't do any good, but it'd sure let off some steam."

"Carry on, Bill."

"Aye, aye, sir."

Byron relieved Kiles in the cockpit. After an arduous night of keeping *Baby* headed into the wind, the exhausted copilot retreated for some much-needed sleep. Between the gentler swells and the sea-anchor bucket, it was now possible for Byron to handle both helm and look-out duties.

While Bill kept tabs on the radio below, hoping for better news, Sparky stretched out on the wing, trying to find some relief. Because there were no life preservers onboard, John had insisted that anyone leaving the cockpit be secured via a jack line. They had made sure Sparky's line was tied on tight, as he spent much of the time hanging over the side, dry heaving. He was literally at the end of his rope.

As the hours ticked by, Byron sensed the pressure John was under and tried to engage him in casual conversation.

"John, when the *Aroostook* does get here, how much fuel you figure we should take on? My hunch is you've already done the math."

Rodgers lowered the field glasses, "Yup, I did. I figure we only need to top off the primary tanks. That'll give us a range of 550 miles—more than enough. We may even want to offload the fifty-five-gallon drums now that they're empty, but that's not critical. With most of the extra fuel weight gone, if the seas stay like this, we should lift off easy as pie."

"You know, that starboard wing float isn't in the greatest shape . . ."

"Yeah, but bent up at the front like that, it shouldn't affect our takeoff."

"Have you calculated our position since your sunrise sight?"

"We're about the same distance as before."

Byron shook his head. "Tantalizing, isn't it?"

John thought of Akiko waiting for him in Honolulu. "Yeah. So near, and yet so far away."

1:52 PM Eastern Time

In New Jersey, the weather continued to vacillate. Even though it had dawned clear on-site, occasional threatening clouds had drifted through the Lakehurst Air Field all day long. Lieutenant Commander Zachary Lansdowne felt painted into a corner. He expressed his reservations privately to his wife Margaret, who had come to see him off.

"I don't feel right about this tour. If the weather turns bad, the *Shenandoah* will be a sitting duck. This time of year, there's just no way to know what it's going to do out there."

"Darling, you have to make the final decision. Call it off if you're not sure."

"There's more to it than that. Two weeks ago, top navy brass accepted my decision to postpone the tour. But now, they're getting antsy. They see glorious fall weather and don't understand my reluctance. Plus, they keep reminding me of the 25,000-plus miles the *Shenandoah's* already flown in all kinds of weather."

Accustomed to her husband's balanced ruminations, Margaret remained silent as he talked his way through the dilemma.

"Dammit, I grew up in Ohio—I know how suddenly late-summer storms can blow up. But on the other hand, I can't continue to put off the tour on the basis of what *might* happen. This trip was already going to be a key PR turn for the navy. Now that Moffett's got his hands full with a potential black eye in the Pacific, the navy needs a big win more than ever. Everyone and their brother wants to see the 'Battleship of the Sky.' They're going to flock to the state fairs we're scheduled to fly over; the navy's counting on it. We've got to get underway. Plus, I think if I continue to delay the trip, I'll be relieved of duty."

"My darling, it sounds to me as if you've made your decision."

"You know me too well, Margaret." He took a deep breath. "Well, that's it then. The crews are onboard and the ship is ready. I guess we're good to go." With one final look up at the sky, Zachary Lansdowne shrugged his shoulders and kissed his wife goodbye.

10:00 AM Hawaii Time

The Honolulu Advertiser lay flat across Akiko's desk. Its grim headline spanned the full width of the paper. Printed in somewhat smaller type than yesterday's editions was: "HOPE FOR RODGERS FADES." The article continued, "Flagplane lost 15 hours as searchers start dawn vigil.

Fate of flagplane rests with concentrated air and land rescue . . ." And yet it also reported, "Officials optimistic."

A distracted Akiko mechanically went through her duties at the office. The radio had been on since her arrival early this morning, but up until now, there had been nothing new. She hoped the top of the hour would bring a long-awaited update. After the sponsor's commercial jingle, the announcer began.

"Aloha, ladies and gentlemen. We know you've all been anxious for the latest on our intrepid aviators. It seems the navy has lost all touch with Commander Rodgers and his brave crew. They were last heard from yesterday afternoon. No further communication has been received since then. The Associated Press wire service now reports that they have been officially categorized as lost at sea. The bulletin also notes that the entire resources of the United States Navy in the Hawaiian district have been mobilized in an effort to locate them. In their official communiqué, the navy has expressed every confidence in Commander Rodgers. And in other news . . ."

Akiko fell to her knees, physically ill from the report. Her Mr. John Rodgers was lost at sea. Alone in his office, Masahiro had heard the news. He appeared in the doorway, then crossed the room and sat on the rattan sofa next to his kneeling daughter. This time he followed his impulse to reach out to her. Putting his hand on her bowed head, he stroked her hair silently. Akiko fell forward into his lap, sobbing.

After several minutes, Masa said softly, "Not to worry, they will find him."

Akiko wiped her eyes, eager to cling to any reason for optimism. "Do you really think so?"

Answering honestly, Masa voiced the opinion shared by so many in Hawaii. "Yes. After all, the whole United States Navy is looking for him."

12:00 PM Hawaii Time

Onboard the *Aroostook*, the ship's intercom rang eight bells. The *Langley* had joined the search earlier that morning, and although not within sight, she already had reconnaissance planes in the air. The *Reno* had also joined the operation, as had the *Tanager*, having made a record run for her small size. They, too, were somewhere over the horizon. Several other navy ships at sea had been called in as well, and would soon join the effort.

As a result of the extra ships and airplanes at his disposal, Van Auken was able to expand the grid considerably. The entire search area had almost doubled in square miles and was now larger than the combined land area of all the Hawaiian Islands. This would have been very good news for Rodgers and his crew, had Van Auken not also shifted the grid 110 miles to the west-southwest, based on his estimation of the drift that the PN9 would have experienced over the past twenty-two hours at five to eight knots. This was a gross miscalculation. Unbeknownst to the searchers, the enlarged grid still left the PN9-1 bobbing well outside of it.

12:12 PM Hawaii Time

With the addition of the *Langley*, the *Tanager* and the *Reno*, the radio chatter being received aboard *Baby* had increased dramatically since sunrise. From the ship-to-ship communication, the crew learned that aircraft from the *Langley* had joined the search. Now their pastime of watching the horizon expanded to watching the skies as well. Their spirits rose as they heard that the navy was pulling out all the stops; surely they would be found soon.

After catching the latest chatter from the *Aroostook*, Bill passed the newest search grid coordinates to John, who took the paper and weaved his way back to his navigation station. He put on his new glasses and was dismayed to find he could hardly read the notes. He was greatly relieved to discover it was only because the lenses had filmed over with salt from the omnipresent sea spray, and just needed a good wipe. Cleaning them with his shirttail, he put them back on and turned to the business at hand. When the new coordinates came into focus, John did a double take. *My God—they've shifted even further south!*

Once again, he gathered the crew.

"Men, there's good news and bad news. As you've picked up from the chatter, the navy's going all out to find us. That's the good news. The bad news is, they're moving in the wrong direction."

Wild Bill cocked his head, "Are you sayin' those coordinates I passed you are wrong, skip?"

John shook his head. "The coordinates aren't wrong, Bill—the trouble is they're right. It's the ships that are all moving in the wrong direction. Our true coordinates are north and east of where they're looking. And there's no way to let them know."

Sparky managed to rally. "Skip, if they're bringin' all those ships in to hunt for us, and they keep increasin' the search area, one of those tubs is gonna get lucky, you'll see."

Bill added, "I'm with Sparky, skip."

Kiles nodded, and Byron summed up the situation. "John, they're hell-bent and determined not to stop until they find us. We just have to sit tight until they do."

Rodgers shook his head, inspired by the optimism of his crew. "Well, men, I'm sure you're right. Anyway, for the time being there's not much else we can do."

As the meeting broke up, Kiles Pope volunteered to spell Bill at the radio, giving him some needed rest and fresh air. In short order, he regretted his offer. The motion in the closed quarters of the radio hold, mixed with the foul smell of fuel, soon found Kiles following Sparky's path to the open hatch.

The day wore on and still nothing appeared on the horizon. In the afternoon, the hot tropical sun beat down, reddening the exposed flesh of the crew; all of them suffered from hunger and thirst. Given the errant, albeit expanding, search grid, the food and drink onboard now seemed considerably less abundant than they had the day before.

4:04 PM Hawaii Time

In Honolulu, KGU Radio had broadcast several new reports throughout the afternoon. Quoting from the latest edition of *The Honolulu Advertiser,* the news had been disheartening. "With hope fading as long hours of a tragic night grew into another day, a colossal search-and-rescue effort went into effect at dawn this morning."

A little later, Masahiro and Akiko had sat in stunned silence as yet another dire report came over the radio.

"We now have the details of some of Commander John Rodgers' last communications with the USS *Aroostook* over twenty-four hours ago. Rodgers said, and I quote, 'Are you in this hellish rain too? We will be gone if we have to land in this rough sea with no motors.' In a later message, Rodgers radioed, 'We are not interested in the wind now. We haven't enough gas to last five minutes. We are getting low.' The situation sounds grave, indeed. I call on all you listeners out there in Hawaii to pray for the safe recovery of these five brave men. Stay tuned to KGU Radio for further updates." The Hawaiian slack-key guitar music that followed sounded inappropriately upbeat.

Masahiro and Akiko sat frozen in their now-customary places in front of the radio while the music played. Although it was not yet time to close the office, Masahiro indicated that he had to run an errand and would be back shortly. Akiko numbly nodded and her father slipped out.

Akiko's mind wandered as the gentle music bounced off her like soft rain. She clutched a wrinkled envelope in her hands—her security blanket—but at this point, John's last letter didn't offer much solace. Throughout the interminable day, Akiko had not been able to eat. A half-hour later, when the little bell signaled Masa's return, she was still sitting where he had left her, nearly comatose.

Masahiro carried a large sack that appeared heavy. He set it down on Akiko's desk and sat down next to her on the couch. In another rare gesture of physical affection he put his arm around her tiny shoulders and pulled her to his side, but Akiko was too numb to be surprised by it. Masa stroked her hair in silence, then said at last, "It's time to close, Akiko. Let us go home."

Obediently Akiko stood and shuffled to her desk to retrieve her pocketbook and hat. She carefully placed the treasured letter back in her handbag. Masahiro picked up his package from her desk, and turned to open the door. He flipped the sign, and reset the cardboard clock hands. The mood in the little shop was bleak. Even the tinkling bell had a melancholy ring to it.

Masahiro and Akiko left the office in silence and headed toward the bus stop. As they walked, Masa said "I've bought us something for the house." He held the handles of the shopping bag open. Peeking in, Akiko couldn't believe her eyes. It was a Crosley tabletop radio. Fresh tears welled up, as she took Masa's arm. "Thank you, Father," she whispered.

They were soon seated on the bench at the bus stop. A paperboy came by, hawking a late edition of *The Honolulu Advertiser*. Masahiro took a nickel from his pocket and bought a copy. The bold, black headline read: "PLANE NOT FOUND." An Associated Press story from the States followed: "FAILURE OF FUEL MAY HAVE SENT FIVE AVIATORS TO THEIR DEATH."

5:52 PM Hawaii Time

John thought it prudent to institute a modest rationing of the remaining supplies; each man was given half a ham sandwich and a pint of water for dinner. When they gathered by the cockpit to eat, Byron tried toasting his meat on the still sun-warmed surface of the wing. When Wild Bill teased him for the idea, Byron protested that it really had improved the taste. The others agreed to try "cooking" their ration of ham the next day as well—if they hadn't already been picked up.

As the twilight skies darkened, Bill went back to monitoring the radio. He felt better after the food and his brief respite in the fresh air. Listening to the chatter, he was excited by a strong signal from the *Aroostook*. It was the loudest message they had yet received, and was intended specifically for the PN9-1. *Damn, they must be close!* The message read, "If you see *Aroostook* near you, fire a star shell or show light. We thought we saw a flare ahead."

Bill let out a whoop and immediately shared the good news with the others. Everyone, including a woozy Sparky Stantz, climbed outside. Even though they knew the flare the *Aroostook* had seen wasn't from them, they still fired a series of three star shells. The signal strength of the radio broadcast led them to believe someone had to be very close.

The crew listened intently for any response over the radio to their aerial display, fervently praying someone just over the horizon would have seen the flares. After several minutes, though, they realized they had not been observed. Disappointed, all hands returned to their positions and prepared to settle in for another long night.

The September 2, 1925 11 AM extra edition of *The Honolulu Advertiser*. The headline expressed the concern everyone in Hawaii had for Rodgers and his crew. Also noted was the optimistic but incorrect story that the PB1 would attempt a crossing the next day.

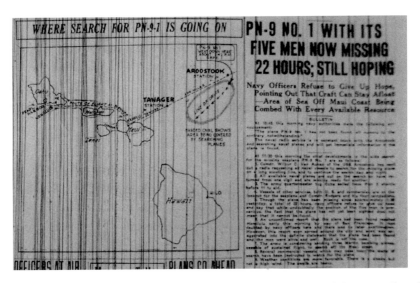

This damaged image comes from microfiche records of *The Honolulu Star-Bulletin* for September 2, 1925: The map and search area shows just how far off the navy was from the actual location of the PN9-1. Rodgers and crew were quite literally off the chart, being north and east of the noted position of the *Aroostook*.

A Crosley table radio from 1925

Chapter 38

Thursday—September 3, 1925

1:09 AM Pacific Time

Admiral Moffett paced the suite in the dark of the wee morning hours. While others of his staff had taken turns spelling each other, the admiral had worked around the clock, with only short breaks for an occasional catnap. Now, fatigue was catching up to him. Determined to fight it off, he refreshed himself with a shower and a shave and got back to work.

Desperate for news, he sent a message ordering an update from the *Aroostook*, even though he knew it was not yet midnight in the search area. Specifically, Moffett wanted to know if there had been any sightings at all during the night.

The last response from the *Aroostook* had infuriated him. Van Auken had radioed that the twilight signal previously reported had in fact been someone's mistaking the planet Venus for a parachute flare. Moffett had been somewhat mollified to hear that there was additional flare activity reported by the *Langley* that was currently being investigated. For the moment, though, all Moffett could do was wait, and as any sailor who served under him knew, the admiral hated to wait.

The situation deteriorated when a telegram for Moffett arrived from Washington. As his sleepy aide handed over the familiar yellow paper, Moffett growled, "Someone in D.C.'s up mighty early. This can't be good."

Sure enough, the wire said the top navy brass was following the Rodgers story closely. They had read the latest Associated Press reports and wanted an update immediately. This caused Moffett to check and recheck all of the messages that had come in overnight as he awaited a response from the *Aroostook*.

At last, a new radio report was relayed from Van Auken. The latest flare activity was now confirmed to have been initiated from the *Reno* and misinterpreted as having come from Rodgers. Frustrated and chagrined at having to relate such incompetence to his higher-ups, Moffett reluctantly composed a response for Washington. In it, he did his best to explain both false sightings, then dispatched an aide to the Western Union office with the handwritten message.

Somewhere along the line an enterprising reporter got wind of the contents of this telegram, and Moffett's awkward message soon appeared in headlines across the country, greatly embarrassing the navy. But even the distressing plight of the PN9-1 was about to be monumentally eclipsed.

5:28 AM Eastern Time

The first signs of morning lightened the horizon as Colonel Billy Mitchell checked out of the Army and Navy Club hotel. He asked the bellman to hold his bags, as he would be taking breakfast in the hotel before departing for the train station. His leave in D.C. completed, Mitchell had been ordered to return to his duty station at Fort Sam Houston. After his last burst of unauthorized grandstanding, even Mitchell would have agreed he was probably lucky that the brass had only stripped him of his star and packed him off to Texas.

Mitchell strode briskly into the dining room to join two favored Washington, D.C. reporters and Lieutenant Smith, his aide. The journalists eagerly awaited whatever tidbit the controversial colonel might throw their way during the course of the meal. One had brought material to prime the pump.

As Mitchell took his place at the table, the crafty reporter shoved a newspaper over to him. "Colonel, just take a look at this . . . !" The headline read, "LOOKOUT ON THE AIRCRAFT TENDER *AROOSTOOK* 'THOUGHT HE SAW A FLARE.'" Mitchell quickly read the story of the two false sightings. Slapping the paper down, he exclaimed in disgust, "You've got to be kidding! Those navy clowns can't tell the difference between a planet and a flare?!" The reporters took out their notebooks and waited for what was sure to be juicy headline fodder.

Mitchell continued, "If I didn't know better, I'd say the navy's doing its level best to bolster my case for a separate air service!"

Over coffee, Lieutenant Smith and the reporters began to gloat over the U.S. Navy's ever-growing malfeasance. Much to their surprise, Mitchell urged restraint.

"Remember, it's possible that there are still five sailors out there struggling to survive. They're the heroes. It's the big boys running the show in Washington that are the idiots. We must be careful that our rhetoric doesn't cross the line with the public."

Lieutenant Smith cleared his throat. "Gener—uh, sorry sir, I mean Colonel, may I speak freely?"

"Go ahead."

"Sir, every moment that goes by leads the public, and everyone involved, to believe that those men have bought the farm. There hasn't been a peep from them in two days. Even the navy's close to admitting it."

"Your point?"

"Sir, they're dead. And they're dead because the navy tried to use this foolhardy mission to rally public support. Someone needs to hold the U.S. Navy accountable for this tragedy, and with all due respect, sir, you're that someone."

At this, Mitchell pushed himself back from the table and cleared his throat. "Gentlemen . . ." And the reporters' pencils began to fly across their pads.

5:35 AM Eastern Time

As dawn crept over his shoulder, a refreshed Lieutenant Commander Zachary Lansdowne was back at the helm of the USS *Shenandoah*. He had gotten several hours of sleep during an uneventful night. The watch had just changed, and after being relieved, nine tired sailors climbed the ladder up from the control car into the main body of the dirigible and headed for their hammocks.

On the first day and night of the tour, they had crossed the Delaware River, the Pocono Mountains, and all of Pennsylvania. The ZR-1 was presently cruising at just over fifty knots, 2,000 feet above Nobles County, Ohio. This was a somewhat lower altitude than normal, as they were bucking a fairly strong headwind and Lansdowne had hoped to find less resistance at this lower altitude.

In the early morning, the country farmers who first saw the *Shenandoah* flying overhead gaped in amazement at the massive, shiny silver aircraft. The airship's external control car hung twenty feet below the horizontally ribbed framework, and carried nine of the forty-three souls aboard. The men in the control car could be seen from the ground, but they seemed infinitesimal next to the vast body of the zeppelin.

No doubt about it, she was a first-rate showpiece for the navy, and she had been decked out accordingly. The massive airship sported the "U.S. NAVY" designation on each side amidships, and a large "ZR-1" was painted on both sides of her nose and her modern, raked-back, curvaceous upper tail fin. Three thirty-foot-tall five-pointed stars—the same red, white, and blue insignia found on U.S. Navy warplanes—decorated both sides of her stern quarter, as well as the belly of her bow. "*Shenandoah*" was boldly painted on each side of the forward portions of the aircraft.

So far, the flight from Lakehurst had been calm and uneventful. At the moment, Lansdowne and the others with him in the control car savored the stunning views of the countryside. The fields, forests, and rolling hills beneath were scored with eerily long shadows from the newly risen sun.

Both Lansdowne and his aerologist Lieutenant Joseph "Andy" Anderson had been relieved by the favorable weather conditions encountered thus far. Unfortunately, they would not last.

5:47 AM Eastern Time

In the small rural community of Caldwell, Ohio, several miles ahead in the zeppelin's flyover path, a farmer was awakened by a loud crash. He jumped from his bed and ran to the front door. Outside, gale-force gusts were banging storm shutters against the window frames, but the crash had been louder than that. Opening the door he saw that all the front porch furniture had been overturned and thrown against the house in the freakish windstorm. Looking to the western sky, he saw a huge, purple-black cloud rising to an incredible height. As he would later describe to friends, it was "as though two storms had gone together."

5:55 AM Eastern Time

As the *Shenandoah* flew further into the Ohio Valley, the weather system continued to build. Zachary Lansdowne was about to come face-to-face with the nightmare scenario he had dreaded. The treacherously unstable front the Caldwell farmer had encountered was rapidly turning into a monster, complete with powerful thunderheads and rapid wind shifts.

Onboard the dirigible, Lansdowne's first warning came from E.P. Allen, the elevatorman whose sole duty was keeping the *Shenandoah* flying straight and level and in proper trim by continually adjusting the huge horizontal tail surfaces. His voice betrayed a tinge of nervousness: "Captain, the ship has started to rise."

Lansdowne swiveled around and ordered, "Check her. Nose down." He then spun back to his aerologist. "Andy?"

"Sir, the barometer is dropping like a stone." Anderson looked worried, knowing a dramatic drop in barometric pressure would make the airship rise. He also knew if the drop was too sharp, the dirigible would quickly become difficult to control.

With nervous perspiration breaking out on his brow, elevatorman Allen called out, "She's rising two meters per second. I can't check her, sir."

Lansdowne responded, "Throttle up engines three, four, and five to assist descent."

Despite the increased power, the giant continued to climb, even though she now had her nose pointed on a sharp fifteen-degree downward angle. At this point, most of the crew in the main body were aware that something was wrong. Those in their hammocks tumbled out and double-timed it to their stations.

"Sir, I still can't hold her down."

Trying to check the rising panic onboard, Lansdowne spoke calmly. "Don't exceed that angle. We don't want to go into a stall." Lansdowne then ordered a new heading in an attempt to evade the front: "Change course to due south."

"Aye sir," said the rudderman, throwing his considerable weight into turning the large ship's wheel. "Hard over, sir." But the *Shenandoah* refused to respond. Seconds later he called, "Sir, she won't take it."

The tension in the control car ratcheted up as the elevatorman added, "Sir, I've got the flippers full down and she still won't check!"

"Don't worry, we'll bring her in." While Lansdowne's confidence was reassuring, the ship continued to shoot skyward, heading straight up into the oncoming turbulence.

5:59 AM Eastern Time

Closer still to the approaching airship, in the small town of Ava, Ohio, a woman who had felt the storm brewing had gone out in her yard to tend to the chickens. Looking up, she cried to her husband, "Good Lord Almighty—come out here and take a look at this sky! Those thunderheads're all boilin' up, almost like they're alive!" As he joined her in the yard, they both caught sight of the zeppelin coming from the other direction. As big as the *Shenandoah* was, she looked tiny next to the storm front. The silver surface of the airship reflected the bruised purple of the roiling clouds she was fast approaching.

6:01 AM Eastern Time

A new set of problems arose for the crew of the ZR-1. Her steep, uncontrolled nose-down attitude was disrupting the gravity-fed fuel lines, as well as overloading the engines' water pump cooling systems. The engines soon began to overheat and sputter from fuel starvation. But these were the least of her problems.

Before the *Shenandoah* left Lakehurst, the decision had been made to overload her precious helium bags by an extra six percent, topping them off at ninety-one percent of capacity. This was because their planned route would not force them to fly very high. As altitude increases, helium expands in response to the subsequent reduction in air pressure. Because of the extra helium she was carrying, the dirigible's maximum altitude ceiling was 4,000 feet. Any higher and the bags would begin to push dangerously outward on the duralumin framework. This fact was foremost on everyone's mind as the elevatorman called out, "Sir, still rising at two meters per second."

Lansdowne commanded, "Have the riggers pull the covers from the automatic release valves." When this order was relayed, CPO Donovan and his men scrambled the entire length of the dirigible removing the covers from the control valves of the twenty gas bags.

Turning again to his aerologist, Lansdowne asked, "Barometric pressure?"

"Still dropping, sir."

Looking at the gauges, Lansdowne realized they were in serious trouble. The altimeter was fast approaching 5,000 feet—well above the safe maximum. He hated to valve off any of the precious helium but recognized that he had no other option.

"Open the maneuvering valves." Within moments, thousands of cubic feet of the gas were expelled, in an attempt to slow the ship's ascent. Lansdowne monitored the passing seconds on his watch. If too much gas was released, it could cause a descent that they would not be able to slow—an occurrence that had happened often during the Great War, with disastrous results.

"Close the valves," he ordered into the intercom, and above them, twenty valves were simultaneously shut. The ship was quiet as all waited to see the result.

"Slowing sir. But still rising one meter per second."

By then, the zeppelin was nearing 6,000 feet. Lansdowne turned to Lieutenant Anderson. "Andy, go up and check on the bags. I need that tail down to get this bird flying level."

"Aye, aye, sir." Anderson quickly headed up the ladder, braving the fifty-knot wind that raked the unprotected space between the control car and the belly of the ZR-1.

Suddenly, a powerful wind shear battered the helpless *Shenandoah,* tossing her up and then stopping her abruptly at 6,300 feet. The shear alarmed Lansdowne. He knew that because of the ship's enormous size, it was possible for her nose to experience different weather than her stern, which could dramatically intensify the structural stress.

Directly in front of them, a bolt of lightning lit up the wall of weather. Then as if triggered by the flash, the *Shenandoah* suddenly dropped.

"She's falling fast, sir—very fast!" was the report from the harried elevatorman, but the announcement was unnecessary. It felt as if the floor had just dropped out from under them. The giant airship plummeted at the unheard of speed of twenty-five feet per second.

"Dump the water ballast!" called out Lansdowne, and immediately tons of water poured out onto the farmland below. "Now, pull that nose up!"

CPO Allen responded, "She's still falling sir."

"She's all right, Allen. We'll stop her." Lansdowne's calm demeanor seemed to will the ship to slow, and the dirigible soon leveled out at 2,500 feet. With order somewhat restored onboard, Lansdowne commanded, "Now, let's get her turned south."

The ship began her turn, but the maneuver was sluggish as both the first and second engines had overheated and shut down. The storm front edged ever closer. The elevator man nervously suggested, "Sir, perhaps we should drop the nose a bit to assist the turn." Lansdowne nodded and picked up the intercom.

"Down bubble five degrees." Then he called the aft-most station. Four hundred and fifty feet away, the flashing phone light drew an immediate response.

"Frame sixty, rigger Donovan here."

"Donovan, how are the cells aft?"

"OK aft of sixty, sir. Fully intact."

"Pass the word forward. Everyone on their toes. We may have to go through this together."

Donovan hung up and began the long walk forward, to pass on the skipper's words. As he proceeded carefully along the ten-inch catwalk, an earsplitting burst of wind shrieked. The rigger watched in horror as the taut duralumin skin of the storm-tossed zeppelin rippled along the length of the entire craft, distorting the framework and taking a full forty-five seconds to travel from end to end. As the wave passed him, Donovan was forced to hold on for dear life. The ship began to rise uncontrollably, her bow leading the way this time, aiming the ZR-1 nose-up.

The great airship shot upward to 3,500 feet and abruptly leveled out. Then, just when it seemed she had stabilized, the *Shenandoah* shot up again, so fast they lost all control of her. The angle and speed of the precipitous ascent forced several sailors to their knees. In seconds, the monstrous vessel had climbed to over 6,000 feet, all the while spinning in a tight circle. While the crew desperately fought to regain control and slow her climb, the *Shenandoah's* bow hit a ferocious downdraft so strong that it felt as if she had bounced off a mountain. The ship then nosed over and dived at an angle so steep that the entire crew was knocked to the deck. Some of the men within the main body were brutally battered as they struggled to hang on to the internal frame.

Despite the steep angle, Lansdowne and his men somehow regained a modicum of control, and for a moment, they thought they were safe. Then the *Shenandoah* struck another wind shear—this time plunging headlong toward the earth.

1:10 AM Pacific Time

Sparky Stantz seemed to get sicker at night. In the dark, the plane's constant rocking motion brought on a vertigo that intensified his nausea. Even with nothing in his stomach, he continued to retch uncontrollably. His condition forced the first real discussion of diminishing supplies.

As he lay in a corner of the cabin, curled up in agony, John spoke quietly with Byron. "I'm worried about Stanz. We're all pretty thirsty, but he's getting seriously dehydrated."

"What else can we do?"

"See if you can find a clean piece of cloth. Maybe if we soak it with the juice from one of the oranges we can get him to suck on it."

"Will do. I'll see what I can come up with."

John nodded and poked his head into the pilot's cockpit. Kiles was back on duty trying to keep the plane headed into the wind and swells. Before John could speak, Kiles said, "Skip, we've got a whole lot of nothing out there tonight. The cloud cover's closed in and you can't even see the horizon."

John checked for himself, and Kiles was right. "Damn—can't even see the waves right in front of us!"

"Roger, sir. How's Sparky?"

"Not good. We've got to keep him hydrated."

"Yeah. I guess we're all going to have to start watching that."

John agreed reluctantly, "Yeah, I guess so." While no one had yet voiced the possibility that they might not be found soon after all, by now the thought was on everyone's mind.

6:14 AM Eastern Time

The pending arrival of the Shenandoah was proving to be a huge draw for the residents of the Ohio Valley. Everyone wanted to witness this monster of the midway; there was hardly a soul who hadn't carved out some time to make sure they'd have the chance to see it. The route the great dirigible would take had been published in all the local papers.

Those with vehicles had loaded up their families, and actually planned on following the ZR-1 as best they could. The vast majority planning to attend the county fair made sure to arrive very early this morning, as it had been announced that the *Shenandoah* would make a flyby directly overhead. They had even endured an unexpected windstorm, brief but violent.

At last, the ZR-1 appeared on the troubled horizon in all her glory. Her silvery shape stood out starkly against the dark clouds. She drew gasps from the crowd as she climbed quickly in what everyone thought was a display of her agility. The dive that followed may have seemed reckless to some, but was also assumed to be a show for the crowds. But it wasn't long before the spectators recognized the ship's violent maneuvers for what they were—her death throes—and their gasps of delight turned to screams of horror. Fearing a colossal crash, the terrified onlookers scattered, scrambling for cover.

6:15 AM Eastern Time

The last drop in the *Shenandoah's* maniacal roller-coaster ride had seriously compromised the aluminum structure of the airship. Lieutenant Joseph "Andy" Anderson had just made his way back from the bow and was preparing to descend into the control car with his report on the helium bags, when he heard a horrendous screeching of metal-on-metal. He was thrown to the deck as the structural girders above him gave way. Looking down, he saw the suspended control gondola began to sway and jerk erratically. Before his eyes, the bow section directly above him ripped vertically from the bottom, and two men aft of him were thrown from the craft into the void. Although completely torn, for the moment the *Shenandoah's* bow was still held together by her many control cables and hoses, but these now came under horrendous stress.

As he hung face down above the control car, Anderson saw the support girders twist, and the thin duralumin skin below him split wide open. Then, as if in slow motion, the entire car broke free and plummeted thousands of feet to the earth, taking Commander Zachary Lansdowne and seven other souls to their death.

Still fairly aft, rigger Donovan thought he smelled something burning. A sharp noise behind him caused him to turn in time to see a mass of severed control cables violently whip-snapping along the length of the keel. Lying prone, he hugged the catwalk, and they somehow missed him as they shot forward.

Meanwhile, Anderson's section of the ZR-1 had been torn free, along with the bow. The piece of catwalk he clung to was now suspended by several cables, with nothing between it and the ground. Above him, seven sailors dangled from girders in the upturned bow, staring blankly down at where the rest of their ship used to be. Another great shriek of metal, and the stern broke free, leaving the crippled craft in three pieces.

Four men were in the center section. It had lost most of its helium, and was weighed down by two of the engine pods. Consequently, it began to fall at a deadly speed. Both engine nacelles ripped free in mid-air, and the section's terrifying descent slowed precipitously. After a protracted crash landing, all four men tumbled out alive. However the four unfortunate mechanics in the engine pods that broke away were all killed instantly.

The stern section was the largest fragment—about 350 feet long. Weighted down by three heavy engine pods, and with little helium left, this section rocked clumsily to the ground, bouncing tail-first in a slow-motion collision. It then split into two sections, the larger piece tumbling swiftly along the ground.

As the desperate men inside jumped one by one from the ship, it looked as if the ZR-1 was spitting them out. Even after they had escaped the dirigible, the men were still in danger. To witnesses, it appeared as though a massive, mortally wounded beast was trying to crush her victims as she undulated in a chilling dance. She continued in this madcap chase for a third of a mile before finally coming to rest.

Once she had stopped, dozens of spectators rushed to the aid of any possible survivors. Other frightened onlookers raced in the opposite direction, expecting a huge hydrogen fireball. They were unaware that because the *Shenandoah*, as the first helium-filled airship in the world, was incapable of exploding. Miraculously, all twenty-one sailors in this section escaped with their lives.

The conical bow section of the craft suffered a very different fate: it stayed aloft. With some helium compartments still sealed, the nose rose dramatically and floated across the countryside like an errant toy balloon. The seven other sailors inside had rescued Anderson from his precarious perch, and together they all clung to the duralumin girders as the section rocketed upward to over 8,000 feet, bouncing wildly in the turbulent air.

Luckily, the helium compartments eventually started to leak, allowing the cone to level off and begin to drop. Nearly an hour later, and eight miles downwind, they banged and scraped against a large oak tree. The impact catapulted a navy rigger into the tree, where he ricocheted like a pinball among the branches. He woke up in an area hospital two days later with a concussion and two broken collarbones, but alive.

The seven other captive passengers continued rocketing along at too fast a clip to jump safely. They also feared their deadly chariot might again climb too high for them to jump at all, which it soon did. They had no choice but to hang on through the second ascent. Eventually, the runaway descended once again and started to swoop closer to terra firma.

At last, after an interminable, erratic cross-country ride, they floated over the small township of Sharon, Ohio. By now, the craft was flying so low that some of the nosecone's control lines had begun to drag along the ground. A farmer named Ernest Nichols watched as the elliptical globe bobbled across his field toward him in slow-motion. The men onboard saw him and yelled for help. Farmer Nichols reacted by grabbing the bow's longest line, and in the best naval tradition slammed a half-hitch knot around an old tree stump, stopping the recalcitrant aircraft cold. The seven badly shaken sailors climbed to safety.

7:05 AM Eastern Time

The primary scene of the crash quickly deteriorated into a macabre circus. The news spread like wildfire and people from the surrounding counties poured in to see the grisly spectacle. The actual fairgrounds were deserted for two days, during which souvenir hunters stripped the wreckage as cleanly as maggots feasting on a carcass. Armed police were finally called in to forestall further souvenir hunting.

Fourteen men died with the *Shenandoah*, including her skipper—a true navy hero. Admiral Moffett's prized trophy, the $1,500,000 ZR-1, had been completely destroyed just one day short of her second birthday. The disaster was a terrible bloody nose for the U.S. Navy—and now, an incendiary PR bomb was about to explode, delivered by none other than Colonel Billy Mitchell.

5:45 AM Pacific Time

Although the news of the *Shenandoah* disaster would soon shock the world, Admiral Moffett was one of the first to hear of it. Word reached him in his suite by phone at dawn. Ashen faced, he listened to how at least fourteen of his men had been killed, among them Zachary Lansdowne, one of his most favored officers.

"Send me the list." Moffett hung up the phone and slumped into the big leather chair, feeling sick to his stomach. He'd had many friends and acquaintances onboard the airship. He closed his eyes in prayer for a moment, and then growled "Damn it!" Staff members around him in the suite assumed the worst for Rodgers and crew. Seeing the expressions on their faces, Moffett stood and relayed the devastating news.

"Gentlemen, there's no easy way to say this: the *Shenandoah* has crashed in Ohio. There are fourteen confirmed deaths including Lieutenant Commander Lansdowne. There are survivors. We should receive a further update within the hour."

In the stunned silence that followed, Moffett called for his stenographer, and the two of them retired to the adjacent anteroom. His first order of business was to dictate telegrams of condolence to the families of the dead men. A list of the deceased eventually reached the suite but was unnecessary, as Moffett had remembered every name from the short phone conversation. He'd helped handpick the crew and had known each of the victims personally. It was a devastating task.

When the admiral finished the last of the fourteen letters, the stenographer stood, expecting to be dismissed. Moffett wearily shook his head and motioned for the scribe to sit back down. He started to dictate similar telegrams for each of the five men aboard the PN9-1. When he finished, he had the stenographer read them back. Hearing the second batch of letters out loud, he changed his mind and asked the man to delete the passages officially confirming death, and replace them with the phrase "lost at sea" instead. When this had been accomplished, Moffett and the stenographer reemerged into the main room of the suite, where Moffett ordered his aide to send all nineteen telegrams immediately. Messages in hand, the aide saluted and departed on his sad mission.

The admiral let himself slump into the leather armchair. He looked at the list of the *Shenandoah* dead, then crumpled the paper into a ball and threw it across the room. He closed his eyes and rubbed both temples.

The phone rang again in Moffett's suite, and although it sat right next to him, he was too drained to answer it. An aide finally picked up, and after a few words turned and offered Moffett the receiver.

"I'm sorry, sir, but it's Lieutenant Strong for you. He says it's urgent."

Moffett glared at the junior officer, then grabbed the phone and growled, "Moffett here. What is it, Strong?"

"Sir, I have my crew working round the clock to get our plane back in service, but we've run into a roadblock. Your executive officer, Commander Moses, has refused to sign the purchase orders for the parts and overtime needed to repair the PB1.

"Sir, there is no way we should be delayed any further. It's not fair. I must ask you to tell this ill-informed officer to get his orders straight. We need those parts now. I . . . my men and I deserve the opportunity to get back in the air and on our way to Hawaii."

A deadly silence followed. At last Moffett replied, "Mr. Strong. Let me assure you that my exec has his orders straight. Let me also advise you in the strongest possible way that you and your men are not going anywhere—*is that clear?*" With that, Moffett slammed the receiver back in its cradle. It had been a hell of a couple of days.

Crew quarters along the keel of the *Shenandoah*. Note the ten-inch-wide catwalk, and the straps on the hammock so that the crew could secure themselves while they slept.

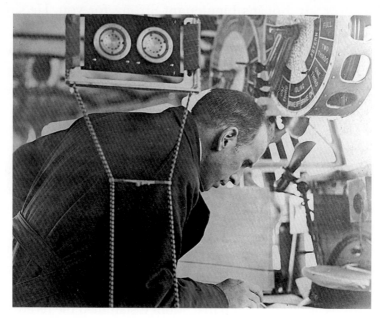

Lieutenant Commander Lansdowne aboard the control pad of the *Shenandoah*.

The *Shenandoah*'s bow section's final resting place was more than eight miles further downwind. Note the line that secures the bow section to an oak tree.

The officers lost in the *Shenandoah* crash.

Aft section of the *Shenandoah*

Fairgoers soon turned into souvenir hunters as people from miles around flocked to the site of the disaster.

Crowds grew so large that the National Guard had to be called in.

The bow section, which had been calf roped to the ground.

Lieutenant Commander Zachary Lansdowne.

Chapter 39

Thursday—September 3, 1925

6:22 AM Hawaii Time

John Rodgers began the fourth day since leaving San Francisco by taking his sunrise sight with the sextant. He plotted their position, as he had done so many times before, and compared it to the search grid and position reports of the ships that were looking for them. It was only getting worse. It was as if he and his men were engaged in a nightmarish chess match—not only was their queen nowhere near the board, but the players in charge kept moving the table.

Chess . . . ? Even in his frustration, an idea began to take shape. Given the circumstances, they were certainly in check. An avid player himself, Rodgers thought back to his more satisfying matches—times when he had been able to pull out of check and turn the tables on a sharp opponent. *Think, John! What made the difference?* As he reflected, he recalled that almost every time, victory had come from a dramatic shift in strategy. No less was called for now. He entered his decision in the ship's log and called the crew together.

"Men, it's clear that we're going to need to try a different tack and come up with some alternate solutions. If we have to cannibalize the plane to make 'em work, so be it." He turned towards Kiles and Bill.

"OK, guys, it's time for you to earn your keep. We need to build some kind of battery-based transmitter."

The idea galvanized Wild Bill. "Skip, what if we connect some batteries to one of the starter motors, and then somehow jury-rig it straight to the generator? We just might be able to drive the generator fast enough to power up the transmitter."

"Sounds good to me, Bill. Let's give it a try."

Immediately all hands pitched in scavenging for parts to implement Bill's idea. Morale onboard rose at the prospect of taking positive action.

12:03 PM Eastern Time

The train carrying Colonel Billy Mitchell to Texas pulled into the Virginia train station and slowed to a stop. The conductor announced "Roanoke. Roanoke. Ten minutes." As a few passengers disembarked, Mitchell's aide, Lieutenant Smith, got off as well to stretch his legs. Putting his back to the wind, he lit a cigarette and walked along the covered platform past porters loading suitcases and packages into the baggage car. When he reached the tiny newsstand by the station door, he caught sight of the headlines blaring from the racks and pulled up short.

Crushing out his cigarette, he hastily dug for some change. To the newsstand attendant's surprise, the lieutenant bought one copy of every morning paper. Double-timing it back along the station platform, he bounded up the stairs to Mitchell's passenger car.

Smith saw the colonel at the other end of the aisle, engaged in conversation with fellow travelers. Shouldering past those in his way, Smith interrupted Mitchell, pushing one of the papers into his superior's hands. "Colonel. Sir. Excuse me . . . Sir, you need to see this!"

Mitchell stared in shock at the bold black letters: "SHENANDOAH CRASHES."

7:21 AM Hawaii Time

As Wild Bill struggled to remove the port engine's aeromarine starter, he spotted smoke on the horizon. He couldn't believe his eyes. *A ship!* He hollered to all below and then grabbed the flare gun from the cockpit holster. He loaded and fired the gun before anyone else could scramble on deck. The flare arced upward about five hundred feet, then burst, trailing sparkling red phosphorescence as it drifted slowly down. Kiles Pope climbed out onto the upper wing and started yelling. He ripped off his shirt and waved it frantically in the air.

The excitement was contagious, and soon all the men had joined him topside, shouting and waving their shirts—even Sparky. The ship was, of course, much too far away for them to be heard but the men yelled anyway. John and Bill scrambled below for the metal bucket that had been serving as their little sea anchor. Bill soaked a rag in some motor oil, then they put it in the bucket and set it afire. As the rag began to smolder, John took the bucket on deck, where it belched forth a copious amount of foul smelling, beautifully visible black smoke.

The freighter was on a contrary but parallel course, sitting on the far edge of the horizon, but the men felt certain rescue was imminent. They broke out the binoculars and everyone took a look. There was even excited talk about repairing the newly-started cannibalization so *Baby* would be ready to refuel and take off. They launched a second flare, and then a third. In the cabin, Bill helped John by scrounging for more material to burn. When they added the oily remnants, the smoke became considerably more intense.

Thinking that there might be radio traffic to monitor, Sparky climbed down from his sickbed to take up his station at the radio console, but the airwaves were silent. He had an idea.

"Skip, I bet I could tap out an SOS in Morse code by creating a spark between the battery terminal and the hot lead. I don't know if a signal that weak'll be picked up, but it's worth a try."

"By all means, give it a shot, Stanz."

The signal went out, but even though the ship was within five miles, it gave no sign of recognition. Wild Bill was all for sending up more flares, but John suggested they save their flares until the ship was closer. "Let's stick with the smoke for now—it's more visible at this range."

Despite all their efforts, the freighter never varied its course. It sailed on, oblivious to the plight of the little band of five. Crushed, they watched as it finally disappeared over the horizon, leaving only a thin trail of smoke, until even that evaporated. The crew was frustrated, but not inconsolable.

Wild Bill shrugged, "Well skip, looks like it's back to Plan B—scavenging."

"Roger, Bill." And all hands fell to cannibalizing *Baby* once again.

9:29 AM Hawaii Time

The early morning newspaper lay on Akiko's desk. The Associated Press headline read, "HOPE IS DIMINISHING." The latest radio news had included the earlier report of flare sightings, and the possibility of contact with the plane had given Akiko something to hang onto. But the next update corrected the previous report, with the story of the comet-flare confusion. At this news, Akiko sank to the floor in front of the radio.

In his office, Masahiro overheard the latest report and decided it was time for him to take action. He set down the spectacles he had been working on and headed into the front office, where he discovered Akiko in a state of collapse. He gently helped her into a chair and told her he would be back in an hour. Moving quickly, he was out the door before she could question him. He was on a mission.

Twenty minutes later, he stepped quickly along the commercial pier at Fisherman's Wharf. His pressed slacks and dress shirt looked out of place in the rough, working-class environment. He stopped and asked for directions from a burly, rubber-booted, dockworker on a cigarette break. Soon after, he was standing on the bulkhead next to the stern of the *Nippon Maru*, a commercial fishing boat. He called out in his native language, and a stout Japanese man walked out on the fantail. The man recognized his old friend, Masa, and after wiping his hands on a rag, welcomed him onboard.

3:51 PM Hawaii Time

As the rations grew smaller, acute hunger pangs complicated the already arduous work onboard *Baby*. The men had consumed the remaining coffee and sandwiches the night before. The last oranges had been shared this morning, and the water was all but gone. They still had the can of corned beef and the tin of crackers, but they were saving them for later. No one could say when "later" would be.

The day passed into late afternoon while all the men, even a nauseated Sparky Stantz, toiled at various tasks. The limited number of tools and spare parts made every job even more problematic. Kiles and Bill were attempting to free the heavy starter. The cramped space inside the port-engine compartment meant that once the bolts that held it in place were loosened, they could only be rotated a twelfth of a turn at a time, and the box wrench the men were using had to be flipped over between each microscopic turn to take advantage of the offset angle of the tool. Meanwhile, Bill and Sparky labored to remove the batteries from the right-side engine; but their movements had to be slow and deliberate, as their combined weight on the outboard side of the starboard cowling tended to seesaw the plane. This motion was particularly hard on Sparky.

At last, Kiles and Bill finally freed the reluctant starter and used a piece of hose and a couple of hose clamps like a drive belt, to connect it to one of the large generators. They had already removed the generator from the lower wing and rewired it to the transmitter. Then they lifted off one of the floorboards and tightly secured both the starter and the generator to the deck, tying the former jack line with truckers' hitch knots in a block and tackle configuration. A longer antenna had been rigged from the bow, up and over the upper wing, back to the tail, and then down through the aft cockpit. Four batteries had been wired together with the negative lead secured to the plane's frame. All in all, it was a set-up reminiscent of something the cartoonist Rube Goldberg might have dreamed up.

When the jury-rigged contraption stood at the ready, the crew looked on expectantly as Sparky donned his headset and prepared to transmit. Bill stood poised to connect the hot lead to the post on the starter. All turned to John for the signal to begin, and he nodded.

"Let'er rip!"

Bill clamped the batteries to the starter and it jumped to life, immediately pulling the hose off the generator's axle. The starter spun madly before Bill could release the hot-wire clamp.

They solved the problem by using a shorter length of hose to eliminate some of the torque, and brought in two more hose clamps to secure the ends. A second try and the generator started to turn, but this time the starter jerked the generator so erratically that it was of no use to the radio. After several more tries, the men stopped to take stock.

Sparky spoke first: "It's not workin', Bill."

"Yeah, an' you know what? If we keep on tryin' we're just gonna drain the batteries, leavin' us without any radio at all."

Kiles shrugged. "Got any other ideas?"

Sparky shook his head. "Let's go back to what worked before." As they reconnected the batteries back to the earlier configuration, they received a message that an "all ships" bulletin was about to be sent. Moments later, they heard their comrade, Commander W. R. Van Auken. His familiar voice sounded grim.

"I have a message for all United States vessels on the open sea within sound of this broadcast. Early this morning, September third, nineteen twenty-five, while flying over Marietta, Ohio, the United States Navy dirigible *Shenandoah* broke apart and crashed in heavy weather. Fourteen men and officers died in the tragedy, including her skipper Lieutenant Commander Zachary Lansdowne. May God have mercy on their souls." The broadcast then ended abruptly.

The men were stunned. For all its size, the navy was, in reality, an intimate congregation. Each of the crew knew someone who had been assigned to the airship. In Rodgers' case it was Lansdowne—a fellow pilot and Naval Academy graduate, two years his junior. Their paths had crossed on occasion and they had become casual friends. Sensing a need for some gesture to commemorate their comrades' tragedy, John led the men in the Lord's Prayer.

As the afternoon wore on toward evening, the sun dipped low and the weather began to change. Heavy tropical humidity enveloped the men like a warm, wet blanket. Fat cumulonimbus clouds mounted in the sky, and the ceiling dropped. Streaks of reddish-gray appeared along the cloud bottoms, and the air smelled of negative ions. The sea deepened in color to an ominous blue-black.

"Men, let's knock off for the day and prepare for what looks like nasty weather ahead. Check around and see what you can find to catch rainwater."

"Roger, sir."

"Aye, aye, skip."

The rain held off, but the seas grew in size as the sky darkened. The men deployed the little sea anchor once again, trying to keep *Baby*'s bow into the wind, but the swells soon tossed the plane about like a child's toy.

After an hour of heavy seas, John began to be concerned for the damaged starboard wing float. In the darkness, he could just make out the waves crashing on top of the lower wing. With each wave, the yawing increased, and John feared the pressure of the water on the wing would buckle the float, or worse yet, break the wing. Either way, the plane could easily be rolled over on its side, then swamp and sink. Given their situation, with no life raft or life vests, this would be disastrous. As the pounding continued to get worse, Rodgers realized that desperate measures were needed.

7:34 PM Hawaii Time

With the exception of the time Commander Van Auken had taken to relay the news of the *Shenandoah* disaster, he had spent most of the day reviewing the plots and tracks of all the ships and planes assisting the search effort since Tuesday. He had arrived at the conclusion that a mistake had been made. At last, he correctly believed that the PN9-1 must have been north of the *Aroostook* at the time of the plane's last broadcast.

Operating under this new assumption, Van Auken put out a call to move the search area farther north, and all ships had responded. However Van Auken's latest grid still assumed a drift that was much faster than *Baby* had actually traveled, and unbeknownst to him, although the vast area the grid now covered was at the correct latitude, it was still too far to the west.

Soon after he ordered the grid moved, Van received a note from the radio operator that a radio call had just come in requesting his presence. Hoping for good news, he double-timed it to the radio room and personally took over the microphone.

"Yes, this is the USS *Aroostook*, Commander Van Auken; over."

An unfamiliar voice responded in heavily-accented Japanese-English pidgin.

"You ruse prane, we rike hep. Many Japanee fishy boat stay Hawaii. We stay watch for Mistah John Lodges, yes? Ovah."

Van Auken responded, "Captain, we certainly appreciate your help, but I think your fishing boats will not be able to come far enough out to assist us. Over."

There was silence, and Van thought they had lost the connection. Then the speaker crackled to life.

"We come stay moa fah. What fleakensee? Ovah."

Perplexed, Van asked the radioman nearby, "What the hell is he saying?"

"Sir, I think he wants to know what frequency they should monitor."

"Cripes, between figuring out what these guys're saying, and trying to keep them from getting into trouble in deep waters . . ." He trailed off, shaking his head. He keyed the microphone and addressed the fisherman. "Captain, thank you again for your kind offer, but I think it would be better if you just stick to your fishing. Over."

But the man insisted, "We no stick to feesh . . . What fleakensee? Ovah."

Shaking his head, Van Auken conferred with the radioman, then keyed the mike, "Very well, Captain, please monitor twenty-two hundred kilocycles. Again that's twenty-two hundred kilocycles. Over."

"Twenny-two hunned kirosikes. Ovah-out."

Van shrugged and replaced the microphone. "I'm not sure this is a good idea, but we've come up empty so far. Can't hurt, as long as they don't get into trouble out here. Let me know if they find anything."

"Aye, aye, sir."

"Oh—and send this message out: 'Cheer up, John, we'll get you.'"

7:56 PM Hawaii Time

The desperate crew received the *Aroostook*'s encouraging message, but they were too busy fighting for survival to take the time to appreciate it. As *Baby* shuddered violently, battered by the high seas, something needed to be done—fast. Watching the powerful waves pound across the surface of the wings, Rodgers got a radical idea.

Over the roar of the storm, he explained his plan to his crew, "I want to cut the fabric off the lower wing so that the waves can pass through the framework unimpeded. If I'm right, I think it'll keep *Baby* from turning turtle.

Wild Bill immediately volunteered. "I'll go out and take a knife to her, skip."

"No, Bill. Thanks, but the wing could buckle before you complete the job, especially with the added weight on it. This job's mine."

As *Baby* bucked and rolled, Bill and Kiles rigged a rope boatswain's chair harness around John. Having learned from Kiles's experience, Bill then wrapped some rags around his already-gloved hands as he looped the line behind his back. Kiles secured the loose end to a floor rib.

At last, John clenched his knife between his teeth and climbed out onto the lower portside wing. Once he worked his way past the propeller and engine mounts in the wildly gyrating waves, he held on to a guy wire and knelt on the wing. He grabbed the knife with his free hand and almost lost it overboard as a wave broke over him. Totally drenched, he started to cut away the fabric between two fore and aft ribs. He sawed through the top layer and then started on the bottom layer, several inches below the upper skin. Another wave broke over the wing, and for a moment, the bottom fabric held the water. John quickly cut away a large section of fabric, and by the time the next wave hit, the water ran right through the framework, just as he had hoped. At that, John started furiously cutting away the fabric that covered the next section of the wing.

By this time, the wind and surf had overpowered the little improvised sea anchor and *Baby* swung dangerously around, tail into the storm. With the wind now at his back, John sliced a large wing-wide, U-shaped cut between the next two ribs. A fierce gust blew the fabric up vertically against the guy wires, making it easier for him to cut the bottom section free. As John started to crawl to the next section, a wave crashed unimpeded through the two new openings, and the wind pushed hard against the piece of fabric now held in place vertically by the crossed supporting wires for the upper wing. *Baby* responded as if someone had just unfurled a spinnaker, and the plane sailed down the swell.

The idea struck John and Byron simultaneously. The two sailing partners hollered back and forth between the cockpit and the wing about how John should proceed with the operation that would transform *Baby* from a plane into a sailboat.

As Rodgers proceeded to cut matching U-shaped sections of fabric out on the wing, Byron yelled for the crew to find some wire so that John could rig the makeshift sails. Bill was busy hanging on to John's lifeline, so Sparky, still sick as a dog, managed to chop up some of his useless spooled antenna wire into two-foot lengths. When John finished his surgery on the port wing, he carefully picked his way over the central fuselage, pocketed some of the pieces of wire, and climbed out onto the starboard wing, where he repeated the procedure. It was tedious, difficult work in perilous conditions, but the starboard wing held as well.

Rodgers' next task was to secure *Baby*'s new sails in place. As he crept along the naked wing frame, a huge wave knocked him down, but he managed to straddle one of the ribs. Catching his breath, he climbed back onto the framework and punctured the top corners of the inverted

U-shaped panels. He strung the two-foot lengths of wire through the stiff cloth and secured them to the braces and guy wires. Before he had completed the task, the plane swung about again, and the starboard sail spun the plane like a top.

Exhausted, he scrambled back over the fuselage and repeated his needlework on the portside panels. When the job was finally completed, he crawled back to the cockpit, so tired he could hardly hold on. The crew was ecstatic. Not only had they managed to avoid disaster, they had also hit on a possible solution to their predicament.

Rodgers called to Byron, "How's she handle?"

"She's a little dodgier than a two-man scow, skip, but I think we can sail her now."

The Honolulu Advertiser September 3, 1925 9:00 AM extra edition: The first news of the ZR-1 disaster hits Hawaii. The number of dead was later corrected to fourteen. The Rodgers' search drops in importance. The Boeing PB1 flight is cancelled, and the PN9-3 sinking is finally reported.

A 10:30 AM extra edition of *The Honolulu Advertiser* moves the search for Rodgers into still smaller type.

Chapter 40

Friday—September 4, 1925

8:00 AM Pacific Time

At the Olympic Club, an early-morning press conference had been called, and the small ballroom was jammed with reporters hungry for an update on the navy's most recent disaster. After reading a brief prepared statement about the *Shenandoah* crash, Admiral Moffett underwent a brutal barrage of questions. He was steeled for the worst, and he got it. The reporters were merciless.

"Admiral, isn't it true that Lansdowne begged to either put off or cancel that trip, anticipating storms over Ohio?"

"Admiral Moffett, why would the U.S. Navy deliberately put that crew at risk for what was little more than an expensive publicity stunt?"

"Sir, it appears that the navy views human life as expendable. Can you address that issue?"

Stressed and exhausted, Moffett struggled to keep his patience, fielding the thorny questions as best he could. At last he tried to bring the painful conference to a close.

"One more question, gentlemen, and then that's it."

One particularly aggressive reporter shouted, "Admiral Moffett, it's been three days since any word has been heard from Commander

Rodgers. How much longer will the navy continue to waste taxpayer dollars on what looks more and more like a hopeless effort?"

Jesus Christ. Moffett lowered his head for a moment, steadying himself at the podium. "Gentlemen, we have just lost fourteen valiant men in a terrible accident in Ohio. You now want to put a dollar value on the search for five courageous sailors lost at sea? You astonish and dismay me. These are five brave Americans! You imply that I should call an end to the search—because of what it costs?

"Well, sir, I will not! In fact, I have already redoubled our search efforts. I have ordered all naval vessels in and around Hawaiian waters to assist in the hunt. Already there are numerous naval planes combing the air from both Maui and Oahu. I have requested that the army launch all available island-based aircraft to help. Hell, even volunteer fishing boats from Oahu have joined our efforts.

"We are going to continue this search until we are positive there is no chance these men are still alive. And I would like to publicly request that all residents of Hawaii report any unusual ocean sightings or unfamiliar flotsam on the beaches, especially on the Windward coasts of the islands.

"Lastly—and this may surprise you—I realize that the possibility exists that the search may be futile, but we will see it to a proper conclusion."

Unfortunately, Moffett's last sentence would be the one all the news wire services picked up and quoted.

8:18 AM Hawaii Time

Aboard the USS *Langley*, most of the stormy conditions from the night before had dissipated with the dawn, and now the visibility was unlimited. Two of the carrier's planes had launched shortly after daybreak and were now scouring the northeastern reaches of the grid. Aloft in the clear but windy weather, they were only about fifteen miles west of *Baby* and her crew. Flying incrementally eastward on alternating north-to-south and then south-to-north sweeps, the planes were actually outside Van Auken's designated search area, and consequently as close as anyone had come to the PN9 since she had gone down. It was almost certain they would be within sight of the seaplane on their next pass.

8:37 AM Hawaii Time

Returning to the office on Friday morning, Masahiro and Akiko encountered a newsboy hawking papers on the street. Masahiro handed the boy a nickel and bought a copy. He noticed that Akiko seemed reluctant even to glance at the headline. The lead banner read, "SURVIVORS TELL OF WILD RIDE IN ZEP." The dirigible's horrific demise had pushed the PN9 story out of the limelight. *"SIXTY HOURS PASS WITHOUT TRACE OF PLANE"* appeared in smaller, italicized typeface.

Masahiro quickly skimmed the front page, then focused on the smaller feature article: "HOPE FAST FADING THAT FLAGPLANE WILL BE FOUND." When he saw the news wasn't good, Masa quickly folded the paper and threw it into a nearby trash can.

Father and daughter passed Bishop Park and the Hawaiian Trust building. The large tote board had been dismantled and taken away. Hoping Akiko had not noticed, Masahiro attempted to distract her gaze and ushered her quickly past the site.

9:12 AM Hawaii Time

By the midmorning of their fifth day of the ordeal, the stalwart crew had some reason for hope. The heavy seas had subsided, and the breeze was blowing constant at twenty knots from the east-northeast. Although exhausted from the wild night, the men were buoyed by the fact that they were finally doing something to help their cause. *Baby's* tiny rudder made her a handful to steer, but they nonetheless found they were able to sail along at about five knots, as long as they headed dead downwind.

The wind-generated waves coming from astern helped keep the plane moving toward the search area, and the Hawaiian Islands beyond.

Occasionally, *Baby* swung about sideways to the wind, but Byron and Kiles soon got the hang of keeping their charge on course. The plane could not go as fast as the swells, so it was a constant roller-coaster ride. Each wave would first raise the tail, causing *Baby* to gain a little speed as she slid lazily down the front of the swell. She would coast a bit as she leveled out and the wave passed underneath. When the wave reached the front of the plane, it forced her nose upward, slowing her down again. All of the men found this monotonous rocking sequence a pleasant relief from the earlier random buffeting—even Sparky.

John's most recent calculations indicated that they were only twenty miles east of the latest search area. If they could maintain their speed they could be within the perimeter of the grid in four hours. And, as thirsty and hungry as they were, the prospect of lunch onboard a navy ship brought smiles all around.

Aware that the crew sorely needed sustenance, John opened the tin of crackers. Given the scarcity of drinking water, it was lucky they were unsalted. The contents of the tin were shared, and the men ravenously gobbled the bland, dry squares, polishing them off in no time.

Their optimism got another boost when Bill intercepted a message from what he thought was one of the *Langley*'s search planes. Intense static made the conversation almost unintelligible, but Bill was still elated. He reasoned that because any radio message from a plane was transmitted with a weak signal, the sender had to be very close.

He forwarded the good news via clothesline telegraph to John, who immediately went aft to check on the radio traffic, telling Byron and Kiles about the message on his way. Energized by the ever-increasing possibility of imminent rescue, the men scanned the horizon, hoping for a visual.

Sparky crouched next to Bill, who was still manning the headset. As *Baby* had settled into a more regular motion, Stanz had started to feel better, and had even been able to keep his share of the crackers down. He stood as Rodgers entered the cramped radio area. John smiled, "Well, Stantz, good to see you're back in the land of the living."

Sparky nodded sheepishly, "Aye, aye, skip. Sir, I'm sorry, I . . . I'm afraid I haven't been much help."

Rodgers interrupted, "No apology necessary, Sparky. Besides, as awful as you felt, you came through for us every time we needed you—that took guts. Just do me a favor and drink what's left of your water ration. We're hoping to spot someone soon, and you need it now."

Wild Bill turned to John. "Skip, that plane could be close. Don't you think it's time to launch a flare?"

9:39 AM Hawaii Time

The USS *Whippoorwill* had been patrolling along the westernmost reaches of the search grid when she sighted flares to the north and west of them. After radioing in their sighting, the ship began a diligent search. Upon receiving the *Whippoorwill*'s message, Van Auken ordered the *Langley*'s two aircraft to assist, redirecting them westward, miles away from the downed seaplane they had come so close to discovering.

Several hours of searching yielded nothing to explain the sighted flare. However, the *Whippoorwill*'s report had raised a possibility that worried Van Auken. One of the worst scenarios would be for Rodgers and his plane to somehow slip past the ships searching for them, and float westward through the Kauai Channel.

The channel was a hundred-mile-wide opening running to the north and west of Oahu, between Oahu and Kauai. The narrow gap between the huge undersea mountains that formed the bases of the two islands funneled the prevailing current through this pass. Although not quite as fast as the Molokai Express, the current was still formidable. If the seaplane had somehow drifted past the searchers and through the channel, there was nothing but the vast Pacific for thousands of miles beyond. They would surely be lost forever.

With this in mind, Van Auken decided to shift the grid once more. He radioed all of his charges, and the armada crabbed farther to the west—away from the PN9.

12:31 PM Hawaii Time

Onboard *Baby,* Van Auken's message had come through loud and clear. Wild Bill and Sparky raced to find Rodgers with the bad news.

"Skip, you're not gonna believe this!"

"What is it, Bill?"

Sparky jumped in. "Damned if they aren't shifting the grid again, sir!"

Bill handed the coordinates to Rodgers. "Where's that gonna put us in relationship to them now?"

John studied the notations and did the math in his head. *Damn it!*

"We're gonna be at least a hundred miles away from the eastern edge. Again."

Rodgers passed the depressing news to Kiles and Byron.

"Why the hell can't they just sit still?" Kiles said to no one in particular. Byron just gritted his teeth in stone-faced disappointment.

Realizing the danger of despair, John gathered his men.

"Gentlemen, this news is a blow, but we can't give up now. Can we refocus on the radio generator? Any ideas?"

Wild Bill perked up a little at this. "Skip, what if we put one of the engine's heavy flywheels between the starter and the generator? That just might deal with the herky-jerky motion that stumped us before."

Rodgers nodded, "Good man—let's give 'er a try." And they set upon the port engine once more.

Several hours and innumerable curse words later, they had managed to remove the heavy flywheel. Now they had to find a way to both connect it and suspend it securely: not an easy problem to solve. After considerable time and effort, though, they finally coupled the flywheel hard to the shaft of the generator. Using some of the wire rope, which they still had in abundance, they secured the flywheel axle and the starter to the plane's frame. If the first setup had looked peculiar, it was nothing compared to the wiry spider web they had now.

The men held their breath and watched to see what would happen this time. At first, the contraption seemed to work as planned. Once the batteries were connected, the flywheel steadied the spasmodic motion from before. However using this setup, the flywheel was only geared to turn at a rate of slightly more than one revolution per second—slower even than the speed of a record player—nowhere near fast enough to transmit a signal. Without a way to speed up the generator to 2,500 rpm, they were once again out of luck.

4:36 PM Central Time

Despite his deep sorrow at the loss of his friend and wartime compatriot, Zachary Lansdowne, Colonel Billy Mitchell arrived at Fort Sam Houston energized by the support he had received along the journey. During the remainder of his train ride, many had recognized him and expressed their support for the independent air force he was pushing to create. More importantly, several important congressmen had signed on to his initiative as well.

Mitchell entered his office to check for mail and messages, and spied the local paper on his desk. Picking it up, he read the bold headlines flashing the latest statement distilled from Admiral Moffett about the missing PN9: "THE SEARCH MAY BE FUTILE." As he stared at the quote, Lieutenant Smith's words came back to him. *Someone needs to hold the U.S. Navy accountable.* Mitchell slammed the paper down on his desk.

He picked up the phone and barked at the operator, "Call Lieutenant Smith and tell him to set up a press conference for tomorrow. I have something to say to the country."

2:41 PM Pacific Time

Admiral Moffett's telegram had arrived at Ethel Rodgers' Burbank apartment the evening before. Livid at the implications of the message, she had spent the entire day trying to track the admiral down. At last, her call made it through to Moffett's suite at the Olympic Club in San Francisco. Almost apoplectic with frustration, she leaned against the hallway wall, tightly clutching the heavy black receiver. Admiral Moffett's voice finally came on the line: "Yes, this is Admiral Moffett."

Ethel wasted no time on pleasantries. "Admiral, this is Mrs. John Rodgers, Commander John Rodgers' wife. I received your telegram last night."

Moffett prepared himself to offer whatever slim hope he could still hold out, "Yes, Mrs. Rodgers . . ."

"I assume that by now the navy still hasn't heard from or recovered that plane."

The admiral was taken aback. This was not the tack he had expected, "Well, yes that's correct, but—"

Ethel cut him off, "Admiral, I must say your telegram was a disappointment. You know they're dead, I know they're dead. Why don't you just come out and admit it?"

"Well, Mrs. Rodgers, that's just not true. We have been . . ."

Again she interrupted, "Look Admiral, I can't collect on John's survivor's pension until he's officially declared dead. That's going to take time because there's no body, so why, for God's sake, don't you go ahead and get the process started? All of us wives should get that money as soon as possible."

Moffett knew there was actually only one other wife involved, but it was clear this was not the time to address that issue. "Mrs. Rodgers, I assure you we will keep you and the others advised of any developments."

"You see that you do. Don't drag this thing out. It's already tough enough for us grieving widows." With that, she hung up.

12:45 PM Hawaii Time

The crew sat huddled around the failed contraption while Kiles manned the helm. They were frustrated but far from beaten, even though no one had been able to come up with a way to get the transmitter working. Then Sparky came up with an idea. "Since we can't figure a way to power the transmitter, maybe we could build a spark set. We'd have to cannibalize the transmitter and one of the engines for ignition parts, but I think we have most of what we'd need."

Byron was puzzled, "Haven't we already tried that?"

Sparky grinned mischievously, "Yeah, kind of . . . but this would be about a hundred times more powerful."

Wild Bill knew exactly what his buddy had in mind, and he loved the idea. "Sparky, if you can pull that off, we'll be calling you Marconi."

John and Byron were lost. Bill quickly brought them up to speed. "A spark-gap transmitter is the most basic type of radio. It makes current jump across open space, kind of like a spark plug does. What we have to do is link up a battery to a capacitor and a resistor on one end, and an inductor on the other. When the space between the capacitor and inductor gets small enough, a spark jumps the gap. That spark pulse will then send energy out through an antenna in the form of radio waves. That's why a radio can pick up the tapping of spark plugs in a poorly grounded car engine."

John and Byron exchanged a glance. John shrugged, "Sounds good to me, Bill. Let's get started."

It took time and effort to get the starter and the flywheel removed, but this project was relatively simple. Once the necessary parts had been rounded up, Bill and John set to removing the engine coil, distributor, and other bits from the starboard engine, while Sparky and Byron pulled the cover off the transmitter and tore into it, extracting the loading coil, a resistor, and the condenser.

Once Sparky and Byron had finished their portion of the project, they worked on stringing as long an antenna as possible. The longer the antenna, the farther the signal would travel, and the better chance they would have of someone's receiver picking up their Morse code distress signal. They insulated the wire everywhere it touched or was secured to the plane. They used an assortment of hose sections, manila rope, and rubber insulation stripped from other wires. The antenna they produced ran from the tip of the bow up on a twenty-degree angle, over the top wing, and all the way back to the tip of the tail assembly, before turning vertically down and entering the aft radioman's cockpit hatch.

In a surprisingly short time, the crew had completed the assembly process. The new radio set used the large Packard flywheel—horizontally this time—to turn the distributor head to make and break the coil-fed connection. There was no prelude to their test. This time, even before the hot lead could be fully secured to the batteries, a powerful spark jumped the gap, surprising them all. Sparky quickly turned the flywheel and broke the contact. He spun it back and the blue lightning struck again. Success!

Byron was impressed by the size of the spark. "That thing looks like it could transmit a message around the world!"

Chief Radioman Sparky Stantz was back in business. "Well Bill, I bet ole' Marconi's smilin' now." He immediately started turning the horizontal flywheel like a bus driver, sending out an SOS. *Dot-dot-dot, dash-dash-dash, dot-dot-dot* crackled over the crude spark-set transmitter. In a matter of minutes the repeated electrical flashes caused the cabin interior to smell mildly of ozone.

Bill wanted to check if the signal was being sent, so he climbed up on the fuselage and raised his right index finger over his head and went to touch the antenna wire. He never made it. A huge blue-green flame arced across the void and zapped him so hard that it almost knocked him off the plane. He lay crumpled in a heap as Byron rushed to his side. "Wild Bill! Are you OK?"

Wild Bill groaned and massaged his jaw. "Damn—feels like all my teeth got knocked loose. Guess it's puttin' out, all right." Bill shook his hand to ease the pain as Byron helped him to his feet. They both stared warily at the overhead wire, then headed back toward the cockpit.

Later, the sky turned a spectacular mix of pinks and oranges as another sunset neared. The rolling seas had calmed even more, and the breeze remained steady from their stern. Helping Kiles sail *Baby*, Rodgers mentally reviewed their situation. He knew that no matter how impressive the spark generator appeared, the maximum range of such a crude device was probably less than ten miles. Although this was better than nothing, for the sake of morale, he chose to keep the information to himself. Sparky and Bill probably knew it as well, but they too kept mum. At last, Byron came to relieve Rodgers so that he could take the sunset fix.

Once back in the nav station John grabbed his trusty sextant. He poked his head up through the opening to take a sight, and as he did, a gigantic spark leaped from the antenna wire and zapped him on the back of his skull. The spark burned his neck and knocked him to the floor. Groggily shaking his head and rubbing the back of his neck, he looked up at the antenna and made a mental note: *You'll only do that once.*

As John carefully took his position fix, an idea struck him. He disappeared back down to his desk to further explore it. With his glasses on, he strained to discern the new coordinates as the twilight dimmed. When he had finished his calculations, he set aside the results and started again from the beginning. Navigation was at best an educated guess, and he had to be sure he was right in order to undertake the gamble he had in mind. It would call on all his skills and talents as a navigator. When he had finished double-checking himself, the results indicated that his idea just might work.

John returned to the cabin and assembled the crew. "Gentlemen, enough of this waiting to be rescued. We're going to sail this bird to Hawaii." Greeted by stunned silence, he continued, "Since we landed, we've drifted eighty miles towards the islands. That leaves us 390 miles away. But now that we are actually sailing, if we can maintain our course at an average speed of five knots, we could make it there in just over three days."

At first, the crew was slow to respond. They were all so thirsty, hungry, and tired that the thought of three more days at sea might as well have been three years. Then Kiles broke the silence, "Well hell, it's not like we've got much choice—if the damn navy's gonna play hide-n-seek with us, we might just as well head for home ourselves."

Bill jumped in. "That's right, and you know what? If we do sail all the way there, we'll have completed our mission to fly to Hawaii! I mean I know it's a long taxi after landing, but still . . ." At this, the men all grinned through their chapped, cracked lips and prepared to finish what they had started.

The September 4, 1925 *Honolulu Advertiser:* Both air tragedies continue to dominate the headlines. The possibility of a Boeing PB1 flight anytime in the future is scrapped as the navy licks its wounds.

The USS *Langley*, America's first aircraft carrier: The twin vertical masts, which were removable helped support the outboard booms. The booms, in turn, were used to assist in recovery of amphibious seaplanes, such as shown here closest to the bow.

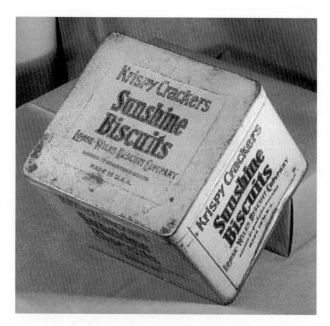

A tin of crackers, presumably like the ones aboard the PN9-1.

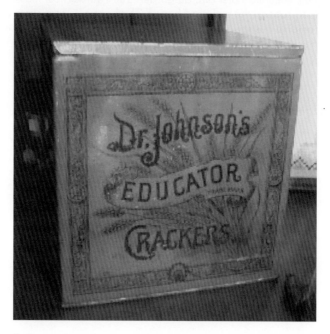

Another brand of period crackers, possibly the same as were carried aboard the PN9-1 as emergency rations.

USS *Langley* launching a DT-2 plane while at the pier in San Diego harbor, circa 1925.

Chapter 41

Saturday—September 5, 1925

6:27 AM Hawaii Time

Aboard the *Aroostook,* Commander Van Auken awoke feeling guilty after the first full night of sleep he'd had in almost a week. He knew someone would have roused him had any significant message come in overnight, but he wanted to check for himself. He quickly showered and dressed, then headed straight to the bridge, forgoing breakfast.

The seas were not large, but the wind was blowing at a brawny twenty-two knots out of the northeast. *Where were these conditions when John needed them?* A mug of steaming black coffee was passed to the skipper. Van's first move, after reviewing the few messages that had come in during the night, was to initiate a roll call check-in of all the boats involved in the hunt.

Many of the search vessels reported that they were running low on fuel and supplies and needed to return to Pearl Harbor. Losing them, Van would be left with far too few vessels to properly cover the present grid. At 7 AM, he dismissed the vessels that needed fuel. Wanting to make sure the PN9 did not slip through the treacherous Kauai Channel, he ordered the four remaining ships under his command to once again move west—farther still from Rodgers and his crew.

8:51 AM Hawaii Time

Saturday was a working day for Akiko and Masahiro. The little bell over the door rang dully as they entered the office. Akiko immediately turned the radio on, and a familiar Hawaiian melody filled the room. Akiko assumed her position on the wicker sofa next to the radio. Masahiro turned their cardboard sign to *Open,* then unfolded the newspaper he had just purchased and placed it on her desk. The headline of importance was now below the fold. It read, "HONOLULU OFFICIALS CLING TO HOPE THAT FIVE AVIATORS WILL BE SAVED." In the story, a naval officer was quoted recalling the rescue of Lieutenant Locatelli, a navy flyer who went down in the North Sea during the war and was recovered alive and safe after drifting for several days.

"You see, Akiko, this man was in much worse trouble than Mr. John Rodgers, and he made it home." Heartened by the hope he saw flash in his daughter's eyes, he continued, "Mr. Rodgers and his men are floating in the warm Pacific. Maybe they swim as they wait for rescue? And remember the article we saw about their supplies? They have food and water for several days more, maybe."

The door bell again tinkled weakly as a long-standing female customer entered. After greeting Masahiro, she noticed the paper open to the ongoing saga of the lost seaplane and snorted, "Hmmph. It's ridiculous, isn't it? Everyone knows they're dead." There was a muffled gasp from Akiko, as the color drained from her face, and Masahiro quickly ushered his client into the back room.

9:28 AM Hawaii Time

Sparky, Bill, and Kiles all took turns at the flywheel spark set, sending out the SOS followed by their position report and drift rate at regular intervals. So far, though, from the radio chatter they monitored, there had been no indication that anyone had heard them.

Meanwhile, Byron and John alternated at the helm, trying to keep *Baby* traveling down their course at speed. Whoever was not at the wheel scanned the horizon with the binoculars. Because of their crude sail setup, they were manifestly reliant on the direction of the wind and current, and could make only minor course corrections. Any more than five degrees off of dead downwind and they would lose both steerage and speed.

In order to monitor their progress, Rodgers took new sights at regular intervals, calculating their position, speed, and distance traveled. Leaving Byron at the helm, John headed back to the nav station to update *Baby*'s coordinates. As he entered the tiny space, he found a ten-inch-long flying fish flopping on the chart table. He brought it back to the main cabin and quickly scaled and gutted it. Without the means to cook it, he sliced what little flesh there was and divided it into five pieces. The ravenous crew gobbled the raw flesh in no time flat. Unfortunately, while providing necessary protein, the meager scraps of fish both reinforced their hunger and intensified their thirst; their water was all but gone.

John had once more relieved Byron at the helm when Wild Bill had an idea. "You know, there *is* water in those engine radiators."

Kiles perked up at this. "You think there's any way to convert that into something we could actually drink?"

"I dunno. That damn Liquid X is about as deadly a cocktail as you'll ever find—lead suspended in a petroleum-based liquid. Seemed like a blessing when we needed it to plug leaks back in San Fran, but now . . ." he trailed off dubiously.

"Yeah, but if the lead chunks are big enough to plug leaks, maybe we could strain most of the bad stuff out?"

"It's worth a try, at any rate." And they were off and running.

Draining some of the foul water from the port radiator into the indispensable little bucket, they strained the viscous solution again and again through various pieces of cloth. Stepping back, they surveyed their results.

Bill sighed, "Well, I don't see globules floatin' around any more, but it's still pretty rank. Looks like we've got an oil spill floating on the top."

Kiles was a little more optimistic, "Maybe it doesn't taste as bad as it looks." Cupping a little into his hand he sipped it cautiously, and then gagged and spat vociferously, "Hooooowee! No way, no how."

Bill shrugged, dipped his finger into the fluid and licked it. Spitting and wiping his tongue, he quickly dumped the contents of their failed experiment overboard.

John called from the cockpit, "I think we've got a squall headed our way."

Without a word, everyone scrambled for makeshift containers to catch rainwater. The storm came up on them in no time. As it began to rain, Rodgers reminded the men to wipe the salt off the surfaces first. John stayed at the helm while Bill and Kiles climbed atop the upper wing, intending to try and pool water in the concave fabric areas between the ribs. Byron and Sparky used their shirts and other bits of cloth to mop up what water they could, and then wring out the moisture into the bucket.

When the short-lived squall had passed, John called from the helm, "How much did we come up with?"

Byron eyed the contents of the bucket, "Skip, I'd say we got about a quart of water." Fresh from his experience with the radiator experiment, Kiles shook his head, "I'd say it's a stretch to call what's in there 'water.'" He was referring to the hundreds of tiny flecks of the gray dope paint floating throughout the liquid. The dope-based paint was probably every bit as poisonous as Liquid X, and even after they strained the liquid repeatedly, it tasted so bad it was undrinkable.

As the crew returned to their duty stations, Bill answered nature's call. Although he had little fluid to excrete, he hung on to the vertical frame and attempted to relieve himself out the main hatch. As he gazed out at the horizon, an unexpected motion caught his eye in the water off to the side.

He nearly fell from his perch when he realized what he was looking at. He bellowed a warning to the others, "Sharks at three o'clock!" He turned back to watch as the two ominous gray dorsal fins headed straight for the crippled plane. As they closed in, he yelled, "Jesus Christ, they've gotta be sixteen feet long!"

2:00 PM Central Time

In San Antonio, Lieutenant Smith had done a good job getting the word out about Billy Mitchell's press conference. Local reporters had flocked to Fort Sam Houston for the statement from the notorious army maverick. Exactly on the hour, the audience was called to attention. The excited buzz in the austere meeting room hushed as a ramrod-straight Colonel Mitchell in full dress strode purposefully up to the podium on the dais. Starched, polished, and clean cut, he was the epitome of a first-rate military officer.

Grasping the sides of the varnished podium, he took a moment to survey those gathered before him. Firmly in command, he began: "Gentlemen, at ease. I would first like to thank all of you for coming today on such short notice. This past week, our great country has been deeply shocked by a pair of tragedies. I refer, of course, to the *Shenandoah* and the PN9 disasters. The *Shenandoah* was a frightful aeronautical accident: loss of life, equipment, and treasure, and for what? An ill-advised publicity stunt. Along with the rest of America, I mourn the dead, and offer my sincere condolences to the grieving families and friends."

Next he tore, at length, into the navy for the PN9s' mission; ". . . then to get publicity and make noise about what it was doing with aircraft, this so-called Hawaiian Flight was arranged for." By now Mitchell was practically spitting with disgust.

"Three airplanes were built to participate in it. One never got away. Another flew for a few miles out. And one was lost on the high seas!

"Patrol vessels were stationed every two hundred miles, a distance entirely too far apart for an experimental flight of this kind. With such primitive flying machines as the PN9s are, double or triple this number should have been there. In fact the whole Pacific Fleet should have been employed there."

Mitchell was unrelenting in his attack. "What happened to this really good-for-nothing big, lumbering flying boat when its brave navigator began to run short of gas over a heavy sea? The probability is that they held her up for as long as they could. As they neared the water, caught by a sudden gust, she might have been thrown into a stall and gone straight down under the waves."

Mitchell paused dramatically, and then dropped his bombshell, in measured, stentorian tones. "These accidents are the direct result of incompetence, criminal negligence, and almost treasonable administration of the national defense by the Navy and War Departments." At this, the room exploded. Flashbulbs went off like Roman candles on the Fourth of July, and reporters scribbled the headlines that would soon stun the country.

1:51 PM Hawaii Time

Commander Van Auken walked briskly to the *Aroostook*'s tiny radio room where an urgent message awaited him. The radio man on duty passed him the microphone. "Same fisherman as before, I think, sir."

Van keyed the microphone. "This is Commander Van Auken. Over."

The heavily accented reply came back. "Commandah, we find prane. If dey need gas, da *Nippon Koto* goin' geeve 'em. Ovah."

Van was not sure he trusted his ears. "Captain, please repeat your message slowly and give your coordinates. Over." The fisherman obliged—and language difficulties notwithstanding, what Van understood was that one of the volunteer Japanese fishing vessels had found the missing PN9, and was going to attempt to refuel it for takeoff. Their position was about fifty miles north of Kahuku Point on the northeast corner of Oahu, just east of their present area of focus. While this location was outside the grid, it was certainly a possible location for the PN9.

The news shot through the fleet as Van requested several planes be sent from the carrier *Langley* to confirm. Ship-to-ship radio chatter increased markedly with the news. Van Auken actually had to request radio transmissions be kept to a minimum so that messages confirming the sighting could get through. In the meantime, he also ordered the *Farragut*—the ship closest to Kahuku Point—to respond to the coordinates given by the

Japanese fishing boat. The mood onboard the *Aroostook* was one of guarded jubilation, but until they were sure all five onboard the PN9 were safe, no one wanted to jinx their rescue with premature celebration.

2:10 PM Hawaii Time

Akiko needed to escape. She slipped quietly out of the office. The tinkle of the bell was muffled as she carefully closed the door and began to walk, with no destination in mind. Her heart ached as she moved slowly along the busy street, oblivious to her surroundings, angry, confused, and desperately in love.

Ever since John had taken off on Monday, news of the PN9 had swept Akiko along on an emotional roller-coaster ride so extreme that she had been physically ill on several occasions. Now, from the news on the radio and in the press, it seemed that everyone was ready to give up on the aviators. But Akiko refused to believe that her Mr. John Rodgers would not be coming back to her. Whenever her energy ebbed, she scolded herself, *I must be strong for him.*

To Masahiro's concern, she had hardly eaten or slept in days. He feared she had regressed to the darkest times of her mother's illness, believing on some level that by depriving herself she could somehow bestow food and rest on John, wherever he was.

The truth was that she avoided sleep, because whenever she did sink into a fitful slumber, terrible nightmares quickly chased her back to consciousness. Each night she stayed up listening until the radio station went off the air. Then she would listen to the dull electric hum for hours, just in case the station came back on with a news flash—anything to avoid returning to the bad dreams. Between sleep deprivation, lack of nourishment, and her incessant anxiety for John, Akiko was growing more fragile by the day.

She walked aimlessly around the block and before long, was back at the office. As she let herself in, the little bell gave only the ghost of a jingle. Masahiro promptly appeared in the doorway between the offices, a concerned frown on his face.

"Akiko?"

She avoided his eyes. Softly she lied, "It's all right, Father. I . . . I just had to run an errand."

"Akiko, you are not well. I will make an appointment for Dr. Lee to come see you as soon as he can." Akiko started to protest feebly at the prospect of a house call from the aging family doctor, but felt suddenly light-headed and had to reach out to a chair to steady herself. Sinking into it, she sighed. "Very well, Father. If you think it best."

3:03 PM Hawaii Time

A little over an hour after their launch, the planes from the *Langley* approached the coordinates the Japanese captain had called in. One of the pilots radioed back to the *Langley* with incredible news. He reported excitedly that a fishing boat and a gray navy seaplane were indeed bobbing about fifty yards from each other. This news rocketed around the fleet and cheers rang out on all ships. The two *Langley* planes had just begun their descent for a closer look when the seaplane below them started to taxi for take-off. The pilots were ecstatic. If the plane could fly, that meant the fishing boat must have managed to refuel them already, and Rodgers and his men would be once again safely en route to Honolulu.

Before the *Langley* planes could get close enough to read the seaplane's identifying tail numbers, she skipped across the ocean's surface and lifted off. The two carrier plane pilots moved in to flank her and could now discern the tail numbers. To their intense dismay, it was not Rodgers' plane after all. Once airborne, the seaplane unfurled her antenna and was able to broadcast again. The crew identified themselves by radio, quickly clearing up the confusion. The plane was an F5L, almost identical in design to the PN9. She was based out of Lahaina Roads on Maui and had been assisting in the search. The plane had experienced a fuel blockage, which forced them to land. The crew had subsequently replaced their fuel filter with a spare, and was now ready to rejoin the hunt for the missing PN9. Disappointment settled like a pall over the fleet.

3:40 PM Hawaii Time

The increased radio traffic led *Baby*'s crew to scan the horizon with renewed vigor. The confusing reports coming in left the crew all the more puzzled and frustrated. What plane? What fishing boat? They felt as if they were listening to a bad radio play. The only things the crew had seen in the water were the two enormous sharks that had menaced the plane. When the massive predators had swum away after circling for almost an hour, all onboard had breathed more easily.

Hunger and thirst continued to take a toll, and all the men had weakened perceptibly. The only edible thing left was the emergency supply tin of corned beef, which looked suspiciously like it had been left over from the war. As sunset approached, Rodgers decided it was time to open the "canned Willy." He figured the six pounds of meat would sustain them for several days. Plus, he assumed the juice it was packed in would help slake their thirst.

Using a knife, Kiles punctured the can along its edge and rocked the blade slowly until he had worked the top off. Being careful not to spill a drop of the precious liquid, he carefully removed the chunk of meat. John sliced off five equal pieces, and returned the remaining slab to the can.

While it didn't look rotten, the meat smelled so foul that as hungry as they all were, the odor kept them from wolfing it down. Knowing that they needed sustenance, the men tentatively nibbled at the dreadful stuff, but it tasted so vile that both Sparky and Kiles vomited straight away. Plus it was salty beyond belief, and had obviously been canned too long ago to still be edible. Although John, Byron, and Bill managed to keep what they had eaten down, it gave them a horrible, burning thirst. Rather than go from bad to worse, the men gave up and pitched their portions overboard. They were all in favor of dumping the rest of the meat in the tin as well, but Rodgers cautioned them against it.

"Bad as it tastes now, you never know when we may need it to hang on."

John saved his frustration for the log: *How could this ancient can of over-salted beef be considered appropriate for emergency rations?*

As the sun went down on their fifth day at sea—the sixth since they left San Francisco—things looked bleak. Thanks to the wretched corned beef, Sparky's nausea had returned with a vengeance. He was now worse off than before, and there was nothing any of them could do to help him. Bill and Kiles were struggling with their own thirst and could think of little else, while John and Byron, although just as dehydrated, focused on the fact that the wind was dying and their speed had slowed. They were all exhausted, and about to head into another long, tough night.

Colonel Billy Mitchell Vintage snapshot images of the controversial officer.

The September 5, 1925 edition of *The Honolulu Star-Bulletin:* The headline has shifted to focusing on the critical comments made against the Navy and War Departments by Colonel Billy Mitchell.

Support Urged for Airport to Be Named for Commander Rodgers

The Honolulu Chapter of the National Aeronautic Association of U.S.A. suggests that no more fitting testimonial of the appreciation of our community to the pioneering work of Commander John Rodgers, U.S.N., could be expressed than by providing a splendid airport on Oahu named after that gallant officer.

A special committee of the Chamber of Commerce of Honolulu is now soliciting contributions to a $20,000 fund required to be raised under the terms of Act 176, S. L. 1925, to be added to a territorial appropriation of $45,000, making a total fund of $65,000 available for the purchase of land fronting on Kalihi bay for a territorial airport.

Any surplus over cost of the land will be expended by the territory in clearing, grading and otherwise improving the site.

The undersigned appeals to every member of this community who can afford to do so to contribute according to his or her ability to a fund to be used for the purpose of further improving the proposed Rodgers airport on this island.

This fund will be in addition to the Chamber of Commerce fund and expended under the direction of the Airways and Landing Field committee of our Honolulu Chapter.

(Signed) A. W. VAN VALKENBURG,
Chairman Airways and Landing Field Committee,
Honolulu Chapter, N.A.A. of U.S.A.

Contributions to the Rodgers Airport fund may be left at the office of this paper if desired, or checks may be mailed direct to A. W. Van Valkenburg, chairman, Postoffice Box 3288.

The Honolulu Advertiser: Centered under the major headline on the front page was the first printed suggestion that Hawaii's planned territorial airport should be named in memoriam after "John Rodgers . . . that gallant officer." This proposal reflected a general consensus in Hawaii that the crew was dead.

This compromised image is of a peculiarly timed cartoon from the September 5, 1925 *Honolulu Star-Bulletin*.

An F5L seaplane. It is similar enough in design to be easily misconstrued as a PN9. A plane identical to this one caused considerable confusion when it was unexpectedly forced to land north of Oahu and east of the search coordinates due to a fouled fuel filter.

Pictured below, two sample tins of period corned beef. This "Canned Willy" would have been similar to the emergency rations that the PN9-1 crew had onboard.

An airplane landing on the USS *Langley*.

Chapter 42

Sunday—September 6, 1925

10:37 AM Pacific Time

Rear Admiral William E. Moffett stood leaning over the large table in his Olympic Club suite. Both of his huge hands were spread out on the table, palms down on either side of the front page of the *San Jose Mercury Herald*. The *Herald*'s headline echoed those splashed on newspapers all across America. It read: "PRIDE OF THE NAVY IS NOW A TANGLED WRECKAGE."

While the headline was harsh, the articles that followed were even worse. One side of the page featured a blistering account of the *Shenandoah* tragedy, and included a list of the dead. The other side was devoted to an attack on the foolhardy "Race to Hawaii" and the navy's abysmal failure to locate the wreckage of the missing plane. The news was so widespread that even the uninformed few who had not previously heard of Commander John Rodgers, certainly knew of him now. Thanks to Colonel Mitchell's tirade the day before, the two separate stories were now inexorably linked.

Virtually every paper in the nation featured in-depth coverage of Mitchell's scathing press conference, in which he had charged the navy with nothing less than treason. Top navy brass were outraged, both by Mitchell's blatant insubordination, and for being caught in such a vulnerable position. Admiral Moffett, although not mentioned by name in Mitchell's speech, was implicitly linked to both disasters. As a result, he now came under a firestorm of criticism.

Moffett was being pushed from all directions, most significantly the Department of the Navy. Sick of the negative press, the brass wanted a quick, clean resolution to the PN9 situation. Messages and telegrams from all over inundated Moffett's suite. Many called for him to cut his losses and move on, while others encouraged him to call out the whole Pacific fleet, not knowing that it was exactly what he had done. Unfortunately, because of the need to refuel and resupply the search vessels, the "fleet" now consisted of only four ships, the *Aroostook*, *Farragut*, *Reno*, and *Langley*. To make matters worse, those four had all been initially assigned to rhumb-line positions, and had been at sea for a considerable time. They, too, would soon need refueling.

For his part, Moffett's faith that the five men might still be alive out on the open ocean was beginning to waver; there had been absolutely no sign of life for six days despite the vast, intensive search. And his doubt was edged with practical concern, as he was also starting to question his rationale for assigning so many ships to what appeared to be a hopeless cause. Maybe Colonel Mitchell was correct. Maybe the aviators were beyond help.

As he paced the room, an aide delivered the latest edition of the *Mercury Herald* and exited rapidly. This latest front page headline referred to Moffett's own BURAERO directly: "MITCHELL THROWS BOMB INTO RANKS OF WAR BUREAUS." Moffett sighed and slumped heavily into the maroon leather chair to review the circumstances yet again. After a few moments, he made his decision. He turned to an aide and ordered a message sent to Van Auken on the *Aroostook*.

9:24 AM Hawaii Time

Akiko sat alone on her bed, her sheet wrapped around her, waiting for Dr. Lee to come into her room. In response to the message Masahiro had sent, and out of deference to his long-standing professional relationship with the Mikamis, the venerable old family doctor had agreed to make a special house call this Sunday morning.

In the hall, just outside the door, Dr. Lee listened as Masa described Akiko's symptoms. Then he entered the room and performed a thorough examination. Wiping his hands on a clean linen towel, and covering Akiko back up with her sheet, he pronounced his diagnosis.

"There is no doubt about it. You are going to have a baby." Stunned, Akiko was unable to speak.

Dr. Lee inquired gently, "Akiko, do you understand what I have just told you?" Akiko nodded numbly.

"Dr. Lee, how long . . . I mean when . . ." she faltered.

"I cannot tell precisely, but you are somewhere between six and eight weeks along in your pregnancy." Akiko sat quietly as her mind raced through the complicated consequences her condition would introduce.

Dr. Lee finally broke the silence, "Akiko, your father tells me you have not been eating or sleeping. It is very important for you to start taking better care of yourself."

"My father . . . how can I tell him? What will he . . ."

"I will address this situation with him if you like."

Akiko blushed and whispered, "Thank you."

"I will need to see you again soon, so please make some time to come by my office in the next week."

Akiko nodded almost imperceptibly, and Dr. Lee slipped out of her room, closing the door behind him.

6 to 8 weeks . . . she knew exactly when this child had been conceived: the last weekend in July, her magical two days at the Moana with John; the weekend they had decided to spend their lives together.

While Dr. Lee conferred with Masahiro down the hall, Akiko wrestled with a kaleidoscope of emotions. She feared her father's reaction. For a daughter to get pregnant out of wedlock meant a scandal for any family; but for a traditional Japanese father like Masahiro, she knew it would be a tremendous loss of face. She found the thought of bringing him shame almost more than she could bear. And yet, knowing that she carried the child of the man she loved beyond life itself, she was filled with joy.

Akiko got dressed, then waited until she heard her father and Dr. Lee bid their farewells. Timidly she opened her door and walked down the hall to the kitchen, where she was certain her father would be making himself a pot of tea. Sure enough, he had put water on to boil, and was carefully measuring tea into the little round pot. She stood in the doorway and waited for him to notice her there. Masa had heard her soft steps approaching, but chose not to look in her direction until he could corral the thoughts racing through his mind. Watching him go through the motions of preparing the tea, Akiko was unable to read his expression. Feeling her eyes on him, Masa turned away from his daughter. The awkward silence stretched uncomfortably.

At last, she ventured, "Father, I think that I will take the sampan bus to Kailua today. I would like to walk along the ocean there. I will be back in time for dinner." With a little bow, she started back to her room to gather her things.

Masa turned and called down the hall after her, "Akiko!" his voice tight with emotion. "I . . . I would also like to walk on the beach today."

Puzzled, she nodded. "Of course." And whatever scene that was to play between them was postponed for the time being.

9:49 AM Hawaii Time

Aboard the *Aroostook*, Commander Van Auken was having a frustrating morning. During the night, the *Reno* had finally been forced to return to Pearl Harbor for refueling, leaving only the *Farragut*, the *Langley*, and themselves—a ludicrously small flotilla to cover such a vast area. All Van could do was to play shortstop and attempt to block the hundred-mile channel between the Islands. Although the *Langley* still had sufficient fuel, the *Farragut* and his own ship would soon be forced to withdraw as well.

Knowing how futile their search must appear, Van was concerned that navy brass would soon call it off—and what better time to do it than when the ships were forced to return to Pearl Harbor. As Van mulled the situation, an aide appeared with a copy of Moffett's latest message:

"Submarine fleet maneuvers south of Oahu temporarily suspended. All available submarines report immediately to USS *Aroostook* on location 21 degrees 32 minutes north, 159 degrees 15 minutes west for search and rescue duty." It was wonderful news, and Van Auken was relieved. Moffett had not caved in to those pressuring him to give up; he was, in fact, providing him with additional eyes and ears.

As Van considered how best to take advantage of the submarines, a runner came in from the radio room with a message from a commercial inter-island steamer. The ship had reported a seaplane adrift in the channel about five miles offshore from Poipu on the southern coast of Kauai. Van's hopes rose once again. *Could this be the real thing?*

He quickly made his way to the radio room and contacted the *Langley*. Despite markedly increased winds, he gave orders to launch reconnaissance planes. He figured if the wind continued to increase and it became too rough for a carrier landing later, the planes would be close enough to Kauai to easily put down there. He also commanded the *Langley* and the *Aroostook to* respond at flank speed to the new location.

The airplanes arrived on scene first, and radioed their findings directly to Van Auken.

"Sir, no sign of the missing seaplane at the designated coordinates. Nothin' here but a beat-up old fishing boat that was probably towed out to sea to be scuttled. Don't know how she's still afloat—she's obviously been holed to sink. Over."

Frustrated by yet another cruel disappointment, Van seized the microphone and barked into it, "Open fire, mister, and don't stop until you see that nuisance go down!"

10:32 AM Hawaii Time

An hour later, Akiko and Masahiro were headed up the Nuuanu Pali road in the back of the little hand-painted violet and cadmium-red sampan bus. They sat stiffly side by side as the rattletrap vehicle swayed and bounced its way up the verdant valley. Neither had spoken since leaving the house. The charged silence was broken only by the creaking of the bus and the "braap, braap, braap" of the exhaust as the engine periodically misfired. Sitting across from them, a young couple who only had eyes for each other were the only other Sunday passengers.

Masa stared straight ahead, oblivious to the lush scenery they were passing through. Through lowered lids, Akiko peeked at her father from time to time, hoping to glean some indication of what he was thinking, but to no avail. His face was an impenetrable mask. Figuring she would know his opinion soon enough, Akiko sighed softly and turned her thoughts inward.

In the thirty-five years Masa had lived in Honolulu, he had only made this trek once before, years ago, and there was a reason. Unbeknownst to Akiko, her father had been plagued all his life with a desperate fear of heights. He had managed to conceal his acrophobia, even from his wife. Now, the prospect of riding the rickety little bus over the Pali terrified him.

As they approached the top of the pass, he struggled to suppress his rising panic. The wind gusted and the ungainly vehicle rocked violently, teetering dangerously close to the edge of the narrow road. Masa's face was absolutely inscrutable as he did his best to mask the terror he was feeling.

Eventually, after the little bus had navigated the most treacherous portion of the trip without mishap, Masa was able to relax a bit and turn his mind to Akiko's situation. The long jungle descent into Kailua gave him time to compose himself.

Once they arrived at their destination, Masa descended first, then turned to offer Akiko his hand as she stepped down. As soon as he saw that she was safely down, however, he withdrew it, averting his eyes. Chagrined, Akiko pointed the way and the two of them found their way through the tall ironwood and coconut trees to the beach. A stiff breeze blew straight onshore, churning the surf and whipping the sand into small dunes. Low, dark gray clouds scudded across the sky.

Akiko removed her shoes to walk on the damp sand at the water's edge, but Masa kept his on. Akiko understood. Even though it made walking more difficult, for her traditional father to do otherwise would have been undignified. That side of him was part of the barrier between them now. They turned north and began a slow walk along the water's edge. As she waited for her father to speak, Akiko searched the stormy horizon, yearning for John Rodgers' plane to magically appear. *Then everything would be all right.*

On and on they walked in silence, stopping occasionally for Masa to empty his shoes of sand. The windswept deserted beach, whitecapped seas, and the empty horizon served as a dramatic backdrop for the tension between them. At last, Masa stopped at a sheltering dune and indicated for Akiko to sit and rest. Again, he offered her his hand to help her to the sand. He then sat down himself, managing to do so with dignity, Akiko noted, even on the beach.

Seated stiffly next to his daughter, he looked out to sea for several long moments, and then cleared his throat. *Here we go,* Akiko thought, and braced herself for the bitter scolding she anticipated. Masa looked briefly at his daughter, seeming to be at a loss as to how to begin. Akiko broke the silence, prompting gently, "Yes, Father? Please tell me your thoughts. I am so sorry . . ."

He interrupted, "Akiko, what I have to say does not come easily. I have thought very hard about your mother, and how she might have guided me now."

"Father, I know I have brought shame to you. For that I cannot forgive myself but . . ." She hesitated, unsure how to continue.

Masahiro looked out to the ocean, as if searching the horizon for a way to put what he was feeling into words. "I . . . I loved your mother, Akiko. I am not one to show my heart, but I loved her very much. When I lost her, I lost part of myself. I have said before I see her spirit in you. It is that which kept me alive when she left us.

"I see that you care deeply for your Mr. John Rodgers. I am glad you have known love with him. Now, whatever happens, you will bring his child into the world."

Masa shook his head gently and continued, "To lose the one you love so early is unthinkable. You must not add to your pain by worrying about my feelings."

Caught completely by surprise by a side of her father she had never seen, Akiko asked, "Father, what *do* you feel? Will this child not mean disgrace for you—for our family?"

Masa considered her question thoughtfully, as if putting all the pieces together for the first time. "I am not the man I was raised to be. I suppose I have you and your mother to thank for that. I lost her, Akiko. I could not bear to lose you as well. Watching you weaken has taught me that. No. You must carry this child with joy. Whatever happens to Mr. John Rodgers, he has given you a reason to go on, as you have done for me."

Having unburdened his heart at last, Masa again cleared his throat, and self-consciously reached out to pat his daughter's hand. "So?"

"Father . . . you . . . I—I cannot . . ." Overwhelmed by her father's response, Akiko gave up trying to find words. Placing her hands on her lap, she honored him with a traditional seated bow, and then threw her arms around his neck and hugged him. Tears flowed on both sides. Masa was the first to recover. Turning away to wipe his eyes, he stood, and gently helped Akiko to her feet.

"Now, we must see that you take better care of yourself and your passenger. We shall start with lunch, yes?"

Akiko smiled through her tears. Arm in arm, father and daughter walked back along the windswept beach.

Back in the center of the little town, they stopped at a small market near the sampan stop. Masa approached the shopkeeper sitting on a bench by the door and discreetly asked a question. The elderly gentleman smiled, and leaned forward conspiratorially to whisper his reply. Masa nodded to Akiko. "I'll be right back," and strode off behind the market, as if on a mission. Assuming her father was responding to nature's call, Akiko entered the store and purchased the makings for a large sandwich—a round loaf of homemade Portuguese sweet bread and some kalua pork. To her surprise, she found she had an appetite for the first time in weeks. As she looked for a place for them to sit, Masa reappeared with an open, unlabeled bottle of bootleg beer.

Akiko looked at him in surprise. "Alcohol, Father?"

Masa nodded sheepishly. "A little liquid courage, Akiko. To get me back over the mountain. Now you know my secret." For the second time that day, Akiko hugged her father.

Afterward, the two of them bounced and jostled back into town on the little bus. This time the silence between them was profoundly peaceful.

3:41 PM Hawaii Time

Later in the afternoon, the *Aroostook* received a radio message from the first submarine reporting for duty, the R-4, a World War I vintage sub under the command of Lieutenant Donald R. Osborne, Jr. She had made the voyage from the waters just off Oahu in record time. Van welcomed the new addition.

"Lieutenant Osborn, glad to have you with us. Over."

"Roger, Commander, thank you. How can we be of help? Over."

"As you know, we have had to scale back our search area. We have now confined ourselves to the throat of the Kauai Channel. I need you to report to the northernmost end of the grid; coordinates 21 degrees, 47 minutes, 85 seconds north, by 158 degrees, 49 minutes, 60 seconds west. This location will be the infield of your racetrack. Run a twenty-five mile-long north-northwesterly pattern—and Lieutenant, look sharp. We can't let that plane slip through the channel and disappear out into the Pacific. Over."

"Aye, aye, sir. We are proceeding to station. We'll keep our eyes peeled, sir. Over."

An hour later, a second sub reported in and was similarly assigned. Van was glad to have the two subs on vigilant watch, as he knew he would soon be forced to abandon his station and return to Pearl Harbor for fuel.

As the afternoon wore on, the wind increased, and the resulting whitecaps hindered visual reconnaissance, especially from the the short conning towers of the low-riding submarines. The chance of sighting a vessel as small as the seaplane would also decrease as the light faded.

At sunset, Van Auken was forced to make one of the most painful decisions of his career. He ordered the *Farragut* and his own ship the *Aroostook* to return to base. As they turned for Pearl Harbor, Van called for a midshipman and dictated a message which he ordered sent to John and the crew of the PN9.

7: 15 PM Hawaii Time

As the sun set on *Baby*'s heretofore uneventful sixth day at sea, the breeze stiffened and they were soon maintaining their best speed yet. A wan and dehydrated Sparky picked up a radio call. It was an encouraging message directed to them from the *Aroostook*. "We'll get you yet. Subs have joined search effort. Hammer hull so submarines will hear on oscillators."

Inspired by this idea, Kiles and Bill found two wrenches in the tool kit and started beating out a signal on the seaplane's metal hull. Sparky rallied and renewed his spark-set SOS and position report. The drum-and-spark trio did their best to send a syncopated signal, hoping to raise an audience. Their enthusiastic pounding worried Byron.

"Skip, I dunno. At the rate they're going they'll beat a hole right through the hull."

Watching the frantic pounding, John shook his head. "They know this plane inside out. They'll know what's too much." He thought to himself, *At least they're doing something that might work—and it's better for morale, in any case.* The hopeful beating continued.

About an hour after sunset, the wind intensified even further. At first, the crew hoped this would mean a corresponding increase in *Baby*'s sailing speed. Unfortunately, the anticipated increase in boat speed was nominal, as they were just about at maximum hull speed. The wind continued to rise, and in another hour was approaching gale force, clocking in at over thirty knots on the mechanical anemometer. Rough waves battered the seaplane.

The rapid change had come faster than the crew was able to react. Kiles fought valiantly at the helm, but suddenly *Baby* spun on her own axis and back-winded her sails. Instantly they all realized they should have reduced their windage earlier. The old sailor's adage flashed through John's mind: *When you first think you need to shorten sail, do it, or it'll be too late.*

The plane bounced in the swells and then gyrated erratically, taking a terrible beating. The sails were being buffeted so severely that John worried that they would disintegrate. Despite the dangerous conditions, Byron and Bill scrambled up onto the wings' open framework and tore down the jury-rigged sails while John and Sparky manned the safety lines. As soon as Bill had dropped back down into the fuselage, he and Sparky once again rigged the indispensable little bucket anchor off the bow. Once it caught, *Baby* turned 180 degrees. In response, the plane curtailed its crazy Charleston and Kiles was able to keep her somewhat under control. He now struggled to slow her down and keep her pointed straight into the wind; the opposite of what they had been doing since they rigged the sails.

Even so, the wing-tip pontoons were taking a dreadful thrashing, and they quickly became the crew's main concern. If one were to break off in these rough seas, a rollover capsize would be inevitable. Although there was very little they could do to forestall this disaster, Rodgers nonetheless instructed the crew to sit on the port side of the fuselage, to try and minimize the stress on the already-damaged starboard pontoon. With Kiles alone at the helm for the first watch, the rest of the crew huddled together and rode out the storm below, praying the float would hold together.

The Sunday, September 6 *Honolulu Advertiser:* The news of Mitchell's virulent attack on the Navy and War Departments is reported in column two. Centered was the repeated suggestion that the planned Honolulu airport be named after John Rodgers. The far-right column indicates that the navy was still not ready to give up their search. In that same column, reference was made to the Japanese fishing fleet's offer to help in the search effort.

An advertisement as it appeared in *The Honolulu Advertiser.* Although cropped and tiny, this image refers to KGU Radio, one of two stations broadcasting in Honolulu at the time.

The narrow Nuuanu Pali pass

View looking north toward Kaneohe from the Nuuanu Pali lookout today.

The USS *Langley*

Planes in the belowdecks "hangar" of the USS *Langley*.

Chapter 43

Monday—September 7, 1925

9:36 AM Pacific Time

Labor Day dawned bright and clear in Southern California. Ethel's high heels clicked along the sidewalk as she briskly made her way to a chic sidewalk café on Hollywood Boulevard, where new friends awaited her for breakfast. She was not wearing black. *It doesn't suit my complexion.* Instead, she was fashionably clad in a deep scarlet silk blouse and a knee-length indigo skirt.

Running late, she nevertheless stopped at a corner newsstand to check for the latest word on the PN9. Picking up a paper, she had to scan the front page carefully, as the story no longer commanded the bold headlines it had earlier. Frowning, she tossed her head. *Those idiots in Washington should get the message; the press and public are ready to move on.* All she could find, in fact, was a half-column article on Rodgers; the only new information offered was the story of the derelict fishing boat which had been misidentified as the PN9, and then sunk. While no official conjecture was offered as to the fate of the missing crew, the tone of the article implied that their demise was becoming generally accepted as fact.

Ethel tossed the paper back onto the stand. *They're dead, damn it. If I can face it, the navy should be able to. Declare them dead and get it over with!*

8:03 AM Hawaii Time

By morning, the gale had abated. The bedraggled crew could have reconfigured the plane back into a sailboat before the sun came up, had they not been so exhausted from the terrible night. The lack of food and water, together with the ongoing mental and physical strain, continued to sap what little strength they had left. It took them two hours to rerig their sails.

Byron relieved John at the helm, and Rodgers immediately went forward to his navigation station. The morning sextant sight brought terrible news. His vision blurring with fatigue, John focused on his figures and went over them once more. He considered all the variables, the wind velocity and bearing, the speed of the current and direction, their speed over ground, the velocity made good, and the maximum angles of sail. The conclusion was inescapable. There was no way they could make landfall on Oahu. The plane just wasn't that good a sailboat. It couldn't overcome the prevailing winds and current. Worse still, if they continued without correction, they were headed straight for the neck of the funnel—into the Kauai Channel and the open Pacific beyond.

What else can we do? There was only one option. John reckoned that if they pushed the plane as far north as they could, they might be able to point 265 degrees. If they could hold that course, almost due west, they had a chance of making landfall on the southeasternmost corner of Kauai. The problem was that Kauai was another hundred miles beyond Oahu. John doubted any of them could last that long without water.

As John emerged from his tiny nav station to clear his head, he was startled by the sight of a young Golden Plover perched on the flat bow of the fuselage. The bird was so weak that it didn't fly away despite John's sudden appearance. It was obviously bound for Oahu on the last leg of its epic flight from Alaska, and wanted to hitch a ride. John studied the spindly-legged aviator standing on the bow. *I wonder which of us is more tired, you or me?* Sighing, he disappeared back into his cave to break the bad news to his men.

Returning to the main cabin, John called the crew together once more. He didn't mince words. "OK, at this point, we're 120 miles from the North

Shore of Oahu. By my reckoning, with the present conditions we can't sail far enough south to make it there. The search grid is now two hundred miles west of us, confined to the area between Oahu, Kauai, and beyond. If they continue to search for us, the grid is bound to move still further west. The way I figure it, our only chance is to alter course right away and try to make it to Kauai. Otherwise, we could slip right through the channel. I don't need to tell you what that would mean."

Rodgers surveyed the long faces surrounding him. All hopes had been pinned on their making it to Oahu, and now those hopes were dashed. Time was running out on them, and attempting to sail any farther could prove to be a death sentence, especially for Sparky. Kiles asked, "How much further is Kauai?"

"A little over a hundred miles," came the flat response.

Trying to be positive, Byron said, "Aye, sir, 265 degrees it is," and retired to the cockpit along with Kiles to adjust their course.

Wild Bill pulled John aside and whispered, "Skipper, isn't there any chance we could still make Oahu? I don't think Sparky'll last another day without water, let alone the time it'll take us to sail to Kauai."

John stared at Sparky, crumpled listlessly on the deck, and shook his head. "Bill, we can't do it. We just can't make Oahu. I'm sure of it."

"Sir, then we've got to get him some water, or *I'm sure* he'll be dead."

8:40 AM Hawaii Time

The USS *Aroostook* was tied to the familiar pier in Pearl Harbor. The crew had not been dismissed and was, instead, busily loading food stores onboard. Several ink-black hoses snaked across the wharf, pumping water and diesel into the appropriate holding tanks. Sailors scurried about tending an assortment of necessary duties around the ungainly ship, like drones servicing a queen bee.

Van Auken was on the bridge, watching the frenzy of activity beneath him, when a message from Admiral Moffett was handed to him. Although the message did not contain the command to stand down that Van had anticipated, the Admiral requested Van's opinion regarding the continuation of the search. In Van's mind this was almost as bad. In order to answer honestly, he would be forced to come to grips with the fact that despite his hopes to the contrary, he doubted the crew was alive.

Commander Van Auken responded to Admiral Moffett as follows:

> *Considering all attendant circumstances and radio messages, it is not understood why radio communication ceased without warning . . . between the plane and Aroostook without even a sign of SOS, and where the plane was about to land. Also considering that the plane could not make out the dense smoke of Aroostook . . . it is believed that the plane must have been over twenty miles, at least, from Aroostook, when the radio communications ceased. As the plane was in a rainsquall . . . and as gasoline was about gone, it is possible that the plane, in landing without motors, was damaged. It is the Commanding Officer's opinion that if the plane or personnel were not damaged or injured that some message of a forced landing could, and would have been, transmitted before, or after, the plane was on the water. Also, that if the plane were not damaged, with the sea experience of Commander Rodgers, the plane would have been kept afloat, and its course and drift so regulated that it could not pass unseen through any of the channels of the Hawaiian Islands . . . But if visibility in the rainsquall were bad, combined with the nervous tension of the pilots at that time, after twenty-four hours in the air, and worry over gasoline shortage; it is possible that a sudden loss of motors with a tail wind in a moderate, choppy sea might have caused a nose dive upon landing. In this unfortunate event, it is probable that with a damaged pontoon and injured personnel the plane went down.*

8:58 AM Hawaii Time

Although Labor Day was a holiday in Hawaii as well as on the Mainland, Masa rose early, intending to head to his office and catch up on paperwork. Entering the little kitchen to make tea for himself, he found Akiko sitting by the radio.

"Have you been awake long, Akiko?"

"Yes, Father. I . . . I didn't sleep well. I was hoping there would be some news this morning, but . . ." she faltered, "It is so hard, Father, this not knowing."

At a loss for words, Masa only nodded and reached out awkwardly to pat her shoulder. He made tea, and they sipped it together in silence, listening to the radio report. There was nothing new. At last, he stood to leave. "I'll be home by noon. You should try to take a nap." Akiko nodded halfheartedly, but stayed seated by the radio.

On his way to the office, Masa wracked his brain. He was determined to find some way to ease his daughter's pain, to distract her from the terrible suspense as hopes for the downed plane diminished. He was desperately worried about what would become of her should the worst come to pass. As he had many times before, he wished Hiroko were still alive. *Surely she would have known what to do for her child.* And then it came to him.

At the office, Masa found what he was looking for in a pile of magazines and unopened mail, and spent an hour preparing it for Akiko. Then, heartened by what he had hit upon, spent the rest of the morning taking care of business. When he had finished up the paperwork, he tucked his gift under his arm and hurried home.

He found Akiko in the kitchen by the radio, waiting for the noon news report.

"Anything this morning?"

"No father, nothing yet."

"Ah so." The words of comfort he had rehearsed in his mind on the way home suddenly felt hollow. Without fanfare or explanation, he placed the present on the table. "For you." Then he busied himself going through the day's mail. Akiko looked at her father, then at the large volume he had set down beside her. It was the current Sears catalogue. She saw that Masa had bookmarked a number of pages. Curious, Akiko opened to one of them and found herself staring at an assortment of babies' clothing.

"Oh, Father . . ."

"We must plan for the future now, Akiko. No matter what happens, you must be brave. Your Mr. John Rodgers would want no less for his child."

Akiko nodded, eyes bright with unshed tears.

2:05 PM Hawaii Time

The exhausted crew rallied, putting their faith in John and his navigational skills; they had no choice. The wind was constant and the sun shone brightly in the clear sky as the men pushed the plane as hard as they could, inching toward Kauai.

They all had another go at the rancid corned beef, this time trying to make it more palatable by cooking it on the wing, but the results were still unfit to eat. Gagging and spitting, the men weakly cursed anyone that had ever had anything to do with the wretched stuff.

After that dismal failure, Byron manned the helm, while Bill and Kiles spelled each other, either pounding on the plane's hull or sparking an SOS. Sparky lay motionless, moaning faintly, drifting in and out of consciousness.

John took another reading with the sextant and joined Byron in the copilot's seat. He was amazed to find that the Golden Plover had hardly moved from his original position on the flat-topped surface of the fuselage.

"Would you look at that? It's our very own living hood ornament!"

"Right, skip. I'd like to think it's a good omen. I mean, if he can make it all this way . . ."

"Roger."

As the seaplane sailed westward the two men began talking to their scrawny-legged, feathered hitchhiker. They appreciated the diversion. Sitting in the twin cockpit, John began to ramble on about his favorite bird.

"Did you know that Golden Plovers can't perch in trees? They live on the ground—do everything there—eat, mate, nest—usually in grassy areas and marshes. They use that needle-nosed beak to feast on worms and insects, and find their drinking water in small puddles, or from the moisture that collects on the underside of leaves in brackish shallows—" John stopped himself in mid-thought. "Wait a minute . . . The moisture under the leaves is from evaporation from the water below, like the rain cycle in the atmosphere . . . that's it!" John jumped from the copilot's seat and scrambled down to talk with Bill and Kiles.

"Guys—we need to make a still! We'll need a piece of metal or glass for the cover. We've got copper tubing in our spare parts, I think, and if not, maybe we can cannibalize some of the fuel lines. We'll need to find something to make a decent fire; something to burn. I bet this'll work."

Bill and Kiles immediately saw the possibilities. John unearthed a few feet of new copper tubing. He and Kiles removed the glass from one of the cockpit windscreens. Bill scrounged up some scraps of material to burn, and some engine oil. Then he studied the wooden framework in the lower wing.

"Skip, if we can strip alternate pieces from the wing, we can collect a fair-sized pile of kindling without weakening the wing structure. Whaddaya think?"

"I say give it a shot." And with that, Wild Bill set to work.

In the meantime, John and Kiles rigged the indispensable little bucket as a fire pit and modified one of the wide-mouthed empty water jugs to be suspended over the center of the bucket. The piece of glass was cleaned and positioned over the jug on a slight angle. A collection tray was fashioned by splitting a section of the copper tubing lengthwise. The tubing tray was then attached to the lower edge of the glass by carefully pinching it. A second section of tubing was set up to run from the collection tray to an empty coffee thermos standing next to the pail.

When they had completed the construction, they climbed out on the wing to help Bill collect kindling. Gathering strips from the rib sections was arduous work in their weakened condition. It took several hours, as they had to bring in the pieces one at a time while standing on the exposed ribs, similar to a high-wire act. They used jack lines and a harness again as Bill, Kiles, and John each took their turn out on the tightrope.

Once they had collected enough firewood, they wasted no time. They filled the jug with seawater and then started a fire in the bucket. They stoked the fire and carefully tended the contraption. As they watched, droplets of water eventually formed on the lower side of the glass. The droplets then turned into tiny rivulets that trickled into the collection tray and dribbled down the tube. Finally, at the base of the copper tube, pure distilled water started slowly dripping into the thermos. Success!

Two hours later, when the last of their firewood was burned, they had magically extracted almost a quart of fresh water. Dolling out meager rations in a small cup, each man marveled as they drank the lifesaving liquid. As Bill helped Sparky with his portion, John took Byron's share up to the cockpit.

"Thanks, skip."

"Will you look at that—our little hitchhiker's still with us."

Indeed, the magnificent speckled Golden Plover was standing in the same spot on the fuselage, staring straight at the disheveled pair as Byron sipped his precious water. Byron lifted his cup to toast the little traveler. As if in response, the bird bobbed his head twice, whistled a chipper "Tsu-eet!" and took off to the south. He was obviously headed to Oahu, unlike the valiant crew of the PN9.

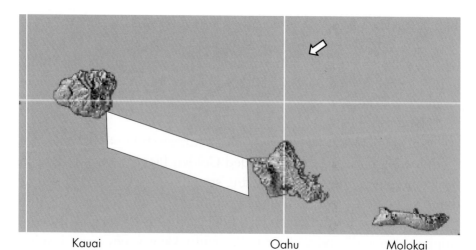

Kauai   Oahu   Molokai

The search area on September 7, 1925

The magnificent Pacific Golden Plover (or *Kolea*): This small but heroic and swift-flying aviator annually completes a 6,000-mile round trip from Hawaii to Alaska to mate and hatch their young. The nonstop migration takes them approximately seventy-two hours. They return to Hawaii each year to the same small parcel of land, which they dutifully defend from other plovers. They have been known to live for more than twenty years.

Males normally return to Hawaii in late July or early August. Females follow two to four weeks later. The newborn chicks, left in Alaska, must fend for themselves after the females leave. Amazingly, the surviving chicks manage to find their way to Hawaii by themselves; arriving in late September, early October.

The Pacific Golden Plover in fast flight

Sears, Roebuck and Co. catalogue from the 1920s. In 1925, Sears claimed to be the world's largest store. They sold everything from undergarments to toys to cars to houses. Although less than pristine, this image is the cover of a period Sears Roebuck catalogue.

Chapter 44

Tuesday—September 8, 1925

5:52 AM Pacific Time

As Admiral Moffett stared out the window of his suite in the early morning hours, the island of Alcatraz looked almost inviting. The solitude of the moment matched his overall sense of isolation. His staff no longer followed radio reports around the clock, catching catnaps when they could. Instead, for the past several days, they had taken to retiring to their own rooms for the night. This simple difference reflected the futility of the situation. Moffett couldn't blame them; the initial excitement of the search-and-rescue operation had devolved to utter boredom.

Moffett paced across the floor to the temporary comfort of the leather wing-backed chair and sat down heavily. He read through Commander Van Auken's report once again. Moffett should have anticipated the gist of the report, but he had hoped that Van Auken would somehow reinforce his own flagging optimism. This was obviously not the case. Van Auken's report was pragmatic and concise, exactly what Moffett would expect of a naval officer. Nonetheless, the admiral pored over the words for any hint of a reason to continue the search.

Moffett was expecting a couple of aides to join him momentarily, when he heard a knocking from the hall.

"Room service!"

The admiral heaved himself out of the chair and lumbered wearily across the room to open the door. A uniformed bellman entered carrying a tray loaded with breakfast, a silver pot of coffee, and a newspaper. Seeing that the dining table was still covered with a week's worth of maps and correspondence, the man set the tray on the coffee table, tipped his cap, and left. At this point, two of Moffett's aides entered and saluted sharply, fresh from a full night's sleep.

"Good morning, sir."

"Reporting for duty, sir."

Moffett responded, "At ease, gentlemen. Let's start the day, shall we?" And the three men set to work at the large dining table. Ignoring the dome-covered breakfast waiting for him, Moffett poured a cup of coffee and snatched the paper off the tray. To his dismay, the morning headline read, "HOPE IS GIVEN UP FOR RESCUE ALIVE OF FIVE AVIATORS." He growled, "Who the hell gave this quote?" He quickly scanned the attached article, then held it up to his aides in disgust, "Will you look at this? Now they're running editorial commentary as hard news headlines! That does it." He took a big gulp of the black coffee and barked, "Take down this message and get it off to Van Auken immediately."

6:18 AM Hawaii Time

Commander John Rodgers took his sunrise position fix as Byron manned the helm, and Kiles and Bill beat their staccato tattoo on the hull. The frequency of their hammering had decreased to half-hour intervals, as had the spark-set SOS attempts. Curled up in fetal misery, Sparky was completely incapacitated, so Bill and Kiles alternated radio duties. By now, between hunger, dehydration, and fatigue, all the men found even the simplest jobs daunting.

The latest position reports coming in over the radio chatter were the most depressing to date. The command of the search had been temporarily deeded to the *Langley* and overnight she had responded to yet another false sighting, this one west of Kauai. Consequently, the search area had been temporarily shifted beyond the Kauai Channel, moving the grid more than two hundred miles farther away.

There was some middling good news this morning. *Baby* had sailed well last night and had maintained almost five knots; a good speed, although the direction was somewhat problematic. John's calculations showed that they had been unable to steer to their goal of 265 degrees and had actually sailed at 261 degrees overnight. John knew this was not high enough. Their absolute minimum course was 265, and John would have preferred sailing above that course to—in sailing jargon—"put some in the bank." He knew that for every degree lost now, they would have to make up the difference later. Their course to steer now had to be at least 266 degrees—an almost impossible task.

6:40 AM Hawaii Time

The USS *Aroostook* was still docked at her berth in Pearl Harbor. Pacing impatiently on the bridge, Commander Van Auken ordered all onshore personnel immediately recalled. He made it very clear he wanted to be underway in twenty minutes. A half-hour later, and short some tardy crew, the *Aroostook* sailed past Hospital Point and out the narrow ship channel that fed Pearl Harbor. Van scanned the terse communiqué from Admiral Moffett once again. "Permission to continue search for one more day." Van had decided to interpret the message liberally, and continue the hunt through the next full day.

As soon as they were clear of the harbor entrance, Van pushed the seaplane tender to top speed—twenty-three knots—heading due west. The much faster destroyers, *Reno* and *Farragut*, followed soon after. They caught up with the *Aroostook* as they rounded Barbers Point on the southwest corner of Oahu, and the three ships headed north toward the Kauai Channel. Two hours later, they rejoined the *Langley* and the subs, and began patrolling the hundred-mile-wide waterway.

Van Auken resumed command and personally radioed all the other vessels involved in the search, requesting one last all-out effort. Replacing the microphone, he muttered to himself, "We've got to give them one more shot, even if it's like looking for a needle in a haystack."

9:42 AM Hawaii Time

A bleary-eyed pair sat in *Baby*'s twin cockpits, Byron at the helm and Rodgers beside him. Byron grumbled, "Sorry skip, there's just no way to sail the 266-degree course we need. This damn plane makes a lousy boat—she can't sail any angle much off a dead-downwind course. If we had a keel or even a dagger-board we might be able to reduce the side slip and point a bit, but . . ."

John knew just what he meant. A keel was a rigid, relatively flat piece of material anchored north/south to the lowest part of the hull. It allowed greater directional control and stability. A keel would act as foil, and use the forward motion of the boat to generate lift to counter the lateral force from the sails. A decent keel would also stabilize *Baby* and give her a pivot point to help the rudder.

"You're right there." Of course a keel was out of the question, but maybe . . . "Wait a minute!" John's eyes widened "What about a leeboard?"

Byron perked up at this. "How. . . ?"

"What if we tore up one of the floorboard sections and somehow secured it to the side of the fuselage?" John had left his seat before Byron could respond. Down in the cabin, John interrupted Kiles's drum solo and suggested his plan. Kiles immediately saw the possibilities. They enlisted Bill's help, and soon had a section of cross-braced aluminum, twelve feet long and four feet wide, standing on its side. With some of the still-unused wire rope, they rigged the floorboard with several lines.

John surveyed the outer side of *Baby*'s fuselage and determined the best way to secure the ungainly piece of metal to the side. Together, the three of them manhandled the floorboard out the main hatch behind the wings. John then had Byron weave the plane gently to slow her progress to a near-stop. John, Kiles, and Bill eased the aluminum slab vertically into the water until it was half-submerged. It took the better part of an hour to lash the exposed flooring tightly in place. Finally they stood back to survey their handiwork. Through cracked lips, Kiles pronounced, "Voilà! A leeboard, even if it isn't very pretty." Rodgers countered, "Beggars can't be choosers. Let's see if it helps."

Byron eased the plane from its downwind heading and broke into a huge grin as the makeshift leeboard immediately increased their point of sail. This would allow them to sail further up from the direction of the wind. The five-degree improvement in direction of sail produced a one hundred percent improvement in morale.

12:53 PM Hawaii Time

Masahiro Mikami stood quietly in the doorway of his little office and watched as Akiko sat at her desk, poring over the Sears catalogue. The radio was on low as time for the news at the top of the hour approached. The copy of that morning's *Honolulu Advertiser* occupied the wastepaper basket. It hadn't helped that right under the major headline on the front page, there was a feature about the Honolulu City Council voting to name the new airport after John Rodgers, in honor of the fallen hero.

But Masa was relieved to see that Akiko seemed to be pulling out of the terrible depression that had threatened to overwhelm her before she learned of her pregnancy. It had frightened him to see her sinking back into the shell she had become during her mother's long and agonizing death.

His goal now was to keep her focused on her future with the child she carried. Consequently he had encouraged her to go through the Sears catalogue and make lists of the things a newborn would need—and beyond that, to the items she might want to order in the years ahead. "You never know, Akiko," he would gently remind her, "You may discover things that you have not even thought of." The process seemed to help make the baby more real to her.

From where he stood, Masa cleared his throat, "It is time for lunch, Akiko. Would you like to go out to eat?"

Startled, Akiko looked up from the catalogue, "Oh, I think not, Father. The news will be on soon, and I am not hungry."

"You must eat, Akiko. Stay and listen to the broadcast. I will go find us something good and bring it back."

"Thank you, Father." With that, she went back to the catalogue, and finished writing down the specifics of the crib she had just selected.

1:00 PM Hawaii Time

Byron was still at the helm, Kiles had laid down to rest, and John had returned to the forward nav station to calculate what the increased angle of sail would mean. Wild Bill was on headsets at the radio and picked up a local Honolulu radio station's newscast. His jaw dropped open in shock as he heard, "Naval officials have given up hope of finding Commander Rodgers and his crew, and all search vessels have been recalled." Setting down the earphones, he stumbled forward to the navigation station.

As Bill burst in, John looked up, realizing too late that he had his glasses on. John sighed and removed the forbidden spectacles.

"What's the matter, Bill?"

Wild Bill swallowed his surprise at the glasses, and blurted, "Skip, I've just picked up a local report that says they're givin' up on us!"

"What?!"

"Local commercial broadcast out of Honolulu says all search vessels have been recalled."

Rodgers fought the rising panic with logic. "Bill, you're on headset—have you heard anything going back and forth between the ships that would confirm that report?"

Bill thought for a second and then brightened, "Nah, skip. I'm still pickin' up all kinds of chatter about the ongoing search—haven't heard beans from anyone out there about callin' it quits."

"Then we have to assume the local broadcast got it wrong. Let's us keep this between us, though. I don't think it's anything the rest of the crew needs to hear at this point."

"Aye, sir."

1:03 PM Hawaii Time

At her now-familiar station by the radio, Akiko knelt, white-faced and motionless. She had just heard the same report. Her body had gone numb, and one thought reverberated in her mind, keeping time with the pounding of her heart.

He's gone . . . he's gone . . . he's gone . . . !

4:36 PM Hawaii Time

Reviewing his records of the past week's search activity, Van came to the conclusion that they might have somehow overestimated the drift of the seaplane. Unwilling to abandon the throat of the Kauai Channel with so few ships, he radioed the *Langley* for air reconnaissance. After a brief discussion with her skipper, Van persuaded Commander Kenneth Whiting to send another patrol plane to search east of the present grid. As was later determined, in the late afternoon, that plane flew the closest anyone had been to the PN9 since the search began—but in an unbelievable twist of fate, a broken air-pressure line caused the small biplane to abort the search and return to the carrier posthaste.

At sunset, as the sky deepened into a fantastic palette of pinks, reds, and oranges, Van initiated a roll call check-in of all vessels and then announced, "Continue to maintain your search stations. Vigilant effort is required tonight and tomorrow, as the search will continue for twenty-four more hours." He released the microphone and muttered under his breath, "Will *only* continue for twenty-four more hours."

7:14 PM Hawaii Time

At *Baby*'s helm, Kiles Pope surveyed the spectacular sunset and murmured to himself, "Red sky at night, sailor's delight." Not surprisingly, no one else aboard the PN9-1 commented. They were all too drained.

Wild Bill copied the latest message from the *Aroostook* and handed it to Rodgers. John took the scribbled note and pulled his glasses from his shirt pocket. Surprised, Byron shot a glance at Bill, and then looked back at John, who calmly hooked the glasses over his large ears and read the message in the declining light. When he had finished it, he tucked his glasses back in his pocket and looked at his companions.

"Well, that's it. Just twenty-four more hours, and the grid's still almost two hundred miles away."

Byron shook his head, "At our best speed, we can only hope to sail 120 miles by sunset tomorrow." The mood was somber as the reality of their situation set in. Rodgers squared his shoulders, "Gentlemen, it's up to us now. If we're going to get home, it'll have to be under our own steam."

With Sparky curled up in the stern of the fuselage, the three men moved to the area just below the cockpit so Kiles could hear their discussion. The facts were brutally clear: the ever-elusive search grid would disappear entirely at sunset the next day. Their only hope now was to sail to Kauai, a two-day sail away. The unspoken certainty was that because of his acute dehydration, Sparky couldn't last two more days. The water they had so ingeniously distilled was all but gone, and there was no additional fuel with which to conjure more. While Oahu was tantalizingly close, even with their new leeboard and the best possible sailing conditions, they still couldn't make landfall there.

The men knew what lay before them. Silently, each confronted his own inner demons, praying that he could last two more days. As *Baby* sailed her course for Kauai, the talk turned to family and loved ones. For the first time since their ordeal had begun, the men discussed affairs of the heart.

Kiles spoke of his concern for his wife and kids. A staunch Catholic, he was comforted by his faith, and knew his wife would be too. Lilly was a rock, and their kids were tough, at least the older ones were, but he still worried how they would all handle life without him. He speculated about whether or not they would all move in with Lilly's parents. At least that way, his in-laws could help with the kids.

Byron wondered out loud whether he shouldn't have settled down by now, instead of always juggling several different girls at once. This might have normally elicited a round of good-natured razzing, but not under their present circumstances.

Considered by the group to be something of a rake, Wild Bill surprised them by confessing his love for Lei, the taller of the two Akana sisters. They had been dating for a year now, and while Bill had been in California, he had decided to ask her to marry him. After admitting his plans, he became upset that he had never shared his decision with Sparky. He headed aft to try to comfort his friend and tell him his news.

John was more reserved. Instead of talking about his feelings, he slipped away to his navigation cave. Once there, he removed his favorite, well-worn picture of Akiko standing barefoot on the sands of Kailua Beach; her long, shiny black hair flowing softly over her shoulder, constrained only by the hat with the pretty ribbon. On the back was the short inscription he knew by heart: John tightened his dry, cracked lips, and using one of the spare clothespins from the messenger line, clipped the picture to the edge of his chart table.

8:53 PM Hawaii Time

Akiko had been distraught since the terrible news she heard on the radio earlier that afternoon. Drawn and worn out from an afternoon of weeping, she had retreated to her room directly after a dinner she hadn't touched. Masa had tried in vain to suggest the report could have been mistaken, but she had been inconsolable. He felt helpless in the presence of her profound grief. He might have expected Akiko's lack of appetite. But what really worried him was that she hadn't turned on the radio all evening. She seemed convinced that all was lost.

Now Masa slumped in the hard-backed kitchen chair, an untouched cup of tea in front of him. In his concern for her, he had moved the radio to the kitchen table and turned it on as low as it would go. He sat mute and still as a statue of Buddha, listening for anything remotely hopeful. There was nothing.

10:09 PM Hawaii Time

In the dark, Kiles called out excitedly from the helm, and John quickly climbed into the copilot seat. "What's up?" Bill and Byron huddled directly below them. Kiles pointed to the left. "I think I see lights."

Placing the binoculars to his weary, reddened eyes, Rodgers scanned the portside horizon. Although actual pinpricks of light were not visible, the cloud cover reflected the aura of a faint electric glow, the first sign of life since the freighter they had seen a week ago. "Yep, that's Oahu's north shore," he said evenly.

"Skip, it's not that far!"

Rodgers shook his head, "I know it looks close, Kiles, but it's more than forty miles away."

Reluctant to accept the truth, Bill challenged, "Sir, are you sure there isn't *any* way we could make it?"

With the binoculars still glued to his eyes, John sighed, "I only wish, guys—I only wish."

The Honolulu Advertiser, September 8, 1925: The Rodgers headline mirrors the commonly accepted opinion that the plane sank soon after it landed. The sub-headline reflects concern over a possible U.S./Japan conflict. The second/third column article finds Colonel Billy Mitchell's opinion on the disparity in the numbers of United States aircraft compared to other major powers gaining some traction. He properly claimed that the United States was ranked eighth in airpower worldwide—right behind Poland. Specifically mentioned is the fact that Japan had a two-to-one numerical superiority in aircraft. The next to last column indicates that many people were rallying to Colonel Mitchell's defense.

Toys available in the 1925 Sears catalogue.

A home built sailboat with a leeboard attached amidships.

Chapter 45

Wednesday—September 9, 1925

7:21 AM Pacific Time

Admiral Moffett was surprised to receive word that the search had continued throughout the night, and it seemed from the tenor of the messages that Van Auken planned on having the fleet continue until sunset, "per your instructions." At first, Moffett considered correcting the misinterpretation and terminating the fiasco, but opted to let it pass. It would be over soon enough—and he had other issues to deal with.

When his staff assembled in the suite, the admiral sat them down and gave them what would be their final update.

"Gentlemen, I am afraid there is nothing new to report—nothing came in overnight. I will be calling off the search this evening, barring any new information to the contrary.

"I want you to know how much I appreciate your hard work and dedication. I am only sorry that the long hours you have diligently invested in this operation could not have been justified by a successful conclusion. You have earned a twelve-day leave, effective tomorrow. I expect you back in Washington by Monday, September twenty-first."

Moffett then focused on the most unenviable of tasks: condolence telegrams for the families of the crew—his second set in less than a week. As he dictated the sad messages to his aide, he did his best to craft the messages carefully, knowing the contents might eventually become family heirlooms. He put off Ethel Rodgers' telegram until last; it was by far the hardest. When he had finished, he ordered the telegrams held until the search was officially called off. He asked his aide to schedule one last press conference for Thursday morning, then retired to his bedroom to pack.

7:28 AM Hawaii Time

The cloud-fringed mountains of the Waianae range on the north-western side of Oahu had been clearly visible off Baby's port wing since sunrise. Their towering heights, peeking out from the cloud cover, had made the island seem even closer. The sight of land was both a blessing and a curse. It gave the men hope that they were not alone on the vast ocean, but it also made them wonder where their rescuers were. Worst of all, it was heartbreaking to sail away from the very visible Oahu toward the unseen island of Kauai.

Earlier that morning, Sparky had taken a turn for the worse. He had started shaking and mumbling incoherently. Bill had comforted him when he could, but was beginning to realize that without water, he would soon be dead. Wild Bill had tried to strain the water from the radiator again, but the result was even worse than before, and totally unfit to drink.

Knowing that today was the last day for their searchers, Bill had set to pounding out his primitive electrical SOS more frequently. John, Byron, and Kiles alternated piloting duties. When not at the helm, Byron and Kiles pounded on the hull in hopes of attracting a submarine, while John plotted and replotted their speed, position, and course.

As weak as they all were, they made yet another attempt to gain better steerage. The four men removed a second section of floorboard and secured it on the opposite side of the fuselage from their first leeboard. It helped to further stabilize the steering some, but did little to improve their angle of sail.

John had another concern. He knew they would lose sight of Oahu before Kauai ever came into view; such was the width of the channel.

He worried about how this would affect the morale onboard, as he knew that stretch in the watery void would be a serious test of faith.

8:03 AM Hawaii Time

Masa stood outside Akiko's bedroom door. It was not like her to oversleep. He tapped on the door lightly. "Akiko? Akiko, are you all right?" He could hear the rustle of bedclothes within, then her weak reply: "Father, I am sorry . . . I do not feel well. Please forgive me, but I do not think I will be able to come to work today." Masa thought quickly. He was not about to leave her alone.

"Ah. I, too, awoke feeling unwell. We shall stay at home today." Trying to lighten the situation, he added, "I believe the city of Honolulu will get along without us for one day, yes?"

There was no answer. Loosening his tie and collar, he sighed and shuffled back toward the kitchen.

4:46 PM Hawaii Time

As the day wore on, the sailors watched as the colors of Oahu faded into the distance. The afternoon clouds muted the greens of the Waianae Mountains, making them increasingly difficult to see. This was the period of time John was worried about. His most recent position fix had them still more than fifty miles from the eastern edge of the grid, thirty miles north of Oahu and ninety-five miles east of Kauai.

Retiring to the navigation station, John wrote at length in the ship's log. He wanted the record to survive, even if they did not. He did his best to describe all they had done to prevail during the course of the nine days since *Baby* had gone down. Although his writing style was concise and factual, as befit a naval officer, his indomitable spirit shone through. It was clear he truly believed they would somehow make landfall on Kauai.

He then wrote a short note to Akiko:

My darling Akiko,

If I should die without seeing you again, know that my last conscious thoughts will have been of you, and the joy you have brought into my life. I will always love you.

John

He sealed the letter in a small white envelope and printed "Akiko Mikami" in his artistic block letters across the front. He secured both the letter and the log book in the sextant's waterproof box, then attached a three-foot section of stiff wire rope as an antenna and tied on a small piece of white shirt cloth as a flag. He placed the box on the dashboard of the navigation cockpit so that it would float free should the plane sink. As John turned and made his way back to the main cabin, the late afternoon sunlight streamed through the opening of the cockpit, dramatically spotlighting the box.

At sunset, the radio crackled to life once more. Bill removed his headset, and put the announcement on the small speaker so that all onboard could hear. Ironically, the signal was the strongest yet, and the familiar voice of Commander W. R. Van Auken came through loud and clear.

"Attention all U.S. Navy vessels and all ships assisting in locating downed U.S. Navy seaplane PN9-1. Be advised that this officially concludes the search. All vessels are hereby ordered to return to port or resume original assignments. Thank you for your assistance. That is all." And then came the sound of a solo bugle, playing "Taps."

7:31 PM Hawaii Time

The clouds had begun to build in the twilight skies as the *Aroostook, Langley, Farragut,* and *Reno* headed south for Pearl Harbor, and the two subs resumed their prior patrols. In his captain's quarters onboard the

Aroostook, Commander Van Auken sat alone with his thoughts. It had been nine days since the rescue attempt began, and more than eight since anyone had heard from the missing crew. The search had covered literally thousands of square miles without a sign of any part of the PN9. Van was convinced they had done everything possible. Rodgers and his crew were gone. There was just no way they could have missed them.

Now Van faced another tough but necessary job. He dictated a curt message for Admiral Moffett. "Effective 19:40 HST search for missing plane PN9-1 terminated. Results negative. Crew presumed dead. All vessels released." A palpable sense of failure hung in the air as the ships sailed away.

The flotilla had hardly left the Kauai Channel when the weather began to change. At first the temperature dropped, and the wind slowed to a whisper. The seas calmed and became a sparkling black mirror, reflecting the harvest moon. Before long, though, ominous clouds blocked out the moon and stars, turning the entire area into an ink-black void. As the storm gathered, the clouds became charged with static electricity. All hell was about to break loose.

7:56 PM Hawaii Time

Onboard their seaplane-turned-sailboat, the crew of the PN9-1 sat in stunned silence. Van Auken's announcement and the playing of "Taps" had cast a tangible pall. Their lips were cracked and sunburned, their throats were parched, and their tongues swollen and heavy. Their thirst was unbearable.

As the skies darkened into night, they could smell the pungent scent of negative ions as the storm approached. Watching the pregnant clouds roil in the angry skies, the men were afraid to speak their hopes for rain, for fear that would somehow jinx them. John finally broke the silence. "We need to be ready, just in case." Each of them knew exactly what he was talking about. Shirts and rags were placed at the ready, as were containers of all shapes, from the cracker tin to the precious bucket.

In the calm before the storm, the breeze died altogether and *Baby* slowed to a stop, bobbing erratically in the gentle swells. Suddenly the ominous quiet was shattered as the sky lit up with a series of ferocious lightening bolts. Ear-shattering thunderclaps crashed all around them as the clouds let loose with a furious, drenching downpour. The excited crew scurried about in the miraculous deluge, leaving the helm unmanned. The raindrops were as big and heavy as copper pennies, quickly washing the crusted salty residue from the wing and fuselage surfaces. The job of gathering water became reasonably easy, despite the men's feeble condition. They filled every vessel to the brim, drinking at will and even pouring out some of the first liquid caught to replace it with cleaner water.

While it was still raining, Wild Bill carried one of the thermos bottles to Sparky. He carefully trickled some water into his buddy's mouth and then gently washed his face. In response to the life-giving liquid, Sparky's eyes fluttered open. Through cracked and peeling lips he managed to murmur, "Thanks pal." Seeing that Sparky was conscious and able to swallow, Bill continued to pour small amounts of water between his lips. Then, after drinking more himself, Bill raced back to top off the thermos bottle once again.

As Bowlin reappeared, Rodgers shouted over the storm, "How's Sparky?"

Bill yelled back, "He ain't outta the woods yet, skip, but you can bet this storm saved his life!"

Kiles and Byron tried to funnel some of the pouring rain into one of the empty 55-gallon fuel drums. In their excitement, though, they failed to scrub the drum well enough first, and the small amount of water they managed to collect was tainted. However, by the time the rain subsided, the crew had collected enough water in clean containers to last them several more days. They had also been blessed with a much-needed, invigorating cold shower, and their spirits were high.

When the rain had stopped, the men secured the water they had collected in creative ways. They didn't want the rocking of the plane to reduce their reservoirs, so they created gimbals from the extra wire rope and suspended open-topped containers inside the cabin; the containers could swing with the plane's motion, minimizing spillage. Closed containers were carefully stacked inside the partially cleansed fuel drum.

As fortuitous as the storm had been, once it had passed, they were left in the doldrums. The sea was like glass and there was no wind at all, not even the whisper of a breeze. *Baby* was dead in the water. They all realized that the rain had been a lifesaver, but now they needed the wind back if they were to avoid drifting through the now-unguarded channel, and make landfall on Kauai.

The September 9, 1925 *Honolulu Advertiser:* By now, news of the search for the PN9-1 has been reduced to a small fourth column article report on the continuing efforts of the navy to find Rodgers and crew.

BEGINNING OF THE LAST FLIGHT OF THE PN-9 No. 1

The September 9, 1925 *Honolulu Star-Bulletin:* The caption at the top of this picture speaks volumes. Honolulu had come to the conclusion that Rodgers and crew were dead. The picture shows the PN9-1 leaving San Francisco and flying through the Golden Gate.

Memorial to Rodgers and Crew Proposed

Only the headline can be read in this image of an Associated Press story from September 9, 1925: A San Francisco city official proposed that a memorial be constructed to honor Commander John Rodgers and the crew of the PN9-1.

Chapter 46

Thursday—September 10, 1925

7:40 AM Pacific Time

Admiral Moffett showered and shaved for the last time at the Olympic Club. He dressed in a starched white shirt and freshly cleaned uniform jacket, replete with gold bands and ribbon boards. His uniform slacks had a razor crease, and his shoes were immaculately polished. Moffett saw his duty clearly, and was prepared to face the press one last time. It was his intention to leave for Washington immediately after his press conference, and face whatever music might be waiting for him there as well.

His previously written condolence telegrams had been sent late last night after he received Van Auken's final transmittal. He wanted the families to receive them before the general public got wind that the search had been called off. He imagined that they had all been delivered by now.

He eased himself once more into the maroon wing-back leather chair to review his prepared statement. As he underlined his points of emphasis, he wondered absently if this would be his last official speech. Once back in Washington, it was altogether possible he would be reassigned, demoted, or even asked to resign. It had been ten days since the PN9s had taken off, and a week since the *Shenandoah* disaster—ten harrowing days that might well be the death knell for naval aviation.

Checking his watch, Moffett stood heavily and crossed the room to call the front desk for a bellhop to pick up his suitcases. He made a final tour of the suite to make sure nothing had been overlooked when his staff had packed up the night before. All seemed in order. Once his luggage had been collected, Moffett picked up his attaché case, squared his shoulders, and strode purposefully down the hall to the now-familiar stairwell and the lynch mob waiting below.

7:55 AM Hawaii Time

Masa was up and dressed in his customary dark suit. He sat silently in the kitchen, drinking his tea. He was running late for work, but Akiko hadn't risen yet and he didn't want to leave her alone. Then he heard Akiko running water in the bathroom. He padded quietly down the hall and knocked gently on the door, "Akiko, are you feeling well enough for work today?"

A very quiet "Yes, Father," came from within.

"Good. I, too, am better today. We will go when you are ready."

"I will not be long, father."

With that, Masa returned to the little kitchen and poured himself more tea. He turned on the radio and lively music filled the tiny room. It seemed out of place, but he left it on. By the time he had finished his tea, Akiko appeared at the kitchen door, pocketbook in hand, dressed and ready to leave.

"No tea, Akiko?"

She shook her head, murmured "No, thank you, Father," and walked toward the front door. Masa placed his teacup in the sink, turned off the music, and followed her out. As they waited for the bus, Akiko was quiet. They had missed the morning news report. Perhaps it was just as well.

8:52 AM Hawaii Time

Onboard *Baby*, the crew had been revitalized by the deluge the night before. Even Sparky showed marked signs of recovery, although he was still too weak to do much besides sleep. Rodgers allowed the men to drink their fill of water. He felt confident they had more than enough to last for several days, and if they hadn't made landfall on Kauai by then, water would be the least of their problems. The crew went back to working the spark set and pounding the hull with vigor. On his breaks, Bill continued to minister to Sparky.

At 9 AM, John recorded in the log that the trade winds had returned an hour ago, and the shell of a seaplane was sailing her proper course at almost four knots. The swells were listed at a modest two-to-four feet. John also noted some personal observations: *Oahu is no longer visible—cloud cover makes it impossible to determine whether this is because of distance or weather. A quiet tension has fallen over the crew since we lost sight of the island and are again on our own in the vast Pacific.*

Several squalls obscured the horizon, making it more difficult for John to navigate. His first fix of the morning had scared him, as it indicated they would never lay Kauai. To his relief, an immediate reshoot with the sextant proved his first figures to be incorrect. Although *Baby* was still not heading quite high enough, she was holding close to their intended course. It would be touch and go.

The restless crew strained to see the impossible—beyond the curvature of the earth. It was as if they hoped that John's calculations could somehow move them magically closer to the island of Kauai. John continued to take additional sights, both to try and ease the crew's worries, as well as to diminish his own doubts. Each plot was painstakingly recorded in the plane's log book, and after each entry John carefully secured the log back in the watertight box—hoping that, if nothing else, the chronicle of their saga would survive.

The radio was eerily quiet now that the search had been disbanded. Bill switched it over to one of the two commercial Oahu stations, and an eclectic mix of music came from the small speaker. When it was time for the 9 AM news report, the Honolulu announcer's voice rang loud and clear as he read from his prepared script. "The navy has disbanded the intensive search for Commander John Rodgers and his four-man crew. The navy last heard from the aviators on September first, as they neared completion of an historic nonstop transpacific crossing." The announcer continued with a brief description of the mission and then proceeded to launch into short eulogies for each of the five sailors. The men were dumbstruck. Each, in turn, listened to his life boiled down to a few sentences, for better or worse.

When the announcer completed his final tribute, that of Commander John Rodgers, he concluded with, "May they all rest in peace." As the men stared in shock at the little speaker, Wild Bill broke the tension. Grinning like a madman, he yelled at the radio, "Not yet, damn it! Not yet!"

9:08 AM Hawaii Time

When the bus deposited Masahiro and Akiko at their downtown destination, Masa bought his daily newspaper. A quick review of the front page showed that the PN9 story had all but evaporated from the news. He folded the paper quickly and tucked it under his arm.

The little overhead bell thudded flatly as Masa and Akiko entered the office. Masa made a mental note to get a ladder later and see what was wrong with it. Akiko turned on the radio, and then silently slipped behind her desk and busied herself with the mail. Masahiro stood watching his daughter for a moment. She seemed paler than normal, but surely that was not unusual, given the circumstances. With a sigh and a tiny shake of his head, he headed into the back office.

1:52 PM Central Time

"Sir, your newspapers."

Colonel Billy Mitchell looked up as Lieutenant Smith placed a pile of assorted editions in front of him and saluted.

"At ease, Lieutenant. What's the latest?"

Pointing to the top paper, Smith replied, "Sir, the Washington, D.C. press is having a field day. The overdue acknowledgement of Commander Rodgers' death has been one more log for the fire. Inside there are both editorial and public cries for a complete overhaul of our aeronautical defense programs."

"Good—that's good!"

Pulling one folded paper from the stack, Smith continued. "Sir, this article picked up on your concern that the U.S. air forces are lagging miserably behind France, Russia, England, Germany, Italy, and Japan. And that most U.S. military aircraft are outdated and poorly maintained. Here, look, they even repeated your quote, 'The birthplace of winged flight is a second-rate air power.'"

"The public will never stand for that. America wants to be first in everything. Lieutenant, this is all very good."

"Uh, yes sir." There was a meaningful pause, and Smith lowered his gaze, clearly uncomfortable. "There's, uh, well, I'm afraid there's more, sir."

Mitchell prompted impatiently, "Very well, Lieutenant. Out with it."

Lieutenant Smith responded cautiously, "Sir, there's talk. Talk about your comments from the press conference."

"Well, I would hope so," Mitchell said.

"Sir, if I may speak frankly?"

Mitchell nodded brusquely, and Smith continued, "Sir, your idea for a single air corps is not getting the traction we'd hoped. It seems the public is calling for better aircraft, but for all the services."

Sensing still more, Mitchell probed, "And . . . ?" Another pause. Mitchell looked Smith in the eye and barked, "Dammit, give it to me straight, Lieutenant!"

"Sir, there is talk of insubordination. Some of the brass feel you overstepped your authority, kicking the navy when they were down." As his superior glared, Smith reluctantly continued, "And they believe your statements denigrated the abilities of the aviators at a time when they should have been eulogized instead."

Mitchell placed both hands on his desk and leaned forward, hanging his head briefly in frustration.

"That was not my intention. I knew those navy flyers were qualified, but I had to wake up the brass and the goddamned politicos! Now you say I've alienated them instead?" Mitchell lifted his head and fixed his aide with a steely gaze. "Don't tell me there's more."

"Colonel, your treason comment . . . Sir, I'm afraid there's talk of a court-marshal."

10:00 AM Hawaii Time

Masahiro was deep in concentration, fitting a set of bifocal lenses into a new frame, when he heard the news come on the radio. Frozen at his counter, he listened as the announcer reported that the search for the missing PN9 had officially been called off. Masa bowed his head as the announcer began the brief eulogies for each crewman. After the final tribute to Commander John Rodgers, Masa heard an anguished wail from the front room. He hurried from his office in time to see Akiko struggling to her feet in front of the radio. Ashen faced, she backed slowly away, shaking her head and pointing an accusing finger at the console. Wracking sobs welled up from deep within her.

She had shifted her office chair out of place earlier, to move to her post on the floor in front of the console. Now, as Masa watched in horror, she backed into it, knocking it over. Struggling to keep her balance, she twisted, then fell heavily on top of it and rolled to the floor. Too late, Masa rushed in to help. Trying to calm his daughter, Masa cradled her where she lay. When she seemed to quiet a bit, he murmured,

"Come. Come, Akiko, let me get you over to the chair. Do you think you can stand?"

She nodded numbly, and Masa struggled to lift her to her feet. Her slight frame felt oddly heavy. As Masa maneuvered Akiko over to the waiting room chair, she continued to weep softly. He managed to set her down gently, and had just started to fetch her a glass of water, when, without warning, she gasped, emitted a low moan and slipped unconscious to the floor in a heap. A crimson stain began to spread from under her skirt.

Placing a seat cushion under her head and a patient drape over her to keep her warm, Masa did his best to make Akiko comfortable on the floor. Then he raced off to find Dr. Lee.

10:23 AM Hawaii Time

The crew struggled to keep *Baby* on course. The wind had stayed light but consistent all morning, and they were now pacing at just under three knots. The unremitting question, though, was whether they could sail high enough to make landfall on Kauai.

The ocean seemed more desolate than ever, and the vast emptiness fueled their frustration. However, they all understood that now it was up to them to save themselves.

10:35 AM Hawaii Time

A grave-faced Dr. Lee stood in the front office with Masahiro. He had just finished with Akiko, who was conscious and resting in her father's office.

"I'm afraid she has miscarried. Her nervous anxiety, the shock of the news this morning, and the fall—any one of these could have caused her to lose the baby. With all three together, it would have been a miracle had she not. Well . . ." The old family doctor trailed off, tactfully leaving unspoken that he thought it might be for the best. He continued, "I'll prescribe a sedative. Try to keep her calm and quiet. I'd like to see her in my office on Monday for a follow-up examination."

Masa nodded, "Is there anything she should do in the meantime?"

"Make sure she gets plenty of fluids, and see that she eats. Give her some time before you take her home. She needs to rest."

"Yes, doctor."

"Very well, then, Masahiro, I will see the two of you on Monday."

"Thank you, Dr. Lee. Thank you for coming."

Masa escorted his old friend to the door and bowed respectfully as he left. Then he took a deep breath and steeled himself for Akiko's grief.

Entering his office, he found her curled up on the reclining patients' chair where Dr. Lee had examined her. She looked very small and pale. He called her name softly.

"Akiko . . . ?"

She didn't respond. He moved closer to the chair and touched her shoulder lightly. Still no response. She simply stared straight ahead. Masa cleared his throat and tried again.

"My child, Dr. Lee has said you must rest. You must take some nourishment. I will go out and see if Mrs. Katsumoto will sell me some chicken broth from her restaurant. Does that sound good?"

There was only the slightest flicker of recognition from Akiko at this. Masa interpreted it as a "Yes." Patting her tentatively, he said "I will go, then. It should not take long. You rest here."

Akiko nodded almost imperceptibly, then she turned her face away.

10:38 AM Hawaii Time

As Wild Bill sparked the rudimentary semaphore, Kiles took his turn banging on the hull. John climbed into the copilot's seat next to Byron for a private conversation. "We should be able to see Kauai soon."

"Skipper, all this damn cloud cover isn't making that easy."

"I know. I know. But keep your eyes peeled. Maybe in an hour or so."

"Skip, do you really think we can make it?"

With a confidence he was far from feeling, John replied, "Yeah. Yeah, I do."

12:29 PM Hawaii Time

Carefully balancing the glass mason jar of chicken broth from Mrs. Katsumoto's restaurant kitchen, Masa unlocked the office door.

"Akiko? Aki-chan, I am back." His call was met by silence. Perhaps she was sleeping.

As quietly as he could he walked into his office. There he found the patient drape neatly folded on the reclining chair, which had been restored to its upright position. The bathroom was empty and the back door was closed. On his desk, a white business envelope sat on top of the Sears catalogue, simply addressed to "Father." Akiko was gone.

2:30 PM Pacific Time

In San Francisco, Admiral Moffett's train pulled out of the 4th and King Street Station on time. He was traveling alone in so many ways. After changing into civilian clothes in his private Pullman-car compartment, he made his way to the club car and found a seat. He decided against reading the newspaper the porter offered, and instead lit his pipe and stared out the window as the train trundled out of the busy city. Emotionally and physically drained, he was eager to put the past week and a half behind him. He hoped the anonymous privacy of the transcontinental train trip would provide him some respite.

12:32 PM Hawaii Time

After reading Akiko's note, Masahiro chastised himself for leaving her alone for so long. If only the restaurant hadn't been so busy. He hurried to the front door, threw it open and searched the street in both directions. There was no sign of her. Turning around, he flipped the shop sign from *Open* to *Closed,* and shut the door. In his hurry, he forgot to lock it, and never noticed that the little bell had not rung at all. Jamming the note into his pocket, he again scanned the street. He caught sight of a sampan bus crossing an intersection several blocks away, and suddenly he had a good idea where Akiko would have gone to mourn. He scurried to the Bishop Street sampan stop. There were already a number of people waiting, but none of them Akiko. *She must have caught an earlier one.* Masahiro anxiously joined the queue.

Moments later, a rickety black, pink, and purple sampan bus approached and juddered to a stop. As soon as the passengers had squeezed tightly onto the facing benches, the modified Model-T truck pulled away from the curb.

After dropping a Chinese woman carrying two large sacks loaded with fresh vegetables off at Punchbowl, and a Filipino couple off at the base of Pacific Heights Drive, they were soon puttering up the wandering road into Nuuanu Valley. Masahiro's anxiety intensified as they climbed unsteadily towards the Pali, but his concern for Akiko eclipsed his fear of heights. This time he willed the bus to go even faster.

1:24 PM Hawaii Time

Another multihued sampan bus that had left Honolulu shortly after noon chugged to a stop in Kailua. A petite female passenger hung back until the other passengers had disembarked, and then climbed unsteadily down the two stern-mounted steps, clutching whatever she could find for support. Uncharacteristically oblivious to the concerned driver's parting "Aloha," Akiko wandered silently away, her face streaked with the tears that had trickled nonstop along the lonely trip. Her straw hat sat slightly askew atop her raven hair. She carried her small pocketbook in both hands in front of her waist, as she made her way toward the beach.

3:26 PM Pacific Time

Ethel Rodgers stepped daintily from the cab in the Hollywood business district. She marched into the new Art Deco office building. Extinguishing her lipstick-stained cigarette, she pushed the button to summon the elevator with a carefully manicured index finger. When the doors slid open, she stepped onboard, barely acknowledging the uniformed elderly operator. "Fourth floor," was all she said as he worked the brass lever to close the doors again.

Ethel exited the elevator and turned left. Her high heels clicked sharply on the polished concrete floor, reverberating sharply as she marched down the hall to the last office on the left. The frosted glass in the doorframe read, Thomas John Weigand, Esq., Attorney at Law.

In short order, Ethel was seated across from her lawyer at the conference room table. All business now, she passed the pale-yellow telegram to him.

"Here. The navy finally came to their senses."

Reading the abbreviated message, her attorney replied, "Mrs. Rodgers, this won't make any difference in your settlement."

Barely concealing her irritation, Ethel retorted, "I know *that*. The point is, how long will it take for me to collect John's insurance?"

Masking his surprise, Weigand responded, "Didn't my secretary reach you?"

"No, I haven't been at home all day."

"Mrs. Rodgers—Ethel—John hasn't been officially declared dead yet, and the judge ruled on your divorce decree earlier today. That's why I thought you were coming in. As a divorcee, you don't have any claim on John's survivor benefits. His insurance has been otherwise assigned."

1:47 PM Hawaii Time

To Masahiro, the trip through the pass and down the mountain was a blur. They rocked their way past the wind and switchbacks at the top, and the road slid down into the tropical gardens. Once the sampan was on more level terrain, Masahiro caught his breath and unfolded Akiko's note to read it yet again. Her words chilled him.

> *Dearest Father,*
>
> *You have been so kind and understanding. I am sorry if I have disappointed you. Please forgive me for any disgrace I*

may have brought on you or our family, but the man I love
was worth risking everything. Thank you for the catalogue
but we will not be needing it now that I have lost our baby.

Your loving daughter,

Akiko

1:54 PM Hawaii Time

To John's concern, an hour had stretched to almost three-and-a-half, and they still hadn't spotted Kauai. Just when the anxiety onboard had become almost unbearable, Byron called out, "I think I see land!" and the smudged gray volcanic peaks of Kauai emerged just above the clouds. As the makeshift sailboat drew ever closer, the sun broke through the mist and the island gained some color. Soon the tall green summit of Kawaikini came into clear view, right where John said it would be. The crew was all smiles, pumping John's hand and slapping his back. Wild Bill toasted Rodgers with a cup of water and led the men in a rousing three-cheer salute. They all applauded happily.

John repaired to his navigation station, recorded the time of the sighting, and took a position fix. He calculated they were twenty-two miles due east of Nawiliwili, the main port located on the southeastern corner of the Garden Isle. Unfortunately, John now had something new to worry about, and it was a serious problem. He tried crunching the numbers once again.

1:57 PM Hawaii Time

The afternoon sun was warm and the breeze was gentle. A calm, sapphire-blue sea lapped playfully at the smooth, ivory-white, crescent-shaped beach. Occasional coconut palms leaned longingly toward the surf. To anyone unfamiliar with the vagaries of the windward climate, it would be hard to believe this peaceful scene had been the same blustery beach of four days ago. Akiko, however, was oblivious to the weather.

She shed her shoes, leaving them in the sand near the start of the path to the ocean. When she reached the water's edge, she turned left and walked barefoot in the damp sand, seeming not to notice as the waves lapped at her tiny feet. After a bit, she stopped, opened her purse, and pulled out two well-worn photographs.

The first was a sepia-toned, hand-colored print of her mother as a young woman. In it, Hiroko was dressed in a traditional Japanese kimono. Except for the obvious age of the photograph, it looked as if she might have been Akiko's sister. Akiko kissed the image and slipped the photo back into her pocketbook.

The second photograph, although much more recent, showed even more signs of wear and tear. The scalloped edges of the black-and-white Kodak print had been worn smooth by loving hands. The image was of her Mr. John Rodgers on this very beach. Tears coursed down Akiko's cheeks as she caressed the print, then held it to her bosom.

2:02 PM Hawaii Time

Returning to the cabin, John called the crew together.

"Men, we've got a problem. Nawiliwili is twenty-two miles away at 271 degrees. We should be able to hold that course, but at our present rate of speed, we won't make the harbor entrance until well after dark." The men looked uneasily at each other. Wild Bill shrugged. "What's so bad about that, Skip? Can't we sail 'er in at night?"

John shook his head ruefully. "The entrance to Nawiliwili Harbor is only about fifty yards wide, with a half-mile-wide strip of razor-sharp coral on either side. The surf crashes onto the leading edge of the reef, rolls across the shallow surface, and slams smack into the lava cliffs. Even if we could somehow steer straight enough to navigate the entrance, the channel itself is a nightmare. It takes a ninety-degree left, followed a hundred yards later by a ninety-degree right, and you know we can't sail those angles."

Byron spoke up, "So give it to us straight, skipper, what are you saying?"

"I'm saying there's no way we can attempt to enter that harbor at night. We'd be cut to ribbons. It'll be hard enough to do it in daylight, and we'll need help even then."

Silence fell like a dense fog as the reality sunk in.

"I'm sorry, men, but we've got to slow our approach radically so that we don't turn *Baby* into kindling during the night."

True to the grit they had shown thus far, the crew took action. Byron spun the plane around to face the wind once more, and the bucket was again rigged to the bow as a sea anchor. Then Bill and Kiles climbed out onto the skeleton frame of the lower wing and furled *Baby's* improvised sails. As expected, the plane slowed in response, and the men resigned themselves to yet one more night at sea.

2:07 PM Hawaii Time

Twenty minutes later, Masahiro's sampan bus stopped at the now-familiar intersection in the little town of Kailua. Desperately hoping that his hunch was right, Masa quickly descended from the back of the bus and headed straight for the beach lane he and Akiko had trod only a few days before. He shuffled quickly down the ironwood-lined path that opened onto the calm, picturesque vista.

Masa's relief was palpable when he saw Akiko's petite sandals carefully placed at the head of the path. *She is here!* As he struggled out onto the soft sand, he decided to head to the left as they had done previously. After ten sinking steps, he threw dignity to the wind. Abruptly sitting down on the sand, he quickly pulled off his shoes and socks and returned, placing them carefully by the *naupaka* bushes next to Akiko's sandals. Then he hurried down the wide beach to find his daughter.

2:09 PM Hawaii Time

After walking almost two miles of nearly deserted Kailua Beach, Akiko felt suddenly woozy and stopped to rest. Looking out to sea, she thought she caught sight of something white that appeared to be floating some distance from shore. Mistrusting her tear-blurred vision, she carefully placed Rodgers' photograph safely back in her pocketbook. When she turned her attention back to the object she had seen bobbing out in the water, it was gone. She blinked hard and rubbed her eyes. There it was again. It seemed to be beckoning her.

Dropping her hat and purse on the deserted beach, Akiko waded slowly into the surf, oblivious to the currents that dragged at her skirt. When the water reached her waist, she stood on her tiptoes and jumped as the waves rolled past her towards the shore. Whatever the thing was, there was something oddly familiar about its puffy, square shape. And then it disappeared behind a wave, as if teasing her. *What . . . ?* She shook her head to try and clear her mind; and there it was, now shimmering a little above the sapphire blue.

She leaned into the next wave and started to swim toward the elusive object. The sea around her felt warm and soothing as she stroked farther and farther out. The incandescent white square danced just a few swells ahead of her now.

As long-repressed memories flooded back, she suddenly recognized Hiroko's special pillow—the one she had used when her mother had begged her to end her suffering. *What in the world is it doing out here?* To her surprise, Akiko found this discovery comforting, and continued to swim toward the vision.

The September 10, 1925 *Honolulu Advertiser:* All hope is finally gone for the rescue of John Rodgers and crew. The single related article notes that two life preservers were found two hundred miles south of Honolulu, near Hilo on the Big Island. These were later shown to be not from the PN9-1, as she carried no life preservers of any kind.

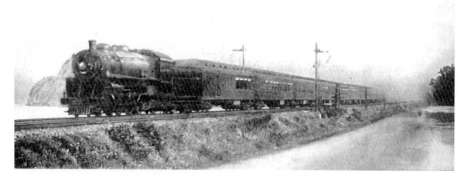

A Union Pacific train, circa 1925

Pullman compartment

Chapter 47

Thursday—September 10, 1925

2:22 PM Hawaii Time

As *Baby* continued to drift toward Kauai, Rodgers realized that as useful as the makeshift bucket sea anchor had been, it was not slowing their progress enough. They were being pulled along by a current that grew stronger as they approached the island—and it was sucking them toward the throat of the channel.

"Kiles, Bill—at the rate this current's got us accelerating, we'll be on the rocks or too far south before sunrise."

Bill spoke first. "Gotta do better than the bucket, Skip. Somethin' bigger, heavier . . ."

Kiles brightened. "How about one of these fuel tanks? They're sure big and heavy."

John nodded. "I think that's the ticket. Let's fall to."

At that, the three of them set to tearing apart one of the empty tanks, feverishly banging and swearing as they wrestled with the stubborn metal in their efforts to cut away a section and punch holes in it. In their distracted state, none of them noticed at first that Sparky had gone back to manning his battery-powered Jacob's ladder. When Bill saw what Sparky was up to, he tried to get him to lie back down, but Sparky would have none of it. Bill shrugged, glad that his friend was feeling well enough to help, and returned to the job at hand.

When they had finished, Bill, John, and Kiles manhandled the large partial drum out onto the fuselage and attached it to a three-sided bridle. The bridle was tied to a mooring line, and the line was, in turn, secured to a forward cleat. They pushed the cumbersome contraption off the bow as the plane slid backward down a swell. Kiles stood poised with a knife, ready to cut the line if the tank jeopardized the plane. When the line to the new anchor became taut, the bow of the plane dipped suddenly, and Kiles started to saw the line. John called him off, and as if on command, the bow rose with the next swell. It was working. They had managed to slow the plane to a crawl.

John was pleased, but had further concerns that he chose not to share with the rest of the crew. Instead he recorded them in the log book. *As we slow the drift, the current might still push us too far south. If that happens we could overshoot the southeast corner of the island. This would mean certain death for all souls onboard.*

4:01 PM Hawaii Time

By now, *Baby* drifted stern first, pointed into the wind and current and facing away from Kauai, which was still nearly twenty miles away. The large sea anchor had slowed their drift rate to under a knot. With his eyes glued on their destination, Wild Bill observed, "Ironic, ain't it, Skip? Yesterday we couldn't get *Baby* to move fast enough, and today, we're doin' everything we can to hold 'er back."

For the first time in ten days the plane didn't need someone on helm duty, as the light trades and the new sea anchor worked together to keep her on track. The crew took turns manning the spark-gap transmitter; even Sparky insisted on taking short stints. The men also continued to drum on the hull, though they knew the subs had been dismissed, on the off chance that one was still around. When not on duty, they could be found standing on the fuselage, staring wistfully at the cloud-shrouded peaks of the lush, emerald-green island visible off the stern.

While John was on such a break, an idea struck him.

He called back to the crew on duty, "Gentlemen, Nawiliwili Harbor's home to a small fleet of fishing boats. Most are just weekenders, but I bet at least a couple try to make a living at it. They just might be returning home about now. It's worth trying to signal." Byron was instantly on John's wavelength.

"That little bucket's free now—let's use it as a smudge pot." Wild Bill disappeared to scrounge scraps of material to burn. When he'd deposited them in the bucket, John dripped some oil from the crankcase of the starboard engine on top of them and set the gooey mess alight. A dark black choking smoke billowed forth and trailed distinctly behind the rudder.

Stepping back to survey their latest effort, John said "Looks great, all right. Sure hope someone out there sees it."

4:12 PM Hawaii Time

Released from the search the day before, the U.S. submarine R-4 had resumed its normal patrol of the Hawaiian Islands. It was cruising on the surface, heading north due east of Kauai, when the radio operator suddenly picked up an anomaly. He thought it sounded like metal banging on metal. Recognizing it as an SOS, and knowing that they had been hoping for days to hear just such a signal, the radio operator instantly reported to Lieutenant Junior Grade W. S. Price.

"Sir, I've got an SOS and it's loud as hell. It sounds like someone is tearing a ship apart."

"Do you have a directional fix?"

"Aye, sir." And he wrote it down.

Price grabbed the note and his cap and climbed the ladder out onto the conning tower to relay their finding to the skipper, Lieutenant Donald R. Osborne. Armed with the coordinates and a heavy pair of binoculars, Osborne instantly swiveled to look just aft of port. Without taking the glasses from his eyes, he immediately ordered the sub to change course to 255 degrees, dead downwind.

4:20 PM Hawaii Time

Baby continued to drift slowly, stern first, toward the southern tip of Kauai. Wild Bill, standing with the others on the fuselage, watching for fishing boats that might have spotted their signal, decided to check on Sparky. The seasick radioman had emerged from the cabin and was sitting in the unoccupied seat of the rear cockpit hatch, staring longingly at their hoped-for destination.

After some time, Wild Bill, who had been standing on the fuselage facing aft with the others, went to join Sparky. On his way, Bill, still fairly weak himself, slipped and almost fell overboard. As he picked himself up, he couldn't believe his eyes. Straight past *Baby*'s bow, a submarine was so close it could have fouled the sea anchor. When Bill realized it wasn't a mirage, he hollered to the others, "Hey . . .*hey*! There's a submarine back of us!"

4:42 PM Hawaii Time

Lieutenant Osborne deftly slowed the sub and pulled alongside. For a moment, he, too, thought he was seeing a mirage. When the search had finally been called off, all involved had given up hope that the crew of the PN9 had survived, as had the rest of the country, and indeed, the world. Yet, here in front of him were five beaming survivors bobbing on the carcass of a flying boat. They were sunburned and haggard, to be sure, but very much alive. Concerned about their obviously weakened condition, Osborne suggested they come aboard the submarine. John put his invitation to the crew and to a man they declined; even Sparky. They wanted to finish this trip and had no intention of abandoning their plane.

Knowing that the crew had to be desperate for supplies, Osborne called for a monkey-fist messenger line. The softball sized, macramé knot with a long, thin trailing string was tossed across to the plane and captured. The end of the string was then secured to a heavier line, and that, too, was pulled onboard the plane. A wire basket was attached to the heavier line, and a jug of water, a loaf of bread, some cooked sausages, and some canned peaches were thus transferred to the plane. The aviators requested coffee, and to their dismay, a small sack with whole coffee beans soon came over. Although there was nothing they could do with the beans, they didn't want to offend their benefactors, so nothing was said.

The next order of business was to rig a tow. However, as Osborne attempted to maneuver his long, slender, semi-submerged tube, the sub bumped the edge of *Baby*'s starboard lower wing near the already damaged wing float. Fortunately, the collision caused only minor damage and the procedure continued.

Byron and Bill pulled in and then cut the large improvised sea anchor free. Then they refashioned another bridle, this one to the plane's bow, and affixed it to the towline. The line should have been longer, but it was the best they could rig. By 5 PM, the sub was edging slowly toward the Garden Isle with its ungainly companion in tow.

Onboard the seaplane, the crew quickly adjusted to being towed by the sub; traveling in its wake made for a much smoother ride. Once they saw that the tow arrangement was functioning properly, they fell upon the food, quickly dispatching the water, bread, and peaches. They only nibbled at the sausages, though, as their stomachs were so weak. As good as the bread and water tasted, the peaches covered in their own sweet juices were like manna from heaven.

The conversation shifted to what each man most wanted once they arrived onshore. Decent meals, cigarettes, and candy topped the lists. Then Kiles Pope asked the question that was in everyone's mind. "Sir, are we gonna have to spend the night on the sub?"

John smiled broadly, "I should say not. Gentlemen, we've done our time on the water. We'll go to a hotel and have a good meal."

5:28 PM Hawaii Time

Onboard the submarine, Lieutenant Osborne sent a radio message once the plane was safely under tow.

"Plane, prep-negative-niner-one, located by sub roger-four. Fifteen miles east of Nawiliwili, Kauai. Personnel safe. Am towing same to Nawiliwili." This message electrified the fleet and would soon be repeated throughout Hawaii, the Pacific, and then across America. However, *Baby's* travails were by no means over.

Nearby, the USS *Tanager*, and somewhat further away, the USS *Pelican*, responded to the happy message and headed toward Nawiliwili to lend assistance. Although this seemed an unnecessary gesture at the time, *Baby* would turn out to need it.

8:45 PM Hawaii Time

The submarine and the seaplane, along with the newly arrived *Tanager*, approached the outer reaches of the harbor entrance in absolute darkness. It was difficult to see the channel markers, let alone discern the narrow passage through the reef. The pounding surf echoed ominously off the sheer cliffs, making them sound very near, and the swells all but closed out the channel. The sub was forced to slow, and as she did the towline sank. With the next swell, the seaplane ran up on the sub's stern. The submerged line then fouled the sub's propeller, stopping it cold, and the R-4 instantly floundered. Osborne quickly dropped an anchor to keep his boat from drifting onto the reef, but the anchor chain snapped immediately. *Baby* swung helplessly and pulled on the stern of the R-4, further imperiling the sub. Osborne quickly dropped a second anchor and dispatched divers to cut the propeller free.

Rodgers saw what was happening, but knew they couldn't cut *Baby* free until they had an anchor, or she would be tossed onto the jagged coral. He shouted this information across to Osborne, who sent a swimmer to the plane with another line. A mushroom anchor was then hauled across to the plane. Once it was onboard, the aviators warped it to their longest line and dropped the anchor, cutting the fouled towline at the same time. Unfortunately, either the scope of the tackle proved to be too short or the anchor too small, and the plane started dragging anchor, moving inexorably towards the reef.

Rodgers hailed the harried R-4 once more, and Osborne radioed a message to the *Tanager,* hovering just outside the channel entrance. Monitoring the situation by radio, the *Tanager* had followed the problems out in the darkness, and was already lowering their sailing launch into the water. Equipped with a hundred-pound anchor, the sailboat headed in towards the sub.

On the shore, an alert group had noticed the commotion, and a large four-oared rowboat was heading out to the channel entrance. By the time it arrived on the scene, the sub and the sailing launch were already engaged, but by now the seaplane had drifted perilously close to the reef. The sailing launch would have had difficulty maneuvering close enough to *Baby,* so the launch crew asked the men in the rowboat to take the much-needed heavier anchor to the plane. The men in the rowboat agreed, and the larger anchor was shifted over. But the anchor never made it to the plane.

At this point, two civilians who had raced out to the seaplane in a powerboat arrived on the scene. John requested a tow, and the men obliged. Unfortunately, the skipper of the powerboat became confused in the darkness, took a straight-line route, and missed the channel. The powerboat accelerated way too fast, and started pulling the plane directly over the reef. All onboard the PN9-1 yelled for the boat to stop, but couldn't make themselves heard over the roar of the engine. Nor could the aviators loosen the towline; it was pulled too tight. Within seconds, the hulls of both the powerboat and seaplane scraped, bounced and screeched across the jagged coral. *Baby's* crew hung on, expecting the bottom of the plane or the boat to be torn out at any moment, but miraculously, neither craft was holed. Once across the reef, the powerboat slowed and the aviators were able to sever the towline. *Baby* was on her own once more, only now she was inside the placid waters of the harbor, bobbing in shallow water.

By this time, the swimmers had cleared the sub's props and the R-4 and the *Tanager* both entered the harbor, where they were rapidly secured at the commercial pier. While that was occurring, John and his crew rigged the old aeromarine starter and two batteries as an auxiliary anchor. They dropped the heavy mass into the inky calm, and to their relief, the makeshift anchor held. In the calm confines of the back bay, *Baby* was finally at rest.

By the time the aviators had made sure the seaplane was properly secured, both the four-man rowboat and the sailing launch had come to their aid. At exactly 11:30 PM on September 10, 1925, after an unbelievable ten days at sea, the crew finally stepped onto dry land, greeted by a hero's welcome.

Nawiliwili, Kauai harbor entrance. The narrow channel is guarded by rocky cliffs (out of the picture), and a vicious reef to the left of this photograph. This vintage image gives an idea of the challenges Rodgers and crew faced sailing into the harbor.

Cliffs outside Nawiliwili Harbor

Submarine R-4: Commanded by Lieutenant Donald Osborne, Jr.

The September 10, 1925 *Honolulu Advertiser* extra edition. (Although shown as a "morning edition," it was obviously printed much later in the day.) With the incredible news that Rodgers and crew had been found alive, the paper reported that "the city literally went wild. Telephone wires hummed, children—and their elders—dashed from house to house crying the glad news. Women wept tears of joy, children shouted with laughter, and staid men tossed dignity to the winds and capered with delight."

Chapter 48

Friday—September 11, 1925

8:52 AM Mountain Time

Rocked by the constant motion of the Union Pacific train, Admiral Moffett had been fast asleep in his private compartment for almost eleven hours, catching up on the rest he had missed over the past ten days. He had been so deeply asleep that now, as he awakened, he felt drugged. Moving slowly, he swung his legs over the edge of the narrow berth and squinted groggily at his watch. It was almost eight in the morning–or was it nine? He figured they had to have crossed into the Mountain Time Zone by now. For an early riser like Moffett, that was like sleeping past noon. *What the hell, I must have needed it.*

The admiral stood carefully, swaying slightly to compensate for the gentle rocking of the train. When he had his balance, he took the two short steps to the small basin, where he splashed some lukewarm water on his face. Looking in the mirror, he saw the reflection of an older man than he remembered. Shaking his head, he opened his small ditty bag and took out his toothbrush, razor, and other essentials to start his day.

Half an hour later, dressed in civilian clothes, Moffett careened his way through the train to the dining car, where he found an empty table, and seated himself. A waiter in a stiffly starched white shirt appeared almost instantly, and set a folded newspaper on the table with a one-sheet menu on top of it. He poured the admiral a cup of freshly-brewed coffee, black and strong. Placing his napkin in his lap, Moffett gratefully sipped the steaming-hot brew.

The dining car was filled with an assortment of sounds: a number of muted, but animated, conversations; the occasional tinkling of dishes and breakfast utensils being either set down or gathered up; and the rhythmic, continuous clickety-clack as the steel wheels rolled over the expansion joints of the rails—but his mind was elsewhere. Musing about what might lay ahead in Washington, he watched the scenery go by as he savored his coffee. When he felt suitably awakened by the caffeine, he turned his attention to the breakfast menu. As soon as he had made his choice, the waiter appeared even before Moffett had signaled, took his order, and removed the menu.

Looking back out the window to the vistas flying past, Moffett overheard snippets of the conversation between the two businessmen breakfasting across the aisle from him.

"Isn't it incredible? After all this time."

"I still can't believe they made it. Talk about ingenuity!"

"I know . . . I know. It's a testament to their training."

"The navy must be ecstatic."

At this, Moffett nearly dropped his cup. Opening the newspaper in front of him, he was stunned by the huge banner headline: "FLYERS SAFE. TURN PLANE INTO A SAILBOAT." He couldn't read the article fast enough. When he had finished, he set the paper down and murmured to himself incredulously, "My god, they made it!"

Union Pacific dining car, circa 1925

Whole City Goes Wild When Astounding News Of Rescue Is Confirmed

Honolulu received the news of the rescue of Commander John Rodgers and his four companions on the seaplane PN-9 with a tumultous outburst of joy and thanksgiving. Scenes only equalled on Armistice Day or Maefking Night in London, signalling the end of the Boer war, were enacted in the downtown district and every home was filled with rejoicing when the tidings spread through the medium of extra editions of The Advertiser and telephone messages from friend to friend.

"Rodgers and his crew are safe," was the word flashed to The Advertiser shortly before 6 o'clock in the evening. A few minutes later an extra edition of the newspaper was on the streets, followed a short time later with a second edition giving further details.

COMMUNITY STUNNED

Ten days at sea in a wrecked plane! It was incredible, and the shock stunned the community. But not for long. As the truth of the report was realized the first awed silence was broken and the city literally went wild. Telephone wires hummed, children—and their elders—dashed from house to house crying the glad news. Women wept tears of joy, children shouted with laughter and staid men tossed dignity to the winds and capered with delight.

DRIFT 300 MILES

Two hundred or more miles off their course when they were forced to land, the airmen drifted for 300 miles in a southwesterly direction, before they were picked up at sea by a submarine, if early reports were accurate.

Honolulu gasped in amaze. It couldn't be. But it was. Rodgers and his fellow flyers have lived to tell the tale.

And we were about to erect a memorial to them," gasped one breathless dignitary as he executed the finishing steps of an impromptu war dance. "We'll do it yet. Why not? Honolulu would rather erect a memorial to the living than to the dead." And he did a few more fancy steps by way of letting off steam.

NOT YET STARVING

Although they were doubtless hungry when they were picked up it is believed here that the flyers were far from starvation. They carried rations that, distributed conservatively, should have lasted during the ten days they were adrift.

When they left San Francisco each flyer had 10 sandwiches, a quantity of ham and corned beef, half a gallon of black coffee, three pints of soup, five oranges, 40 cubes of sugar, one pickle and chocolate tablets.

In addition to these rations the ship carried 30 gallons of water, eight pounds of corned beef, crackers and hardtack. This emergency ration was counted on to last for three days. It is believed that it could be stretched over a much longer period in case of necessity.

THE ILL-FATED PLANE IN FLIGHT

This is one of many *Honolulu Advertiser* articles reporting on the incredible adventure. The story was repeated in virtually every newspaper across the United States.

The September 11, 1925 edition of *The Honolulu Advertiser.*

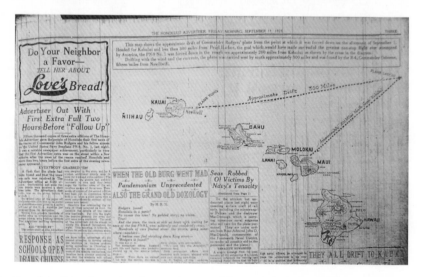

The Honolulu Advertiser printed a rough map of the route the crew drifted, and then sailed, after their crash landing. The hundred-mile-wide channel between Oahu and Kauai is evident. If they had just drifted on the current, they would have been funneled between the two islands, and the next possible landfall would have been thousands of miles away.

This picture was taken off the coast of Kauai with a "vest-pocket camera." Supposedly the entire five-man crew was standing between the engines.

The September 11, 1925 edition of *The Honolulu Star-Bulletin:* These page-two stories followed joyous headlines set in enormous type on page one. The picture shows the Nawiliwili Harbor entrance, with a ship at left, attempting to avoid both cliffs to the left and reefs to the right, while entering the circuitous channel.

AT ANCHOR IN THE BAY

The PN-9-1 at her anchorage at Ninmalu, in Nawiliwili bay.

While barely visible, this image from the September 11, 1925 *Honolulu Star Bulletin* shows the PN9-1 finally safely at anchor in the calm waters of Nawiliwili Harbor, facing seaward.

Chapter 49

Saturday—September 12, 1925

9:31 AM Hawaii Time

As John had promised them, the crew had enjoyed the night in a Kauai hotel, eating and drinking their fill. After sleeping in late and enjoying a sumptuous brunch, the men had spent that afternoon overseeing the loading of their somewhat forlorn flying boat safely onto the stern of the USS *Pelican*. By sunset on Friday, *Baby* and her crew had become simple passengers for the trip back to Pearl Harbor. During the overnight voyage, they each underwent a thorough physical, and although Sparky Stantz was still fairly weak, the ship's surgeon had pronounced them all fit—remarkable, considering the ordeal they had survived.

When the *Pelican* finally entered the broad expanse of Pearl Harbor, she was greeted by a huge flotilla of boats, each packed to the gills with jubilant well-wishers. Horns and whistles blared as those on the water waved flags and screamed in delight. A fireboat led the procession, shooting tons of water skyward in celebration. The midmorning sunlight reflected through the misty spray, producing a spectacular double rainbow as the USS *Pelican* with the beat-up PN9-1 strapped to her fantail made her way toward the docks. John, Byron, Kiles, Wild Bill, and Sparky—commander, lieutenant commander, CPO, chief mechanics mate, and chief radio operator—all clad in clean, borrowed uniforms, stood proudly at the ship's rail.

While the men had been treated royally since making landfall on Kauai, nothing could have prepared them for the reception they were about to receive on Oahu. The navy had ordered the gates to Pearl Harbor opened wide to allow the press and public to greet the returning heroes. This morning, literally thousands of people lined the wharf, barely held in check by roped barriers and spit-shined Shore Patrol. Almost every civilian there was either wearing or carrying flower lei for the heroes. As the *Pelican* was tying up to the pier Wild Bill elbowed Sparky and joked, "All the plumeria trees on Oahu must be naked."

Once the *Pelican* was properly secured, the crew of the PN9-1 thanked their hosts, saluted the ship's flag, and descended the gangway. The navy band struck up a rousing rendition of "Anchors Aweigh," and the crowd on shore broke into song. The exuberant throng cheered and applauded wildly as the men were led, smiling and waving, to a hastily erected dockside platform. The Hawaii-based navy brass had turned out in force, as had the Territorial governor, the mayor, and scores of lesser politicians.

The voracious press swarmed the platform, their cameras clicking, popping, and whirring in a mechanical symphony. Live radio coverage was being broadcast via phone lines; a breakthrough for Hawaii in the history of broadcast journalism. The two Honolulu newspapers had each printed extra editions, which many in the crowd held aloft. Even the mainland press was represented, with some of the correspondents who had originally been dispatched for the planned September 1 arrival, and had luckily not yet sailed for home. Because the flight of the PN9-1 had originated from San Francisco, that city had adopted a particularly proprietary attitude toward the crew's miraculous accomplishment, and several Bay-area reporters were in attendance.

As the introductory speeches blared from the loudspeakers, a close-formation flyby from a dozen navy seaplanes silenced the crowd for a moment, after which the cheering grew even louder. Those trying to pay tribute to the crew of the PN9-1 were hard put to make themselves heard over the din. It was as if everyone present wanted to raise their voices in celebration of the extraordinary accomplishment. At last, to everyone's relief, the laudatory speeches ended, and the press began to pepper the heroes on the podium with questions.

John was amazed that people didn't care that his team had failed to complete the original mission—a nonstop transpacific flight to Honolulu. Instead, the man on the street seemed to be much more interested in celebrating the crew's survival as an example of American ingenuity at its best. The public loved the fact that the team had not floundered helplessly, or given up, but had instead taken the initiative to transform their plane into a sailboat, and beat all odds to not only survive but navigate across hundreds of miles of open ocean to make landfall. One reporter even suggested, as Wild Bill had earlier, that by making it to Kauai in their plane—whether by sea or by air—the crew had actually accomplished their goal. Rodgers demurred, quipping "Well, 472 miles isn't exactly a taxi; it's more like a cross-country train ride." At this, the crowd burst into enthusiastic applause, charmed by the commander's self-effacing response.

Individuals in the crowd called out to the crew, and to Rodgers in particular, begging to hear more. Increasingly uncomfortable at the unbridled adulation, the men were growing impatient, as well. Leaning over to Rodgers, Wild Bill hissed, "Skip, how long do we have to stay on display up here?"

Sparky added, "Yeah, sir, we kinda want to see our girls."

Nodding, Kiles Pope said, "Sir, I'm sure my wife and kids are out there waiting, and who knows how many ladies are lined up to welcome Byron." At this, Connell just grinned and shrugged.

Rodgers understood completely. He ached to see Akiko again. Leaning over to the U.S. Navy public relations officer, he whispered "Can't we wrap this up? All of us have loved ones who've waited long enough."

The PR officer nodded, stepped up to the microphone, and tried to quiet the excited crowd. "Thank you—no more questions now. Thank you, ladies and gentlemen, for your show of appreciation for these brave men. And now, let's let them go find their families. Thank you, and aloha."

At this announcement the band leader took his cue and the band played "Aloha'Oe." The crowd immediately joined in singing Queen

Liliuokalani's beautiful song, while Rodgers and crew shook hands with all of the dignitaries on the podium. But even after the song was over the jubilant crowd was reluctant to disperse. They wanted more.

The band then struck up a rousing rendition of Sousa's "Hands across the Sea." As the music played, a determined Aunty Momi Akana, dressed in a long, multicolored muumuu and a fine *lauhala* hat, elbowed her way through the crowd toward the restraining rope barriers. Her two beautiful nieces followed dutifully in her wake. She hailed the shore patrol sailor guarding the nearest barrier.

"Eh, you! Han'some sayla-man! Watchu t'ink—dis one beeg day, yeah?"

Having caught the young man's attention, Aunty Momi latched onto his arm, continuing to talk animatedly while signaling behind her back to Lei and Lani. Taking full advantage of their aunty's diversionary tactics, the two sisters, piled deep with flower lei, slipped under the ropes, and scampered giggling across the tarmac. As they reached the platform steps, Wild Bill and Sparky waved off several well-intentioned sentries, then pulled the young women up onto the stage and into their arms. Tears flowed like water, as Lei and Lani draped their boyfriends in dozens of fragrant plumeria, tuberose, and *pikake* lei. The crowd loved the display and applauded the two couples. A loud wolf whistle came from behind the rope lines generating even more enthusiastic approval.

Next, a young boy managed to slip past the flimsy barrier. Little Bobby Pope, Kiles's eldest son, zigzagged past the guards, imitating his football hero, Red Grange. As Bobby reached the edge of the stage, Kiles, jumped down, hugged him briefly, then lifted him up onto his shoulders, much to the crowd's delight. Not far behind Bobby, his sobbing mother ran after him as best she could, with an infant in her arms and four young children in tow. By the time Lilly Pope reached her husband, Kiles enveloped her in a passionate embrace—baby and all—as the rest of his children hugged whatever part of their daddy they were tall enough to reach. Everyone watching roared in approval.

At this, the excited crowd overwhelmed the ropes and surged toward the stage. The Shore Patrol sailors tried in vain to maintain some order, but in the end they were barely able to prevent the crowd from climbing right up onto the stage.

True to Kiles Pope's earlier crack, Byron had a crowd-control issue of his own brewing. From the podium he could see at least two of his lady friends, only feet apart, waving and calling his name.

Smiling sheepishly, he turned to John. "Uh-oh. This could be trouble." Byron shrugged his shoulders. "Oh well, here goes!"

John smiled as Byron headed down the steps to his welcoming committee, and then went back to scanning the throng for Akiko. *She's here—she's got to be here.* Tiny as she was, he knew she would be hard to spot in the crowd, but given her spunk, he was surprised she hadn't worked her way to the front, as the others had done. He couldn't wait to take her in his arms and tell her over and over again how much he loved her.

4:45 PM Central Time

At Fort Sam Houston, two ramrod-straight MPs entered Colonel Billy Mitchell's outer office. Mitchell's aide, Lieutenant Smith, stumbled to his feet as the senior MP saluted,

"Sir. Audience requested with Colonel Mitchell."

Smith responded cautiously, "Do you have an appointment with the Colonel?"

"No sir," came the brusque reply. "We're on official business."

Smith tried to stall. "I'll see if the Colonel is available . . ."

"Sir, he will see us. We have orders."

At that moment the door to the inner office opened, and Mitchell himself entered the room. The MPs saluted, and despite the colonel's intimidating presence, attempted to continue, "Colonel Mitchell. We have—" Mitchell raised his hand to silence them.

"Gentlemen, I know why you're here. Let me see what you have."

The junior MP passed a legal-sized manila envelope to Mitchell, who withdrew the document, perused it rapidly, and then nodded. "So, gentlemen, am I to be your prisoner?"

Stammering ever so slightly, the MP replied, "Uh, sir, no sir. You are on your honor as an officer and a gentleman. You are, however, required to report with all due haste to the Provost General's Office in Washington, D.C. in response to the charges stated therein."

"If that is all, gentlemen, then please consider me properly served. You are excused."

Stunned, Lieutenant Smith watched as the door closed behind the MPs. "Sir, I . . . I don't know what to say."

"Lieutenant, don't concern yourself. I fear I have said enough for both of us."

1:23 PM Hawaii Time

The black Franklin taxi made its way down King Street, as the lone passenger in the back willed it to go faster. John was on his way to Masahiro Mikami's shop to try and find Akiko. He wished Masahiro had a phone. He hadn't known whether to go to the office or their house, and had finally decided on the office.

Although disappointed not to have seen Akiko at the ceremony, he knew there were many possible explanations for her absence. After all, Masahiro did keep Saturday store hours. Maybe he had needed his daughter to work. Maybe Akiko hadn't known the base would be open to the public today. And even if she had, with her characteristic thoughtfulness, she might have been afraid of embarrassing him in front of his superiors. He was, after all, still a married man, at least as far as he knew. He made a mental note to check on how the divorce was going.

The cab turned left on Fort Street and as they neared the little optometrist shop Rodgers told the driver to stop. He leaned forward to pay, but the cabbie turned around in his seat, smiling broadly. "Sorry, Commander, but your money's no good . . . least not today. All Hawaii's proud of you."

Embarrassed, John mumbled a sincere thank you and got out of the car. The cabbie called out the window after him, "Aloha, brah—welcome home!" John acknowledged the tribute with a sheepish wave, and the taxi pulled away from the curb.

John turned toward the storefront shop and was surprised to see that the cardboard sign in the window read *Closed*. The lights were on, so he tried the door anyway. It opened, but the familiar little bell was silent. He stepped through the door, hoping to find Akiko at her desk. Not seeing her, he called out, "Hello. Anybody here?"

Masahiro appeared in the doorframe between the two offices. "Mr. Rodgers. I guessed you would come here. I have been waiting for you." Trembling with emotion, he handed John the white envelope and whispered, "Akiko wrote this to me. I'm sure she would have wanted you to read it. I am so sorry, Mr. Rodgers." With this, Masa crumpled onto the little rattan sofa, grief overwhelming him.

With a terrible, sinking feeling, John put on his glasses, and took out the note. When he had finished reading it, Commander John Rodgers, American naval hero on the most triumphant day of his life, slumped next to Masahiro Mikami and wept.

The USS *Pelican* with the PN9-1 secured onboard. You can clearly see the lower wing, which was stripped of all its fabric for sails, and some of its ribs for firewood. The plane was repaired at Ford Island in Pearl Harbor and flew again less than a week after this picture was taken.

The September 12, 1925 edition of *The Honolulu Advertiser:* Part of the huge crowd which greeted the aviators upon their arrival in Honolulu.

Commander John Rodgers: this dark newspaper image captures the returning hero.

Chapter 50

Friday—August 27, 1926

10:42 AM Eastern Time

With clear skies and unlimited visibility, Commander John Rodgers flew north in a Vought VE-9—an open-air, single-engine, wheeled navy biplane. Ostensibly, he was winging his way from Anacostia Naval Air Station to the Philadelphia Naval Air Field to inspect the progress of an innovative plane design—part of his new job at BURAERO. But there may have been personal reasons as well. This visit would reunite the intrepid crew of the PN9-1.

Almost a year had passed since the amazing conclusion of the attempted transpacific crossing. The public and the press had showered John Rodgers and his crew with accolades for their ingenuity and fortitude. They had been embraced and rewarded as true American heroes. Their navy training had also received rave reviews, and any blemishes that been associated with naval aviation had been forgotten.

In Hawaii, it had been decided that even though Rodgers was very much alive, the nearly finished airfield in Honolulu would still be christened the John Rodgers Airport; such was the adoration there for their champion. The fact that Ethel had divorced Rodgers had affected neither his career nor his star status.

After their mission, Rodgers' crew had been offered their choice of plum assignments. As it turned out, their individual requests mirrored each other, and ultimately led all of them to the Philadelphia NAF, where they were all now stationed, designing and testing new planes.

All four members of the quartet had happily settled down. Wild Bill and Sparky's friendship continued stronger than ever, and the two buddies were still inseparable. Not surprisingly, they had married the Akana sisters in a double wedding shortly after their miraculous return. Duke and Samuel Kahanamoku had come in from California for the nuptials, and had given away the girls in a joyous Hawaiian ceremony on Waikiki Beach. Byron had wooed and married a childhood sweetheart from his hometown. He had never seemed happier. To everyone's amazement, Kiles and his wife had not produced another child—yet.

The Philadelphia Navy Air Field had grown in importance. It had become the epicenter for testing and developing of all types of new and better long-range aircraft. Although the Philadelphia NAF would remain the mecca for emerging naval aircraft technology for some time to come, Boeing, Curtis, and several other civilian airplane manufacturers were now also producing planes under contract to the U.S. Navy.

In the wake of *Baby*'s celebrity, Admiral Moffett had ridden out the *Shenandoah* debacle with hardly a scratch. One positive consequence of that disaster was that Americans had learned that the U.S. Navy's dirigibles were filled with helium, not hydrogen. This fact alone fed their hope and belief that America was still technologically superior to other countries. The successful launch and countrywide tour by the *Shenandoah*'s enormous new sister ship, the *Los Angeles*, did much to bolster the navy's claim to the skies. It was also widely reported that the *Los Angeles* had even been able to use some of the precious helium recovered from the remains of the *Shenandoah*, a fact not lost on budget-minded politicians and voters.

The *Langley*, Moffett's aircraft-carrier prototype, had received more public notice in her small role in the search for the missing PN9 than she had during all the time since she had been put into service. The public had been enthralled by the repeated launches and landings of her planes during the course of the rescue attempt. Congress and the public now demanded more and better aircraft carriers. As a result, Moffett was once again deemed a visionary, and allowed to continue as the head of BURAERO.

A month after the transpacific flight, Colonel Mitchell was court-martialed. He was found guilty of insubordination, and resigned from the service. Two weeks later, Congress had not only declined to eliminate naval aviation but had, instead, approved a five-year plan for the development of more than a thousand new planes for the U.S. Navy. Promoted to Admiral Moffett's chief assistant at the expanded and now well-funded BURAERO, Commander John Rodgers' responsibility was to make sure the designs and development moved ahead as planned.

Today, as he flew in the clear, warm summer air, John gazed at his favorite well-worn photo of Akiko, clipped to the control panel and fluttering in the breeze of the open cockpit. He reflected that however much he accomplished, there would always be a hole in his heart. Akiko had drowned in the surf off Kailua Beach; whether by suicide or accident, he would never know. All he knew for certain was that he missed her terribly. That she had lost their child as a result of the stress of those ten terrible days had been a double blow. The pain she must have suffered haunted him to this day.

He shook his head to focus on the landing ahead. The Philadelphia NAF runway ran north to south, and the wind that day was blowing in from the south. As John set up his approach over the Delaware River, he was flying dead downwind. Closing in on the facility, John descended to 150 feet above the water before banking hard to the left and diving for the runway.

As the plane banked sharply halfway through the 180-degree turn, the wind ripped Akiko's picture from the dashboard. It shot across the cockpit, and was momentarily pinioned against John's leather-jacketed chest. Desperate not to let it blow away, John instinctively grabbed for it, and in that split second, he lost control of the aircraft. The VE-9 dived straight for the river shallows and smashed hard into the chest-deep water, yards short of the runway.

Several sailors working outside a hangar witnessed the crash. They shouted for help, jumped in a car, and sped to the accident. Splashing into the shallow water, the men raced to the scene as fast as they could. They found Rodgers conscious but in bad shape. He had sustained extensive injuries—both internal and external—and was wedged so tightly in the wreckage that they would need tools to pry him free. One of the sailors recognized Rodgers and the word soon spread. In less than ten minutes, all four of his old crew had joined the rescue effort. It was taking too long to free him, though. They could see they were losing him.

Kiles, Wild Bill, and Sparky hovered close by as a distraught Byron Connell clung to the wrecked cockpit, talking to his old friend, trying to keep him awake. Clutching a crumpled photo, Rodgers looked around at each of them; and then, with a curious smile, spoke his last words.

"Tell them it wasn't my eyes."

Colonel Billy Mitchell receiving the guilty verdict at his court-martial in October 1925.

The August 28, 1926 edition of *The Honolulu Advertiser:* The paper announced to a stunned Hawaii that Commander John Rodgers had died in a plane crash almost a year to the day of when he had started his epic flight. The yet-to-be-completed airport, which was already to bear Rodgers' name, would now become a monument to this intrepid pioneer aviator.

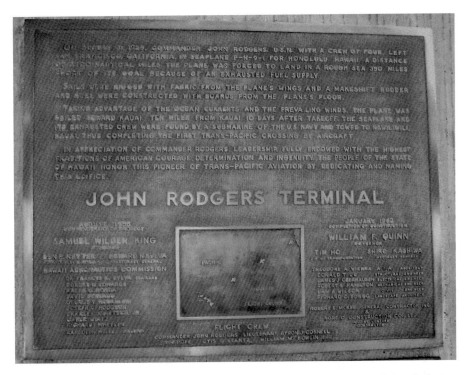

The dedication plaque that adorns the main terminal building at the arrivals level of what is now the Honolulu International Airport

Rodgers Boulevard: Today this sign indicates the entrance road from Nimitz Highway to Honolulu International Airport, formerly named John Rodgers Airport.

Acknowledgments

Thanks to Eden-Lee Murray, my editor, for your patient advice, enthusiasm, forthright attitude, talent, and friendship. To Roger Jellinek, my agent, for your willingness to take on this project, and for your sage counsel, experience, and guidance. To Jack Lopez, my archivist, for your many hours of research. To Carol Williams, who helped with early edits.

I am blessed by so many wonderful friends who have tolerated me during this journey. Thank you to all of them. Thanks also to Dick Baldwin, Dennis Major, Allan Riddle, Douglas Riddle, Kit Beuret, Chris Brigham, Wayne Millar, and Debra Perry for your feedback on the work-in-progress.

And finally, special thanks to my beloved wife, Linda Riddle, for your kind patience, stalwart optimism, and unwavering support throughout this entire endeavor.